"Your father called me a couple months ago," Lynne said. "He said he'd gotten a letter. He was convinced I was being hunted by a serial killer."

Kir sucked in a sharp breath. "Why didn't you call and let me know he'd contacted you?"

"To be honest, I didn't pay any attention to his warning. He'd called the office when I was in the middle of delivering a litter of pups, demanding to speak to me. When I got on the phone his words were slurred, as if he'd been drinking, and he just kept saying over and over I was going to be murdered. When I pressed him for details, he said he had been getting letters from a serial killer who was intending to kill the women of Pike. I honestly thought he was confusing the plot of a movie he was watching with real life."

Kir moved forward, grabbing her hand to give it a small squeeze. "Don't apologize, Lynne. I'm just on edge. And trust me, you weren't the only one to dismiss my father's ravings. The sheriff did. I did. . . ." His voice broke and he was forced to clear the lump from his throat. "Or at least, I assumed that if he truly was getting letters, they must be from someone who was trying to screw with him. What else could we think when there were never any bodies?"

"Until now . . ."

Books by Alexandra Ivy

Published by Kensington Publishing Corp.

DON'T LOOK

ALEXANDRA IVY

ZEBRA BOOKS
KENSINGTON PUBLISHING CORP.
www.kensingtonbooks.com

ZEBRA BOOKS are published by

Kensington Publishing Corp.
119 West 40th Street
New York, NY 10018

All Kensington titles, imprints, and distributed lines are available at special quantity discounts for bulk purchases for sales promotion, premiums, fund-raising, educational, or institutional use.

Special book excerpts or customized printings can also be created to fit specific needs. For details, write or phone the office of the Kensington Sales Manager: Attn.: Sales Department. Kensington Publishing Corp., 119 West 40th Street, New York, NY 10018. Phone: 1-800-221-2647.

Zebra and the Z logo Reg. U.S. Pat. & TM Off.

First Printing: December 2020
ISBN-13: 978-1-4201-5142-8
ISBN-10: 1-4201-5142-8

ISBN-13: 978-1-4201-5143-5 (eBook)
ISBN-10: 1-4201-5143-6 (eBook)

10 9 8 7 6 5 4 3 2 1

Printed in the United States of America

*A huge thanks to Dr. Rachel Goehl
and the entire staff at the Canton Veterinary Clinic.
Not only are you generous with your time and expertise,
but you take the very best care of my spoiled Levet.
Thanks for all you do!*

Chapter 1

Eyes aren't the windows to the soul, funerals are.

They reveal precisely how the deceased lived their lives, and how those who remain behind want them to be remembered.

Some are glorious celebrations of a generous heart. Some are garish displays of wealth and power. Some are small, intimate gatherings that are too painful to be shared with others.

This one was . . . bleak.

There was no other way to describe it.

Standing next to the open grave that had to be chiseled into the frozen ground, Kir Jansen cast a restless glance around the smattering of guests. Pike, Wisconsin, was a small, rural town in the heart of dairy country where neighbors were closely acquainted with one another, but Rudolf's last eighteen years had been a downward spiral into the dark chasm of alcoholism. He wasn't surprised that there weren't many who were willing to brave the bitter January weather.

His attention moved to the preacher, who was reciting a prayer in a monotone voice.

Pastor Ron Bradshaw was a scrawny man in his late twenties with pasty white skin and dark hair that looked as if it'd been trimmed with a pair of dull scissors. He'd kept the service blessedly short, merely mentioning the deep loss that would be felt by Rudolf Jansen's family and community at his death.

Kir didn't mind that there hadn't been any mention of the positive aspects of his father's life. Although there had been plenty of things to make a man proud.

Rudolf had once been a highly respected sheriff in Pike with a wife and son he adored. It wasn't until he'd been attempting to arrest a petty drug dealer that his life had gone in the crapper. The shootout had left the criminal dead and Rudolf with a bullet in his brain that had forced an early retirement. Without the job that had been at the core of his self-worth, nothing had been the same.

Shuffling through the old memories to happier times had felt like ripping open ancient wounds to Kir as he'd prepared to attend the funeral. He'd tucked away his life in Pike the day he'd packed his bags to head to college in Boston. And he'd never looked back. Being forced to recall the childhood days when he'd been a part of a loving, secure family had only emphasized what he'd lost.

With a last plea for Rudolf's salvation, Pastor Bradshaw motioned that the funeral was over and Kir turned to greet the mourners with grim determination. It was the least he could do after they'd braved the brutal weather to pay their respects.

First up was a distant cousin, Dirk Jansen. He was a large, gruff man in his late sixties who had visited Rudolf the last Sunday of every month. He called it his family duty to try and make Rudolf repent his evil ways. Kir's father had called it a pain in his ass.

Now Kir politely shook the man's hand even as he blocked out the droning lecture on the damaging effects of alcohol. The idiot had no idea he was far more a pariah in this small community than Rudolf had ever been. A perpetual drunk was an annoyance, but there was nothing worse than a pompous blowhard.

Dirk at last moved on to allow the clutch of elderly women to surge forward en masse. Kir assumed they attended every funeral in the area, regardless if they personally knew the deceased or not. He accepted their sympathies with a distracted nod and barely noticed as they scurried toward their waiting cars.

Instead his focus was locked on the young woman who was holding out a slender hand. Kir experienced a strange sensation as he reached to squeeze her fingers that were covered in a leather glove and skimmed a quick glance down her slender body.

Dr. Lynne Gale was a tiny woman with light brown hair she kept pulled into a messy ponytail. Her skin was pale and smooth with a smattering of freckles across the bridge of her slender nose, making her look like a teenager although he knew she was just a couple grades behind him in school. Which meant she had to be at least thirty. Her eyes were dark and penetrating and surrounded by long lashes he suspected were real. He'd never seen this woman wearing makeup when they were younger, or later when they crossed paths during his infrequent trips to visit his dad.

To combat the bitter cold, she was wearing a sensible parka that fell to her knees and a pair of heavy snow boots.

"I'm so sorry for your loss, Kir."

There was a gentle sympathy in her voice that threatened to bring the tears to his eyes that had been lacking during the preacher's sermon.

His father had always admired Lynne. He called her a traditional small-town girl with a big heart. It was true she had a big heart, but there was nothing traditional about her. From a young age she'd been blunt and opinionated, and ruthless when it came to protecting the vulnerable. Especially if they happened to be furry.

It hadn't always made her a favorite with the other kids, including himself. Now that he was older, it was a trait he truly admired. You always knew where you stood with Lynne Gale.

He cleared his throat, forcing himself to release his grip on her fingers. "Thank you for coming, Lynne."

She shrugged. "My father and Rudolf were friends their entire lives."

A bittersweet sensation tugged at Kir's heart. Her father had been the local vet, and like Rudolf, his wife had walked out on him, leaving behind a young daughter to raise.

"Gavin was one of the few people in this town who stood by my father," he murmured. "I'll never be able to repay his loyalty."

"He sends his sympathies."

"I assume he's still in Florida?"

"Yeah." Lynne wrinkled her nose, which was pink from the cold. "He hated to miss the funeral, but it's been hard for him to travel since he fell and broke his hip."

"I'm relieved he didn't risk the trip," Kir assured her, glancing toward the thick layer of snow that coated the landscape in white. It was beautiful, but deadly. "This weather isn't fit for retired veterinarians."

"It's true that he prefers the warm beaches these days."

"Who wouldn't?" He glanced back at her. "I can't believe you stayed here when you could be living in the sunshine."

"It's home," she said without hesitation.

Kir flinched as her words struck a raw nerve. Pike had once been home. Until the night his father had been shot. And Boston . . . Well, it was where he lived. He wasn't sure that qualified as being his home. "For some."

"I suppose you'll be returning to Boston?" she asked, as if sensing she'd unwittingly intensified Kir's feelings of grief.

"In a few days. I want to clean out the house and talk to a Realtor about putting it on the market. I hate to have it sitting empty."

"If you need anything, just give me a call," she told him.

They were the customary words offered at funerals. Pleasant platitudes. But suddenly Kir was hit by an overwhelming desire to see this woman again.

He wasn't sure why, he just knew that he had an urge to connect with someone in Pike before he walked away forever. And there was always the possibility that she might have talked to his father or seen the older man. Kir needed . . . what? Closure, perhaps. He felt as if his anchor had been cut and he was floating in a sea of regret, guilt, and something perilously close to relief that he would never see his father suffering again.

"How about lunch tomorrow?"

She blinked, clearly caught off guard. "I usually eat something in my office at the clinic."

"Good." His tone left no room for her to politely wiggle

out of his invitation. "I'll bring my famous deconstructed sushi on *pain de seigle*."

She blinked again. This time in confusion. "Excuse me?"

"Tuna fish sandwich on rye bread," he translated.

Her lips quirked in a genuine smile. "Okay. I usually take a break around noon."

"See you then," he said.

She turned to scurry toward the red truck parked near the road. Kir watched her pull away before he turned to face the man who was stoically waiting near the open grave.

"Thank you, Pastor," he said, forcing himself to move forward, holding out his hand.

"I was pleased to be able to help in your father's time of need."

"I appreciate you stepping in on short notice."

The clergyman lifted his brows at Kir's words. "It wasn't."

Kir dropped his hand and stepped back. He didn't want to stand where he could see the glossy casket that was waiting to be covered by the piles of frozen dirt. It somehow made his father's death irrevocable.

Stupid, but there it was.

"I beg your pardon?" he asked, confused by Bradshaw's response.

"It wasn't short notice," Bradshaw said.

"I don't understand."

"Your father asked me if I would officiate his funeral service."

Kir stiffened. When he'd received the call from the sheriff that his father had been found dead at the bottom of the stairs, he'd asked for his body to be sent to the local funeral parlor. Everything had been such a blur since then that he hadn't questioned why this pastor had been selected to perform the service. He'd assumed it was some sort of package deal that went with the grave plot, the headstone, and the flowers that had been placed on top of the casket.

Now he frowned in confusion. "When did he ask you?"

"A couple weeks ago."

"I didn't realize the two of you were acquainted."

"It's a small town, so of course, our paths had crossed, but I can't say that we were acquainted," Bradshaw admitted. "His request came as something of a surprise, to be honest. It isn't uncommon for elderly parishioners to contemplate the end of their lives. Many even make arrangements for their funeral. But your father was in the prime of his life and he assured me that he wasn't ill."

Kir winced. His father's death had come as a complete shock. Despite his heavy drinking, he had always maintained robust health. It had taken a fall down the stairs that cracked his skull to kill the stubborn old fool.

"No. His liver wasn't in great shape, but he certainly wasn't on death's door," Kir said.

Bradshaw shrugged. "Ah, well. He did say something about being tired. Perhaps he had a premonition. It does happen."

A shiver threaded its way down Kir's spine. Was it possible his father had some sense that the end was near? No. His rational mind fiercely dismissed the ridiculous explanation. If his father had reached out, there was a logical reason.

"Why you? I mean . . ." Kir paused as he tried to imagine his father seeking out a pastor. Rudolf rarely left his house unless it was to go to the neighborhood bar. "He didn't attend your church, did he?"

"No. To be honest, I'm not sure why he chose me. I was returning to the church after spending the morning at the local thrift shop and your father suddenly pulled his truck into the parking lot and jumped out, waving his hands to get my attention. I thought at first there must be some sort of emergency."

Kir frowned. Had his father been drunk? Perhaps delusional? "What did he say?"

"He introduced himself and we spoke for a couple minutes. Then he asked if I would arrange his funeral." Bradshaw glanced toward the leaden sky as if trying to remember the encounter. "I asked him to come inside and discuss why he'd sought me out and if perhaps there was something I could do to assist him in his time of need, but he refused. He insisted he had to get home. When I read in the paper that Rudolf had passed, I contacted the funeral director to inform him of your father's request."

"How . . ." Kir's words faded. It was simply impossible to imagine his father appearing on a church doorstep with the sole purpose of asking a complete stranger to officiate his funeral.

"Weird?" Bradshaw offered.

"Yeah."

"'It is *He* who reveals the profound and hidden things,'" the pastor quoted from the Bible.

"I suppose." Kir wasn't in the mood to discuss theology. He wanted to know what was in his father's mind. "Did he say anything else?"

"Not really." Ron's eyes abruptly widened. "Oh. Wait. I almost forgot." He dug into the pocket of his heavy jacket, pulling out a folded piece of paper. "Here."

Kir allowed the man to shove the paper in his hand. Was it a bill? Maybe he expected to get paid on the spot.

"What's this?" Kir demanded, even as he mentally calculated how much cash was in his wallet.

"I don't know." Ron shrugged. "Your father handed it to me before he left the church and asked me to give it to you after the funeral. I assume it's a personal note he wanted you to have once he died."

The vague sense of unreality was laced with a strange prickle of fear as Kir stuffed the paper into the pocket of his coat.

"You really didn't know my dad," he muttered, suddenly needing to get away from the snow-smothered cemetery and the pastor who was regarding him with a sympathetic smile. "Thanks again."

"The doors to the church are always open," Ron called out as Kir turned to hurry down the narrow path to his waiting SUV.

"Rest in peace, Dad," he prayed as he drove away.

Dear Rudolf,

I'm sorry to say you had a shitty funeral. The attendance was sparse and the few who were there hurried away as soon as the preacher said amen. I did warn you that I was the only one who truly cared about you.

Why did you threaten to betray me?

Now you're gone and my lust is no longer leashed. It's exploding out of me as if a dam has burst. And I've already chosen my first . . . hmm, should I call her a victim? She's not innocent.

She spread my most private treasures across the

*snow as if they were trash. She gutted me to reveal
my innards to the entire world. And then she
laughed. The harsh braying laugh of a donkey.*

No, she's not innocent.

*This time I will be the one laughing as I watch
her crimson blood stain the pure white snow. Life
spills from warm to frozen. The pain is gone.
Don't look.*

Revenge is mine. . . .

Sherry Higgins sat on a high stool in the small office building overlooking the Pike Trailer Park. She was a large woman with a square head and a matching square body she currently had stuffed in a velvet jogging suit. Her father had spent her childhood calling her a worthless blockhead—only one of the reasons she'd spit on his grave. The only decent thing he'd ever done was die when she was a young woman, giving her sole ownership of the park. It wasn't a great living, but the rent from the trailers, plus utilities, provided enough to scrape by.

On the other side of the counter a young man with a haggard face and messy red hair was glaring at her with bloodshot eyes.

"You . . ." Spittle formed at the edge of his mouth. "Bitch."

She rolled her eyes, returning her gaze to the television set on the corner of the counter. The idiot had stormed into the office when she was watching her favorite reality show.

"Your job is to throw families out of their homes in the middle of winter?"

"Wanna stay warm? Pay your rent," she told him.

"I'm going to. I have a new job I'm starting on Monday."

"That's what you said last month."

"Yeah, but—"

She waved a silencing hand in his direction. "I don't want to hear it. Pay or get out."

"Where are we supposed to go?" the man whined.

It was the same conversation Sherry had endured a thousand times over the past twenty years.

Boo hoo, I lost my job, my kid is sick, my car broke down . . . blah, blah, blah.

Everyone had an excuse why they couldn't fulfill their obligations.

"I run a trailer park, not a charity," she told him. "Call the government, they're always handing out money to lowlifes who can't keep a job. People who work never get nothing but the bill."

"At least give me a few days to find someplace we can stay," he pleaded. "We have a baby."

"Not my problem. You have . . ." Sherry glanced toward the large clock attached to the cheap paneling that lined the outer office. "One hour left to pay the rent or I'll turn off the electricity and water. Ticktock, ticktock."

Without warning the man slammed his hand down on the counter. "Someday you're going to get what's coming to you."

Sherry leaned forward, glowering at the intruder. "There's a camera right there." She stabbed a sausage-shaped finger toward the ceiling where a small hole was drilled. There wasn't anything there—she was too cheap to actually buy security equipment—but the threat was usually enough. "You say another word and I'll have you charged with harassment."

The man's face turned a beet red, but he turned and

stomped across the floor. "I hope you rot in hell," he yelled as he slammed shut the door behind him.

Sherry snorted. "I've been rotting in hell for years," she muttered.

With a shake of her head she returned her attention to the television. She was far more interested in what was happening with the naked people trying to survive in the wilderness than the people who rented her trailers. Bunch of losers.

Darkness thickened outside, the sound of the wind whistling through the windows. It was past five, but Sherry made no move to go and check if the delinquent tenants had made their exit from the park. If they were there in the morning, she'd have the sheriff kick their asses out. It was too damned cold to do anything tonight.

Flicking off the television, she stood and moved to lock the front door. Her own trailer was at the end of the park, which meant she didn't have to face the icy roads to get home. Still, she wasn't excited by the thought of the frigid walk through the dark.

Not for the first time she considered moving closer to the office. She wouldn't have the yard that currently surrounded her mobile home, or a view of the lake, but she could avoid the trudging back and forth.

Heading out through the back-storage room, she didn't bother to turn on the lights. It was easy enough to follow the narrow path between stacked boxes and old, broken furniture. She could do it with her eyes closed.

It wasn't until she heard the unmistakable tread of a footstep that she regretted the thick darkness that made it impossible to see.

Her heart thudded, the pizza she had for lunch churning uneasily in her stomach.

"Hello? Who's there?" Reaching out her hand, she tried to find something she could use as a weapon. There was nothing. "How the hell did you get in here?"

"I'm sorry, Sherry."

A portion of her terror lessened. There was something familiar about the voice. Was it one of her tenants?

"You better be sorry," she told the intruder, reaching into the pocket of her jogging suit to pull out her phone. "This is breaking and entering. Don't think I won't call the sheriff."

There was a sound like someone clicking their tongue. "You brought this on yourself."

"Bullshit. If you needed something, you should have come through the front door during normal business hours."

Sherry hit the flashlight on her phone and swung it toward the intruder. The idiot was too far away to make out more than the fact that he or she was bundled in a heavy coat with a stocking cap on their head and something clutched in their hand.

A gun?

Shit.

"You never change," the intruder drawled. "All that squawking in an effort to disguise just how weak you are."

"Weak? I'm not weak," she tried to bluff, cautiously inching backward. If she could get into her office, she could lock the door and call the sheriff. "Just ask anyone."

"Terrorizing helpless victims doesn't make you strong. Most cowards are bullies." The arm lifted, pointing the gun straight toward the middle of her chest. "Laugh for me, Sherry."

Her mouth was so dry she could barely speak. "What?"

"Laugh."

"I can't—"

"Do it."

The words were low . . . almost gentle . . . but they sent a blast of terror through Sherry. This wasn't some weird-ass joke. The intruder was going to shoot her if she didn't find some way to get out of there.

Parting her lips, she forced a hoarse laugh past the lump jammed in her throat. It echoed through the room, sounding unnaturally loud in the silence.

"Just like a donkey." There was disgust in the voice.

Sherry flinched. Her father used to say that. *You bray just like an ass. . . .*

She slid her thumb to the corner on the screen of her phone and pressed. That was emergency service, wasn't it? Then, praying that someone was on the way to save her, she tried to distract the intruder. "What did I ever do to you?"

He stepped forward. "You didn't see."

"See what?"

"Me."

Sherry scowled. Why was the weirdo talking in riddles? If they had a beef with her, then just spit it out.

She was on the point of demanding an explanation when she heard the sound of a click followed by a sharp pain in her right shoulder. Had he shot her? It didn't sound loud enough to be a gun, but maybe he had a silencer on it.

Terrified to even look, Sherry forced herself to glance down at her shoulder, not sure what to expect. What she saw wasn't a gaping hole or spurting blood from a bullet wound. Instead it looked like a long metal tube was sticking out of the velvet material of her jogging suit.

She tried to puzzle out what was happening, but her brain felt fuzzy. As if it was being stuffed with cotton. And her dry mouth was now parched.

What the hell?

She took a stumbling step in a futile effort to escape, but her weak knees abruptly gave way and she landed flat on her back. She grunted in pain. She was a large woman who hit the cement floor with enough force to knock the air from her lungs. It wasn't the impact, however, that caused her heart to halt in pure horror.

It was the dark form that moved to stand directly over her.

"Laugh for me, Sherry."

Chapter 2

After a night of tossing and turning, Dr. Lynne Gale had barely managed to fall into a deep sleep when a wet tongue swiped over her cheek.

With a groan, she shoved away the furry face. "Go away." There was another lick and she reluctantly cracked open one eye to discover Barkley, a fifty-pound rescue mutt, perched on the bed. She'd brought the wiggling mass of goofiness home from the rescue sanctuary to give him a good grooming before his new owners picked him up at her veterinarian clinic. "Stop tugging on the sheets," she muttered. "We need to do something about your manners. It's far too early to play."

As if to mock her words, a shrill alarm blasted from the nightstand.

"Arg." Lynne glanced toward the clock that claimed it was four thirty a.m. How was it possible? She'd just closed her eyes. "Okay, okay," she told the dog. "Let go of the covers and I'll feed you."

With a bark that was far too happy for this time of morning, Barkley jumped off the bed and headed to the door. Lynne grabbed a thick robe and followed at a much slower pace.

Usually she didn't mind the ungodly hours her job demanded. She loved what she did and was always eager to enjoy the day, but her restless night had left her feeling lethargic. The unexpected death of Rudolf Jansen had obviously hit her harder than she'd realized, and combined with the sight of Kir after so many years . . . She'd been weirdly unsettled.

What she needed was a hot shower and a mug of coffee. In that order.

An hour later she'd showered, swallowed a gallon of coffee, and switched on the bedroom television as she pulled on a half dozen layers of clothing. Braving the early morning farm calls in Wisconsin wasn't for the faint of heart. Or the underdressed.

Frostbite wasn't a joke.

She was struggling into her coveralls when the sound of an urgent voice on the television captured her attention.

"We have breaking news exclusive to Channel Four," a smooth male voice said as the morning talk show was replaced by a man seated behind a news desk. "The naked body of an unidentified woman was discovered on the property of Raymond Warren three miles west of Pike. The authorities confirm her death is being investigated and they are asking for citizens to contact them if they noticed anything suspicious. More details at six tonight."

Lynne switched off the television and headed out of the house. Any crime was unusual in their small community, let alone one that involved a naked woman. She could only assume the woman had been killed somewhere else and her body dumped.

It didn't make the story any less horrible, but it did allow Lynne to dismiss it as she concentrated on driving to the first dairy farm on her list. She had a full schedule that included a milk cow with an infected udder, a horse with an abscess on his hoof, and a newborn calf who refused to nurse. That didn't include any emergency that might come in.

Four hours later she at last finished her rounds. Driving to her clinic, she was nearly frozen to the bone and desperately hungry, but there was no time to do more than grab another cup of coffee and a donut before dealing with the waiting room full of patients.

By noon she was sitting in her office, breathing a sigh of relief as her receptionist and two temporary interns headed out to lunch. There was blessed silence, or at least as close to silence as you could get in a clinic that had an attached kennel for those animals scheduled for surgery, or who were simply too sick to go home.

At least Barkley's new owners had swung by to pick him up. There was nothing more satisfying than watching a neglected dog go to a family who were anxious to smother him with love.

She was sprawled limply in her chair when she heard the sound of the front buzzer. The clinic was technically closed during lunch, but everyone in town knew she was here in case of an emergency.

Rising to her feet, she walked down the hall and into the reception area of the clinic. It was a long, narrow room that was lined by plastic chairs, and at the end was a high counter for her receptionist. Eventually she hoped to build on an addition that would include a larger lobby as well as two more exam rooms. That would allow her to hire another vet to ease the workload that was threatening to overwhelm her.

Reaching the door, she pulled it open to reveal the tall man standing just inches away. Kir Jansen. Instantly, her heart gave an odd leap. Not out of surprise—she'd been expecting him. But because he looked so absurdly handsome as he smiled down at her.

He'd been cute as a teenager, with his golden blond hair, impossibly blue eyes, and square chin. Now his features had hardened to a stark beauty and his body had filled out with the sort of muscles that revealed he spent precious little time sitting behind a desk. At the moment that very fine body was emphasized beneath his leather jacket and black slacks.

"Lunch, as promised," he murmured, holding up a small basket.

Lynne glanced toward the parking lot, wondering why she hadn't heard his car pull in. When she didn't see a vehicle, she sent Kir a startled glance. "Did you walk here?"

"It's only two blocks," he reminded her, then shivered as a sharp breeze whipped around the corner of the brick building.

She waved him in and hurriedly closed the door to prevent the icy air from entering. Her electric bill was shocking during the winter months. And the action gave her the opportunity to appreciate the man's very fine backside.

When she was in high school, she never understood why the other girls giggled when Kir passed them in the hallway. She was too busy with her schoolwork and helping her dad at the clinic to have time for boys. Now, however, she understood.

This man could make any woman giggle and flutter in all the right ways.

Clicking the lock, she turned to lead him out of the reception area and into her office. The scent of his warm skin brushed against her like a caress, and she sucked in a deep breath without bothering to hide the shiver of pleasure that raced through her.

Why not enjoy having Kir as her lunch companion? It wasn't like she had a plethora of gorgeous, sexy men in her life.

In fact, she had exactly zero.

"I don't suppose you included something to drink?"

She moved to the long table at the back of the office, shoving aside the stacks of files to give Kir space to set down the basket.

"I have a few bottles of water," he said, pulling out the containers of food along with the water.

She heaved a teasing sigh, settling on one of the folding chairs. "I was hoping for whiskey, but water will do."

He arched a brow, taking a seat beside her. "Rough day?"

She shrugged, watching as he filled a paper plate with precisely cut sandwiches and a pile of potato chips. "Farm calls in this weather are always rough," she admitted, arching her aching back before she reached for the sandwich.

"Do you enjoy your work?"

"I love it. I can't imagine doing anything else," she said without hesitation. She took a bite, surprised by the flavor that hit her tongue. She'd made tuna fish all her life, but this was different. It had spices and egg and relish. *Yum.* She swallowed. "Your father mentioned you'd opened your own businesses in Boston. I never thought of you as an entrepreneur."

His lips twitched, as if he knew she was recalling the reckless, out-of-control boy who lived on the edge of danger.

"It actually started as a fluke," he told her. "I was trying to earn extra money to pay for tuition when I started running errands for my professors. I walked their dogs, washed their cars, picked up lunch, and even took their cars to have the oil changed. Eventually I realized if I concentrated on taking care of the tasks no one else wanted to do, I could make a lot more money than an entry-level accountant." He opened a bottle of water and set it in front of her. "Now I have over a hundred employees throughout Boston and Philadelphia. Whatever you need done, we'll take care of it."

She finished the tuna fish and reached for the water to wash it down. She had a healthy appetite after her morning in the cold.

"Including making sandwiches?"

He chuckled. "It's my specialty."

"They're delicious," she assured him, turning so she could directly face him. "If you are as good at all the other services that you offer, I can understand why you're such a success."

"It was a combination of hard work and luck that paid off."

"Your father was very proud of you."

He flinched, almost as if he'd taken a physical blow. "I wish . . ."

"What?"

"That I'd come back more often." He abruptly shoved back his empty plate, his expression grim. "There always seemed to be some catastrophe that demanded my immediate attention while I was building my business. And to be honest, my dad got put at the bottom of the list." He shook his head. "I thought there would be more time. Now—"

His words were cut short as the front buzzer once again

sounded. A rare annoyance stabbed through Lynne at the unwelcome interruption. Since her father had retired two years ago, she'd grown accustomed to being on call 24/7. It'd never bothered her. Not until this moment. Suddenly she wanted to yell at the person interrupting her lunch that she deserved a few minutes of peace.

Instead she forced herself to her feet. "Sorry, I need to see if this is an emergency."

He nodded as she turned to hurry from the room. A moment later, Lynne was pulling open the front door. "Parker," she muttered in surprise, her gaze taking in the local news anchor, who was shivering on the porch.

He was a few inches taller than her, which made him short for a man, with dark hair that she'd heard he drove all the way to Green Bay to have trimmed. His features were exactly what you would expect for a television personality. High, perfectly chiseled cheekbones with a strong jaw, a bold nose, and piercing gray eyes. Most people thought he was handsome, but Lynne was turned off by the perpetual tan and super-white teeth that didn't look quite real. Still, she had to admit that he had a polished charm that made him a welcome addition to Pike.

Plus, he was a fellow animal lover.

"Hello, Lynne," he said, flashing his white teeth.

Lynne glanced toward the nearby van with the local station's call letters painted on the side. "Is something wrong with Norman?" she asked, referring to the rescue dog that Parker had recently adopted.

"No, no. He's fine," he assured her. "Fat and happy."

"Good." She started to inch the door shut. The sun was shining, but it only made things worse. The air was cold enough to make her fingers go numb. "I'm closed for lunch. Is there something you need?"

He stepped forward, as if he was preparing to stick his foot in the threshold to keep her from slamming the door in his face.

No doubt that happened a lot in his line of work.

"I have a few questions."

"Questions about what?"

"Can we talk inside?" The practiced smile widened. "It will only take a couple minutes."

"Is this for your 'Pets' Corner' segment?" Lynne inquired as she reluctantly stepped back to let the man into the reception room.

As much as she wanted to run him off and continue her lunch with Kir, she was in Parker's debt. He'd been the only one who was willing to listen to her idea of featuring a rescue animal on the evening news. More than that, he'd pressured the owner of the station to give it a try.

Thankfully, the spotlight had not only helped the local sanctuary, but it'd been so popular with the public that they added an extra ten minutes on Friday nights for Lynne to discuss the proper care and training of pets, as well as promoting one of the animals in need of a home each week.

"Unfortunately, no."

Lynne frowned. "What's going on?"

"You didn't catch my special report this morning?"

It took a second for her to recall the news alert she'd heard before leaving her house. "Oh, right. The body that was found."

He heaved a dramatic sigh. "Yes. Poor woman."

"Do they have an identity yet?"

"They haven't made an official announcement, but I have an inside source who told me it's Sherry Higgins."

Lynne jerked in surprise. She hadn't considered the possibility that the dead woman might be from Pike. "The lady who owns the trailer park?"

"That's her."

Lynne didn't know Sherry very well. The woman had kept to herself most of the time, but it was still disturbing to think that she was dead. And that someone might have deliberately hurt her. "How awful."

"Tragic." Parker's voice held a smooth compassion that Lynne assumed he practiced. It was the same tone he used to reveal there had been a fire at the local lumberyard, or that there were budget cuts to the school. "According to my sources, Sherry was found with her naked body posed in the snow and her throat slit. The only thing the killer left was a crimson ribbon tied around her neck."

Lynne lifted her hand to touch her neck. It was an instinctive reaction to the horrifying thought of what Sherry must have suffered. "Do they know who's responsible?"

"The sheriff isn't offering any information." Parker leaned toward her, as if sharing a secret. "But my initial investigation has revealed that Ms. Higgins wasn't a very nice person. She regularly had families evicted from their homes, she charged outrageous fees for basic services, and she was caught peeking through the windows of her tenants. I would guess there's going to be an overabundance of suspects."

Lynne tried to hide her disapproval. She never listened to gossip. It was rarely accurate and always destructive.

"People don't kill someone for evicting them," she protested.

Parker snorted. "I've known people who will kill someone for spilling their coffee." He paused, as if considering the murder. "Of course, it's one thing to strike out in the heat of anger, and quite another to kill someone, strip off their clothes, and arrange the body in the snow like some sort of pagan offering."

A shudder raced through Lynne. It was disturbing to think such evil could touch her town. "I don't know her family. Are they in the area?"

"Her parents are dead. She had a live-in boyfriend." Parker pulled his hand out of the pocket of his long, black coat to glance at his phone. "Wes Klein," he continued, obviously glancing through the notes he'd already gathered on Sherry Higgins. "She called the sheriff two weeks ago to have him forcibly removed from her trailer."

Lynne took a step back. She felt sorry for the dead woman, but she didn't have time to waste chitchatting. In less than a quarter of an hour her staff would be returning along with the afternoon rush and her brief time alone with Kir would be over. She didn't know why the thought bothered her, but it did.

"It's sad," she assured Parker. "But I'm not sure why you're here."

Parker glanced around the empty office, as if making sure they were alone. "My source says that when they searched the back office at the trailer park, they found a silver dart that looks like it came from a tranq gun." He deliberately paused. "The sort used by vets on large animals."

She studied him in confusion. "Why would there be a dart there?"

"The sheriff assumes she was knocked out so she could be taken without a struggle and killed somewhere more private."

Lynne stiffened. Was Parker sniffing around her clinic because he thought she was somehow involved in the murder? "What does that have to do with me?" she asked point-blank. She wasn't a subtle sort of woman.

"I need an expert on how a person could go about getting their hands on the drugs you use and how they would affect a person who was injected with them."

She was only partially mollified by the smooth explanation. "No."

"It can be off the record," he wheedled. "Just some background information that would help my audience understand—"

"No." Her tone was sharper.

Not surprisingly, Parker wasn't deterred. He was a journalist. They didn't allow rejection to stop them from getting what they wanted. But even as his lips parted, there was the sound of a male voice speaking from behind Lynne.

"I believe she told you no."

The newscaster twitched, clearly caught off guard at the realization they weren't alone. Then, with a practiced ease, he turned to flash his toothy smile. "I'm sorry, I didn't know Lynne had a patient." He held out his hand. "Parker Bowen."

Kir strolled forward, his face oddly pale as he shook the man's hand. "Kir Jansen."

"Jansen?" Parker paused, as if testing the name. Then he snapped his fingers. "Any relation to Rudolf Jansen?"

It was Kir's turn to look surprised. "You knew my father?"

"No, but I did read his obituary in the paper. I'm sorry for your loss."

"Thank you."

Parker tucked his phone back in his pocket, his expression distracted as if he was already thinking of his next task. Perhaps finding another vet who would give him the background information he wanted. Turning, he walked toward the door.

"Call me if you change your mind about helping with the investigation," he told Lynne. "That dart had to come from somewhere."

Chapter 3

Kir was shaken.

Bone-deep, to-the-soul shaken.

He hadn't meant to eavesdrop, but the door was open, and the voices easily carried as the unknown man had talked about some woman being found dead and posed naked in a field. At first he'd been vaguely horrified. Murder was rare in such a small town. Still, the majority of his attention had been focused on how long it was going to take to get rid of the intruder. He'd been thoroughly enjoying spending time with Lynne and was anxious for her to return to their lunch.

Then the man had mentioned the crimson ribbon, and the words he'd dismissed for years whispered through his mind.

Crimson blood stains the pure white snow. Life spills from warm to frozen. Don't look. The pain is gone.

Those were the words at the end of each letter his father had received from his mysterious pen pal. The letters Rudolf had been convinced came from a serial killer, and Kir had been convinced were the work of some nutjob.

What actual killer would write to a sheriff, even if he was retired, Kir had argued when his father would call to say another letter had arrived at his house. And where were the bodies? You couldn't be a serial killer if you weren't actually murdering people.

Kir told his dad it was far more likely that someone was playing a cruel game. Or perhaps it was someone sick in the head who imagined he was a killer. Stuff like that happened all the time.

"Kir." A slender hand touched his arm. "Kir. Is something wrong?"

"Crimson blood stains the pure white snow," he murmured, still lost in his escalating fear.

"What?"

He shook his head, focusing on the woman who was regarding him with a worried expression. "The letters."

"I'm sorry, I don't understand what you're talking about."

He waved an impatient hand toward the front door. "The guy who was just here."

"Parker Bowen? He's the local newscaster."

Kir grimaced. He'd barely spent two minutes in Bowen's company and he already didn't like him. He had a slick charm that usually hid a devious personality. But that wasn't what was causing his racing pulse. "He said they found the body naked except for a crimson ribbon around her neck," he said.

Her lips slowly parted. "You didn't know poor Sherry, did you?"

"No." With jerky movements, Kir returned to Lynne's office to grab his leather jacket. "I need to go look for those letters."

"Letters?"

"I'm sure my dad didn't throw them away," he muttered. "They have to be in the house somewhere."

"Wait." Lynne appeared beside him. "Are you leaving now?"

Kir swallowed a sigh. He'd spent last night and most of this morning anticipating his lunch with Lynne. It'd been the only way he could bear the grim task of packing up his father's belongings. And if he was honest, he was eager to spend some time discussing the past with someone who had shared it with him. Lynne might not have been his best friend growing up, but they'd gone to the same school and enjoyed the same local hangouts.

He'd devoted so much effort to blocking out the broken man his father had become that he'd forgotten there had been good times in this town. He needed to make sure that they were the memories he took back to Boston.

"I'm sorry, I know we didn't get to finish our lunch," he said, his regret genuine.

"Don't worry about it." She stepped toward her nearby desk, which was nearly buried beneath stacks of files. "Obviously you're upset. I'll drive you home."

"There's no need."

She glanced back at him, her expression still worried. No doubt she was thinking that his father's sudden death was making him a lunatic. And maybe he was.

"Kir."

"I'm fine," he assured her as he walked toward the door, pausing to glance back at his companion. "Make sure the doors are locked while you're here alone."

She thankfully didn't look at him as if he'd lost his mind. She simply nodded her head. "I always do."

Kir lingered, oddly reluctant to leave. Then, clenching his teeth, he forced himself to turn and walk out of the clinic. As much as wanted to spend a few hours in Lynne's company, he couldn't shake his sense of foreboding.

It was almost as if his father was whispering in his ear, warning him that danger was stalking the women of Pike.

Two hours later, he had just finished boxing up the papers from his father's file cabinets when there was a knock on the door. He froze. Did he answer it? Or did he pretend he wasn't there?

He wasn't in the mood for the condolences of a well-meaning neighbor, or more likely, the intrusive demands of the real estate agent he'd hired. In fact, all he wanted to do was find the damn letters and set his mind at ease that they had nothing to do with the dead woman.

Unfortunately, whoever was outside was determined to get in. They pressed their finger to the ringer, refusing to let it stop until he'd stomped through the house to yank open the door.

The angry words that trembled on his lips died as he realized it was Lynne standing on the porch.

"What are you doing here?" he demanded in surprise.

She was bundled from head to toe in winter gear, but she still looked cold. "I thought you could use some company."

Kir hurriedly stepped back, allowing her to enter the living room so he could close the door. "What about your patients? Or whatever they're called."

She kicked off her boots on the small mat before moving toward the center of the living room. It wasn't a large room, but it felt empty. Maybe because the walls were bare, and the only furniture was a worn recliner and an old television on a rickety stand in a far corner. Or maybe it was because his father wasn't there.

"The animals are my patients, and the owners are my clients." She pulled off her stocking cap and coat, laying them on the worn brown carpet before sending him a smile. "But I usually call them friends and family. That's who they are to me. Especially the animals."

His heart lurched. Why hadn't he ever noticed her smile? It was captivating.

He stepped toward her. "You always did have a preference for four-legged creatures."

"They're a lot easier to understand."

"True." His lips twisted as he considered his years of dealing with angry customers. It'd made him appreciate the thought of retiring one day with a loyal dog and a cabin in the middle of nowhere. "So shouldn't you be taking care of your furry friends?"

She shrugged. "I'm finished with the surgery I had scheduled, and my interns can deal with the routine cases. If an emergency comes in, they'll call."

"I know I ran out of your clinic like a madman, but I really am okay. You don't have to keep an eye on me."

He used a light tone, trying to hide his abrupt realization that he was glad she was there. He hadn't been aware of how many ghosts haunted this house. Not until she stepped through the door and battled them back with her smile.

"It wasn't just concern for you that brought me here," she said.

"No?"

"After you left, I finally realized what you were talking about."

His lips twisted into a wry smile. "It was more a babble than actual talking," he conceded. "I was a little distracted."

"I get it." She held his gaze. "When Parker mentioned

that a dead woman had been found, you were afraid it might have something to do with the letters your father had been getting, weren't you?"

Kir made a sound of surprise. It wasn't what he'd been expecting. "You know about them?"

She hesitated, considering her words before she spoke. "Your father called me a couple months ago."

"Was that unusual?"

"Yes. I tried to stop by and visit when I had the time, but after Butch died, I didn't come here as often as I should have," she admitted, referring to Rudolf's beloved hound dog. "We drifted apart over the past year."

Pain sliced through Kir. How many times had he told himself that he needed to call his father? And how many times had he told himself that he would do it later? A shrink would no doubt call it "avoidance." He called it being a shitty son. "What did he want?"

"He said he'd gotten a letter."

"Why would he involve you?"

"Because he was convinced I was being hunted by a serial killer."

Kir sucked in a sharp breath. "Why didn't you call and let me know he'd contacted you?"

She waved her hand in an apologetic gesture. "To be honest, I didn't pay any attention to his warning. He'd called the office when I was in the middle of delivering a litter of pups, demanding to speak to me. When I got on the phone his words were slurred, as if he'd been drinking, and he just kept saying over and over I was going to be murdered. When I pressed him for details, he said that he had been getting letters from some mysterious lunatic who was intending to kill the women of Pike. I honestly thought he was confusing the plot of a movie he was watching with real life." She glanced toward the empty chair in the corner, her expression one of regret. "After work I ran by his house and he didn't even remember calling me. I just dismissed it. I'm sorry."

He moved forward, grabbing her hand to give it a small squeeze. "Don't apologize, Lynne. I'm just on edge. And trust me, you weren't the only one to dismiss my father's ravings. The sheriff did. I did. . . ." His voice broke and he was forced to clear the lump from his throat. "Or at least, I assumed that if he truly was getting letters, they must be from someone who was trying to screw with him. What else could we think when there were never any bodies?"

"Until now."

He started to nod, then he released his breath with a low hiss. "Christ," he muttered, hurrying across the room and into the old-fashioned kitchen.

It was a boxy space with old wooden cabinets and a white sink that was chipped and rusting where the water had leaked for years. The fridge hummed with a sound that warned it was on its last legs, and the oven was coated in grease.

He'd tried to keep his stuff contained here and in his old bedroom, so nothing got lost among the stacks of boxes he was filling with his father's belongings.

"Now what?" Lynne followed behind him, her expression puzzled as he reached for the wrinkled piece of paper he'd tossed on the worn dining table.

He turned the paper so she could see the letters scribbled on the front. "I was given this by Ron Bradshaw."

She stepped closer, studying the initials. "What is it?"

It was a question that had plagued him since Bradshaw

had shoved it in his hand. Last night he'd sat at the table, eating his solitary meal and trying to puzzle out what the letters could mean. They were written in the form of initials. S.H. R.D. Did they refer to names? Places? Or nonsense from a delusional man on the edge of death?

All he'd gotten for his efforts was a headache.

"I have no idea, but my father left it with the preacher to give to me after his death," he told Lynne.

"It looks like initials." She guessed the obvious.

He pointed a finger at the bottom letters. "Here."

"D.R.L.G." she read out loud. Then she lifted her head to meet his steady gaze. "Does it mean something to you?"

"Dr. Lynne Gale."

Lynne made a sound as if she'd taken a blow to the stomach.

In fact, it felt like she'd been punched.

She'd come to this house because she'd remembered the strange phone call from Rudolf. And she honestly had been worried about Kir after he'd charged out of her clinic. But now that he was implying that those were her initials on some sort of weird list he'd been given, she found herself eager to dismiss his suggestion.

"That's a stretch," she argued. "It could mean any-thing."

"The only way to know for certain is to find those letters."

She bit back her protest and squared her shoulders. He was right. She hadn't known Rudolf as well as her father. The two old men had been friends for fifty years. But she'd often stopped by to check on Rudolf's dog, knowing that the poor man was going to be devastated when the old hound finally died. And each time she rang the doorbell, she never knew which Rudolf would answer.

The funny, self-deprecating man with a razor-sharp memory who loved to chat. Or the bleary-eyed, drunkenly muddled man who barely recognized her.

One thing was for certain. He'd never lied to her. He might have been confused, or mistaken, but he never lied. So, assuming he hadn't been delusional, then some nutjob had sent him letters that had terrified him enough to call her. Which meant he would have kept them. They had to be somewhere. "Where have you searched?"

"Dad's bedroom, and I just finished his office," he told her.

"Does he have a safety-deposit box at the bank?"

He shook his head, even as he abruptly turned toward the narrow door across the room. "He has a safe," he said, opening the door. "Follow me."

"Where are you going?" Lynne asked as he disappeared from view.

"The cellar. There's an old safe down here where dad used to keep his gun locked. I think there were some personal papers in there as well," he called out.

Lynne passed by the fridge that vibrated with enough force to make the floor shake and headed down the narrow flight of stairs to the basement. The smell of damp hit her before she reached the bottom and she hesitated on the last step.

She hated creepy, enclosed spaces. "Is there a light?"

"Yeah, hold on."

There was the sound of a click and a barren bulb in the center of the ceiling glowed to life, revealing the damp, musty space. There wasn't much to see. A washer and dryer along one stone wall, a hot water heater, a bookcase with well-used paperback books. And in the very center of the dirt floor was a three-foot safe.

"Shit." Kir's gaze was locked on the safe's door, which was wide open. "Someone was in here."

"Are you sure?" Lynne forced herself to follow Kir as he surged forward. "Maybe your father lost the key."

Kneeling down, he grabbed the crowbar that had been left beside the safe. "He would have had a new one made. He wouldn't have had the strength to use this."

That was true. In the past few years Rudolf had lost enough weight to make him appear gaunt. It was doubtful he could have wedged open a steel door. Even with a crowbar.

"Do you know what was in there?"

"Most of his important documents I took to Boston with me," Kir told her in absent tones. "I was afraid they might get lost. But his gun is gone, along with the bullets."

He knelt down, pulling out the only object left in the safe. A large shoebox. Flicking off the lid, Kir peered inside.

Lynne could tell by his disappointed expression that the letters weren't there. "Empty?"

"Yep." He dropped the box and straightened. "Let's get out of here."

Lynne didn't argue. She desperately wanted out of the dismal cellar. How could anyone breathe in the dark, cramped space?

Once back in the kitchen, Lynne sucked in the relatively fresh air and studied Kir's tense expression. "Do you think someone broke in after your father died?"

His nod was jerky. "I do."

"For the gun?"

"I think the gun was taken to cover up the truth of what the thief really wanted," he said. "The letters."

His face had paled, the blue of his eyes darkened with worry. She understood. It was one thing to talk about Rudolf receiving letters from a mystery person, but now they had a dead woman, and someone willing to break into Rudolf's home and destroy his safe.

"Why risk stealing them?" she asked.

"Fingerprints. DNA." A grim smile twisted his lips. "Proof my father wasn't crazy."

She reached to touch his arm, her heart melting with sympathy. Kir had just buried his father, but for the past eighteen years he'd been mourning the loss of the man he'd once loved. She couldn't even imagine how hard it had been to live in this house, watching Rudolf fade from a respected sheriff to the town drunk. "No one thought that, Kir."

He didn't argue, instead he covered her hand and squeezed her fingers in a tight grip. "What if he was right, Lynne?"

"About a killer in Pike?"

"Yes."

Her mouth suddenly felt dry. "There haven't been any murders. Not until today."

"Maybe the killer was hunting in other towns and the bodies haven't been found. Or maybe . . ."

"Or maybe what?

He scrubbed his face with his hands and Lynne was suddenly aware of the weariness that was etched into his face.

"Maybe something just triggered him. I don't know." He reached for his coat. "I'm probably overreacting, but

I didn't listen when my dad was alive. The least I can do is attempt and figure out what he was trying to tell me from the grave."

"What are you going to do?"

He tugged on his jacket, the air of weariness replaced by a ruthless determination. "I'm going to take a drive."

"To where?"

He headed out of the kitchen. "To the place they found the woman."

She hesitated. She should return to the clinic. Although both of her interns had recently graduated from veterinary school and were perfectly capable of dealing with the daily routine, she preferred to be close by in case they had questions. But she knew she wouldn't be able to concentrate.

Not only was she even more worried about Kir than before, but she also wanted the same answers that he did.

Who killed Sherry Higgins? And did it have anything to do with the letters Rudolf might or might not have received? Why had Rudolf given Pastor Ron the strange list of initials? And why not send it directly to Kir if he wanted his son to have it?

This all might be a wild-goose chase. As Kir had said, they could be overreacting to events that had simple explanations. But until she was sure, she wouldn't be able to think of anything else.

She marched into the living room, grabbing her coat to bundle it around her. Next was her stocking cap and gloves.

"I'm going with you," she announced.

"Lynne."

She ignored his exasperated expression. He was obviously like her—used to doing everything himself. For now he was going to have to get used to having a partner.

"The farm belongs to Raymond Warren," she told him, moving to shove her feet into her boots. "He'll shoot you if you drive onto his property without an invitation. Especially now that the sheriff and gawkers are no doubt tramping around the place."

Kir furrowed his brow, as if scouring his memory to place the name. "Old man Warren?" he at last demanded.

She nodded. "I make regular visits to check on his livestock, so he'll recognize my truck. That should give us time to talk to him before he starts shooting."

"I remember him." Kir shuddered. "He threatened to chop me into little pieces and use me as fertilizer when he caught me stealing apples from his orchard. He scared the shit out of me." He zipped up his coat and wrapped a scarf around his neck. "Yeah. Maybe you should go. I'd hate to end up in his wood chipper."

Lynne stilled, studying him with a sudden fascination. She'd already accepted that she was physically attracted to this man. You'd have to be dead not to find Kir insanely sexy. And at the funeral, she'd sensed he'd achieved a maturity that had been profoundly lacking when he'd walked away from Pike. But his easy acceptance of her suggestion touched a raw place deep inside her.

Probably because her last boyfriend, Nash Cordon, had been an egotistical jerk. He'd accused her of being a control freak who emotionally castrated him. Whatever the hell that meant.

"I like that," she said.

He arched a brow. "What?"

"A man who can admit he might need a woman's help."

He smiled, moving to tuck one of her stray curls beneath the knit stocking cap. "My career as a jack-of-all-trades has taught me the wisdom of bringing in an expert when I need one. And you, Dr. Lynne Gale, are an expert with the good citizens of Pike." His fingertips lightly trailed down her cheek. "Perhaps I'll display my own expertise later."

Chapter 4

The drive to Raymond Warren's farm was only three miles outside of town, but it took twenty minutes to navigate the icy roads. Eventually they turned onto a snow-packed drive winding toward the double-story white house and sprawling complex of paddocks and outbuildings.

Lynne had confidently pulled her battered truck to a halt in front of a red-painted barn, smiling when the man who was as broad as he was tall stepped into view. He was wearing a thick layer of coveralls with a flapped hat covering his head, but the ruddy face was scrunched into a scowl and there was a very large shotgun gripped in his gloved hand.

Kir had inwardly congratulated himself on his astute decision to allow Lynne to drive. He hadn't been teasing when he'd told her he had learned to seek the knowledge of others. His business thrived because he offered top-notch services for a competitive price. And that meant handing off duties to those better suited to perform a certain task.

If he'd pulled up in his own vehicle, he was fairly sure he'd be at the wrong end of that shotgun.

Instead the man had greeted Lynne with an unmistakable warmth, and while he'd sent Kir a suspicious glance, he hadn't threatened to chop off any parts of his body. Progress. The farmer had even given in to her request to see the scene of the crime, leading them around the barn and to the top of a low hill.

Kir was instantly struck by the peaceful beauty of the view. Blindingly white snow coated the rolling fields in a thick blanket, dramatically framed by the distant tree line. Here and there a fence row poked through, coated with ice and glittering in the late afternoon sun that peeked through the heavy gray clouds.

It looked like a Norman Rockwell painting. Until his gaze landed on the spot where Raymond Warren was pointing. There was nothing peaceful about that corner of the field.

The snow had been trampled by vehicles and footprints until the frozen ground beneath had been churned to the surface. And worse, in the very center, the snow had been dug away to leave a barren patch. He assumed that was where Sherry Higgins's dead body had been. And that the sheriff had taken everything, including the ground, in case it might have evidence.

It left behind a gaping scar.

"Right there," the man was saying, his voice harsh. "I couldn't believe it. I was headed to the barn when I saw the red ribbon flapping in the wind. I didn't know it was attached to a dead woman till I got close."

Kir could imagine how easy it would be to spot the crimson ribbon against the backdrop of white. Was that why the killer had put it on the body? Or had the woman already been wearing it? "Do you have any security on the property?" he asked.

The farmer sent him a narrow-eyed glare. "This is all the security I need." He waved the gun as if Kir had somehow overlooked the three-foot weapon.

Kir refused to be intimidated. He wasn't a twelve-year-old boy who could be run off with a threat. "Did you notice anything unusual this morning?"

"Besides the dead woman?"

"Yeah, besides the dead woman."

"Nope."

Kir glanced around. He didn't know what he was looking for. Hell, he wasn't even sure why he was there. But he could almost feel his father urging him to continue the search. It was going to haunt him until he did everything in his power to discover whether or not there was a serial killer in Pike.

"There weren't any tracks in the field?" he finally asked.

"To be honest, I didn't pay any attention," the older man admitted. "I was too busy trying to keep down my breakfast."

Frustration bubbled though Kir, but before he could say something stupid and get himself shot, Lynne stepped between the two men.

"What about Rusty?"

Raymond looked confused. "What about him?"

"Did you hear him barking?"

The farmer paused, pondering the question. "We put him inside at night when it's this cold, but if someone had pulled into our drive, he would have let us know."

That meant they had to come from the opposite side of the field, Kir silently concluded. He turned, studying the thick woods. It would be the most secluded way to this area. Did whoever dumped the body know there was a dog here who barked at passing cars? Or had they just wanted to avoid the house?

"I'm sorry this happened to you, Raymond," Lynne murmured. "Did you know the poor woman?"

"It looked like Sherry Higgins," Raymond muttered, his ruddy face tightening at the horrifying memory. "Fraser's daughter."

Lynne offered a sympathetic frown. "I've seen her around town, but I didn't really know her."

"She took over Fraser's trailer park after he died," the older man explained. "She kept to herself most of the time, but I'm not sure she was well liked by her tenants. She kicked my nephew out of his trailer last year after he lost his job at the glove factory. And he wasn't the only one."

Kir was instantly reminded of the dude from the news who'd interrupted his lunch with Lynne. Perkins? Parker? Anyway, he'd mentioned that Sherry Higgins hadn't been the most beloved member of the small community. Perhaps her killing was nothing more than retribution from an angry tenant.

"Do you have any names?" he demanded. "I'd like to talk to them."

Kir swallowed a curse as Raymond stiffened at his abrupt demand. He'd been in Boston too long.

"I need to get back to my chores," the older man muttered.

"Thanks for visiting with us, Raymond." Lynne tried to smooth over the man's ruffled feathers.

Raymond grunted, but before he walked away, he glanced toward Kir. "Sorry about your father, Jansen," he said without warning. "He once spent an entire night helping me search for a missing calf. It must have been twenty below, but he never gave up. He was a good man." There was a short pause. "A good sheriff."

The gruff words meant more to Kir than any flowery speech. "He was."

With another grunt, Raymond stomped toward his nearby barn, entering through the back door.

"Now what?" Lynne asked.

Kir glanced around. They couldn't poke around here. Even if he hadn't managed to annoy Raymond Warren, the farmer had made it clear he wanted them to leave.

Still, he wasn't prepared to give up. He wanted to know who'd killed Sherry Higgins, and how the body had ended up in this field.

Crimson blood stains the pure white snow.

He pointed toward the distant line of trees. "I think I remember a road on the other side of this field. Is it still there?"

She nodded, immediately understanding his desire to check it out. "We can cut through Raymond's orchard to reach it."

They retraced their footsteps in silence, both moving with as much haste as possible, considering the frozen ground. Sherry's body had been hauled away, but the memory of her violent end seemed to linger. Like an echo of evil.

Kir climbed into Lynne's truck. He never thought he'd feel sympathy for the abrasive Raymond Warren, but it was going to be horrible to walk past that spot every morning.

Lynne started the truck and shoved it into four-wheel drive as she turned toward a narrow access path that ran between the barren apple trees. Kir's lips briefly curled at the memory of sneaking through this orchard on a dare from a friend. In those days he would have done anything to experience an adrenaline rush. It was the only thing that drove away the fear his father would never escape his dark quagmire of misery.

They bumped over the ice-coated path, winding their way up the hill and into the wooded area. Then, turning onto the main road that had recently been cleared of the snow, they traveled parallel to Raymond's farm.

"Can we stop?" Kir abruptly demanded, nodding toward the shallow shoulder. Without a word, she whipped the truck to the side and put it in park. "You can stay in here. It's freezing," he assured her.

She snorted, switching off the engine. "I'm used to the cold. You're the city boy," she reminded him.

"I'll admit that it bothers me a lot more than it used to, but I have a feeling it has more to do with age than my current address," he said in wry tones.

Together they climbed out of the truck and walked along the edge of the road. They didn't have to go far for Kir to find the tire tracks that were nearly concealed by the blowing snow.

"There." He glanced around, eerily aware of the heavy silence that shrouded the road. It wasn't just that he was used to the hustle and bustle of a large city. This was the silence of an area that was rarely disturbed by humans. "Do you know who owns this property?"

Lynne furrowed her brow as she glanced from one side of the road to the other.

"I'm pretty sure it belongs to the conservation department."

Kir strolled to where the tracks were the deepest, as if someone had parked there for long enough to sink into the snow. Then, as he turned in the direction of Raymond Warren's farm, his breath caught in his throat.

There was an opening through the trees that looked like it'd once been a cattle crossing.

"That's the field," Lynne said, moving until she was pressed against his side.

If it hadn't been below freezing, he might have hoped she was seeking comfort from being close to him. Instead he was fairly sure she was just trying to stay warm. "From this position it's a clear path to where they found the body."

Lynne nodded. "So either the killer forced her to walk down there and murdered her, or she was already dead."

Kir tried to imagine what'd happened. The newsman had mentioned a slit throat, but they didn't know where the woman had died. In addition, he had no idea if she'd been killed and dumped last night, or early this morning.

Of course, they did have one clue, he abruptly recalled. "There's another possibility."

"What?"

"She could have been unconscious."

Lynne's eyes widened as his words jogged her memory. "Oh, that's right. I forgot Parker said something about a tranquilizer dart."

Kir parted his lips to ask Lynne if she had a relationship with the slick-talking Parker, but he hastily swallowed the words. It wasn't any of his business. Even if he was starting to wish it was. Instead he kept the conversation focused on the reason they were standing in the frigid air.

"He could have knocked her out at the office, then driven her here."

Lynne glanced back at the opening. "Yes. If it was me,

I would have put her body on a tarp or a blanket and dragged her down the slope."

Kir leaned forward, studying the slope, which was steeper than he'd first realized. "It would be the easiest way," he agreed, visualizing sliding the dead woman down the hill. Far more sensible than trying to carry her through the deep snow. "It would also mean a woman could be the killer." A fierce wind managed to penetrate the trees, the shadows lengthening as a reminder that the afternoon was nearly at an end. He didn't want Lynne driving the icy roads after dark. "Let's go."

Dear Rudolf,

What a glorious day. I wish you could have been here to witness my splendid achievement. It wasn't like the first time. Or even my second time. I wasn't nervous. Or lost in my fury. No. I was calm. That's the only way to truly savor my justice.

Sherry hadn't changed, Rudolf. She was just as revolting as ever. Ah, but she tried to hide it. She pretended to be confused when she saw me. Then she acted as if butter wouldn't melt in her vile, nasty mouth. Like she could make me forget her sins.

Then there was her fear.

The magnificent fear that was so thick in the air it seeped into my skin. I can still smell it.

My only regret is that I didn't wait for her to wake. It would have been sheer perfection to watch the life draining from her eyes. The bitter old cow.

But practice makes perfect. And I already have my plans in motion.

Tonight, I'll meet with my prey. She has no idea

*she has been selected to participate in my . . .
Hmm. What should I call it, Rudolf? It's not a
game. Perhaps a quest. Yes, I like that. My quest
for vengeance.*

*She believes she's meeting the man who she's
been chatting with online. People are so gullible. I
put up a profile with the picture of some handsome
jerk, and presto. She couldn't wait to be lured
away from her family.*

I'm going to take my time punishing her.

*I promise you, it will be epic as her crimson
blood stains the pure white snow. Life spills from
warm to frozen. Don't look. The pain is gone.*

Randi with an *i* not a *y* parked her vehicle in the empty
lot behind her flower shop. It was nearly ten o'clock, but
no one would question seeing her flashy red car. Over the
past few years Randi had discovered more and more
reasons to linger at the shop. Anything was preferable to
dealing with her daughter who'd gone from a precious
baby to an obnoxious teenager, and her husband, who
spent their time together bitching about the money she
spent. As if it was her fault he'd stayed in his job at the
paper mill instead of finding a position that could do more
than pay the mortgage. If he thought she was going to live
in squalor and wear clothes from a discount store, then he
was even dumber than he looked.

Switching off the motor, Randi shivered. The snow had
started to fall, filling the night with swirls of white. Sometimes it felt as if she was being smothered. Not an ava-
lanche, but a slow, relentless blanket of suffocating snow.

She had nightmares about it.

How had her life come to this?

Once she'd been the most popular girl in Pike. She'd been dazzlingly pretty with her long, dark hair and big green eyes. And so sexy the boys would beg just to walk next to her in the hallway.

She'd assumed her position as homecoming queen would last forever.

Instead she'd married her high school sweetheart and had a baby before she'd even turned twenty. Since then her life had been on a downward skid straight to the gutter.

Okay, maybe it wasn't the gutter. It was worse.

It was obscurity.

Squaring her shoulders, Randi climbed out of her car and scurried toward the back door of her shop. She'd deliberately chosen this location to meet her mystery man. She might be horny, but she wasn't stupid. This was her territory, and not only did she have a security system, but she also had a loaded handgun in her office. If she got any hinky vibes, she was going to shoot first and ask questions later. She could always claim the stranger broke into the shop and she had to defend herself.

Reaching the door, Randi experienced a flutter of excitement. Her mystery date had been fascinating when they'd chatted online. Charming, funny, and properly appreciative of her opinions. A man who knew how to make a woman feel special. She desperately hoped he was as good up close and personal as he was on the computer.

"Please don't let him be a loser," she whispered, fumbling for her keys.

At the same time, she felt a strange prick on the side of her neck. She reached up, grabbing the object protruding just above the collar of her coat.

What was it?

She tugged it loose, then held it toward the nearby security light. She frowned at the silver tube. Where had that come from?

"Hello, Randi," a voice drawled, but Randi didn't turn her head to see who was standing next to her.

She was mesmerized by the strange object she cradled in the palm of her hand. Besides, her neck felt rubbery. As if her head was suddenly too heavy. She swayed, struggling to stay upright.

As her eyes began to dim, she caught sight of the snowflakes that had already coated her in a layer of white. A hysterical laugh bubbled in her throat.

Her nightmare was coming true.

Damn the snow.

I settle in my seat and take a second to calm my heart. It's beating so hard I can feel the pulse in my throat. It's not from fear. It's pure adrenaline.

And it's glorious.

Sitting in a dark corner, I study the woman lying naked in the center of the room. Far over her head a fluorescent bulb spills out a harsh pool of light. It reveals the slender limbs that are artistically arranged and the glossy curls that frame her pale face like a dark halo.

Most people would no doubt find her beautiful. Despite the years she'd managed to keep her trim body. And her youthful, girl-next-door features were discreetly maintained with layers of makeup. But all I see is a brittle veneer that disguises the ugliness below.

Randi Decker is a vain, shallow bitch who has never cared about anyone but herself. She bullied her classmates throughout school, and I assume she continued the abuse with her employees at the flower shop. She nagged her husband and ignored her daughter.

I smile, recalling how easy it'd been to lure Randi into my web. A few compliments in a chatroom and she was ready and eager for anything. She didn't care that she was betraying her husband or that her daughter would be mortified if her cheating was exposed. Nothing mattered but her own pleasures.

Some things never changed. . . .

No. I rise to my feet. I changed. I'm no longer a victim of fate. Now I control my destiny. Including those who once thought they were immune to justice.

Randi woke with a thick head and a coat of fuzz on her tongue. Ugh. Did she get tanked last night? It wouldn't be the first time. Over the past couple of years she'd spent more and more evenings dulling the sharp edges of her life with a bottle of wine. Sometimes two.

Still, she didn't remember overindulging. In fact, she couldn't remember anything at all. Pressing her fingers against her throbbing temples, Randi slowly sat up and forced open her heavy lids.

The first thing she noticed was that she was naked. Completely and utterly naked. The realization sent shockwaves through her. She was *never* naked. Not unless she was in the shower. Her vanity couldn't bear to reveal the stretch marks that marred her stomach or the droop of her once perky breasts. Even during sex she kept on her nightgown. Not that her husband noticed. He barely bothered to kiss her before he was shoved inside her and done.

Her second realization was that she was freezing.

Shivering, she pulled her knees to her chest and wrapped her arms around her legs. Then, with an effort, she forced herself to glance around. It was a wasted effort. Beyond the small circle of light there was nothing but darkness. A thick, blinding darkness.

Was she in a basement?

Yes. She had to be.

Now the question was how she'd gotten there.

Rocking back and forth, she searched her fuzzy brain. She didn't have a basement at her house or even one at the shop. . . .

Shop. The thought of her flower store stirred her memory. Oh, shit. She'd been going there to meet her mystery man, hadn't she? And then she'd felt a pain in her neck. A needle? Maybe a tranq dart?

She squeezed her eyes shut. She'd been so certain that she held the upper hand. She'd planned for everything. Or at least that's what she'd told herself.

And now she was naked and alone and terrified out of her freaking mind.

Bending her head, Randi did something she hadn't done since she was five years old.

She prayed.

Chapter 5

It was Friday, which meant Lynne was able to sleep in until six o'clock. One intern was covering the herd wellness checks, while she would take care of the morning appointments at her clinic, and her other intern would arrive at noon to deal with afternoon appointments. As a bonus, it was her weekend off.

Usually she enjoyed a leisurely breakfast before heading to the clinic. This morning, however, she was just stepping out of the shower when the familiar sound of Parker Bowen's voice echoed from the television.

"Another day and another body has been discovered in Pike," the newscaster announced, his smooth voice properly somber. "The authorities haven't released a name, but the female was found on the banks of the Keokuk River near the campground. Like the previous victim, she was stripped of her clothes and a crimson ribbon was tied around her neck. The sheriff refused to speculate on whether the two crimes are connected, but she did reveal that both women had their throats slit. Once again, the authorities ask that anyone with information please contact the sheriff's office. I will have more on this continuing story on the evening news."

Another body. Fear tightened Lynne's stomach. Yesterday she'd first assumed that the poor female was a stranger who had the misfortune to be dumped near Pike. Then she'd discovered it was Sherry. This time she was bracing herself for the realization that the victim was from the area. And that it was quite likely someone she knew.

How could this be happening? Pike was a sleepy, tranquil town where nothing ever happened. That's what she loved about this place.

And now the peace was shattered by two violent deaths.

Was Kir's suspicion right? Was there was a maniac out there hunting the women of Pike? And was he holding the list of women the killer was targeting?

"God." With a shudder, Lynne dressed and headed for the clinic. She was no longer in the mood for breakfast.

For the next five hours there was thankfully no time to worry about the news report as she worked her way through the numerous appointments. She'd just finished giving a rabies shot to an overly enthusiastic Labrador when her receptionist stuck her head into the exam room.

Chelsea Gallen was two years younger than Lynne with blond hair, and a short and full-figured body she emphasized with soft sweaters and narrow skirts. Her bubbly personality made her a favorite with the clients, which was why Lynne had hired her after her father's receptionist had retired. Unfortunately, the younger woman wasn't always dependable, more often than not showing up late or dashing out the door long before the day's schedule was done. Still, Lynne tried to be patient. Chelsea was a single mother to a little girl. It couldn't be easy for her.

"The sheriff is here to see you," Chelsea said, her expression curious.

Lynne blinked in surprise. "Why?"

"She didn't say."

"Okay." Lynne headed toward the sink at the back of the room. "Tell her I'll be out as soon as I wash up."

Chelsea disappeared and Lynne heard the distant sound of voices. The sheriff had stopped by the clinic on a few occasions, usually when they'd located a dog roaming the streets and wanted to scan it for a chip. Today, Lynne doubted the local law enforcement were worried about strays.

After scrubbing her hands with a brisk efficiency, Lynne pulled off her lab coat and smoothed back the hair that had come loose from her ponytail. It was ridiculous to feel uneasy, but she had a terrible premonition that the sheriff's visit was connected with the dead woman who had been found that morning. Perhaps she'd been a client. Or a friend.

The thought made her stomach cramp with unease as she stepped out of the exam room and into the reception area. It was thankfully empty at the moment, except for Chelsea, who was standing next to the tall counter, and the current sheriff of Pike.

Kathy Hancock was in her forties with dark hair that was roughly chopped at her shoulders and combed away from her square face. Her eyes hovered somewhere between gray and green and her skin was pale and dusted with freckles. She wasn't fat, but she was solid and looked like she could hold her own in a fight. Probably a useful quality in an officer of the law.

At the moment, she was wearing her brown sheriff uniform with a matching brown parka. Her expression was grim.

"Sheriff," Lynne murmured. She didn't know Kathy in more than a professional capacity. The older woman was competent at her job, but she wasn't the most social person. "Chelsea said you needed to see me. Is there a problem?"

"I have a couple of questions."

"Okay."

"I'm sure you've heard about the two women who have recently died?"

"Yes." Lynne braced herself for the bad news. "It's been on television."

The sheriff reached into the pocket of her heavy brown parka. "What we haven't released is that two dart cartridges were found at the scene where each woman was taken." She pulled her hand out, revealing a plastic bag that contained two silver tubes with a hollow needle at one end and a plastic stopper with wings at the other end. "Do you recognize these?"

Prepared to be told that one of her friends had been murdered, it took Lynne a second to focus on the darts in the plastic bag. "They look like the ones I use," she admitted. "But so do a dozen other people in the area."

Kathy looked surprised. "Who else?"

"Farmers, conservation officers, animal control." Lynne shrugged. "Even a few hunters."

The sheriff nodded. It was hard to tell if she was pleased or disappointed to know that the darts were readily available in Pike. "And you have tranquilizers in your clinic?"

"Of course."

"Can you tell me what kind?"

"Xylazine. Medetomidine. Telazol." Lynne shrugged. "A few others, including a form of cocaine for extreme cases."

Kathy pushed the bag back into her pocket. "I assume you keep all your drugs locked away?"

Lynne frowned. She understood the sheriff had to ask questions. The two dead women had seemingly been hit with tranq darts before they were killed. A veterinarian clinic was an obvious place to start the investigation.

Still, she couldn't prevent herself from bristling defensively at the hint of censure in the woman's tone. It sounded as if she suspected Lynne of being sloppy in keeping dangerous drugs off the street.

"I follow very strict protocols when it comes to keeping my medications stored."

"Do you mind if I see?"

"Certainly not." Lynne squared her shoulders to a rigid angle, waving her hand toward the nearby hallway. "This way."

"Dr. Gale," Chelsea said, her tone urgent.

"I'll be right back, Chelsea."

Leading the sheriff to the end of the hallway, she unlocked the steel door and shoved it open. The spacious room with high ceilings and bright lights had once been the kennels, but Lynne had built a separate space for the animals who were waiting for surgery or too sick to go home behind the clinic. It ensured they weren't constantly being disturbed by the steady stream of patients.

Now the old kennel was lined with glass and steel cases that could be individually locked as well as steel shelves at the back for the daily office supplies.

Kathy stepped into the center of the room, slowly turning in a circle, her hard gaze missing nothing.

"Who has the key to the cabinets?" she at last demanded.

"There are three of us." Lynne held up her keychain. "I have one. Chelsea has one. And there's one for whichever intern is on duty."

The sheriff took out a notebook and pencil from beneath her parka. "Could someone have made a copy?"

"Theoretically." Lynne didn't believe for a second any of her employees would make copies of her keys. She trusted them without question. "Why?"

"Would you know if there were any sedatives missing?"

"Absolutely." Lynne reached out to grab the clipboard that was hanging on the wall and crossed to stand next to the sheriff. "Each prescription is logged in when it's stocked and anyone who removes a vial has to initial the date and time and amount that is used." She pointed to the column that listed the drugs and then the squares next to the names that showed who'd removed it from the cabinet. "They're also recorded into the computer. At the end of the week Chelsea takes an inventory to make sure it all matches."

Kathy studied the clipboard before glancing back at the cabinets. At last she gave a small shake of her head, as if forced to give up on a promising clue. "Where would someone get these drugs?"

"We have a computer program that tracks the drugs and creates an order from our supplier when we are running low."

The sheriff nodded, as if making a mental note. "Can anyone order from your supplier?"

"No. You have to be a licensed vet."

"What about the black market?"

Lynne wasn't sure how to answer. She'd never had experience with the black market. Then again, she'd gone to enough seminars on safeguarding her prescriptions and the disposal of them after their expiration date to know that it was obviously a problem. "There isn't the same demand as for prescriptions for humans, but any drug is worth money on the streets," she conceded.

"And you're certain that none is missing?"

Lynne was a tolerant woman. You couldn't be a vet and not have the patience of a saint. But the sense of being interrogated as if she was a criminal was wearing on her nerves. "I've just told you, we've never had any—"

"Dr. Gale," Chelsea interrupted.

Lynne sent her receptionist a sharp glance. She hadn't realized the younger woman had followed them to the storage room. "Not now, Chelsea," she said, in no mood to deal with whatever was bothering the younger woman.

"It's important," Chelsea insisted.

Lynne turned, belatedly noticing her receptionist's pale face. "What's wrong?"

"We did have a few vials of Telazol missing."

Lynne stared at her employee, certain she must have misunderstood. "What are you talking about?"

Chelsea cleared her throat, shifting from one foot to another. Lynne had never seen her act so nervous. Not even when she had spilled a bottle of soda and they'd had to replace the computer system. "Well, th-they weren't exactly m-missing," she stammered. "They were broken."

Lynne forgot about the sheriff as she stepped toward Chelsea. "When?"

"A couple months ago."

"Why didn't you tell me?"

The younger woman's pallor was replaced by a deep flush. "It was just an accident. I swear."

Lynne frowned. Chelsea had a lot of accidents. She was never this upset about them. "Okay, but it should have been noted in the inventory," she pointed out.

Chelsea continued to shift from foot to foot, looking as if she wanted to turn and flee. "I changed the log."

"Why?"

"I didn't want you to know."

Lynne's confusion was threaded with a hint of anger. An accident was one thing. To deliberately cover it up was another. Still, she hid her annoyance. If Chelsea thought she was being chastised, she would sulk like a petulant child and refuse to answer.

"Did you think you would be in trouble?"

The receptionist hunched her shoulders, as if she was expecting a blow. "Not because of the broken vials."

"Then why?"

There was a long, awkward silence. "Because I wasn't in the storage room alone," Chelsea at last whispered.

"You . . ." Lynne's breath caught in her throat as she realized what her employee was saying. She'd been having sex in the storage room. "Oh."

There was the sound of heavy boots squeaking against the tile floor as the sheriff intruded into their conversation. "Who was with you?"

Chelsea seemed to shrink an inch as she twisted her fingers together. "It doesn't matter. I just wanted to explain any inconsistency in the records."

The sheriff wasn't impressed. "I'll decide what information is important, Ms. . . ."

"Chelsea Gallen."

Kathy leaned forward, her hands on her hips. "Answer the question."

Chelsea shrank another inch. "What does it matter? We were in the storage room and a few vials fell off the shelf."

"You witnessed them break?" Kathy pressed.

"Well . . ."

"Be careful, Ms. Gallen." The sheriff's expression was as icy cold as the weather outside. "It's a crime to lie to law enforcement. Did you see the vials break?"

Chelsea shook her head. "No. I had to answer the phone. When I came back there was glass on the floor and . . ." Her words trailed away as she glanced nervously toward Lynne before returning her attention to the sheriff. "My friend was mopping up the mess. He said he'd bumped into the cabinet and a case of Telazol had fallen out and busted."

Lynne struggled to contain her anger. "I can't believe you didn't tell me."

"I couldn't."

"Why not? I thought we were family here."

Kathy sent Lynne a chiding frown. "You can discuss your trust issues later." She pointed a finger in the younger woman's face. "I want a name."

The younger woman shook her head in mute misery.

Lynne ground her teeth. Why was Chelsea hesitating? Surely the worst part of the confession was the fact that she'd been having sex in the storage room? Unless she'd been in there with a married man.

"You can tell us here or we can go down to the station and talk there," Kathy threatened.

Chelsea sucked in a terrified breath. No doubt she was thinking of her young daughter. It was a small town. Even if the sheriff didn't press charges there would be nasty rumors swirling around her visit to the station.

She abruptly spit out the name. "It was Nash."

Chapter 6

When Kir arrived at the clinic, he was immediately on edge at the sight of the sheriff's SUV parked out front. It didn't help his nerves to enter the reception area and find it empty.

Where was everyone? Had something happened to Lynne? His heart clenched with a startling, painful sensation, but before he could allow himself to overreact, he heard the sound of voices echoing from the back of the clinic.

Cautiously he made his way down the hallway, halting just outside the open door of what looked like a storage room. Inside he could see Lynne along with Sheriff Hancock. Neither of them noticed him as they concentrated on the younger woman, who was visibly trembling. The tension was so thick he could physically feel it pulsing in the air.

Unashamedly eavesdropping, Kir managed to figure out the blond woman had been caught in the storage room getting up close and personal with some dude named Nash, and that there were vials of tranquilizer missing. Presumably the same tranquilizer that was used on the dead women. Why else would the sheriff be there asking questions?

"You know who she's talking about?" Kathy Hancock demanded.

"Nash Cordon." Lynne's voice was laced with an unexpected bitterness. "My ex-boyfriend. He owns the Bait and Tackle bar on State Street."

The sheriff grunted, her expression twisting with a sudden displeasure. "Yeah, I know him."

"I'm sorry, I truly am," the younger woman whispered. "It only happened a couple of times."

Lynne held herself so rigid that Kir feared she might shatter. "Has Chelsea answered your questions?" she asked, her gaze locked on the sheriff.

Kathy shrugged. "For now."

Kir stepped into the storage room. It was obvious Lynne was reeling from what she'd just discovered. And the knowledge that she was so deeply hurt pissed him off. He had a vague memory of Nash Cordon. In school, he'd been a cocky bastard. Clearly, he hadn't changed much in the past few years if he was willing to cheat on Lynne with her own employee.

Still, now wasn't the time to consider the pleasure of tracking down the jerk and punching him in the nose. Instead Kir sucked in a deep breath and forced himself to focus on the sheriff. He couldn't take away Lynne's visible sense of betrayal, but he could bring an end to Kathy's interrogation. That would at least give her the space to gather her composure.

"Hello, Kathy," he murmured.

Kathy jerked her head in his direction, her expression remaining sour as she recognized who had interrupted her grilling of the two women. Long ago the woman had treated Kir like a younger brother. But that'd all changed the day his father had been shot.

No surprise. Everything had changed that day.

"Kir." She offered a stiff nod. "I didn't know you were still in town."

"It's going to take a while to organize my dad's things and get the house ready for sale."

Kathy looked uncomfortable at the mention of Kir's father. She cleared her throat. "Are you here to see Dr. Gale?"

He had been, of course. From the minute he'd opened his eyes that morning he'd been devising a reason to seek out the fascinating vet. Only the knowledge she would be busy had kept him from arriving at the clinic at the crack of dawn. Instead he'd continued his self-imposed task of packing away his father's belongings until it was nearly noon. Then, pulling on his boots and leather coat, he'd headed for the clinic.

He'd hoped to tempt Lynne to join him for lunch. After all, their last date had been interrupted.

"Actually, I need to speak with you," he told the sheriff. It wasn't a lie. He did need to report the missing gun. "I saw your SUV outside."

Kathy hesitated before offering a grudging nod. Heading toward the door, she glared at the two women. "Don't leave town. Either of you."

Resisting the urge to send Lynne a comforting smile, Kir stepped aside to allow Kathy to take the lead as they left the clinic. Once outside, the sheriff stuffed her hands in the pockets of her parka.

The sun was blindingly bright as it shimmered and reflected off the snow, but the wind was biting.

Kathy shaded her eyes with one hand. "What do you need?"

"Can we talk at Dad's house?"

"Why?"

"There's something I want to show you."

Kathy furrowed her brow. "I don't really have time. In case you haven't heard, we have two dead women."

"It's important," he insisted.

"Fine," she muttered. She pressed the side of the small radio attached to her coat. "Anthony, come in."

There was the sound of static, then a male voice answered. "Anthony, here."

"I need you to call Nash Cordon at the Bait and Tackle bar and tell him I want him at the station for an interview ASAP."

"Ten-four."

Kathy dropped her hand and glanced around the parking lot. "Do you want a ride?"

No. What he *wanted* was to return to the clinic and pull Lynne into his arms. He couldn't explain the sensation. He had no reason to feel so protective toward the woman. It wasn't like they'd been best friends when he'd lived in Pike. At that age two years between them meant they were never in the same classes. And since his move to Boston, he'd barely glimpsed her during his fleeting visits.

Still it was an effort to force himself to nod his head. "That would be great."

Together they climbed into the SUV and Kathy started the engine. Pulling out of the parking lot, she turned onto the street heading south.

She drove slowly as they bumped over the thick layer of ice, her fingers clenching the steering wheel. Then without warning she heaved a harsh sigh. "I'm sorry about Rudolf." Her gaze remained locked on the road.

"Are you?"

She sent him a startled glance. "Of course."

Kir turned in his seat. It'd been sheer impulse to ask Kathy to come to his father's house, but he realized this was the perfect opportunity to get some answers.

"Dad said you refused to talk to him." He didn't bother with polite small talk. Kathy had never been chatty, not even when she'd been Rudolf's deputy. She was blunt to the point of rudeness. He intended to be the same. "That you wouldn't take his calls."

Her jaw hardened at his words. "He accused me of refusing to do my job. In fact, he implied that I was assisting a murderer to escape justice."

"He could be difficult," Kir agreed.

Kathy snorted. "He was a pain in the ass."

It was true, but Kir wasn't letting this woman forget that she owed Rudolf Jansen her career. "He was also the only one willing to battle against the prejudices of Pike to hire a woman as his deputy." Kir didn't add that at the same time Rudolf had overlooked her sketchy family. She came from a long line of con men, petty thieves, and moochers. When his father had first hired her, Kathy had been living out of her car.

Kathy's expression was stoic, but the flush that crawled beneath her freckled skin proved Kir had made a direct hit.

"That's true," she muttered. "He hired me and trained me to be a good cop. I considered him to be a second father."

There was a hint of genuine regret in her voice. Kir frowned. "So what went wrong?"

"He got shot."

"You blame him for that?"

"No, he blamed me."

Kir's breath hissed between his clenched teeth. His father might have drowned himself in alcohol and self-pity after the shooting, but he'd never blamed anyone for what had happened to him. Not even the low-life drug dealer who'd pulled the trigger. "That's not true. He never said a word about you being responsible. In fact, he'd always said that every day he walked out the front door he never knew if he was coming home. He accepted the dangers of his job."

"He didn't blame me for getting shot. He blamed me for taking the job he loved." Kathy sent him a quick, bitter glare as she pulled the SUV to a halt in front of the two-storied white house with green shutters and a steeply slanted roof. "And he wasn't the only one. I didn't put the bullet in Rudolf's head, but more than one person believed I was quick to take advantage of the situation."

Kir shoved open his door and slid out of the SUV. Did he resent this woman for taking his dad's place? Maybe a little. It'd been hard to watch his father struggling to accept his forced retirement while Kathy walked around town, doing his job. He'd never actually considered how difficult it might have been for Kathy to step into the shoes of a man who'd been close to a legend in this town.

With a sharp shake of his head, Kir led the sheriff to the side door that opened directly into the kitchen.

"You'll probably want to take off your coat," he suggested as the warmth of the house wrapped around him. "I've had the heater on high since I returned for the funeral. The place felt like the inside of a freezer when I first arrived."

Kathy halted next to the kitchen table that was piled

with boxes. Absently she pulled off her parka, hung it on the back of a chair, and glanced toward the old ceramic mug that was stained from forty years of Rudolf's morning coffee.

"I should have gone to the funeral," she apologized.

"It was a simple graveside service." Kir shrugged, careful not to offer blame or forgiveness.

Kathy could wrestle with her own conscience. God knew he was having enough trouble dealing with his own.

As if sensing his dark thoughts, she squared her shoulders. "Why am I here?"

"It's downstairs." Kir stepped toward the nearby door and pulled it open.

He could sense the sheriff's impatience as they maneuvered the narrow wooden stairs to enter the musty basement.

"Well?" she asked.

Kir pointed toward the center of the floor. "Someone broke into the house and destroyed my father's safe."

Kathy crossed to stand next to the safe, studying the door that had been pried off its hinges. "Did this happen while you were here?" she asked.

"I'm not sure when it happened. It was like this when I came down to see if there was anything that needed to be packed away."

Kir skirted the truth. He didn't want to reveal that Lynne had been with him. He hadn't liked Kathy's parting shot when she'd left the clinic. As if she suspected Lynne or her employee of being involved in something nefarious.

Perhaps even in the deaths of the two women.

"What did your dad keep in here?" Kathy glanced around the basement, which was covered in several layers of dust.

"His service revolver."

As expected, his words captured the sheriff's complete attention. "Damn. You're sure it was in there?"

"No, but that's where he usually locked it away, and I haven't seen it anywhere else in the house."

"I'll look up the registration and get it put in the system as a stolen weapon." She was all business as she moved to study the small window that offered a potential way into the basement. "Anything else he kept in there? Money? Prescriptions?"

"The letters," Kir said without hesitation.

Kathy turned back to face him. "Letters?"

"The ones my dad received from the serial killer."

Anger smoldered in her eyes. "You can't be serious?"

"I've never been more serious."

Swearing beneath her breath, Kathy stomped toward the stairs. "I'll write up a report on the theft of the gun."

Kir hastily moved to stand in her path. Probably not the smartest decision, considering she was carrying a weapon. "What if the letters are related to the current murders?" he suggested.

"They aren't."

"How can you be so sure?"

Her square face looked as hard as a stone. "They aren't."

Kir folded his arms over his chest. Rudolf used to say that his deputy was as stubborn as a mule, but this went beyond stubborn. It was deliberate avoidance of potential evidence. "Did you ever read them?" he demanded.

She paused, her gaze flicking toward the nearby stairs. Was she considering whether to simply walk away? Then, clenching her hands into tight fists, she forced herself to answer. "Your father brought them to the station."

"And?"

"And they were nothing more than gibberish," she snapped. "Vague references to women being killed and something about snow."

"'Crimson blood staining the pure white snow. Life spills from warm to frozen. Don't look. The pain is gone,'" Kir quoted, waiting for the resemblance to the current murders to sink through the sheriff's thick skull.

She dismissed his words with a wave of her hand. "Those letters were written years ago."

"Not all of them," Kir protested. He was personally aware of at least two letters his father had received in the past year, and there might very well have been others. "The letters have to be connected to the current murders. Why else would someone break in and steal them?"

"Someone broke in to steal a gun," she ground out. "Or maybe they were looking for money. The drug epidemic has hit Pike as hard as everywhere else. Even decent people will do crazy things when they're addicted."

"Then why didn't they take the laptop my father had on his desk? Or the silver tea tray in the china cabinet?"

"Maybe they were scared off by something. More likely, all they wanted was the gun."

"Or the letters."

She made a sound somewhere between a growl and a muffled curse. "If the weapon is recovered, I'll let you know."

Kir swallowed a curse, accepting the sheriff was never going to believe that his father had been right about the letters being a warning. Maybe it wasn't so surprising. If they turned out to be real, it would mean she truly had allowed a serial killer to mature from mere threats to actual murders. The deaths of the two women would be on her head.

Still, he wasn't prepared to give up. Not this time. He reached into the back pocket of his jeans to pull out a piece of paper. "Okay, if you won't take the letters seriously then what about this?"

Kathy allowed him to shove the paper into her hand, slowly unfolding it. "What's this?"

"I'm not sure, but I think it's a list of the women being targeted by the serial killer."

Her head jerked up to stab him with a suspicious glare. "Where did you get it?"

"My father gave it to Ron Bradshaw just a few weeks before he died. He asked the pastor to give it to me after the funeral."

The sheriff returned her attention to the list. "He didn't say what it was?"

"No, but the first letters are S. H. Sherry Higgins," he pointed out.

She visibly stiffened. "We haven't released the victims' names."

"It's a small town."

"Yeah, S. H. could stand for a lot of things. It could be a grocery list for all you know." She dropped the paper as if it was a piece of trash. "In fact, it probably is."

Kir bent down to angrily snatch the list off the ground, carefully folding it and putting it back in his pocket. "Why would Dad give it to a preacher if it wasn't important?"

Kathy glanced at down at the tips of her boots, as if

pondering her response. Then, lifting her head, she met Kir's accusing gaze. "Look, I didn't want to tell you this, Kir, but over the past few months your father had become increasingly erratic."

"What's that mean?"

"He was found wandering the streets late at night searching for his dog that'd been dead for over a year," she said. "And twice he was found passed out in his truck outside the old Shell filling station."

Kir winced at the thought of his dad wandering the streets in search of his beloved hound. But the filling station made him frown in confusion. As far as he knew, his father had no connection to the place. "Why would he be at the station? Isn't it closed down?" He spoke his question out loud.

"He swore a woman had been murdered there."

"Did you check?"

Kathy narrowed her eyes at his sharp tone. "Yes. My deputies did a thorough search. There was nothing inside but a few rats and lots of dust. He was obviously delusional. Or maybe he was confused. I think there was a woman killed there twenty-five years ago. A botched robbery or something." She turned and clomped up the stairs, her heavy footsteps warning she was done with this conversation. "Let this go, Kir," she called over her shoulder. "Your father's delusions drove him crazy. Don't let them do the same thing to you."

Chapter 7

Lynne spent the afternoon at the animal shelter she'd built on her grandparents' farm. She needed to keep her mind occupied, and her hands busy. What better way than cleaning the kennels and unloading a pallet of dog food? There was also the task of vaccinating the puppies that had been left that morning.

Once she'd returned to her house, however, she found herself pacing the kitchen floor. She had paperwork to do, and dinner to cook, but she couldn't stop her feet from carrying her from one end of the narrow room to the other. Almost as if the constant movement helped her to endure the pain that was crushing her heart.

It wasn't pain at the thought of Nash being unfaithful. By the time she'd ended her brief relationship with the creep, she'd accepted that he'd been sleeping with count-less women. He was just a loser in a long line of losers.

No, what hurt was the thought that Chelsea had pre-tended to be her friend and loyal employee even when she was having sex in a storage room with Lynne's boyfriend. And even worse was the fear that because of Chelsea's betrayal, some lunatic was using the drugs from her clinic to kidnap and murder innocent women.

God . . .

Her dark thoughts were interrupted by a glimpse of movement in her backyard. She froze, not sure if she'd actually seen a person or if it had been a tree branch swaying beneath the weight of the falling snow.

Moving to grab her cell phone off the kitchen table, Lynne cautiously headed to the back door. Double-checking the lock, she peered through the window. There was a small glow near her garden shed where she'd installed a security light last year, but the rest of the yard remained shrouded in shadows. It was impossible to see if there was anyone out there.

About to turn away, she was halted as headlights sliced through the darkness. Someone was driving up the narrow alley and parking behind her house.

She lifted her phone, preparing to dial 911 as a man stepped out of the truck. Then the intruder reached the light from the shed and her breath caught in her throat.

Nash Cordon.

Even at a distance she could make out his large six-foot-four frame that had once been hard with the muscles of a high school quarterback but were now sagging toward his middle. Lynne took waspish pleasure in the realization that his jacket had grown even tighter since she'd last seen him.

Jerk.

Watching him climb the back steps, she briefly considered the pleasure of calling the sheriff and having him arrested for trespassing only to quickly dismiss the childish impulse. Not only were the law officers busy trying to discover who'd killed two women, but the sheriff also had rubbed Lynne's nerves raw when she'd been at the clinic.

Lynne would rather deal with Nash than Kathy Hancock.

Pulling the door open, Lynne stepped aside to give her unwelcome guest room to enter the kitchen. Nash shook the snow from his light blond hair. Over the past weeks it'd grown long enough to brush his shoulders. Lynne wrinkled her nose. Once upon a time she'd thought Nash's dark blue eyes and golden features were handsome. Now all she could see was the peevish dissatisfaction that pinched his lips and sallowness beneath his fake tan.

His lips were pinched tighter than usual as he cast a quick glance around the cramped room. Lynne loved this house. Probably because it was where she'd been born and raised. It didn't matter that it was small and simple and more than a little shabby. It was home. Nash, however, had often complained that she lived like a miser instead of a professional woman with a thriving career.

Only after they'd broken up did she realize Nash thought her family was wealthy.

Nash opened his jacket to reveal he was wearing a sweatshirt with the Bait and Tackle bar logo on the front, but he didn't pull it off. Presumably this was going to be a short visit.

Thank God.

"Hey, Lynne." A humorless smile curved his lips. "Long time, no see."

Not long enough, she silently acknowledged. "What are you doing here?"

"Do you want to guess where I spent the past few hours?"

Lynne folded her arms, eyeing him with blatant dislike. "It's late and I'm not in the mood for games."

"Let me tell you. At the sheriff's office." There was an edge she'd never heard in his voice. Nash could be charming, reckless, and sleazy, but she'd never thought of him as dangerous.

"Congrats." She inched backward. "Go away."

"I'm not done." He deliberately closed the distance she'd just gained. "I haven't told you why I was there."

Lynne forced herself to hold her ground, despite the fact she had to tilt back her head to an awkward angle. This was Nash. He might be pissed, but he would never hurt her. "I assume it has something to do with stealing drugs from my clinic," she said, going on the offense.

His smile faded, his expression settling into a peevish sulk. The one he used when he was in the wrong but refused to admit it. "I didn't steal anything," he argued. "The bottles were knocked off the shelf and they busted. Big fucking deal."

It was Lynne's turn to smile. "Busted while you were having sex with my receptionist?"

Nash narrowed his eyes. "Is that what this is about? You're bitchy because you found out I was banging Chelsea, so you called the sheriff and claimed I stole your stupid drugs?"

"One." She lifted her hand with the first finger extended. "I didn't call anyone. The sheriff came to the clinic asking questions about my prescriptions and the protocols I use to keep them protected. Two." She extended another finger. "It was Chelsea who told the sheriff that it was you who supposedly broke the vials—"

"There's no supposedly about it," Nash abruptly interrupted.

"That's between you and the sheriff."

His nose flared as fury darkened his eyes. "I'm not going to jail because you're a petty, vengeful bitch," he snapped. "It was your fault I was in that storage room in the first place."

"My fault?" Lynne's jaw dropped at Nash's outrageous claim. "Not even your ego is that bloated."

"I wouldn't have looked twice at Chelsea if I hadn't constantly been hanging around the clinic waiting for you to finish work," he snarled. "How many nights did you tell me to wait for you to get back from some emergency? 'Just five more minutes, Nash.'" He mimicked her voice. "I wasted endless hours. Why shouldn't I have a little fun?"

Lynne tilted her chin, pretending his accusation hadn't struck a nerve. Okay, maybe she was busy. And there'd been nights when Nash had arrived for their date and she'd been in the middle of an emergency. What did he expect? That she would walk away from a sick animal so he didn't have to wait?

Struggling to control her temper, Lynne was distantly aware of the sound of knocking and then Kir calling out her name as her front door was opened. He sounded worried, but she kept her attention on Nash.

Her ex didn't appear to have heard Kir's arrival. Typical. He rarely paid attention to anything beyond the sound of his own voice.

"You know, Nash, I'm not disgusted with you. It's obvious you can't help being a selfish ass," she said, determined to keep him distracted. Nash was brashly arrogant, but he wasn't overly bright. It wouldn't take much to goad him into revealing the truth. "I'm disgusted with myself for not seeing what you were from our first date."

He sneered at her accusation. "Lie to yourself if it makes you feel better. I've never had a woman who was so eager to lure a man into a relationship."

"Lure? You wouldn't stop following me around," she taunted. "You were like a lost puppy."

Lynne leaned against the counter. It allowed her to see around the bulk of Nash's body to the connecting doorway to the living room. As soon as she caught sight of Kir, she gave him a sharp shake of her head.

Kir stopped, his expression puzzled. Clearly, he was trying to determine if she wanted him to leave or if she needed his assistance. Then, as if recognizing Nash, he moved to press himself against the wall. Out of sight, but easily able to listen to the conversation.

Nash gave a forced laugh, still oblivious to Kir's presence. "Your dad was a vet, now you're a vet. I thought you might have some spare cha-ching to invest in my business. Then I discovered you threw away all your money on that useless sanctuary."

His words were no surprise. They'd been dating less than a month the first time he'd asked her to become a silent partner in his bar. She'd refused, of course, and he'd dropped the subject. At least for a while. Toward the end of their relationship he was badgering her on a daily basis to give him money.

Now, however, she intended to use his inept lack of financial skills to her advantage.

"Speaking of the bar, how's it doing?" she asked in overly sweet tones.

He jerked, visibly caught off guard by her question. "Fine. Great. Business has never been better."

"Really?" Lynne held his wary gaze. "I heard from a reliable source that you've resorted to selling cases of beer to underage kids in the back alley."

"Your reliable source is full of bullshit."

His voice was harsh, but Lynne didn't miss the way his hands clenched and unclenched. A sure sign he was lying.

"I doubt that. But in any case, I'm sure the sheriff would be interested in the rumors," she assured him. "After all, if you'll supply alcohol to underage kids, then why not drugs?"

"You bitch." His faced flushed, that unfamiliar danger sizzling around him as he glared down at her. "You're trying to ruin my life."

"I don't care enough to try and ruin your life, Nash," she taunted, inwardly relieved that Kir was nearby.

She'd never been afraid of Nash, but he was very large, and very angry. Who knew what he might do if his temper snapped?

"Then why are you threatening me?" he grated.

"Because I want the truth."

"You know the truth. I had sex with Chelsea." His hands continued to clench and unclench. "Big deal."

"What did you do with the drugs?"

"I told you."

Lynne lifted her hand that was holding her phone. "I'm calling the sheriff."

"Stop."

"What did you do with them?"

Nash's jaundiced gaze remained locked on the phone. Was he considering whether he could grab it out of her hand before she could hit 911? Then he conceded defeat with a muttered curse.

"Fine." His expression was as hard and brittle as ice. "My cousin from Grange dabbles in drugs. He was approached by a customer willing to pay big coin if he could get his hands on some Telazol." Nash's lips curled into a smirk. "My cousin knew I was dating a vet, so he called me and promised to split the profit."

Lynne considered his words. Nash could be lying, but for the moment she was prepared to believe his explanation. "Who was the customer?" she asked.

"He didn't give his name. It's a cash-only business."

"Did your cousin recognize him?"

Nash rolled his eyes, assuring her that it was a stupid question. "No, he didn't recognize him. In fact, my cousin said the creep gave him the willies and he was glad he never came back even if he was willing to splash around his money."

Lynne blinked. "What could cause a drug dealer to get the willies?"

"He told me that the buyer was covered from head to toe," Nash explained. "He even had his face hidden by a scarf despite the fact it was warm outside. And he insisted they meet in a dark alley. My cousin assumed the dude must be an assassin. Why else pay a fortune for an animal tranquilizer and lurk in the shadows?"

Or a serial killer, Lynne silently added. Out loud she asked, "Your cousin was sure it was a man?"

"Why would he have called him a dude unless he was a man?" Nash pointed a finger in her face. "That's all I know. Screw with me again and I'll make you very, very sorry."

She reached to open the back door. "Go away, Nash."

With a sour expression, Nash turned to storm out of the house, slamming the door shut behind him. A second later, Kir strolled into the kitchen.

"Very nicely handled." He slipped off his leather jacket and hooked it over the back of a wooden chair.

The tension that had clenched her muscles into tight knots began to ease. It wasn't just because Nash was gone. It was having Kir standing next to her. As if his solid presence was providing her with a sense of peace.

Like her own personal Xanax. Only this one came with a gorgeous face and a firm, sexy body she wanted to get her hands on.

Resisting the urge to lean forward and breathe deeply of his warm scent, Lynne wiped her damp palms on her jeans. "I'm glad I'm a vet and not a detective. It's harder than it looks," she admitted. "Plus, I feel like I need a shower after having Nash in my house."

His mouth curved into a slow, enticing smile. "I could scrub your back."

Lynne had zero trouble envisioning standing in a shower with the man, the hot water pouring over their naked, entwined bodies. . . .

Her mouth was suddenly as dry as sandpaper. "Very generous of you."

He took a step closer, as if sensing the awareness sizzling through her. "I'm a generous guy."

Lynne swallowed, eager to distract him. "You shouldn't

tell me that. I run an animal sanctuary at my grandparents' farm and we're always looking for donations."

"Count me in for five thousand," he said without hesitation.

She blinked. "Dollars?"

"Not enough?"

It was the largest donation she'd ever received. Well, except for her grandparents, who'd donated the farm in their will.

She narrowed her gaze. "Are you doing this because you feel sorry for me?"

He looked genuinely puzzled. "Why would I feel sorry for you?"

"Because my ex-boyfriend is a slimy creep who not only slept with my receptionist but stole drugs from me?"

He shrugged. "We all have creepy exes."

"Even you?"

"I dated a woman who asked me to have a DNA test after our second date."

"Why?"

"Her mother was impregnated by a sperm donor and she wanted to make sure we weren't related before we had sex."

"Yikes."

He reached to brush away a stray piece of straw clinging to her ponytail. She hadn't taken a shower since she'd come home from the sanctuary. With shattering ease the image of her and Kir together in the steamy shower once again seared her mind.

"I give to charities on a regular basis," he assured her in soft tones. "My offer was nothing more than that."

Lynne took a step back, hoping Kir didn't notice the blush staining her cheeks. "Thanks. We can use the money."

"Let's make ourselves comfortable. You look exhausted." He pulled out a chair for her before he took a seat. Lynne readily dropped onto the chair. She wasn't offended by his observation. He was right. She was bone-deep exhausted. He watched in silence as she settled across the table. "Do you believe the jackass?"

She knew exactly which jackass he was referring to.

Nash Cordon.

"Yeah." She didn't have to consider her answer. "He might be more involved in the sale of the drugs than he claimed, but I believe a stranger offered a lot of money to get their hands on Telazol and that Nash was greedy enough to steal it." She made a sound of disgust. "That's probably why he seduced Chelsea. Just so he could get in the storage room."

His brow arched, no doubt wondering why Nash hadn't tried to get *her* into the storage room for some afternoon delight instead of Chelsea. Thankfully, he was a well-mannered adult who didn't enjoy embarrassing people with crude jokes and innuendos. Unlike Nash.

"So the question is whether this was all some huge coincidence or if the drug was stolen deliberately from your clinic," he instead said.

"Wait." She held up a hand in protest. "We don't even know if it has anything do with those poor women."

"Sheriff Hancock wouldn't have been at your clinic if she didn't think there was a connection. You're the only vet in the county."

"Nash said his cousin sold the drugs to someone in Grange."

"Which is only fifteen miles away."

Lynne battled her instinct to continue the argument. As much as she wanted to deny any connection, there was the possibility the drugs Nash stole had ended up in the hands of a lunatic. She shuddered.

"It's awful to imagine that something from my clinic could be involved with the murders. Like I'm responsible."

"Yeah, I get it." He leaned across the table to grab her hand in a comforting grip. "It's giving me nightmares to think that my father was being harassed by the killer. And I told him to ignore the letters. Maybe if I'd accepted there was a threat, we might have prevented the deaths."

They shared a glance of mutual frustration. It was impossible to say with a hundred percent certainty that the letters sent to Rudolf or the drugs stolen from her clinic or anything else was linked to the killer. But it felt as if they were being sucked into the evil spreading through town.

Another shiver raced through her. "Did you tell the sheriff that your father's weapon had been stolen?"

"I did. Along with the letters. I also told her about the list of initials."

"I'm guessing she wasn't interested."

"She's going to write up a report on the gun." He shook his head in disgust. "She didn't want to hear the rest."

Lynne heaved a sigh. "Two women dead."

"And a killer still out there." Kir glanced toward the back door. "Could Nash be involved?"

Lynne hesitated, shuffling through her tumultuous memories of Nash, from the day he'd pushed her into a mud puddle when she was five until the day that she'd told him their brief, tumultuous relationship was over. "My first impulse is to say no. Nash is a vain, selfish ass who has more ego than brains," she finally said. "On the other hand, he's immoral, cunning, and capable of manipulating people."

"I have a vague memory of him in school. He played football, didn't he?"

"The star quarterback who took the team to state. He told that story every night at the bar." Lynne rolled her eyes. "He might be thirty-one years old, but he never left high school."

"Glory days," Kir said in dry tones.

"Something like that."

Kir absently stroked his thumb over the tender skin of her inner wrist. The casual caress sent delicious shock-waves through her body.

"He would have plenty of strength to kill the women."

She struggled to concentrate. What were they discussing? Oh yeah, Nash being a serial killer. "It wouldn't take much strength if the women were unconscious."

"True," Kir readily agreed. "He wouldn't have to risk stealing a tranquilizer if he could overpower them." He furrowed his brow. "Unless that was the point."

"What point?"

"Using the drugs taken from your clinic," he said. "Nash could involve you in his sick game. Just like he involved my father with those letters."

The breath was jerked from her lungs at the mere thought. "God."

Kir gave her fingers a tight squeeze before he was abruptly rising to his feet.

"I'll make us some dinner."

Chapter 8

Kir hated the pallor of Lynne's face, and the knowledge that he'd been partially responsible. Unfortunately, they couldn't risk denying the possibility that there was a killer in Pike who'd used the drugs from her clinic to kidnap the two dead women.

Efficiently whipping up two ham and cheese omelets and toasting English muffins, Kir pondered the possibility of Nash being responsible.

The creep didn't seem the type. He was a typical blowhard who lived in his past because he couldn't face a future of mundane obscurity. Even worse, he obviously measured his manhood by how many women he could get naked. Just like a dozen other men in this town.

Then again, did serial killers have a type? They could be quiet, arrogant, a loner, a beloved family man. A woman . . .

With a shake of his head he slid the perfectly cooked omelets and muffins onto plates before returning to the table. They ate in silence, but it wasn't uncomfortable. In fact, there was an ease between them that made it seem as if they were lifelong friends. Or lovers.

Once they were done, he loaded the dishwasher and studied Lynne's face. She still looked exhausted, but the color had returned to her cheeks. He was discovering that she had a kind, giving heart that was easily hurt, but also possessed a spine of steel. She might never forgive Nash or Chelsea for their betrayal, especially if it turned out the drugs had fallen into the hands of a killer, but she wouldn't let them defeat her.

"You're kind of handy to have around," she murmured.

Kir strolled to stand directly in front of her. He'd done his best during dinner to ignore the awareness vibrating in the air. This wasn't the time or place. But then, nothing had been the right time or place since his return to Pike.

He intended to enjoy the sensations that she stirred to glorious life. He hadn't felt such a potent attraction since . . .

Actually, he'd never experienced such an intense need.

It wasn't just lust, although there was plenty of that. It was the way she intruded into his thoughts, and the urge to seek her out no matter how busy he was, and the growing fear that she might be in danger.

He reached out to grasp her hand and pulled her slowly to her feet. "I have several skills."

She tilted back her head to meet his gaze. "Do you?"

"Mmm." Tugging her close enough for the warmth of her body to seep through his sweater, Kir lowered his head. Gently he brushed a kiss over her mouth. A groan rumbled in his throat. Her lips were pure temptation. Soft and sweetly willing. He deepened the kiss, allowing his tongue to dip between her lips. She trembled, as if she was as shocked as he was by the passion that instantly blazed between them. Kir lifted his head to gaze down at her flushed face. "Wow. That was . . ."

"Dangerous," she said.

"Yes."

Long ago Kir had been an adrenaline junkie. There was no dare he wouldn't take, and no risk that was too great. But after moving to Boston he'd focused his energies on creating his business. He'd outgrown his addiction to danger.

Until this woman.

He wrapped his arms around her and kissed her again. Longer and slower and deeper. Until the world melted away and nothing else existed.

"Kir." Lynne pressed her hands to his chest.

Kir lifted his head, struggling to leash his hunger. He wanted to spend the rest of the night tasting Lynne's honeyed passion. Instead he gave in to the curiosity that had been nagging at him all afternoon.

"Can I ask you a personal question?"

He felt Lynne's muscles tense, as if she was preparing for a blow. "Okay."

"Why Nash Cordon?"

"Oh." She grimaced, but she thankfully didn't look angered by his prying. "A momentary insanity. And an inbred need to rescue strays."

"You thought Nash was a stray?"

She shrugged. "He's lost. In his past. In his ego. In his inability to become an adult."

He nodded. That made sense. But that wasn't the entire reason she'd chosen a loser like Nash. "And he wasn't any threat to your obsession with your career," he suggested.

She narrowed her eyes. "You haven't lived in Pike for

years. How could you know if I'm obsessed with my career?"

"When we were still in grade school I watched you run into the road to rescue a bird with a broken wing," he said in dry tones. "I doubt you have changed since then."

Her lips pursed at the reminder of the day she'd stormed off the playground to carefully scoop an injured bird off the pavement and place it beneath a nearby tree. She couldn't have been more than seven or eight at the time. Kir had watched her mad dash with astonishment. Not even he was willing to boldly march directly into traffic.

"Jimmy Schultz threw a rock at it," she said as if her actions had been perfectly reasonable. "I had to do something."

"I remember your teacher was furious."

"Ms. Randall nearly jerked off my arm dragging me to the principal's office," Lynne said. "I didn't care. I got the bird off the road and after school my dad drove me back so we could take it to the clinic."

"See? Obsessed."

"Passionate about my career," she corrected in firm tones, tilting her head to the side. "Aren't you?"

That was a question Kir had been asking himself lately. Certainly he'd been passionate about creating his business. And he would forever be grateful for the financial security he'd achieved. But there were days when he found himself pacing his office, unable to concentrate on the stacks of paperwork that made him feel like he was being buried beneath his own success.

"Actually, I've had an offer to buy the business," he said. "A very, very generous offer."

Her eyes widened. "Are you considering selling out?"

"That sounds like an insult," he teased.

"You know what I mean. I thought by the way you talked about building your business that it was your baby."

"It is. But it might be time for a new adventure." It was the first occasion Kir said the words out loud and he was shocked by how *right* they felt.

She searched his expression, perhaps trying to decide if he was being sincere. Then she nodded. "You were always restless."

"If I keep moving, the demons can't find me."

Lynne smoothed her hands over his chest in a gesture of comfort. "I'm sorry."

Kir shrugged. He wasn't interested in the past. He had enough to deal with in the here and now. The reminder forced him to lower his arms and take a step back. "But first I intend to discover whether or not some crazy-ass killer was tormenting my father."

She wrapped her arms around her waist. Was she missing his touch? The mere thought satisfied him on a deep, primitive level.

"Kir, it's dangerous. Really, really dangerous," she protested. "Maybe we should leave this to the sheriff."

"I don't intend to intrude into the sheriff's territory," he promised.

Years ago he might have been willing to sneak around the cold, dark streets in search of a serial killer. Like Batman, without any of the cool toys. Now he understood that he was more likely to get himself killed than to expose the madman.

"Then what are you going to do?"

"Visit the Bait and Tackle for a drink."

"I should go with you," she immediately decided. "I know everyone there."

His blood ran cold at the mere thought. "Which is exactly why you shouldn't go," he protested. "They won't talk in front of you."

"Why not?"

"Because you're the ex-girlfriend of the owner."

Her jaw tightened. "I'm as involved in this as you are."

"I know." He allowed his gaze to drift over her delicate features. "The thought is giving me an ulcer."

"It's not your job to protect me."

"That's not how it feels."

"Kir."

Kir swallowed a sigh as he watched her jaw tighten with annoyance. She was a woman accustomed to giving orders, not taking them. If he treated her as if she was incapable of taking care of herself, she would kick his ass out the door and slam it in his face.

"I promise this has nothing to do with your gender, Lynne. I just want to find out if Nash was working last night. And if he has any connection to the dead women." He cautiously leaned forward to brush a kiss over her forehead. "I'll call you in the morning and let you know what I discover."

She didn't shove him away.

He was going to take that as a good sign.

"Lock the doors and don't let anyone in." He held her gaze. "Not anyone."

Madeline Randall finished washing her dishes before spraying the countertop with bleach and scrubbing away any stray crumbs. She wasn't OCD. Not clinically. But after working for forty years as a third-grade teacher she had a phobia about touching sticky, grimy things.

She'd hoped retirement would ease her nervous habits, and at long last she could enjoy her life. Unfortunately, the decades of being exposed to the whiny, screaming monsters had taken its toll.

Even after two full years of being away from the school, she was in a constant state of anxiety.

The truth was, she should never have become a teacher. She'd wanted to marry her childhood sweetheart, Donny Burman. But her mother had warned her that Donny was a lowlife who would run off and leave her with a pack of squalling kids.

Her mother had been right.

Donny had married Madeline's best friend and a few years later he'd disappeared, leaving her to raise three small children on her own. Still, Madeline's choice to become a teacher instead of a wife and mother hadn't brought her joy. Just the opposite. She'd spent each day counting down the seconds until she could walk away from the school forever.

She hadn't considered the possibility that after her retirement she would spend each day alone in this tiny house she'd inherited from her mother. Stupid, of course. She'd never made friends with the other teachers, and the few acquaintances she knew from church were all too busy with their families to consider she might be lonely. Or more likely, they just didn't care.

Why should they? She was nothing. To no one.

She turned off the kitchen lights and entered the living room. As she passed by the bay window, she caught sight of her reflection in the glass. Even blurred, her image looked like an old woman. She'd always been slender, but now she was closer to gaunt with a narrow, pinched face that had long ago been drained of any beauty.

She shivered, coming to a sudden halt. She'd been so wrapped in her bitter memories that she hadn't noticed the sudden chill in the air. The snow had started to fall while she was making dinner and the wind was rattling through the trees, but that shouldn't affect the temperature in the house.

Was there a window open?

No, that was impossible. She never opened the windows unless it was to yell at the neighbor's dog that insisted on relieving itself on her mother's prized rosebush.

So why was it so cold?

She was busy puzzling the question when a sharp pain pierced her back.

Madeline grunted, trying to reach around to find out what was biting her. It was hard to believe a bug could survive in the subzero temperature outside, but what else could it be?

It wasn't until her knees collapsed and she fell flat on her face that she considered the possibility she might be in danger. And then it was too late.

The story of her miserable life.

Madeline woke in the darkness. Not just night, but a black void. As if every bit of light had been sucked out of the world.

The unnerving thought clawed through the fog in her brain. Had she gone blind? It seemed unlikely. She'd never had trouble with her eyes. But then again, her father had died of a stroke when he was in his early forties. Could a stroke cause blindness? Maybe.

But that didn't explain why she was lying on what felt like a cement floor. Or why it was so cold.

Shoving herself into a seated position, Madeline squelched the urge to panic.

There had to be a perfectly reasonable explanation. There always was. She hadn't taught a bunch of savages for forty years to be rattled because of a little darkness.

With grim determination, she sought to puzzle together where she was and what had happened.

Her last memory was standing in her living room. She'd finished washing the dishes and she was going to watch TV. A typical evening. Boring.

So what had happened?

There'd been a breeze, right? Had she gone to check the back door and seen something that led her outside?

Madeline licked her dry lips, eager to cling to her theory. Okay, she wasn't outside now, but she had a detached garage. She might have gone there. No, wait. She had an old cellar just behind the house. It was possible that the door had blown open during one of the snowstorms. It wouldn't be the first time. And if she'd gone to fix it she might have slipped and fallen down the stairs. It was pitch dark down there and always cold.

Yes. That made sense.

Relieved by the explanation, Madeline shakily rose to her feet. Her head throbbed as if she'd smacked it on the ground when she fell. And there was a queasy sensation in her stomach. But she couldn't stay there. She was going to freeze to death.

Holding out her arms like the blind people she'd seen

portrayed in the movies, she took a cautious step forward. Then another.

"You're going to be fine," she told herself in a loud, firm tone.

"No, Ms. Randall. You aren't going to be fine. In fact, you're never going to be fine again."

Madeline froze. Where was that voice coming from? It popped and crackled as if it was being broadcast through one of those old-fashioned intercoms she used to have in her classroom.

Was it possible she'd somehow driven to the school in her sleep? There was an old basement where the boiler used to be.

"Who's there?" she demanded.

"This is my playground, Ms. Randall," the garbled voice warned. "And I make the rules here. Understand?"

Without warning Madeline felt a shock blast from her neck to the tips of her toes. The pain buckled her knees and she landed back on the floor.

She lifted a hand and touched the band around her throat. It felt like the sort of thing you put on a dog.

A shock collar.

Oh, heavens.

I chuckle as I watch the woman squirm on the floor.

I'm wearing night-vision goggles so I can see without being seen. Besides, it seems appropriate to watch her flounder in the darkness.

How many children did she lock in the gloomy classroom closet for hours at a time?

I hold the remote to the shock collar in my hand as I speak directly into the intercom.

"Back on your feet."

Ms. Randall pushes herself onto her hand and knees, panting as if she's actually a dog.

Good. I smile in satisfaction.

"You have until the count of three," I snap. Just like she used to do. "One, two . . ."

"I'm doing it," she mutters, managing to straighten and glare around the darkness. "Who are you?"

"The one in charge," I remind her. "How does it feel to be at the mercy of someone bigger and stronger than you?"

Ms. Randall lifts her hand, tugging at the collar. "This isn't funny. I demand that you reveal yourself."

I press the button on the remote, listening to the woman's scream with a shiver of excitement. "You're a slow learner, aren't you, Ms. Randall?" I mock. "Do you know what I do to slow learners?"

The woman licks her lips. Was she remembering how she would call a student stupid and then shove their nose against the chalkboard, forcing them to stand there for hours?

"I think there's been a mistake." Her voice has lost the shrill arrogance that haunts my dreams. Now it is whiny. And equally irritating. "I'm just an old woman."

"Close."

She blinks like an owl. Blink, blink, blink.

"What did you say?"

"You're not just an old woman," I assure her. "You're a dead woman."

I press the button, closing my eyes as the symphony of her screams fills the air.

Bliss.

Chapter 9

The Bait and Tackle bar was sandwiched between the dentist's office and the laundromat just a block from Main Street. It was a plain brick building with a tin roof and large windows that were fogged from the heat inside.

Kir parked in front and allowed his thoughts to travel back to when he'd lived in Pike. This place had been called the Sugarland Saloon back then, and it'd belonged to a woman with garish red hair and false teeth that fell out when she laughed. She was a decent woman, even if she did drink most of her profits, and she would call him when his father was too drunk to walk home.

Hurrying across the icy sidewalk, Kir shoved open the door and stepped into the welcome warmth. Then he stopped, an unpleasant sense of déjà vu jolting through him.

The place hadn't changed. The battered wooden bar was still located in the shadowed back of the room. There were the same old lights that advertised beer and the local hotel flickering on paneled walls. The same tables and stools scattered around the planked floor. He was willing to bet there were the same nasty jokes scrawled on the bathroom walls.

An urgent desire to turn and run out of the bar gripped him with surprising force. He hadn't expected such a violent response. He'd already faced the funeral and packing his father's belongings. So why did he feel as if he was being battered with painful memories?

Perhaps because this was the place where he'd seen his father at his lowest. A once proud sheriff who'd turned into a drunk, feeble man crying alone at a table in the corner.

A strange breeze brushed over him, almost as if his father was urging him forward.

And maybe he was, Kir silently conceded. He didn't really believe in mystical mumbo jumbo, but he wasn't so arrogant to think that he knew everything about everything. Maybe Rudolf could reach out to his son.

With a shake of his head at his morbid imaginings, he glanced around the long room. At the back a middle-aged woman was tending bar, and three younger men were playing pool.

No Nash.

Kir turned his attention to the tables. Most were empty. There was a couple who were cuddled near each other, trying to carry on an intimate conversation over the blare of honky-tonk music. And close to the large window a woman who was sitting alone, a bottle of beer in front of her.

He narrowed his gaze. There was something familiar about her. Perhaps her body was thinner beneath the velvet jogging suit. And the lines had deepened around her weary blue eyes, while her limp brown curls were threaded with silver. But there was no doubt this was Rita King.

Perfect.

The woman was twelve years older than Kir, but she'd been one of his father's regular drinking buddies. He didn't know her story beyond the fact that she'd been brutalized by her first husband, and that she'd had her teenage daughter taken away by the state when she'd tried to run the bastard over with her car. But if there was anyone who could answer questions about what went on in this bar, it was Rita.

Crossing the floor that was disturbingly sticky, Kir pulled out a chair opposite the woman and sat down.

"Hello, Rita."

She studied him with bleary eyes. "Are you buying?"

"Yep." He held up a hand, catching the bartender's attention and indicating he wanted two beers.

Rita leaned forward, trying to focus her gaze. "Do I know you?"

"Kir Jansen."

"Kir?" She released a short laugh, her gaze taking in his expensive leather coat that he'd had fitted to accommodate his wide shoulders. "Good God, you're a sight for sore eyes."

"That I am," he agreed.

"What brings you to Pike?"

"I came for the funeral."

"Oh." Her smile slowly faded. "Damn. I'm sorry about Rudolf. I miss him. He was one of the few men a woman could trust to share an evening without expecting her to take her clothes off." The bartender arrived and set down the beers. Rita reached for one of the bottles and lifted it in the air as Kir paid. "To Rudolf."

Waiting for the bartender to leave, Kir lifted his bottle. "To Rudolf."

Kir took a sip while Rita swallowed the beer in two

huge gulps. She slammed the empty bottle back on the table.

"He was proud of you, you know," she said, her voice astonishingly steady. He'd be gasping for air after downing an entire beer. "He talked about that fancy business you started all the time."

Kir didn't have to fake his expression of regret. "I wish I would have come home more. I thought we'd have more time."

Rita looked grim. "We all do."

Kir leaned back in his chair, considering his words. He'd come to the bar for information on Nash Cordon. Now he realized this was the perfect opportunity to discover more about his father. And any connection to the killer.

"Did you happen to talk with Dad before he died?" he asked, keeping his tone casual.

Rita paused, the effort to think through the beer fog in her brain a visible struggle. "I didn't see him that day," she said slowly. "In fact, I hadn't seen him for a couple weeks, which was strange." She shrugged. "I thought maybe he was sick."

Kir set aside his beer. It really was strange. There were other bars in town, no doubt, but Rita made it sound as if this was his regular spot. So why had he stopped coming?

"I spoke with him on the phone, but he never said anything about not feeling well," he said. He tried to recall his last conversation with his father. The effort was bittersweet. "He was more . . . distracted."

"Yeah, he'd been that way for a while." Rita paused, as if shuffling through her memories of Rudolf. "I think it was because of those letters."

Kir froze. "Did he talk to you about them?"

"He talked about them to anyone who would listen when he'd had a few too many," she said dryly. "No one believed him."

"Did you?"

She wrapped her fingers around her empty bottle, as if wishing it would magically refill. "Not until today."

They shared a glance, silently acknowledging that there was something evil stirring in Pike. "Is there any word on the second victim?"

"Randi Decker. She was married to Ned Decker," Rita told him. "She ran the flower shop on State Street. I seen a whole bunch of trucks with flashing lights in front of her shop this morning and then the television people showed up. I stopped to find out what was happening, and they said they found her body out by the lake. Terrible business."

Kir tucked away the knowledge that the sheriff had been at the flower shop and not her house. Later he would try to discover if she'd been murdered there or if she'd been tranqued and taken somewhere else to be killed.

"I don't recognize the name."

"She was Randi Brooks in high school. She was probably a few years older than you."

Kir couldn't place her. Not surprising. He never tried to be Mr. Popular in high school. He went to class and left. It was a means to an end. "Was she friends with Sherry Higgins?"

Rita's sharp laugh echoed through the nearly empty room. "Christ, no. Randi lived in a big brick house next to the golf course. She thought she was some hotshot in this town just cause she won a few beauty pageants when she was young."

Kir frowned. The two women had to have something in common, didn't they? "Did they go to the same church?"

"I don't think so. Randi went to that new church in Grange. I guess ours weren't fancy enough."

The mention of Grange reminded him of his original purpose in coming to the Bait and Tackle. Nash Cordon. "Did Sherry or Randi ever come to this bar?"

Rita shook her head. "Not that I ever seen."

"Did they know Nash Cordon?"

"It's a small town, but I never seen any of them together. Nash has been sniffing after our local vet."

Kir snapped his teeth together. The next time Nash came sniffing he intended to teach the bastard he wasn't welcomed. As painfully as possible. "Was Nash here last night?"

"Yep." Rita hesitated, her brows drawing together. "Or he was. He was behind the bar when I first got here, but I didn't see him around when I left."

"What time?"

"Ten or so. I don't stay out as late as I used to." She shoved aside the empty bottle with a sigh. "What's going on? Is Nash in some sort of trouble?"

Kir rose to his feet. He'd discovered that Nash had left the bar before closing time, and that his father had been acting strange before his death. That was enough for tonight. "It's freezing outside," he said. "Why don't you let me drive you home?"

"No need." She waved her hand toward the bartender. "Cherry gets off in an hour. She said she'd drop me off."

Kir nodded and shoved his hands in his pockets. His

fingers brushed against a folded piece of paper, and he was suddenly struck with inspiration. "One last thing." He pulled out the note and unfolded it before he set it on the table in front of Rita. "Did my father ever show you this?"

The older woman squinted at the column of initials. "What is it?"

"I'm not sure. My father left it with Pastor Bradshaw before he died and told him to give it to me after the funeral."

"Is that the preacher from the Lighthouse Church?"

Kir was genuinely surprised. "You know him?"

"Not personally. I'm not the churchgoing kind of gal. At least not anymore. But the pastor runs a charity shop out of the old bowling alley." She glanced down at her velvet jogging suit. "I get all my clothes there. I even found a television for my bedroom. The screen is cracked, but it works fine. Course, I had to wrestle it away from Sherry."

Kir stiffened. "Sherry? Sherry Higgins?"

"Yeah. She was in there every week trying to snatch up anything she could get for free." Without warning, Rita flushed. "Oh, I forgot . . . I shouldn't have said that."

Kir waved away Rita's apology, his thoughts racing.

A charity shop. What better place for the community to cross paths? Randi Decker could easily have gone there to donate items. And it sounded as if Sherry Higgins was a regular.

And Pastor Bradshaw.

Something to investigate.

But not tonight.

"So you don't know anything about the list?" he asked Rita.

She grabbed the paper and held it out to him. "I know one thing."

"What?"

"That's not your father's handwriting."

Dear Rudolf,

I wish you were here with me. I've improved so much. I think you would be proud.

Sherry was sloppy, although I won't lie, her death gave me a great deal of pleasure. The ugly bitch had never looked better than when I was slicing open her throat. But I didn't take my time to savor my revenge.

Randi was better. I brought her to my happy place so we could be alone. We played until she couldn't scream anymore, but I was too rough. She was gone before I could finish enjoying her pleas for mercy.

Now I have Ms. Randall. The dried-up bitch looks like death warmed over, but I intend to take care not to end our time together until I'm fully satisfied. After all, she took delight in seeing my suffering. Day after day, she smirked at the sight of my bruises, never doing anything to end the torment.

Well, now she will know what it's like to be small and helpless and afraid. So very afraid.

Crimson blood stains the pure white snow. Life spills from warm to frozen. Don't look. The pain is gone.

Lynne swerved into the icy parking lot and slid to a halt. Then, switching off the engine, she jumped out of her truck and stormed toward the clutch of people standing in front of her clinic.

When Shane, her on-duty intern, called at the crack of dawn, Lynne hadn't been happy. She'd spent most of the night tossing and turning. Not because of what she'd discovered about Nash. He was a horse's patootie she was happy to have out of her life. No, she'd tossed and turned because she was worried about Kir.

He might have matured into a successful businessman, but beneath his polished exterior she didn't doubt he was still the impulsive, adrenaline-junkie kid she'd known years ago. And while Pike wasn't a hotbed of crime, anyone involved in the drug trade could be violent. Not to mention the fact there was a potential serial killer lurking in the dark. The thought of Kir charging into danger twisted her stomach in knots of fear.

So having her phone interrupt her sleep just a couple hours after she'd managed to doze off hadn't done anything for her mood. And then for Shane to tell her that the local television station was filming directly in front of her clinic . . .

Her bad mood had plummeted from annoyed to furious.

Crossing the slippery parking lot, Lynne took in the sight of the large white van with KTRV painted on the side, then to the cameraman who was surrounded by several people. She didn't know if they worked for the station, or if they were just gawkers who'd happened to be passing by, and she didn't care. Her attention locked on Parker Bowen.

The handsome reporter was wearing an expensive

trench coat and cashmere scarf tied around his neck with a microphone in his hand as he spoke directly into the camera.

"The victims have been identified as sixty-year-old Sherry Higgins and thirty-six-year-old Randi Decker, both lifelong residents of Pike. According to law enforcement sources the two women were both sedated with Telazol before they were kidnapped, their throats slit, and their naked bodies dumped in isolated locations. Telazol is a tranquilizer most commonly used by veterinarians and not readily available to the public. The sheriff suspects that the drug was obtained from this clinic—"

Lynne's fury was laced with horrified disbelief as she hurried to stand directly in front of Parker. "Stop right there."

There was the sound of startled gasps from the onlookers. Dammit. She hadn't meant to make a dramatic entrance, but she wasn't going to let anyone link her clinic to a crazed killer.

Parker, however, was a trained professional and his expression never changed as he smoothly stepped to one side, so they were both in the camera shot, and offered her a smile. "And here is the owner of the clinic, Dr. Gale. Can I ask you a few questions?"

Lynne narrowed her eyes. "Get off my property."

Parker's smile never faded, but he waved a hand toward the cameraman. "Give us five."

Lynne didn't care whether the camera was turned off or not before she attacked. "How dare you imply that I supplied drugs to some maniac?"

Parker looked genuinely shocked. "Don't be silly. I promise that no one in Pike would ever believe you were selling drugs. But there's already talk about the sheriff investigating the clinic. Wouldn't you rather go on the record and clarify why she was here?"

A nasty sensation crawled through Lynne. She hated the realization that her friends and neighbors would be speculating whether the drugs that had been in those poor women had come from her clinic. It felt like it tainted all she'd worked to achieve.

Damn Nash Cordon. And damn the sheriff for ensuring everyone in town knew she'd been there investigating.

"No. I would prefer you leave any mention of my clinic out of your report," she snapped.

"I'm sorry, Lynne, but you know I can't do that. It's news."

She clenched her hands at her side. She wanted to argue, but what could she say? She couldn't deny that there was a possibility that the drugs had come from the clinic. Especially after discovering Nash had stolen them. And Parker was right. The murder of two women was the biggest news to hit Pike since the eighteen hundreds when there'd been a fire in the wool mill and ten people had died.

"The second body was Randi Decker?" she abruptly demanded.

"Yes. Did you know her?"

Lynne shook her head. "I think she went to Pike High School but she was older than me."

"I haven't been able to locate anyone who will admit that they were more than distant acquaintances with the woman. And her husband isn't talking."

"Do you blame him? His wife was just found murdered." She sent him a chiding frown. "The last thing he would want to do is have his grief splattered across the television."

"That's my point," Parker insisted. "You would think he would want the killer caught before he strikes again. The more information we can provide to our viewers, the more likely we can stop the madman."

"So you're performing a public service?"

"That's precisely what I'm doing." Parker glanced toward the onlookers craning their necks for a better view. No doubt they were hoping to see the two of them in a heated argument. "Or at least that's what I'm trying to do. I'm discovering the good citizens of this town aren't the easiest people to interview."

"We value our privacy."

He turned back to study her with a faint frown. "I'm not the bad guy here, Lynne."

She arched a brow, but she didn't respond. Maybe he wasn't the bad guy, but he wasn't standing in the freezing cold to make the world a better place. It was all about ratings.

"Randi was killed the same way as Sherry?"

"Her throat was slit. And the sheriff's department is trying to keep it hush-hush, but I have it from an inside source that she had a red ribbon tied around her neck, like Sherry Higgins."

"Was she . . . ?" Lynne's words faltered.

He easily read her mind. "Sexually assaulted?"

"Yes."

He turned so his back was to the crowd and made sure that the microphone was turned off before he spoke in low tones. "She was abused with an object. That's all the information I could get."

Lynne shuddered. "So awful."

"It is," Parker murmured, then he leaned forward to whisper in her ear. "How did your tranquilizers end up in their systems, Lynne?"

She leaned back, glaring at him in annoyance. Did he think he was going to catch her off guard? She dealt with patients who regularly tried to bite, gore, stomp, and pee on her. Besides, there was no way to be certain that the drugs had come from her clinic. Unless Parker knew something she didn't? Before she could ask, however, there was the crunch of boots on the snow and a male voice cut through the tense air.

"Is there a problem here?"

Kir.

An unexplainable relief flooded through Lynne. It wasn't that she needed a man to fight her battles. She'd been taking care of herself for years. Ever since her mother had walked away and her father had struggled to keep up with his thriving business while raising a young child. But she couldn't deny that there was something nice in the sensation she wasn't fighting this particular battle alone.

Parker wasn't nearly so pleased. He frowned as Kir halted next to her. "You again?" His gaze traveled over Kir's expensive leather jacket and then toward the SUV that cost more than most homes in Pike. His lips flattened. "I didn't realize the two of you were so close."

Without warning, Kir draped an arm around Lynne's shoulders. "Is there a reason you should be informed?"

"I consider Lynne a friend."

"Really?" Kir deliberately glanced toward the cameraman, who was stomping his feet to combat the cold.

Parker shrugged. "I'm just doing my job."

Kir leaned forward, his expression hard. "Maybe you should do it somewhere else."

Parker flashed a smug smile before turning to Lynne. "Call me if you change your mind about the interview."

"I won't," Lynne said, but Parker was already walking away.

"I don't like him." Kir watched Parker motion for his cameraman to pack up his equipment and climb into the waiting van with narrowed eyes.

"You don't even know him," Lynne protested, pulling away from Kir's arm. The desire to remained tucked against him was oddly tempting.

Too tempting.

Kir waited for the van to drive away before he glanced down at her. "He's not from Pike?"

"No, he moved here a little over a year ago."

"Where was he before that?"

"I have no idea." Lynne shrugged. "He might have said something about his former career when he took over the anchor position, but I didn't pay any attention. Honestly, I'm usually too busy to catch the evening news."

Kir was silent for a minute, then, with a shake of his head, he seemed to put Parker Bowen from his mind. "Are you working today?"

"Only if I get called on an emergency. Why?"

"I have something I need to do," he told her. "I could use some company."

Chapter 10

Kir followed behind Lynne as she parked in front of her house. A minute later she was climbing into his SUV and pulling the seat belt into place.

The faintly floral scent that he was beginning to associate with Lynne laced the air, teasing at his senses with an enticing promise. He wanted to lean across the console and press his face against her skin and simply absorb her scent. He battled back the urge with a wry smile. He might be increasingly convinced there was something special happening between the two of them, but that didn't mean Lynne felt the same.

He drove out of town, allowing a silence to settle between them. Lynne was still flushed with anger, as if she was fantasizing about the numerous ways she'd like to torture Parker Bowen for plastering her clinic across the morning news. Probably along with whoever was responsible for tipping off the newsman that the sheriff had been there to investigate the missing drugs.

It offered him the opportunity to concentrate on the narrow road that was packed with snow along with a crunchy layer of ice. The local road crews were too busy trying to clear the main streets to do more than pass through these country lanes once or twice a month.

Kir turned onto a private drive that was completely snow-packed before he came to a halt and switched off the engine.

With a blink, Lynne leaned forward to glance out the front windshield. "I don't think I've ever been out here."

Kir allowed his gaze to roam over the rolling hills that surrounded a small frozen lake. At this time of year there was nothing much to see beyond the barren trees that poked through the thick layer of snow.

"This was the Jansen homeplace," he told her. "According to my grandfather some distant ancestor traveled here from Norway in the seventeen hundreds after he decided he wanted to be a farmer instead of following the family tradition of becoming a cobbler."

"A cobbler?" She sent him a wry glance. "Really?"

"Swear to God." He pointed toward the top of the nearest hill. "When I was young there was a huge three-story house on the ridge there." He moved his arm until he was pointing toward the flat pasture that had once been filled with a large herd of dairy cows. "Over there were two barns and a paddock."

"What happened to them?"

"My dad was an only child and he had no interest in being a dairy farmer." Kir heaved a faint sigh of regret. He had a lot of happy childhood memories here. "It all just decayed and eventually collapsed after my grandparents died. A sad waste."

She reached to lay her hand on his arm. "This isn't the only farm that's been abandoned," she assured him. "The rural Midwest is evolving, and it isn't always easy for us to adapt."

He turned to study her sympathetic expression. "The Darwin theory?"

"The species that survives is the one that is able to adapt, or something like that," she said. "I suppose this place belongs to you now?"

He glanced back at the snow-covered hills. It hurt deep inside to think that everyone who'd loved and devoted themselves to this place was gone. "I guess I do, but don't ask me what I'm going to do with the property because I haven't decided. My brain tells me to sell it. It's a prime piece of property that's being neglected. My heart tells me it's my duty to hang on to it. This is my heritage."

"You don't have to make a decision now. This place isn't going anywhere."

"True."

She gave his arm a gentle squeeze before returning her attention to their isolated surroundings. "Is there a reason you wanted to come out here today?"

"My father never wanted to be a dairy farmer, much to the disappointment of my grandfather, but he did love to spend his afternoons fishing at that lake. He called it his little slice of heaven." Kir reached to grab the battered hat he'd placed on the dashboard and opened his door. "The funeral doesn't seem real. It was just a box going into the ground," he told Lynne. "This is where I want to say my good-bye."

She nodded, opening her own door and climbing out of the SUV. Together they battled their way through the snow to reach the edge of the frozen lake.

Kir felt his chest tighten, unexpected tears filling his eyes as he bent down to gently lay the hat on a wooden post that was all that remained from the old dock. At the funeral he'd been too numb with shock to accept that his dad was gone. Really and truly gone. Now the grief hit him with a punishing ferocity.

He didn't know how much time passed, but he sensed it was several minutes before Lynne broke the silence.

"Did you like to fish with your dad?"

He latched onto her soft voice, gratefully allowing it to pull him out of a dark pit where he'd descended. "I never had the patience," he said. "Ten minutes after we got here, I would be climbing a tree or digging holes in the ground. Or more likely, falling over my own feet and ending up in the water. My dad claimed I was a magnet for disaster, and he wasn't wrong."

"You were always . . ." She allowed her words to trail away as she shoved her hands into the pockets of her coat.

"Restless," he supplied. He could still feel the energy that hummed just beneath his skin. "The world always felt like it was spinning too slow for me. And after my father was injured . . ." He shook his head as he recalled his in-exhaustible need for distraction. "I went from restless to reckless."

"And now?"

He studied her upturned face, abruptly realizing that when this woman was near, the relentless agitation disappeared. As if she managed to soothe the beast inside him. "I finally learned to focus my energies on building a successful career." He allowed his gaze to drift down to her full lips. "But I'm not sure that's enough."

Her cheeks were already reddened by the cold, but he suspected she was blushing.

"You'll soon be back in Boston and settled in your life again," she insisted.

"Do you think?"

Their gazes locked, an unspoken heat smoldering between them. Hot enough to make him impervious to the sharp cold. Then Lynne sharply turned away, studying the rolling hills.

"Did your mother ever come out here?"

Kir shook his head. "Not often. She would sometimes bring me here for a picnic, but she didn't really like being in the country. She was born and raised in L.A." He waved his hand toward the empty landscape. "This place was foreign terrain to her."

"How did your parents meet?"

"My father went to college in California," Kir said. He'd never been able to imagine his father anyplace but Pike. This area was imprinted in his DNA. But Rudolf had obviously felt the same reckless need for adventure as Kir, at least once in his life. "It was one of the top schools for criminal justice in the country, and he wanted to experience the world beyond Wisconsin. My mom was there getting her degree in nursing." A wistful smile touched his lips. "She said it was love at first sight, but I'm not sure she truly understood how hard it would be for her to leave her family and move to a small town in the middle of nowhere. Still, they seemed happy until my father was injured."

"Do you stay in contact with her?"

Kir shrugged. "We talk on the phone and usually get together during the holidays for a day or two, but it's awkward."

"Because she left?"

Kir paused. He never discussed his mother. Their relationship was complicated. But Lynne was perhaps one of the few people who could understand his convoluted emotions. "Because she feels guilty for walking away and starting a new family. And I resented her for walking away and starting a new family," he admitted. "Or at least I did when I was younger."

As he'd hoped, there was no judgment in Lynne's eyes, just curiosity. "Why did you stay in Pike?"

"I was just fourteen and I thought I could save my dad." A familiar ache clenched Kir's heart. There was nothing more depressing than watching someone you love slowly destroy themselves. "I was wrong. By the time I turned eighteen, I figured out that he was never going to put down the bottle, so I walked away. Just like my mother. Ironic, really."

"You did what you had to do."

The simple words captured exactly what Kir had known at the center of his soul. He either got out, or he became infected by his father's sickness.

Kir sucked in a deep breath, savoring the crisp, clean air. It seemed to cleanse away the darkness of the past. "What about you?" he demanded. "Do you have any contact with your mother?"

"No." Lynne's jaw tightened with disgust. Obviously, her memories of her mother weren't nearly as complicated as his own. "When she left Pike, she made it very clear she didn't want anything to do with a husband or child."

"You don't know where she is?"

"My parents' marriage wasn't a romance story. They married a week after they graduated from high school. I think my mom assumed being the wife of a vet would give her a life of luxury." Lynne wrinkled her nose. "She hadn't considered the years she would be forced to work as a waitress to put my dad through school. By the time he was done, she wanted out of the marriage. She resented the years of watching her friends out having fun while she was constantly struggling to try and keep a roof over her head." She glanced away, but not before Kir glimpsed the pain that darkened her eyes. "Just a week after she told my dad she wanted a divorce, she discovered she was pregnant. She stuck around long enough to have me, but she skipped town before my second birthday."

Kir knew it must have been difficult for Lynne. Not just because her mother had abandoned her, but he knew any child would wonder if they'd somehow caused their mother to disappear from their life. He'd done it himself.

Still, she'd had a father who'd adored her.

"I'm surprised your dad never remarried," he said.

"I don't think my parents ever officially got their divorce," she told him. "Anyway, my dad was married to his career. He barely had time to take care of me, let alone find a new wife."

"And you followed in his footsteps?"

Her tension eased as a genuine smile curved her lips. "I suppose I did."

He stepped close enough to catch her floral scent. "We have a lot in common."

Her brows lifted. "Because we were abandoned by our mothers and now we're workaholics who can't commit to a healthy relationship?"

"That's not exactly how I was going to put it." He chuckled, then glanced toward the lake as a sharp breeze swirled tiny tornadoes of snow over the ice. His grief was still raw, but Lynne's presence had helped him remember the good times he'd shared in this place. "Thank you for coming with me," he murmured in soft tones. "This is the good-bye I wanted for Dad."

There was a long silence before Kir started to move. It was too cold to linger, but before he could turn away, Lynne was pointing across the lake.

"Is that the old air base?"

Kir glanced toward the low line of buildings surrounded by a chain-link fence. The abandoned base was such a part of the landscape that he didn't even notice it was there.

"Yeah, I forgot it was so close." A wry smile twisted his lips. "I used to sneak in there to party when I was in high school."

She studied the snow-covered runways, the vast empty buildings, and the rusty radar tower that looked like an alien landscape set in the middle of the dairy farms.

"What's in there?"

"Nothing but a bunch of old, broken equipment and trash." A puffy cloud drifted across the sun, stealing the meager warmth it offered. Kir shivered, grabbing Lynne's hand. "Come on. We have one more stop and then we'll have some breakfast."

They waded through the snow and climbed into the SUV. Twenty minutes later they were back on the main road headed north of Pike.

"Now where are we going?" Lynne asked.

"The bowling alley."

"Seriously?" He heard the hint of surprise in Lynne's voice. "If you're in the mood to bowl, you'll have to drive to Grange. The local alley closed down a couple years ago."

He turned toward the outer road that ran along the outskirts of town. Long ago it'd been the place to go in Pike.

There'd been a drive-in theater, an indoor ice rink, and a bowling alley that also served burgers and milkshakes.

Now it looked like a scene from a dystopian novel.

The movie screen had decayed until there was nothing left but the wooden skeleton, and the ice rink had collapsed into a pile of rubble. The bowling alley had fared better, he noticed as he pulled into the large parking lot. The one-story brick building was faded, and the roof looked as if it was groaning beneath the weight of the snow, but it was still standing.

"I heard from an old friend last night that it's now a charity shop run by Pastor Ron Bradshaw." He pulled to a halt near the front door. "I'm going to donate my dad's clothes and stuff from the kitchen."

"Oh." She glanced over her shoulders at the pile of cardboard boxes Kir had loaded into the SUV before leaving his dad's house that morning. "That's generous of you."

"It's not completely altruistic," he admitted, his gaze taking in the half dozen cars and trucks in the lot. "I want to check this place out."

"Why?"

"I've been trying to find a way that Sherry and Randi could be connected. They don't seem to have anything in common beyond the fact they were both from Pike."

She glanced toward the bowling alley. "So why this place?"

"I heard that Sherry was a regular visitor. I want to know if Randi was ever here." He shrugged, not revealing his suspicion of the good pastor. "Like I said, I'm just looking for a connection."

Her lips parted, as if she wanted to remind him that it

wasn't his job to investigate the victims. Then, glancing at his face, she heaved a resigned sigh. No doubt his expression was stubborn enough to convince her any argument would be a waste of time.

She shoved open the door of the SUV, glancing back at him when he left the engine running. "Aren't you coming?"

"I'm going to unload the boxes in the back. I'm assuming that's where the drop-off is located."

She nodded, slipping out of the vehicle. "I'll stroll around. There might be someone who has seen Sherry or Randi around."

"Be careful," he called out.

She sent him a wry glance before closing the door and heading toward the front entrance. He waited for her to disappear into the building before he drove to the end of the parking lot. Then, grabbing the boxes, he crossed the icy cement to push open a door that was marked for deliveries.

As he hoped, he found Pastor Bradshaw sorting through a pile of used shoes at the front of the storage room. The younger man was casually dressed in jeans and a thick sweatshirt.

Strolling forward, Kir set the boxes on a long table that was shoved against the wall before casually turning to glance around the narrow space lined with steel shelves filled with clothes, shoes, old electronics, and piles of china plates. There were also several open bins loaded with coats and boots.

Kir suppressed a shudder. The drop ceiling nearly brushed his head and there was a staleness in the air that made the room unpleasantly claustrophobic. It felt as if the mounds of junk were ruthlessly consuming the space. Like a living organism.

"Hello again," a male voice intruded into his dark imaginings.

Kir turned, pasting a faux look of surprise on his face. "Oh. Pastor Bradshaw."

The man wiped his dusty hands on a handkerchief before stretching one out to offer it to Kir. "Ron, please."

Kir clasped the outstretched hand, hiding his grimace at the man's moist, clammy skin.

"Ron." He pulled his hand away with a jerk that was just short of rude.

Ron didn't seem to notice. "How can I help you?"

"I brought a few boxes from my dad's house. There's nothing fancy, but it's all still in good condition."

"Thank you, Kir." Ron smiled, his thin face pasty in the fluorescent light. "That's a wonderful way to honor your father's memory."

Kir ignored his tiny pang of guilt. "I hope it can help someone in need."

"Yes." Ron's smile faded. "There's a great deal of need in Pike these days."

Kir glanced around the crowded storage area. "It looks like you have plenty of donors."

"Not as many as we used to have. Since the paper factory shut down, the families who used to give are now forced to take. It's been a difficult transition for people who consider it a weakness to accept charity."

"Thankfully, you're here to provide it."

Ron pressed his sweaty hands together in a prayerlike gesture. "I do what I can."

Kir offered a sympathetic smile. "Yes, I'm sure you

do." He paused, then abruptly shifted the conversation. "A shame about Randi Decker."

"Who?" The man blinked, looking confused.

Real or fake? Kir was betting on fake.

"The woman they found murdered at the lake," he clarified. "I believe she ran the local flower shop."

"Oh. Oh, yes. Ms. Decker. Such a tragedy."

"And Sherry, of course," Kir added.

Ron heaved a sigh. "These are dark days for Pike."

"Have you talked to the sheriff?"

The question came without warning and Ron jerked in surprise. "The sheriff? Why would I talk to the sheriff?"

"I just assumed that since you knew both women she'd have questions for you."

"I didn't really know them," Ron protested. "I've seen poor Ms. Higgins in the store, of course. She came every Monday afternoon to see what furniture had been dropped off over the weekend."

Kir didn't miss the edge in the pastor's voice. Sherry was no doubt the type of person who took advantage of his charity, swooping in like a bird of prey to snatch the best furniture to use in her trailers. "Was she here last Monday?"

Ron furrowed his brow, as if trying to think back. "She must have been. I would have noticed if she didn't stop by."

"And Randi? When was the last time she was here?"

The pastor narrowed his eyes, as if annoyed by the question. But his good manners overcame his irritation. "The local PTA collects canned goods at the school for our food pantry," he told Kir. "This year Randi was president, so it was her responsibility to deliver the collection at the end of each month."

Satisfaction flared through Kir. He'd been right. Both women had been regular visitors to the charity shop.

Along with Pastor Bradshaw.

"When was the last time Randi was here?"

"School was closed through the holidays, so I guess it would have been the end of November." Ron pointed toward the back door. "She usually leaves the cans in the large container in the parking lot, so she doesn't have to come in. For all I know it could be her husband, or even one of her employees, bringing them by."

Kir narrowed his eyes. Was it his imagination or did Ron's efforts to deny any interaction with Randi sound forced?

Tucking the thought in the back of his mind, Kir glanced through the nearby door to the actual store that had a half dozen customers strolling along the towering shelves. Including Lynne, who was chatting with a weary-looking woman with three small children tugging on her frayed coat.

"How many people work here?" he asked his companion.

"We have several volunteers," Ron said. "But no one is on the payroll. This is a charity in its truest form."

"Any men?"

Ron lifted his brows at the question. "Sam Lind and Ted Madsen are usually here in the mornings. They're both retired, and coming here gets them out of the house. As a matter of fact, they just left." The pastor paused, before he seemed to recall that Sam and Ted weren't the only men. "And on Mondays the sheriff sometimes brings by parolees who need community service hours to help me with deliveries or pickups."

Kir swallowed a curse. Parolees? That could mean dozens of men and women who'd seen Sherry and Randi around the store. And many of them violent criminals. Instead of scratching Ron off the list of potential suspects, he'd instead added endless possibilities.

"Did you have any of them here the last few months?" he asked, hoping to narrow down the list.

"A few."

"Do you have their names?"

Ron's expression hardened. "That's not something I'm comfortable discussing."

Kir wanted to kick himself. Ron had gone from polite man of the cloth to eyeing Kir with a barely concealed dislike. Kir had not only stepped over the line, but had ruined any hope of getting more information out of the pastor. At least for today. "Of course."

"Thank you for your generosity," Ron said in cool tones. "I'm sure your father's belongings will find a grateful home."

Turning away, the pastor headed into the store.

And that was that.

Chapter 11

Lynne settled in the leather seat of the SUV as they pulled away from the charity shop. Next to her, Kir was focused on the icy streets, his expression difficult to read.

"What did you find out?" she asked.

"I confirmed that both victims spent time at the shop," he told her. "Sherry came to pillage free furniture for her trailer park business and Randi stopped by each month to deliver donations from the school to the food pantry." He paused as they turned onto the main street leading to the center of town. "And then there is Pastor Ron Bradshaw who runs the shop."

"What about him?"

"He crossed paths with both women."

She sent him a confused glance. "So did a lot of people."

"Yeah, but Pastor Bradshaw is the only one who gave me a note with the initials of potential victims on it."

It suddenly hit Lynne why they'd gone to the charity shop. It hadn't just been because he suspected Sherry and Randi had been there. No doubt the two women had also been at the grocery store, the post office, and a dozen other places in town. It was because Pastor Bradshaw ran the charity. "You can't believe he's a suspect?"

"Why not? I only have his word that my father asked him to speak at the funeral or to give me the mysterious note."

"But—" Lynne cut off her protest. She better than anyone knew that the most devoted, seemingly kind people could hide a dark side. She'd seen the evidence in the animals they brought to her clinic. She never let herself be fooled by the façade they showed the world. This was no different. Anyone could pretend to be godly. Still, it didn't make sense that Ron was the killer. "If he was involved in the murders, why would he give you the note?"

"I'm not sure a lunatic has a reasonable explanation for the things he does." Kir's jaw tightened. "But my guess is that he wanted to include me in his sick game now that my dad is dead."

Lynne's mouth went dry. Was it possible? Could the killer now be fixated on Kir?

"Oh God. That's an awful thought," she breathed.

"And nothing more than a wild theory. I have no idea how to discover if the good pastor is involved or not."

Lynne's hands clenched in her lap. She wanted to reach over and give the man a good shake. Or maybe a kiss. Wait, no. A good shaking. "It's not your job to discover if he's involved."

"Maybe not, but I can't ignore the fact that the women of Pike are being murdered."

She frowned. Kir was stubborn—almost as stubborn as she was—but he wasn't stupid. He wouldn't deliberately put himself in danger unless . . . Oh.

"You're doing this because you feel guilty," she accused.

"Excuse me?"

"You think you should have believed your father when he warned you about a killer in Pike."

His fingers tightened on the steering wheel until his knuckles turned white. "It's more than that." He slowed to a mere crawl as they passed the local park where kids were playing in the thick layer of snow. It wasn't unusual for someone to lose control of their sled and end up in the street. "It's almost as if he's whispering in my ear, urging me to stop the madness."

Lynne shivered. She was a scientist at heart. She believed in hard facts, not mystic fantasies. But she couldn't deny the tendrils of dread creeping down her spine, as if there was something or someone trying to warn her of danger.

Was it Rudolf Jansen's spirit?

She shook her head, refusing to let her imagination run wild. "I knew your father, Kir, and the last thing he would want is for you to put yourself in danger."

"Where do you want to eat breakfast?" he asked, changing the conversation rather than admitting she was right. "There's not much choice when it comes to restaurants in Pike. I can cook if you want."

Lynne swallowed a sigh. It was a waste of energy to try and convince Kir to give up his determination to hunt down the killer.

"Let's have it at my house," she said. "It's my turn to cook."

"It's your day off," he protested. "Besides . . ."

"Yes?"

"Ah." He tried to look innocent. "Nothing."

Lynne narrowed her eyes. "Are you scared of my cooking?"

His lips twitched. "I'm sure you have many fine skills, but is cooking one of them?"

She rolled her eyes as he allowed his words to trail away. "I might not have your magical talents in a kitchen, but I can pour out some cereal and toast a few slices of bread."

Kir's tension seemed to ease as he turned onto the street that led to the small, ranch-style house that Lynne had called home from the day she was born.

After pulling behind her battered truck, he switched off the engine and they climbed out of the SUV. "It seems strange to think of this place without your father."

"I still expect him to walk through the door and call out my name," she admitted as they entered the house. They shed their heavy coats and wiped the snow from their boots before she led Kir toward the kitchen. "I'm happy he's enjoying his life in Florida, but it gets lonely without him."

"You could always get a roommate," he suggested.

Lynne shuddered at the mere thought. "I'd be a horrible landlord."

"Why?"

"My hours are crazy, I foster sick animals, and I walk out of the house with the oven on or the door wide open when I'm preoccupied." She moved to the fridge to pull out the milk and butter.

"I'm sure the benefits of sharing a home with you would outweigh any drawbacks."

Lynne shook her head, crossing toward the stove. "Doubtful."

Passing by Kir, she wasn't prepared for him to reach out and swing her toward him. She tilted back her head, her heart missing a beat as he leaned down to press a kiss against her lips.

It was soft. Like a question. Then, when she didn't pull away, he grasped her hips and deepened the kiss. A welcome warmth poured through her, chasing away the lingering chill.

Lynne trembled, instinctively swaying toward his hard body. It wasn't until she felt the carton of milk press against her stomach that she recalled what she was supposed to be doing.

"Breakfast," she muttered.

"In bed?" he whispered against her lips.

The image of lying naked in the arms of this man was terrifyingly easy to summon. Lynne didn't have to guess why. It'd been nestled in the back of her mind, just waiting for the opportunity to consume her thoughts. But she'd just been brutally reminded by Nash's treachery that her ability to choose lovers sucked. Perhaps tumbling into bed with a man who was going to disappear from Pike at any moment wouldn't be her brightest decision.

With an effort, she forced herself to take a step back. "Don't push your luck."

"I just thought I would throw the suggestion out there." He grinned. "What can I do?"

More flustered than she wanted to admit, Lynne turned to stack the ingredients on the stove before waving her hand toward the counter across the room. "The coffeemaker is over there. I'm dying for a cup." She recalled her unexpectedly early morning. "Or six," she added.

"Ah. Coffee is my specialty." He headed in the direction she pointed.

Lynne bent down to pull out a skillet. "Everything is your specialty."

"I'm a talented guy." He ignored her snort at his arrogance, planting his hands flat on the counter as he suddenly leaned forward to peer out the window. "What's that?"

Lynne frowned, crossing to join him. If it was Nash again, she was going to get a restraining order against him.

The horse's patootie.

Standing next to Kir, she searched for any sign of her ex-boyfriend. What she saw was a lot of snow, her utility shed, the empty alleyway, and Mrs. Norris's black cat.

"You mean Tyne Daly?" she asked, her gaze on the cat as it leaped from her picnic table to the nearby tree.

"No. On your shed."

Her attention shifted to the long metal building where she kept her gardening supplies along with her lawn-mower and a snowmobile for the times her truck couldn't make it to an emergency call.

It took her a minute to locate what had captured his attention.

"It looks like a piece of paper is stuck," she said, watching the object flutter in the stiff breeze.

"I'll check it out."

Kir was moving before she could protest, heading out the back door and tromping through the snow. Lynne hurried to the door he'd left open, watching as he reached the shed and yanked the paper off the small hook she used to hang the hummingbird feeder.

He glanced down, and even at a distance she could see him stiffen.

"Kir?" she called out. "What is it?"

He lifted his head, his expression hard. "Call the sheriff."

Kir finished his search of the shed and garage before he returned to the house. Lynne was just placing her cell phone on the table when he entered the kitchen.

Her face was pale, but she held her chin high. She'd displayed the same courage when he'd brought in the enlarged photo of her that had been dangling from a small hook on the shed. The black-and-white photo had been a close-up of her face. She'd been asleep, with a few wispy strands of hair brushing her cheek. The image had been unnerving enough, but someone had altered the photo to look as if there was a red ribbon tied around her neck.

The threat was unmistakable.

Enraged, Kir had forced himself to focus on ensuring there were no other unpleasant surprises hidden outside. He had to keep busy. If he allowed himself time to dwell on the horrifying realization that the killer had snuck into Lynne's bedroom and stood there watching as she slept while he indulged in his evil fantasies, he wouldn't be able to function.

And right now, being able to function had never been more important.

Blowing on his frozen hands, he moved to stand directly in front of Lynne. "Well?" he demanded.

"I talked to Anthony," she told him. Then, as he sent her a confused glance, she continued. "He's a deputy at the sheriff's office. He was in my class at school."

"You didn't talk to the sheriff?"

"No. He said the sheriff drove to Madison yesterday to deliver a packet to the WSC something or other. She should be back later today."

"The WSCLB. The Wisconsin State Crime Lab," Kir explained in absent tones. "I understand why she would personally deliver any potential clues from the murder scenes to protect the chain of evidence. I remember my dad doing the same thing. But I don't know why she'd stay the night in Madison. I doubt she'll get any results this weekend."

"Anthony said he'd drop by later to pick up the picture." Her gaze darted toward the photo he'd left on the kitchen table before skittering away. "I think everyone is feeling overwhelmed."

"I'm feeling a little overwhelmed myself," Kir admitted. "I checked through the shed and garage. I think we should do a quick look through your house to make sure there aren't any other surprises."

She paled, but grimly holding on to her courage she gave a small nod before leading him out of the kitchen. They searched the living room before heading down the hall to the bedrooms. Kir was briefly distracted from his fury at the thought of a pervert intruding into this house as they entered the bedroom.

It looked as if it was ready for Lynne's father to arrive at any moment. The furniture was dark and heavy, with a brown-and-tan comforter on the large bed. The walls had a few framed pictures of Dr. Gale and Lynne together, along with various awards the older man had earned over the years. There was even a pair of boots next to a chair, patiently waiting for their owner to return.

Next they moved to Lynne's room. There was nothing

frilly about it. In fact, it was almost masculine, with solid furniture and beige walls, and a brown-and-black comforter on the bed. But there was a simple coziness that reflected Lynne's personality. She would never be flashy or glitzy, and that somehow made her all the more fascinating.

Who knew solid dependability could be so sexy?

With a grimace, Kir dismissed his untimely thoughts, waiting for Lynne to make sure that nothing was out of place before they returned to the kitchen.

"Oh, I forgot about breakfast." She came to a halt in the center of the floor, staring at the eggs and milk on the stove.

Kir's heart felt as if it'd been put in a vise. She looked unbearably lost. "I doubt either of us can eat right now." He gently urged her to the table, pressing on her shoulders until she took a seat. Then he crossed to the counter. "But I could use some coffee. I think I've been cold since the moment I returned to Pike."

"I'm sure Freud would have a theory."

His lips twitched as he switched on the coffeemaker and grabbed two mugs from the cabinet. "No doubt."

"But it isn't your imagination. It's even colder than usual this year." She shivered. "And, I think there's supposed to be snow later."

Kir stiffened, whirling to face the window. "Snow."

"Has it already started?"

Kir's gaze scanned the backyard and he silently cursed himself for overlooking such an obvious clue. "The only footprints out there belonged to me," he said.

"Okay." She sounded confused.

"That means it had to have snowed since someone

put the photo on your shed." His gaze moved toward the alley beyond the outbuildings. Nothing. The snow was undisturbed.

"It was snowing when you left last night to follow Nash, but it had stopped when I went to bed at midnight," Lynne said slowly. "So it had to have been before then."

Kir turned toward Lynne, leaning against the counter. She was right. It'd been snowing heavily when he'd left the bar and gone home. "Did you notice anything when you first came home from work?"

She shook her head. "I stopped by the animal rescue for a few hours. It was already dark by the time I got here."

"What about before you left for work yesterday morning?"

There was a pause as she considered his question. Then she gave a decisive shake of her head. "The snow had drifted during the night, so I had to go to the shed to get the shovel to clear the driveway. The photo definitely wasn't there."

That was exactly what Kir had expected. He moved forward to tap the photo on the table with the tip of his finger. "That means this was placed on your shed sometime after you went to work yesterday morning and before midnight."

She sucked in a sharp breath. "Nash."

"He's the obvious choice," Kir agreed. He tried to imagine the man driving to Lynne's house and then creeping around the yard to put the photo on the shed. Why not put it on the front door, or even in the mailbox where Lynne would be sure to see it? Then he abruptly recalled Nash storming away. "When he left last night he used the kitchen door. Do you know where he was parked?"

Lynne made a face. "He always blocks the alley when he comes here. He's afraid his truck might get scratched if he leaves it on the street."

Kir's lips twisted into a humorless smile. Now it made sense. "It would have been easy for him to hook the photo on the shed before coming to the house."

"I suppose."

Kir arched his brows. "I hear a 'but' in there."

She reached to pull the photo closer, trying to hide her revulsion as she studied the picture of herself.

"Nash hates computers," she at last continued, pointing toward the red ribbon that had been electronically added to the image. "I'm not sure he even knows how to turn one on, let alone be capable of using Photoshop."

Kir couldn't argue. It was an easy enough process, but if Nash truly didn't know anything about computers, it seemed more likely he would have used a red marker to draw on the ribbon. It would have achieved the same effect.

"Who else would have a picture of you sleeping?"

She released a shaky breath, leaning forward to study the picture. "Wait." She suddenly pointed toward the top corner of the photo where the paneled wall was visible. "This isn't my bedroom. This is the couch at the clinic."

Kir jerked in surprise. The location changed everything. "Do you sleep there often?"

She nodded. "If I'm out on a late call I'll sometimes take a nap during my lunch break, or if there's an animal in need of 24/7 care I'll spend the night."

"That means anyone could have taken this picture." The clinic wasn't huge, but it was busy with people constantly coming and going.

Not to mention the various animals added a layer of chaos

that meant it would be easy to sneak past the distracted staff to Lynne's private office.

"Yeah," she agreed with a shiver.

The scent of coffee had Kir spinning back to fill two large mugs before he returned to the table and took a seat. "Nash is still at the top of the list," he told Lynne, refusing to give up on his prime suspect. "No one would notice him coming or going from your office, and we know he walked past the shed last night."

She looked unconvinced, but suddenly her eyes widened. "Oh, I forgot. There was a shadow."

"What shadow?"

"I was standing there last night." She pointed toward the window. "And I thought I saw something or someone dart across the yard. When I got to the back door, I saw Nash pulling into the alley."

"So he couldn't be the shadow?"

"No."

Kir's jaw tightened. Why was she working so hard to find someone besides Nash to blame as the potential killer? Did she still have feelings for the jerk?

The thought was more disturbing than it should have been.

With an effort, he resisted the urge to force her to admit that her ex-lover was more than likely a serial killer. "I don't suppose you have security cameras?" he asked.

She lifted her brows at the question. "In Pike?"

"Crime is everywhere." He deliberately glanced at the photo. "The good citizens of Pike aren't saints."

She sighed. "No, there are no security cameras."

Kir sipped his coffee, silently sorting through various

means of discovering who had been in Lynne's backyard. The options were seriously limited.

"Maybe one of your neighbors noticed something."

"Doubtful." She squashed his one hope. "Cal and Denise live on the other side of the alley, but they spend the winter in Arizona. And my nearest neighbor, Mrs. Norris, is nearly blind."

He muttered a curse. "Everyone in town would know they could enter your backyard with no one noticing."

"Probably."

A surge of fury raced through Kir. Not toward Lynne. But toward the lunatic who was stalking the women of Pike.

He tapped his finger on the photo. "Whoever left this was sending a warning, Lynne."

Her face was pale, but she was obviously battling against the urge to panic. "We don't know that it was from the killer. It could be a terrible joke."

His lips thinned. He didn't want her having hysterics, but she had to realize this was life or death. "I'm serious, Lynne," he insisted. "Do you have any family you can stay with?"

"No."

He glanced toward the nearby door. It was perfectly fine for keeping out the winter wind, but one good kick would shatter it. "You can't stay here alone."

"You're not going to let this go, are you?"

Kir finished his coffee and rose to his feet. "I'll get my things."

Chapter 12

It was five thirty on Sunday morning when Lynne's phone rang. She was out of bed and pulling on her clothes before she finished the call.

Unlike most professionals, Lynne worked with creatures who had no respect for the fact that it was her day off. Or that the snow was tumbling through the air in thick swirls. Like feathers escaping from a busted pillow.

She'd tried to be quiet as she crept through the darkened house, but she was still pulling on her heavy boots when Kir appeared from her father's bedroom, already dressed.

Lynne hadn't bothered to argue with him as they left the house to drive over the icy roads to the distant farm. She was still freaked out from the picture that'd been left on her shed. She wasn't eager to be completely alone in such an isolated location.

And honestly, it was unexpectedly nice to have someone to chat with as she plowed her truck through the snowstorm. She enjoyed her own company most of the time, but Kir was easy to be around. Smart, interesting, and comfortable with silence when she wasn't in the mood to talk.

It surprised her. When they were young Kir had seemed so shallow. Now she was beginning to realize that he used his reckless charm as an armor to hide his sensitive heart.

Because she kept her speed at a snail's pace to avoid ending up in a ditch, it took almost two hours to reach the farm. Once there, she'd tried to convince Kir to stay in the truck. Not only was it going to be insanely cold in the barn, but she also suspected her work was going to involve a lot of blood.

She'd been right. The pygmy goat had managed to catch his leg on a barbed wire fence and ripped open his flesh down to the bone. It'd taken over an hour to suture the flesh back together. And then another half an hour with the owner so she could express her profuse gratitude. Which meant it was past eleven when they arrived back in town.

Relieved to be on roads that had been packed down by other vehicles, Lynne glanced over at Kir. He'd been quiet on the drive back, and his handsome face was paler than usual.

"Are you okay?" she asked.

He sent her a wry smile. "That's not for the faint of stomach."

"I warned you to stay in the truck."

"I wanted to see you in action," he insisted. "I'm impressed."

She turned her attention back to the road. There was a steady stream of traffic as the citizens of Pike headed to church. "Because I stitched up a goat?"

"Because you climbed out of bed at five thirty in the

morning and drove through a blinding snowstorm to stitch up a goat."

"Seesaw is like family to Jemma. She would be devastated if she lost him."

He turned in his seat, his coat whispering softly against the worn leather upholstery. "You devote so much of yourself to caring for others. Who cares for you?"

Her heart gave a funny jerk. As if it was reacting to some deeper meaning in his soft question.

"I have my father." She cleared a sudden lump from her throat, eager for a distraction. She found it in the small, red brick building with a towering steeple that was just ahead of them. "Isn't that Pastor Bradshaw's church?"

Without warning, Kir was leaning forward, his body stiff with tension. "Pull over."

She whipped the truck against the curb across the street from the church. "What's wrong?"

Kir pointed toward the graveled parking lot. "That van."

Lynne studied it in confusion, not sure why he was so interested. "That's the delivery van from Randi's flower shop."

"Why would it be parked at the church?"

She shrugged. "I suppose they're going to have Randi's funeral here."

"Rita said Randi attended church in Grange," he told her. "She didn't think the churches in Pike were fancy enough for Randi's taste."

Lynne's lips parted to point out her family might want a local funeral, only to have the words falter when she realized she recognized the woman headed toward the van. "That's Jillian Bryant."

Kir studied the short, heavyset woman who was precariously skidding over the icy gravel. She was wearing a thick, quilted red coat and matching stocking cap. Even at a distance, Lynne could tell her cheeks were as rosy as her coat. Whether from the cold or some emotion was impossible to say.

"You know her?"

Lynne nodded. "She was a few years younger than me in school."

"Was she friends with Randi Decker?"

"I don't know about friends, but she works at the florist shop. I remember her delivering a bouquet of roses to the clinic a couple of months ago."

His eyes narrowed. "From Nash?"

Lynne made a sound of disgust. "Not hardly. He was too cheap for roses," she said. In fact, the only gift Nash had ever given her had been a teddy bear he'd won at a local fair. "My dad sent them for my birthday."

"You like roses?"

"I like the thought my dad remembered it was my birthday."

He studied her with a speculative gaze before turning his head to regard the woman who had almost reached the van. "I want to talk to her."

"Why?"

"First I want to know what she's doing at this church."

Lynne furrowed her brow. It didn't seem that odd to Lynne, but Kir was determined to suspect that there was something sketchy about the pastor. "What else?"

"I want to know if Randi mentioned being followed or harassed by anyone," he said without hesitation. "The killer obviously likes playing games."

"Games?"

"He sent my father letters. He left you a photo. It seems

possible he might have taunted the women before killing them."

With a nod, Lynne switched off the engine and unhooked her seat belt. "I'll ask her."

His brows snapped together. "I can do it."

"She's not going to talk to you."

"Why not?"

Lynne grabbed the door handle, glancing in the rear-view mirror to make sure there wasn't any traffic. "You might have been born in Pike, but you haven't lived here in a very long time," she reminded him. "You're a stranger to Jillian. She's not going to gossip about her dead friend with you."

He heaved a harsh sigh, shoving open his own door. "You're right. You talk to her and I'll have a look around."

They both climbed out of the truck. Waiting for Kir to join her in the middle of the street, she sent him a stern frown. "Stay out of trouble," she commanded. "You've already been thrown out of the charity shop. Do you want to get banned from a church?"

He flashed an unrepentant smile. "If it leads me to the truth."

She rolled her eyes, but she didn't say anything as he headed toward the brick building. Instead she concentrated on reaching the parking lot without slipping on the ice. The snow was floating down in the soft, fluffy flakes that always looked so pretty on television, but clung to her skin with icy persistence. The sensation warned Lynne that the younger woman wasn't going to be eager to stand in the cold and chitchat. She needed to get directly to the point if she hoped to get the information she wanted.

"Hey, Jillian." She stepped in front of the woman, who came to a startled halt.

"Lynne," Jillian said in surprise, then she smiled. "Sorry, I suppose I should call you Dr. Gale."

"Lynne is fine."

Jillian nodded, glancing over her shoulder. "Do you go to church here?"

"No, I happened to see you when I was driving past and I wanted to make sure you're okay," Lynne said.

Jillian glanced back in surprise. "Me?"

"I know you worked with Randi. Her death must have been a terrible shock."

"Oh, yes." Beneath the chilled redness of Jillian's cheeks, her skin paled. She appeared genuinely disturbed by her employer's death. "Honestly, I couldn't believe it when I got to work and the sheriff told me she'd been murdered."

Lynne patted Jillian's arm in sympathy. "Do they know how it happened?"

Jillian's lips trembled before she pressed them into a tight line. "I'm not sure. They refused to tell me anything, but I saw Randi's car in the parking lot behind the shop. I have a terrible feeling she was there when . . ."

"When she was attacked?"

Jillian shivered. "Gives me the creeps just to go into the shop."

Lynne squeezed Jillian's arm, using the skills she'd developed over the years to put the woman at ease. Being a vet wasn't just helping animals. It was connecting with the owners so they trusted her to do the very best for the pets they loved or the livestock that provided for their family.

"What a horrible thought," she murmured. "Randi must have come in early to work and the monster was waiting for her."

Jillian slowly shook her head. "No, I don't think so." She hesitated, as if debating whether to continue. At last she leaned forward, speaking low as cars started to pull into the parking lot. Obviously, it was getting close to time for the church service to begin. "I'm not supposed to be talking about it, but Randi's husband told me Randi came home last evening at five just as she always did, but that after dinner she said she had to run back to the shop to arrange flowers for a funeral the next morning. She never came home."

Lynne arched her brows. "Was that unusual?"

"We didn't have any orders," Jillian said. "In fact, we decided not to replenish our coolers because it was going to be a slow weekend."

"She might have gotten the call for the order after she got home," Lynne pointed out. It was a small town. It wouldn't be unusual for someone to call a merchant at home, regardless of the day or time.

"If she did, she would have to wait until our vendor opened this morning to work on any arrangement," Jillian insisted. "So why go that night?"

There was one obvious reason. Still, Lynne chose her words with care. She didn't want Jillian bolting. "I know it's awful to speak ill of the dead, but could she have been meeting someone at the shop?"

"You mean a client?"

"Or . . ." Lynne waited for an elderly couple to pass them on the way to the church. "A friend."

"Oh." Jillian blushed. "Not that I know of."

"Sorry." Lynne wrinkled her nose. "It's just weird that she'd be out on such a cold night unless it was important."

Jillian cleared her throat, looking like she was caught between good manners that insisted you didn't gossip about the dead, and the fierce desire to share what she knew. "I suppose it's possible she might have made plans to hook up with someone," she finally conceded. "She's been complaining lately how boring Ned is, and that she felt as if she was being buried alive." She abruptly realized what she said, shoving her hands in the pockets of her coat. "God."

"Was there anyone she was interested in?" Lynne quickly asked.

Jillian looked sick, obviously regretting mentioning Randi's private complaints. "She's never mentioned anyone. At least not to me. The sheriff took her laptop from the office, so there might be something on there."

Lynne sent her a reassuring smile. If Randi had been cheating on her husband, she was convinced Jillian didn't know. "Well, we all complain about our lives, don't we," she said in light tones. "That doesn't mean anything."

Jillian was instantly relieved. "No. And even if she was . . . indiscreet, I'm sure it wouldn't have anything to do with what happened to her."

Lynne wasn't nearly so convinced, but she nodded in agreement. "True. It's much more likely that whoever attacked her was a stranger." She paused, not having to fake her sudden shiver. "Maybe someone who's been creeping around the shop. Or following Randi."

Jillian nodded. "That's what I think."

"Did you notice anyone?"

Jillian furrowed her brow as she tried to recall if there'd been any mysterious lurkers in the area. "No. No strangers."

An unexpected pang of disappointment squeezed Lynne's heart. It made her realize that a small, secret part of her was desperately clinging to the hope that the killer was an outsider who'd randomly chosen Pike to stalk his prey. Ridiculous, of course. Especially after the picture that had been left on her shed.

With an effort, she forced herself to ask the most obvious question. "Randi was a beautiful woman who ran her own business. Did any of the locals hang around making a pest of themselves? Or expect extra attention?"

Jillian shook her head. "Most people call in their orders and we deliver them," she told Lynne. She shrugged. "The only person we've had any problems with is Nash Cordon."

"Nash?"

Jillian raised a gloved hand to her lips. "Oh, sorry. I forgot the two of you are a couple."

Lynne shuddered. Her relationship with Nash seemed like a lifetime ago. "We haven't been a couple for weeks," she assured her companion. "What did he do?"

Jillian took a step closer as more parishioners funneled past them. In the distance the sound of someone picking out notes on an organ filtered through the frigid air.

"The VFW rent out their building for wedding receptions and banquets," Jillian said. "That's the bulk of our business so they gave us a key to the back door to make our deliveries without needing someone there to let us in. But half the time we can't get through because Nash parks his truck in the alley. Randi finally called the city council to complain. I don't think he was very happy when he found out."

"Yeah, I can imagine." Lynne shook her head in disgust, all too familiar with Nash's belief that the world was created to make his life easier. At the same time, she tucked away the knowledge that Nash had a reason to be angry with Randi.

The evidence was certainly building against him.

"Anyone else?" she pressed.

"I don't think so." Jillian glanced around as the organ warmed up and the choir joined in to spill music through the open doors of the church. "I should get going."

Lynne held on to the woman's arm. She wasn't done with her questions. "Are you working this morning?"

Jillian nodded. "Randi had a standing order with this church to deliver fresh flowers for the altar every Sunday morning."

Lynne lifted a brow. Fresh flowers in the middle of winter seemed an extravagant cost for a tiny congregation. "Every Sunday?"

"Yep." Jillian's lips twisted. "Until now. The pastor just said he wanted to cancel the order." She looked momentarily angered by the loss of business, then heaved a resigned sigh. "I guess I don't blame him. I have no idea what's going to happen to the shop now that Randi's . . . gone."

"Did you have to do the delivery every Sunday?"

Jillian waited for an elderly couple to shuffle past them before she answered. "Actually, I never did them." She lowered her voice. "Randi said the good pastor insisted that she personally bring the flowers."

Lynne swallowed a curse. Maybe Kir wasn't so nuts to suspect both Nash and Pastor Bradshaw. "Why?"

Jillian shrugged. "He said he hoped to convince her to attend his church, but Randi assumed he had a thing for her. Of course, she thought every guy had a thing for her." She halted, her eyes widening with distress. "Oh. That was a terrible thing to say."

"None of us are saints, Jillian," Lynne assured her, a genuine sincerity in her voice. She worked intimately with families in the community. None of them were as perfect as they wanted people to believe. "And it was no secret that Randi could be vain."

"I guess," Jillian conceded.

"Do you think Pastor Bradshaw wanted more than flowers from Randi?"

"He's a guy even if he is a man of the cloth. And Randi knew how to turn on the charm when she wanted something." There was an edge in her voice that suggested Jillian might have been jealous of Randi's popularity. "That's why she was such a good businesswoman."

"Do you think they ever . . ."

Jillian shook her head in a sharp denial. "No way. Randi used to make fun of him all the time. She called him a dweeb." The church doors closed with a loud snap, obviously indicating the service was starting. Jillian shook off Lynne's hand. "Look, I really gotta go. My kids are home alone."

"Be careful," Lynne urged, watching as the woman climbed in her van.

She hated the sensation that the killer was a lurker in the shadows, stalking unsuspecting women. Like a guillotine hovering over the town of Pike, just waiting for the opportunity to execute the unwary.

Chapter 13

Madeline Randall woke, swallowing a scream as she realized she was still in the dark basement.

Or maybe it was hell, she grimly acknowledged.

When her mother had warned that she was going to end up in the fiery pits if she didn't obey her commands, she'd imagined it would be filled with horned devils and putrid lava. Instead it was frigid darkness interrupted by brutal bouts of violence. She never knew when they were going to happen. She would drift off and awaken to a painful assault. For terrifying minutes she would huddle in a tight ball as the attack exploded through her.

It was never the same.

Sometimes there would be vicious kicks to her back. Other times her hair would be yanked out in bloody chunks. She'd been smacked by something that felt like a tire iron. And burned with a cigarette.

Every inch of her body had been tortured in one way or another. Her muscles ached, she had at least one broken rib, and she suspected she had internal injuries.

She wouldn't last much longer.

Worse, she didn't know whether to mourn or celebrate her impending death. It wasn't like her life had been a bed of roses before she'd been entombed in the darkness.

But as if to taunt her morbid thoughts, Madeline heard the faint click that warned her tormentor was returning. That was her only warning. There was no flare of light from another room. No sound of approaching footsteps. Nothing but the click followed by hideous pain.

Madeline tensed, a sob lodged in her throat. There was no use screaming for help or pleading for mercy. She'd tried everything until her throat was raw from the effort.

A minute ticked past. Then another. Her shallow pants became louder as she waited. And waited. Christ. Tears poured down her frozen cheeks. The anticipation was nearly as bad as the actual blows.

At last the cramp in her lower back forced her to roll to the side. She strained to hear the sound of her captor.

There was nothing.

Could he—or she—stay that quiet for so long? It seemed unlikely. So what was happening?

The click was the sound of the door opening. She was certain of that. So this had to be a trick, right? Just some new form of torture.

But what if it wasn't? What if her captor had finally made a mistake?

With a groan, Madeline forced herself to her feet.

It didn't matter if this was a trap or not.

She'd spent her entire life making the safe choice and what had it gotten her? Squashed dreams and bitter regret.

For once she was going to take a chance.

Stumbling forward she kept her arms outstretched as she blindly searched for the door.

Kir sat in the passenger seat of Lynne's truck, his gaze absently studying the church as he allowed the warmth from the heater to drive away the chill from his body.

He'd spent the past twenty minutes creeping around the church grounds. He hadn't really known what he was looking for until he'd noticed the small house at the back of the property. It had to be the parsonage where Pastor Bradshaw lived.

He wanted to see inside, but he wasn't willing to risk being spotted. Not when there were dozens of people wandering around the parking lot and church.

"What are you plotting?"

Lynne's question interrupted his absent musings of how he could reach the house without alerting any nosy neighbors.

He glanced toward her with what he hoped was an innocent expression. "What makes you think I'm plotting anything?"

"I expected you to charge into the church and accuse Pastor Bradshaw of lying to you."

It was exactly what he'd wanted to do after Lynne had repeated her conversation with Jillian. In fact, he'd even taken a step toward the church before he'd come to his senses. "The man was preparing to deliver his sermon in the house of God. I'm not a heathen," he told Lynne in pious tones.

She narrowed her eyes. "Like I said. What are you plotting?"

He chuckled. "I'll admit my first instinct was to confront the pastor."

"But?"

"There has to be a reason he pretended he barely knew Randi Decker."

She paused, as if considering the possibilities. "Maybe because he felt you were hounding him. Or maybe he was embarrassed to admit he had a crush on a married woman."

"Or maybe he was obsessed with her."

Her jaw tightened, but she didn't argue. Even she couldn't deny there was something sketchy about Pastor Bradshaw.

"So when are you going to ask him?"

"I'm not ready to let him know I've discovered he lied to me. Not until I've had a chance to nose around."

"You're going to spy on him?"

He clicked his tongue. "'Spy' is such an ugly word."

"That's not an answer."

He shrugged, not bothered by her accusing gaze as he pointed toward the end of the street. "Drive around to the back of the church."

"Why?"

"I'd like to know more about Pastor Bradshaw and his habits."

Heaving a sigh, she put the truck into drive and slowly drove around the block. "You're going to get yourself arrested," she complained. "Or shot."

"Drop me out here." He wasn't worried about being arrested or shot since he didn't intend to get caught.

She pulled over, her expression concerned. "Kir."

"I'm not going to do anything stupid, I just want to poke around," he promised, jumping out of the truck. He glanced at her before he shut the door. "Are you going home?"

"First I'm going by the animal sanctuary."

"The one at your grandparents' farm?"

She nodded. "There are a couple strays that came in last week that I'm treating for injuries and malnutrition."

Kir clenched his jaw. He couldn't stay next to Lynne 24/7. Not if he intended to track down the person responsible for threatening her. But the thought of her traveling to such an isolated spot made his stomach cramp with fear.

"Will you be there alone?"

"No. Either Grady or Monica will be there."

"Who are they?"

"A young couple who take care of the sanctuary in exchange for living rent-free in my grandparents' house," she explained. "They're both finishing their online degrees so it's a perfect arrangement for all of us. But I still try to check on the animals every couple of days."

A portion of his fear eased. "Be careful."

"I'm always careful." She sent him a chiding glare. "Unlike some people I know." He started to shut the door only to be halted when Lynne leaned across the console of the truck. "Oh wait. You'll need a key to get back in the house in case I have an emergency." She grabbed her worn leather medical bag and dug through a side pocket. At last she pulled out a single key and handed it to him. "Here."

Holding her gaze, he pocketed the key. "Thank you," he murmured, knowing it was more than just a gesture of convenience.

Lynne wasn't a woman who would easily open her house or her heart to others.

For now, he'd take the key to her home.

She flushed, as if feeling exposed by his intense gaze. "You should go before you freeze."

With a nod he closed the door and stepped back. He waited until the truck pulled away before he crossed the street, his gaze sweeping over the small, tidy homes that lined the block. They looked like something off a postcard, with their roofs covered by a layer of snow and smoke curling from the brick chimneys, but Kir was more interested in the heavy curtains across the windows and peaceful silence that surrounded him.

Were the neighbors all at church? Or maybe just sleeping late on a lazy Sunday morning. Either way it offered him the opportunity that he needed.

Maintaining a leisurely stroll, Kir pushed open the front gate to the house directly behind the church. He avoided the porch as he circled to the side of the house. For now he preferred to avoid breaking and entering. He wasn't entirely certain Lynne would bail him out if he was arrested.

He paused at the first window, peering through the crack in the curtains. He could see a narrow living room with green shag carpeting, tan leather furniture, and blank walls. It looked like it was stuck in a seventies time warp. Obviously, Pastor Bradshaw wasn't into home décor. Accepting that there was nothing suspicious to be seen, Kir moved to the next window. This one revealed a kitchen just as dated as the living room. There was an old gas stove and an avocado green fridge with a square table in the center of the tiled floor.

Nothing there.

He moved to the last window. The curtains were pulled tightly closed, but they were sheer enough that he could make out a bed and a heavy dresser. There didn't seem to be anything on the walls, although the shelves were packed with books.

With a grimace, Kir continued across the backyard toward the nearby church. He didn't know what he'd been looking for, but all he'd discovered was a house that looked as if it was as sterile as a hotel room.

Following a narrow pathway that had been tunneled through the snow, Kir headed toward the addition that had been built on the back of the church. He expected it to be locked, but the door easily swung open and he quickly darted inside.

Instantly he was hit by the smell of mold from the piles of old choir gowns and well-worn hymnals. He wrinkled his nose, weaving his way through broken chairs and folding tables precariously stacked on the wooden floor. This was obviously the storage area.

He continued forward to enter the main building. There was a darkly paneled hallway that led to the nave where he could hear Pastor Bradshaw delivering his sermon. His voice echoed and soared through the air, ringing with a sincerity that was impressive.

Kir didn't listen to his words. He wasn't there for the preaching.

After glancing around to ensure he was alone, Kir opened the nearest door to find a coat closet. The next two doors were marked for the men's and women's bathrooms. He inched toward the opening at the end of the hallway where he could glimpse the sparse congregation dotted around the pews. Far from a full house, but that didn't seem to dim the pastor's enthusiasm.

Reaching the last door, he pushed it open and slipped

inside. He smiled with satisfaction as he realized he'd located the office.

It was a cramped room lined with bookcases and a wooden desk loaded with stacks of papers along with a laptop computer. It looked as if the pastor spent more time in this office than he did in his house.

Hopeful he could find something that would connect him to the dead women, Kir did a quick search of the shelves. Nothing. The books were all theological, with a few historical biographies. Next he moved to the desk. Again he came up empty. The papers were all official correspondences for the church or the various charities that Pastor Bradshaw had started. Kir even pulled out the list the pastor had given him to try and compare the handwriting. It didn't look the same, but he wasn't an expert.

Frustrated with the feeling that he was stumbling through the dark even as the killer was creeping closer and closer to Lynne, Kir left the office. He intended to slip out of the church before the service ended, but he'd barely taken a step down the hallway when the door to the bathroom opened and a middle-aged woman was suddenly standing directly in front of him.

She pressed a hand to the center of her chest, as if she was as surprised as he was by the unexpected encounter.

"Can I help you?" she at last demanded, a hint of authority in her voice. Did she work for the church? Then her eyes widened. "Kir?"

Kir frowned, taking in the woman's thin face that was lined with wrinkles and the dark hair sprinkled with silver that was pulled into a knot on top of her head. She was wearing a pink pantsuit with a frilly white top and low, sensible shoes. She looked vaguely familiar.

"Ms. Lockhart," he murmured, finally placing the face with a name.

When he'd been young, she and her husband had run a corner grocery store. She'd always had a stash of candy beneath the counter she would hand out to kids when they came in. Her habit had made her a local favorite, at least until her husband had died and the store had closed.

He hadn't known what had happened to her after that, although there were shadows beneath her eyes and a droop to her shoulders that indicated life hadn't been entirely kind.

"I haven't seen you forever." She studied him with genuine interest. "Are you still in Boston?"

"Yes. I'm just home for Dad's funeral."

"Oh, I heard." She clicked her tongue. "I'm so sorry for your loss."

"Thanks."

She glanced over his shoulder where the choir was performing the farewell song as the congregation rose to their feet. "Are you here for the service?"

Kir smiled, realizing this woman might be able to answer some questions for him. "I actually wanted to see Pastor Bradshaw. He spoke at Dad's funeral."

"Did he?" The older woman looked surprised. "I don't remember Rudolf attending this church."

"He didn't."

"Ah well, it wouldn't matter to Ron." Ms. Lockhart's expression softening with an unmistakable fondness for the pastor. "He loves everyone."

"Everyone?"

"Yes." Her hand moved to touch the pearl necklace nestled against the lacy shirt. "We're so fortunate to have him in Pike. He's not only revived this church, but he's become a vital member of this community."

"So I heard. He started a charity shop in the old bowling alley, didn't he?"

She nodded. "Not only that, he also sponsors the T-ball team during the summer, and volunteers at the nursing home."

He sounded like a saint. Kir never trusted saints. They were usually the most corrupt people around. "What about supporting local businesses?" he inquired.

Ms. Lockhart blinked, as if confused by the question. "I suppose he does."

"Especially the local flower shop."

There was a short silence before the woman sucked in a shocked gasp. "Kir Jansen, you of all people know better than to spread malicious gossip," she chided.

He refused to back down. "You know people whispered about his interest in Randi, don't you?"

"So what if Ron enjoys flirting with pretty women? He might be a servant of God, but he's still a man. Show me one who isn't attracted to flashy baubles. It's harmless." She sniffed, obviously willing to turn a blind eye to the pastor's flirtatious habits.

Kir wasn't as forgiving. "You're certain he's harmless?"

"Yes, I am. Unlike some men, Ron understands how to keep his hands to himself."

"Some men? Do you mean a specific man?"

"Nash Cordon, for one," she snapped.

Kir was caught off guard by the woman's unexpected words. "Nash Cordon is a member of this church?"

A sour expression hardened the older woman's face. "Only because his mother insists he bring her every

Sunday. I expect the place to be hit by lightning each time he walks through the door."

Kir tilted his head, studying the sudden anger that darkened her eyes. "Not a fan?"

Her lips pinched, her body vibrating with emotion. "He dated my daughter Sonja a few years ago. After they broke up, they found Sonja in a cabin near the lake. The sheriff said it was an overdose, but I know in my heart she killed herself."

The bleak confession hit Kir with unexpected force. He had a vague memory of a tiny, blond-haired girl who was always running around the store. She'd been several years younger than him, so he hadn't really known her, but the thought that she was dead was oddly disturbing.

"I'm so sorry."

She sucked in a slow deep breath before she spoke. "It was Ron who offered me a job as his secretary. He understood I needed a purpose in my life."

Kir was starting to understand her unwavering loyalty to the pastor. That didn't, however, mean he wasn't a killer.

"Do you know where he was before he came to Pike?"

"Minneapolis," the woman said before she frowned. "Or maybe it was Chicago." She shrugged. "It was a big city. Too big for Ron. He prefers being in a small town. He says he likes knowing his congregation as more than faces in the pews." The choir came to a halt and Ms. Lockhart squared her shoulders. "The service is ending. I need to open the doors. Have a safe trip back to Boston."

"Thank you."

He followed behind her as if he intended to leave through the nave, but instead halted in the shadows to watch the congregation shuffle out of the pews. His gaze easily located Nash, who was looking bored out of his mind as an older woman next to him was chatting with a gaggle of fellow parishioners. That must be his mother.

About to turn away, Kir stiffened in surprise when a younger woman dashed through the doors that Ms. Lockhart had just opened and made a beeline for Nash.

Chelsea Gallen. Lynne's receptionist.

Kir pressed against the wall, watching as Chelsea stepped between the pews to directly confront Nash. The man looked more annoyed than surprised by the appearance of the younger woman, reaching out to grab her arm and tug her away from his mother and her cronies.

They huddled together, Nash leaning down to speak directly in her ear. From a distance it appeared to Kir that Chelsea was pleading for something and Nash was refusing to give her what she wanted. Then, with a shake of his head, the man was turning to stomp out of the church, leaving his mother and a tearful Chelsea behind.

Kir frowned. The receptionist had assured Lynne that sex with Nash had been a terrible mistake. A brief madness.

Now it appeared she'd been lying. It was obvious she was still obsessed with the arrogant jerk. What would she do to please him? He studied her shattered expression. He was betting the answer was that she'd do anything.

Remaining in the shadows, Kir waited for the congregation to filter out the open doors where the pastor was standing in his heavy robes to shake hands. He briefly considered waiting to confront Bradshaw. The man had lied to him. Then silently he turned and hurried out the back of the church.

He would keep a watch on the man for a day or two. It

was possible he would reveal whether he had any interest in a woman besides Randi Decker. And if his interest was deadly.

Desperate to keep herself busy, Lynne drove to the sanctuary and focused her attention on the variety of wounds and infections that needed her treatment. She gave a medicated bath to the poor beagle who had been dropped off with a skin infection and swabbed the infected eyes of a litter of kittens before replacing them beneath the heat lamp. Next she checked the two boxers who had lost a battle with a porcupine to make sure their injuries were healing.

Once she was done, she grabbed the hose and power-cleaned the kennels while Monica took each of the animals to the enclosed shed for some exercise. It felt good to have both her mind and body occupied. As if the mounting sense of dread couldn't find her as long as she kept moving.

At last, she washed her hands and waited for Monica to join her in the small office she'd built onto the end of the barn. It was amazing how much paperwork went into running a not-for-profit charity.

The younger woman had long, dark hair she kept in a braid and a pretty oval face with large brown eyes. Beneath her heavy coveralls she was so slender she looked incapable of dealing with the duties of running the shelter. But Monica had been raised on a nearby farm and she could handle even the most aggressive animals with remarkable skill, not to mention hauling around sacks of food and supplies as if she was a linebacker.

"Everyone is back in their kennels," she told Lynne. "I'll give them fresh water before I go to bed."

Lynne nodded. "You've cleaned out the pens in the back?"

"Yep, they're ready to go."

Lynne leaned against the edge of her cluttered desk, a sadness tugging at her heart at the knowledge of what the next two weeks were going to bring. It happened every single year. "Unfortunately, the holidays are great for people buying or adopting pets to give as gifts, but once the new wears off they realize it's a lot more work than they want to invest. We need to be prepared," she warned her companion.

Monica nodded. "I hate the thought, but I think we're ready. I asked for extra food donations, plus I found a few blankets we'd stored in the attics."

"Thank you." Lynne smiled with genuine gratitude. She knew she was lucky to have Monica and her husband to keep an eye on the shelter, and she honestly had no idea what she was going to do when they finished their degrees and took the next step in their careers. A worry for another day. "Have you run into any problems?"

"No . . . oh, wait." Monica snapped her fingers. "I almost forgot."

"What?"

"Sheriff Hancock stopped by."

The anxiety Lynne was trying to keep locked in the back of her mind whispered down her spine. "When?"

"Yesterday." Monica furrowed her brow. "Or maybe the day before. She was asking if we keep any medications here for the animals."

Lynne forced a stiff smile, her mouth oddly dry. It wasn't

fear. Not precisely. It was more a jittering sense of unease. "I suppose that makes sense," she said, pretending indifference. "It's no secret that the sheriff suspects drugs were stolen from my clinic."

Monica rolled her eyes. "I saw the news. That reporter is an idiot."

Lynne's smile softened in appreciation at the blunt, unconditional certainty that Lynne couldn't be involved in anything nefarious. "What did you tell the sheriff?" she asked.

"That you always bring any medication with you, unless it's a prescription we need to give every day," Monica said. "And that those are locked in a cabinet in the house."

"Good."

Monica cleared her throat, shifting from foot to foot. "And . . ."

"Yes?"

"I told her that a few months ago Grady discovered someone had pried open the back door to the kennels."

"They did?" Lynne blinked in surprise. "Why didn't you tell me?"

Monica shrugged. "Nothing was missing, and the animals were fine. You were—" She hesitated, as if choosing her words with care. "Distracted, and there was no point in worrying about a door that was easily fixed."

Lynne thought back, trying to figure out why she would have been distracted. Then she swallowed a sigh. That was about the time she'd started dating Nash. The relationship had been in the new, giddy stage when she wanted to spend every spare minute with him.

It hadn't lasted long. In fact, it'd taken only a couple of weeks before she started to suspect she'd made a mistake.

Still, she'd continued to date Nash, a part of her worried that she was too finicky when it came to men. She'd told herself she had to accept that no one was perfect.

What a waste of her time.

"If anything else happens, no matter how trivial, let me know, okay?"

Monica nodded, clearly relieved that Lynne wasn't angry that she'd kept the break-in a secret. "Of course."

"And keep the doors locked when you're home alone," Lynne continued. "I never thought about how isolated this place is until bad things started happening in Pike."

Monica nodded toward the open doorway where they could see the kennels that lined the walls.

"When Grady has to go somewhere, I always have a few friends in the house with me."

"That's not a bad idea." Lynne's gaze moved toward the large English mastiff that had been dumped at the shelter a couple months ago. King was a cream and black beauty who she didn't doubt would be quickly adopted once she finished his heartworm treatment.

He was gentle as a lamb, but his sheer size was enough to terrify most people.

A perfect houseguest.

Chapter 14

Dear Rudolf,

Did you study the Effigy Mounds when you were in school? I did. Our fourth-grade class took a field trip to visit them. The other kids ran around pretending they were cowboys. Or sneaking into the nearby woods to play stupid kissing games. Idiots. But not me. I was fascinated by the mounds. Just imagine capturing the spirit of the dead in those tombs. As soon as I got home I ran to an empty field and built my own mound. It was supposed to be a Thunderbird, but it looked more like a wonky cross. Still, I wanted to see if it would give me the powers I so desperately craved. I had no dead body, but that didn't stop me. I slit the throat of our cat and put it inside.

That's when my mother came to find me.

I thought she would be proud of me. I had created my very own Effigy Mound. Foolish, of course. No one was ever proud of me. She saw the dead cat and assumed I must be doing some sort

*of devil worshipping. She stared at me in horror
and screamed.*

Oh, God. Those screams.

*That's how I remember her, you know. Her
screams echoed through our house night and day.
They were a symphony of anger and pain and
self-indulgent torment.*

*When they were finally silenced, I thought I
would find peace. Just one night without those
incessant shrieks. But there was no peace.*

*Instead there was an aching void deep inside
me. I didn't know what I needed to fill it.*

*Not until last night when I heard those screams
once again. They were vibrating through me as I
found my release.*

Sweet success, dearest Rudolf.

And this morning . . .

*Crimson blood stains the pure white snow.
Life spills from warm to frozen. Don't look.
The pain is gone.*

Lynne woke early Monday morning and prepared for work.

She had slept remarkably well, considering there was a crazed killer loose in her hometown who was leaving creepy photos on her shed. And there was a man she hadn't seen in years sleeping on the other side of the wall. Oh, and she had a hundred-and-twenty-pound dog crowding her bed, who snored like a trucker.

Maybe it was because she wasn't alone in her house. She had her share of courage, but she wasn't an idiot. There was safety in numbers. Especially when the numbers included a massive dog. Or maybe it was the relaxing evening she'd spent watching television and sipping a glass of wine with Kir.

By mutual agreement they'd shared what they had discovered. Kir had told her about Chelsea cornering Nash in the church, as well as his conversation with Ms. Lockhart. She'd told him the sheriff had been to the sanctuary, and that there'd been a break-in months ago. After that, they'd deliberately avoided any subject that would remind them there was a killer in town.

Lynne had snuggled in the couch with Kir just a few inches away, feeling so . . . comfortable. It was almost as if she'd spent years, not a few days, with this man.

How had that happened?

Once, when her father was trying to explain why her mother had left, he'd told her that life wasn't always predictable. Sometimes you traveled along, able to look behind you to see each footstep that led you to a precise point. Other times, you looked around and you had no idea how you'd gotten so lost. It was as if a wave had swept you off your feet and landed you in a place you never intended to be.

It could be good or bad, but it was inevitable. A gift from fate, he'd called it, while Lynne had called it a curse.

Hard to say which one Kir would turn out to be.

Showered and dressed for the day by five forty-five, Lynne strolled into the kitchen to find Kir already up with a hot pot of coffee and fresh toast waiting for her. He'd pulled on a pair of worn jeans and an old sweatshirt, and his golden hair was tousled from sleep. Heat swirled through the pit of her stomach. How could he look so decadently sexy at such an early hour?

More of a gift than a curse so far, a voice whispered in the back of her mind.

She grabbed the mug of coffee he handed her and leaned against the counter to nibble her toast.

"How did you sleep?" Kir asked, his gaze skimming down her cream cable-knit sweater and casual slacks like a physical caress.

She battled back a girlish urge to blush as she swallowed the last of her toast and took a sip of coffee. "King snores."

He chuckled, moving until she could feel the heat of his body. "I don't."

She tilted back her head, meeting his teasing smile. "And you're telling me this because . . . ?"

"Future reference."

"Good to know."

He stepped even closer, his hand against brushing her hip. "I do, however, steal the covers."

Tingles of pleasure shot through her. "That doesn't surprise me."

"It doesn't?"

"You seem like the kind of guy who knows what he wants and goes after it."

His hand skimmed over her hip to the lower curve of her back. "I'm determined."

"Stubborn," she corrected.

"I'm also a realist."

She instinctively arched forward, allowing herself to press against the rock-hard strength of his body. "What's that mean?"

An aching regret darkened his eyes. "It took me years, but I finally accepted that I can't change others. No matter how much I might want to." He paused. "You have to decide I'm worth the risk."

Her mouth was as dry as the desert. Kir was barely touching her but there was a connection between them that was frighteningly intimate.

Instinctively, she took a step back, breaking his light hold. "I'm too boring to take risks."

He blinked, as if she'd just said something outrageous. "Are you kidding?"

"No."

"Lynne, you have bumps and bruises all over you, not to mention at least one bite mark I can see." He pointedly glanced down at her hand that was healing after her battle with a terrified Yorkie. "You drive through blizzards and work insane hours. Your entire life is a risk."

"Not my heart."

"Ah." His hand lifted as if he was going to pull her back toward him. Then, with a grimace, he allowed it to drop back at his side. "What are you afraid of?"

"I don't know." The words weren't an answer, but they were sincere. She briskly moved to grab her jacket, which she'd hung over the back of a chair. "I need to get to the clinic. What are you going to do today?"

Kir folded his arms over his chest, leaning against the dining table. "I thought I might take King on a walk."

Lynne moved to pat the head of the mastiff, who had finished his breakfast and was snoozing by the back door.

"Not too far. His paws will freeze in this frigid weather."

"He'll be fine." Kir smiled at the dog. "Won't you, boy?"

King barked in agreement.

Lynne rolled her eyes and grabbed her purse and

medical bag she'd left on the counter. "If I'm not home for dinner, you can find some stuff in the freezer."

"I'll take care of it." Without warning Kir moved to frame her face in his hands, then he pressed a fierce kiss against her lips. "You stay safe."

He released her before she knew what was happening, and Lynne rushed out of the kitchen and through the living room. Moments later she was seated in her truck, allowing the engine to warm. What was wrong with her? Her heart was racing fast enough to make her lightheaded, and her lips were tingling from his kiss. As if she was a giddy teenager.

Hadn't she learned her lesson with Nash? The words, however, were hollow. Kir was nothing at all like Nash. And her increasing fascination was just the opposite of what'd happened with the men she'd dated in the past. Usually, the closer she got to them, the more she wanted to bail from the relationship. With Kir, the more time she spent with him, the more she respected and liked him.

Muttering at her ridiculous thoughts, she put the truck in reverse and backed out of the drive. Thankfully, Kir had parked across the street so she didn't have to worry about his vehicle blocking her. And the snow had stopped on her way home from the sanctuary, so she didn't have to clean the windows.

But as she put the engine in drive, Lynne frowned.

Something felt weird.

She allowed the truck to roll forward, trying to pinpoint the source of her unease. When she couldn't, she chalked it up to the strangeness of starting her day with a man in her kitchen and put her foot on the gas. She had enough to worry about without adding to the list.

Rolling down the empty street, she turned the corner to head to her clinic. It was early enough that dawn was just beginning to spread across the sky. The lingering shadows made it easy to see the flashes of light coming from the center of town.

Now what?

She braked. Her clinic was to the right. *Just drive straight to work and pretend that nothing is wrong*, she told herself. After all, she wasn't a sheriff or a trained medic—what could she do to help? But a sick curiosity compelled her to drive forward. As she turned down Main Street, Lynne's stomach clenched at the sight of the numerous emergency vehicles circling the park.

Oh God. Something bad had happened.

Focused on the shadowed figures, along with the sheriff she could see moving around the ambulance, Lynne released a squeak of shock when a van coming from the opposite direction suddenly swerved to a halt directly in front of her.

Slamming on the brakes, she cursed as the truck fishtailed before she regained control. She was still shaking when a familiar man climbed out of the van and headed toward her door.

Parker Bowen.

Lynne rolled down the window, resisting the urge to snap at him for nearly giving her heart failure. She assumed he had an important reason for his reckless maneuver. "What's happened?"

Parker stepped into the glow of a nearby streetlamp, revealing his tense expression. "Go to the station."

"What?"

"The television station," he clarified. "I'll meet you there."

She shook her head. There was no way in hell she was ending up on the morning news. "As much as I appreciate all you've done for the sanctuary, Parker—"

"This is important," he interrupted.

Without waiting for her response, he turned and hurried back to his vehicle. Lynne frowned as the van cautiously pulled away. Did she ignore his request? She didn't trust him not to try and urge her to be interviewed. Then again, he did say it was important. What if it had something to do with the murders?

Blowing out a frustrated sigh, Lynne took her foot off the brake and did a U-turn. The sheriff was too busy to notice, and she didn't want to drive past the park. Not when she had no idea who was lying dead in the snow.

And she didn't doubt there was someone dead.

Why else would every emergency vehicle in the county be there?

Trailing behind the van, Lynne was relieved when they pulled into the parking lot next to the station. It was early, but there were already several vehicles in the lot and the lights were blazing from the single-story brick building. It was true—the news never slept.

Parker halted in a space with his name painted on a wooden sign. Lynne parked next to him. She didn't plan on staying long enough to be in anyone's way.

He waited for her to climb out of the truck and led her

through the locked front door. Together they crossed the lobby where a pretty young receptionist was already at a glass desk, her expression perking up at the sight of Parker. Were the two lovers? Probably. Lynne wasn't personally attracted to the man, but he was young and handsome and ambitious. All the things most women wanted in a potential husband.

Without glancing toward the receptionist, Parker led her down a hallway that was heavily carpeted and lined with glossy photos of the current newscasters.

"Where are we going?" she asked as they turned a corner. There was a hushed silence in this part of the building that she didn't like. It made her feel too isolated. She reached in her purse to wrap her fingers around her phone.

"My office." He used his keycard to unlock the door and pushed it open. "Come in."

Lynne tightened her grip on the phone. "I really need to get to the clinic."

"This won't take long."

He stepped over the threshold and disappeared from view. Cautiously, Lynne moved forward, peering into the office. It was starkly masculine with heavy leather furnishings and shelves filled with statues that she assumed were some sort of awards. One wall was floor-to-ceiling glass that revealed a view of the rolling fields that surrounded Pike.

Parker crossed the silver carpet to take a seat behind the heavy cherrywood desk and impatiently motioned for her to join him. "Close the door."

Lynne hesitated, then, squaring her shoulders, she forced her feet to carry her forward. "Actually, I prefer to leave it open."

He frowned. "Okay."

"Sorry, it's just . . ."

"Yeah, it's a strange time in Pike," he agreed with a humorless smile. "And it just gets stranger."

Lynne perched on the edge of a leather seat near the desk. She absently noticed the stacks of notebooks on his desk, along with two laptop computers. On the opposite wall there was a television with the early morning show flickering on the screen and below that was a series of framed photographs of Parker holding up a variety of large fish.

Parker might not be from this area, but he'd obviously developed the local obsession.

Reassured that the office looked exactly like she'd expected for a busy anchorman, she turned her attention to the man watching her with an unreadable expression. "Do you know what's going on in the park?" she asked.

He leaned back in his chair, swiveling from side to side. "I have a few contacts in the sheriff's office. They called me at five o'clock to say a dead body had been found."

It was hard to breathe, as if the air was solidifying in her lungs. "Do you know who it is?"

Parker hesitated, reaching to grab a notebook off the desk. He flipped it open. "Ms. Randall," he read out loud.

"Madeline Randall?"

"Yes. She's a . . ." He grimaced, glancing up from the notebook. "Excuse me. She *was* a retired teacher."

"I had her in the third grade." The fear that Parker was about to name one of her close friends faded, leaving Lynne oddly numb. She hadn't known the older woman beyond the classroom. And if she was brutally honest, she'd hated Ms. Randall as a teacher. Even back then she'd been a bitter, resentful woman who'd been downright cruel to children. "Do you think it was the same lunatic that murdered Sherry and Randi?" she asked.

The anchorman tossed the notebook back on his desk. "By the time I got there the park had been barricaded and they weren't very forthcoming with information. But there was a look on the deputies' faces that tells me it's the same killer."

Lynne nodded. "It's horrible news, but I'm not sure why you insisted I come to the station."

"When I realized I wasn't going to get any footage of the crime scene I returned to the station."

Lynne hid her shudder, trying not to be disgusted. It was Parker's duty to cover the news, whether it was the new STOP sign in front of the bank or a meeting of the 4-H Club or dead bodies.

"That's when I remembered that we have a camera in the park."

Her eyes widened in shock. A hidden camera in the park? That seemed . . . intrusive. Maybe even illegal. "Seriously?"

"We use it for live footage during the morning and evening weather reports."

Oh. Lynne suddenly recalled the early dawn and sunset views that were shown during the broadcast. She'd never considered where the cameras might be located. Now she leaned forward, a surge of hope racing through her. "Are you saying the murder was caught on live television?"

He held up a slender hand. "The camera is in the park, but it's pointed toward the town square. Still, I hoped we might have caught something that would reveal the identity of the killer."

"Did you?"

"Unfortunately, no." His jaw tightened with frustration. "A damned shame. It would have been my shot at the national networks."

"Parker." Her disgust was replaced with bone-deep shock. For a crazed second she wondered if he might actually be responsible for the deaths. What better way to ensure you were covering the hottest story in Wisconsin?

Then she squashed the nasty suspicion. Not even Parker was that ambitious. Was he?

"Plus we could have brought the monster to justice," he continued in smooth tones.

She shook off her dislike for Parker. He had every right to further his career. It wasn't like a small station in Pike, Wisconsin, was a dream job for any anchorman. "There was nothing that could help the authorities?"

"There was only one vehicle caught on camera." He sat forward, grabbing a remote control off the desk. Pointing at the television on the wall, he changed from the live feed to the earlier video from the park camera. "See for your-self."

She frowned. Did he hope she would recognize the vehicle and give him an inside track to the identity of the killer?

The image on the tape was a sharp contrast of light from the streetlamps and the shadows of predawn, giving the town square an artificial quality. As if it was a Hollywood set, not the town she'd known her whole life. The stores were dark, and the streets were empty. Just a sleepy night in Pike.

Then headlights slashed across the park and the camera's shutter opened and closed in an effort to focus.

The technical glitch nearly obscured the vehicle racing down the street, the tires throwing up loose snow in a spray of white. But just before it disappeared off the screen, Parker hit the pause button on the remote control and zoomed in.

Lynne surged to her feet, taking a step toward the television. "That's my truck," she choked out, pointing toward the license plate with the letters PAWSPRO. A joke from her father. "What time was this?"

"Four fifteen this morning," Parker said, his lack of surprise warning Lynne that he'd already known it was her vehicle.

She shook her head. "I don't understand."

"Understand what?"

"How my truck could be driving around town when I was in bed asleep."

"You weren't out on a call?" he asked.

She forced herself to think back. Sometimes her days ran together. Especially when she was crazy busy. It wasn't unusual to get mixed up. "No," she firmly denied. She'd spent the evening with Kir and then slept until her alarm went off at four forty-five. She released a shaky breath. "Someone must have stolen it."

"Hmm." Parker tossed the remote control on the desk and slowly pushed himself out of his chair. "I was coming to speak with you when I saw you drive past the park."

She turned her head to send him a puzzled glance. "Why?"

"You were . . ." He deliberately paused, his lips twisting into a wry smile. "Upset when I mentioned that the drugs found in the dead women might have come from your clinic. I assumed you would be equally upset to discover your truck was filmed passing the park where a woman was being murdered."

She licked her dry lips. "Ms. Randall was killed in the park?"

"Maybe her dead body was just dumped there," he conceded. "Either way, it doesn't look good to have your truck in the area."

Despite her heavy coat and the heat in the room, Lynne was shivering. "Poor woman."

Parker moved to perch on the corner of the desk. "What do you want me to do with the tape?"

"Excuse me?"

He nodded toward the television where the image of her tailgate was still frozen on the screen. "As far as I know I'm the only one who has seen this."

She returned her attention to Parker's handsome face. Was he trying to imply something? She wasn't good at picking up subtle hints. "I'm sure it'll just be a matter of time before the sheriff asks to see it."

He smiled. "I could make it disappear."

"Why would you do that?"

"I'm confident you have nothing to do with the murders, but the sheriff . . ." His words drifted away. Like a warning. After a long pause he continued. "She's looking for someone to blame. I don't want the killer to escape while the local law enforcement is chasing their own tails."

She narrowed her eyes. Did she trust him? No. She was discovering that Parker Bowen was willing to use any situation for his own advantage, whether it was for his career or his personal life. She wasn't entirely sure how he thought hiding the video of her truck could benefit him, but maybe he was one of those guys who went around gathering favors. There was a power in having people in your debt.

"Thanks, but that's not necessary." She offered a stiff smile. "Someone must have stolen my truck."

He arched a brow. "And then returned it?"

Lynne froze, abruptly remembering the strange sensation when she'd first crawled into her truck. Had she subconsciously realized it'd been moved? Maybe the interior was a few degrees too warm. Or the seat not exactly in the right position.

A queasy horror clenched her stomach, but she met Parker's gaze without flinching. She didn't want him to realize how unnerved she was. "Yes."

"You think the sheriff will believe you?"

"I have a witness." It was a struggle for Lynne to form coherent words. She wasn't afraid of the sheriff. Why would she be? She hadn't done anything wrong. But the obscene thought that the killer had taken her truck to commit murder . . .

Parker stiffened, as if astonished by her confession. "A witness?"

"Kir Jansen spent the night in my house."

"Ah." Something that might have been jealousy tightened his jaw. "How fortunate for you."

Desperately needing to be alone so she could process the latest tragedy, Lynne backed toward the door. The last thing she wanted was to reveal how close she was to full-out panic.

"Thanks for the heads-up, Parker." She nodded toward the television. "You should probably give the footage to the sheriff."

He stepped toward her. "Are you going to be okay?"

"Of course."

With a meaningless smile she turned and headed out of the office and down the hallway. It wasn't until she was climbing back into her truck that she allowed the smile to fade and the waiting fear to rush through her.

"Am I going to be okay?" she whispered.

There was no answer.

Chapter 15

Kir watched Lynne pull away, absently patting King's head as unease whispered down his spine. He didn't want to let her out of his sight. Not an unreasonable fear, considering two women were dead. But he couldn't be with her 24/7, he reminded himself. Not if he intended to hunt down who was responsible.

Needing to stay busy, Kir returned to the kitchen and washed the dishes. Then, unable to resist temptation, he cleaned out the cabinets and rearranged them to make the small kitchen as functional as possible. He wasn't trying to intrude, but he'd made a fortune organizing other people's lives. He was an expert.

He smiled wryly, heading into the bathroom to take a quick shower. What was he going to do with his expertise if he did sell his business? He didn't really want to start a new business. The stress had been fine when he was young, but he didn't want to work a hundred hours a week anymore. Then again, there was no way he could lie around doing nothing. He'd rather shove a fork in his eye.

It was the sound of King scratching at the bathroom door that ignited a flash of inspiration.

He didn't want the constant demands of creating a new company, but what about a not-for-profit charity? His organizational skills along with his contacts in the business world were a perfect combination to raise money. Starting with Lynne's animal sanctuary.

An excitement he hadn't even realized was missing from his life tingled through him. A new adventure. Just what he needed. And having that adventure include Dr. Lynne Gale? Well, that was a bonus.

After finishing his shower, Kir dressed and bundled himself into his leather coat and boots. Then he clicked a leash on King's collar and took him for a walk around the yard to check for signs of any unwelcomed intruders during the night. Once he was assured that there were no fresh tracks that would reveal an intruder, he took a jog around the block. If anyone was keeping an eye on Lynne's house, he wanted them to have a good look at the massive dog.

Returning King to the house, he headed to his SUV. The sullen clouds hung low enough to brush the treetops as he drove through town. It was almost nine, but the streets were oddly empty. Or maybe they just felt empty after the hustle and bustle of Boston.

Driving in the city was a gladiator sport, not a solo activity.

It was a relief not to battle traffic, but it did make his SUV stand out. He crawled over the icy roads at a snail's pace, then parked two blocks away from the church. He didn't want to be spotted and spook the pastor before he was ready to confront him.

After heading directly to the small parsonage, he circled around it, peeking into the windows. Empty. Next he strolled up the scooped pathway to the church. The back door was locked. He glanced around, making sure no one was driving past before he rounded the edge of the brick building. It was quite likely that Pastor Bradshaw was busy with one of his charities around town, but he was going to make sure before he left.

He shoved his hands in the pockets of his jacket as he walked past the first window. No one was in the storage area. He moved on, his boots crunching against the frozen layer of ice that covered the snow. Evoking his memory of the interior, he realized he must be passing the bathrooms. The next window had to be Bradshaw's office.

Kir slowed his pace, coming to a halt at the edge of the window to peer inside. He smiled. Even through the frosty glass he could make out the shape of the pastor seated at his desk.

Not giving the man time to escape, Kir hurried to the front of the church. Tugging on the heavy wooden door, he was surprised to discover it was tightly locked. With a shrug, he returned to the back of the building and with one sharp shove of his shoulder had the lock broken. He should feel bad, he acknowledged, silently moving through the cluttered storage area. But wasn't there some saying about one door closing and another one being opened?

He was just taking it from a spiritual level to a literal one.

Reaching the office, Kir cautiously peered around the edge of the open door. Inside Pastor Bradshaw was still seated at his desk, his head bowed as tears streamed down his face. His fingers were absently shredding the flowers that had spilled from an overturned vase.

Kir froze. The man looked pathetic as he hunched forward, his shoulders drooping. Or terrifying, he silently acknowledged. This could be the regret of a man who'd just murdered two women.

It was a timely reminder as Kir moved to stand in the doorway. He needed to be on full alert. If this man was responsible, he wouldn't hesitate to kill again.

Remaining in the doorway in case he needed a quick exit, Kir leaned against the jamb. "Am I interrupting?"

Bradshaw jerked his head up, clearly caught off guard. "You," he muttered, shoving himself to his feet. "How did you get in here?"

Kir shrugged. "Despite being the son of a sheriff, or more likely because of it, I developed several unsavory habits when I was young," he admitted. "One of them was breaking into old buildings to spray graffiti."

"This is a church."

"Doesn't that mean the doors should always be open?"

The pastor flushed, as if Kir had managed to strike a nerve. "The church is open on Tuesdays and Thursdays as well as Wednesday nights for our prayer meeting. I prefer not to be interrupted when I'm working on my sermons."

Kir glanced toward the desk where the flower petals were spread over piles of paper. "Is that what you're doing?"

The man's flush darkened, this time with embarrassment. "I've tried to be patient with you, Mr. Jansen—"

"Kir."

"Kir." Bradshaw's jaw tightened. "I understand you're grieving the loss of your father."

"I am."

"Still, I can't allow you to break into the church," he continued, moving to stand directly in front of the desk. As if he could hide the evidence of the mutilated flowers. "It's against the law."

"Maybe, but I'm not the only sinner in this room, am I?"

Bradshaw shifted from foot to foot. He was wearing a pair of jeans and a sweatshirt. The casual attire emphasized the fact he wasn't just a preacher, but a young man in his prime.

"We're all sinners."

"So true." Kir nodded toward the petals on the desks. "Beautiful flowers. What happened to them?"

Bradshaw took a jerky step forward. "This is your last warning to leave before I call the authorities."

Kir ignored the implied threat. He wasn't afraid the man was going to call the sheriff. Not yet. "What does a bouquet like that—delivered on a Sunday morning—cost?" he demanded. "A hundred bucks a week? That's quite an indulgence for a small church."

The pastor hesitated. Was he going to try and deny he'd ordered them? Then, as if realizing Kir had seen the delivery truck, he tried to look defiant. "I believe it's my duty to support the local businesses."

Kir snorted. "Especially if the owner happens to be a beautiful woman?"

"That had nothing to do with it."

"Then why cancel your standing order now that Randi's dead?"

Bradshaw paled, his hands clenching at his side. His intense reaction assured Kir that his suspicions were right. There was something going on between the preacher and Randi Decker.

"I assume the shop will be closing," Bradshaw tried to bluster. "She was the owner."

"Cut the crap, Bradshaw." Kir narrowed his gaze, resisting the urge to move forward and tower over the man.

He didn't doubt he could beat Bradshaw in a fistfight, but he had no way of knowing if the man had a weapon. He needed to make sure he could get out of the church in a hurry. "Why did you lie to me?"

"I don't know what you're talking about."

"You pretended you barely knew Randi Decker, and now I discover she was meeting you every Sunday."

The man scowled. "We didn't meet."

"Are you claiming that Randi didn't make a flower delivery to your church every Sunday? That's a pretty easy thing to check out."

"Yeah, she dropped off flowers, but that was it." He pursed his lips. "Not that it's any of your business."

His accusation echoed a small voice in the back of his mind. Bradshaw had a point. Kir wasn't a cop, or a Fed, or a private eye. He was a glorified handyman who was grasping at any straw in the hopes he could figure out who had taunted his father and was now threatening Lynne.

But he wasn't going to stop. Not until he had the truth.

He was nothing if not stubborn.

"Why did you lie?" He repeated his earlier question.

Bradshaw licked his lips. "This is bordering on harassment."

"If you think this is harassment, just imagine what's going to happen when the sheriff discovers your secret."

Kir tossed the words out in the hopes of striking a nerve. They were a direct hit. This time the pastor didn't pale. He went snow white with fear.

"What secret?"

Kir's lips twisted. He hoped this man never played poker. His emotions were etched on his face. Unless he was a lot more clever than he pretended to be. "Your obsession with Randi Decker."

"Obsession?" Bradshaw managed a strained laugh. "That's ridiculous."

"Were you having an affair with her?"

"She's a—" His words broke off. "She *was* a married woman."

There was a pain in his voice that sounded genuine. Of course, he'd seemed genuine when he was pretending Randi was barely more than a random stranger. "When has that ever been a barrier?" Kir asked. "I know a lot of men who prefer women who are committed to a husband and family. It keeps them from being too demanding."

With a sharp motion, the pastor turned to pace across his cramped office. "I wasn't having an affair with Randi."

"But you wanted to?"

"You can't prove that."

"I don't have to. I just have to call the sheriff and share my suspicion with her. She can dig for the truth."

The threat hung in the air. Like tossing a hand grenade that landed without exploding—there was no predicting whether it was going to combust or be a dud. Not even Kir knew if he would follow through. The sheriff didn't seem to be overly pleased that he was lingering in town. She would be even less pleased if she suspected he was interfering in her investigation.

Whirling around, the pastor glared at him. "Why are you so determined to destroy me? I've done nothing but try and comfort you during your time of mourning."

"There's a killer out there," Kir said with a simple honesty. "He has to be stopped."

"It has nothing to do with me."

"Then why did you lie?"

Frustration and something that might have been panic twisted the man's features. "I can't risk being involved."

"Involved with what?"

"I just want to tend to my flock without scandal." Bradshaw glanced toward the framed photograph on the wall. It was a picture of him in front of a large, glass and steel building with a wide smile on his face. It looked like one of those megachurches that catered to the wealthy suburbs of Boston.

Why would he leave such a plush position to come to Pike? There was only one explanation. "Like the scandal you had at your previous church?" Kir asked.

Bradshaw swayed. Was he going to pass out? At last he reached to grab the corner of a filing cabinet, visibly trying to regain command of his composure. "How did you know?"

"I have a lot of friends in a lot of places." It wasn't a lie. He did have a lot of friends in a lot of places.

The man made a weird sound. Something between a sob and a curse. "I didn't know that the person I was chatting with online was underage," he finally snapped. "She told me she was twenty-one. I might have many faults, but I have no interest in young girls."

Well, well, well. The good pastor really did have a secret. One that presumably ruined his promising career. "That's an easy claim to make," Kir drawled.

The man jutted his chin. "The police searched through every chat we shared and even subpoenaed my phone to make sure I hadn't contacted her outside the dating site.

They cleared me of any wrongdoing." A raw anger darkened his eyes. "If the investigation hadn't become public, I would never have been asked to leave."

Did he believe him? Kir mentally shrugged. Right now he was more interested in what happened after he came to Pike. "Is that why you were determined to choose an older woman like Randi Decker?"

Bradshaw resumed his pacing, his expression distracted. Was he trying to decide how to get rid of his unwanted guest? Maybe plotting murder?

Eventually he came to a halt directly in front of Kir. "If I tell you, will you promise to leave me alone?"

"Of course," Kir lied without hesitation.

Bradshaw hesitated, then, seeming to accept that Kir wasn't leaving until he confessed his real relationship with Randi, he conceded defeat. "Being a man of God comes with an enormous responsibility. I'm expected to lead by example, and to be above the weakness of the flesh. It's not always easy."

"People don't expect perfection."

Bradshaw's laugh was shrill. "Obviously you haven't attended church in Pike. Everyone knows everyone and they all gossip with each other. The slightest misstep and I will find myself unemployed."

That was true enough. Gossip was the only thing in Pike that moved at lightning speed. That didn't, however, explain Bradshaw's connection to the dead woman.

"You didn't think Randi Decker was a misstep?" he inquired.

The blush returned to the pastor's cheeks. "It wasn't something I planned."

"What did you plan?"

"As a single man I've found it easier to meet women online," he reluctantly admitted. "It's anonymous and it prevents any confusion with the women who attend my church."

Kir hid his smile. Online dating opened a whole smorgasbord of options. Phone sex. Fetishes. Easy hookups. "And?"

A shadow drifted over Bradshaw's face. Grief? Maybe regret.

"Last summer I started chatting with a woman I found fascinating. She was fun and witty and . . ." He glanced away, obviously embarrassed by the conversation. "Sexy. I wanted to meet her in person, but I wasn't going to risk another disaster. So I did some research on her."

"You didn't recognize her from her profile?"

The pastor snorted. "No one uses real names or pictures on those sites."

Kir frowned. He didn't blame the man for his caution. The girl might be underage or, just as likely, a dude from Africa who was trying to catfish him out of his life savings. But his words set off Kir's inner alarms. "How could you research her? I thought you said it was an anonymous dating site?"

"You're not the only one who learned unsavory tricks when you were young. My older brother was a computer genius who taught me how to hack into systems before he went straight and left home to attend MIT," he admitted. "It wasn't that hard to discover I was chatting with a woman named Randi Decker from Pike, Wisconsin."

Kir wasn't convinced. "That seems like an unlikely coincidence."

"Not really." Bradshaw shrugged. "The app I was using

was specifically designed to pair you up with someone within a hundred miles of your location. It makes it easier in case you decide you want to meet." He grimaced, as if recalling his reaction to discovering who'd been on the other end of the computer connection. "Of course, I didn't expect her to live in Pike. And I certainly didn't expect her to be married."

"But that didn't stop you."

The man stiffened, instantly defensive. "I tried. I stopped chatting with her online, and even joined a new dating site. But I couldn't get her out of my mind." His gaze grew distant, as if he was being sucked into the past. "I knew she was the president of the PTA, so I set up the food drive at the school. It was harmless enough. I could create a pantry at my charity shop, and it gave me an opportunity to see Randi in a public area."

Kir arched a brow. It might have seemed harmless to the pastor, but no woman would be happy to discover she was being manipulated so a strange man could ogle her. Even if it was in public. "That's the same reason you ordered the weekly flowers and insisted Randi personally deliver them?" he demanded.

Bradshaw nodded. "After she started dropping the food from the school in the outside bin, I knew I had to find another way to see her."

Kir hid his shudder of distaste. It wasn't the creepiest thing he'd ever heard, but it was . . . disturbing. "Did she know that you were the man she'd been chatting with?"

"No."

"You're sure?"

"Absolutely." Bradshaw's lips twisted into a humorless smile. "To be honest, I think she was already getting tired of our conversation," he admitted. "Before I deleted my profile on the app, she mentioned someone else she'd met online. I could tell she was more interested in her new man."

"Convenient," Kir murmured. If he was trying to convince people he hadn't killed the woman he'd been stalking, the first thing he'd do was imply she had another stalker. "When did you stop chatting online with Randi?"

The pastor thought for a moment. "Late summer. I remember the charity shop was busy with customers looking for back-to-school clothes."

Kir considered the possibility that the man was telling the truth. And that Randi had found a new man to flirt with online. What was the possibility that it was the killer?

"What was Randi's username in the app?" he asked. He had a friend who was a computer whiz. He might be able to track Randi's online activities.

"Roses4ever," Bradshaw answered without hesitation.

"And the name of the app?"

"Local Lover."

Kir tucked away the information. He would call his friend later, but he knew it would take time for any answers. He wasn't going to sit around waiting for something that might be a dead end. Instead he tried to discover more about the dead woman, and what she'd been doing before she was murdered. "When was the last time you spoke with Randi in person?"

This time Bradshaw didn't have to consider his answer. "Last Sunday when she delivered the flowers."

"Did you have a conversation?"

"It was brief." He shook his head in a sad, slow motion. "She seemed distracted."

"Was she scared? Nervous?"

"No. She seemed . . ." Bradshaw struggled for the right word. "Excited. As if she was expecting something wonderful to happen. I even asked her why she had a sparkle in her eyes."

Kir wasn't expecting that. He blinked, trying to shift his mind from a woman who was being hunted by a madman to one who had a sparkle in her eyes.

She certainly wouldn't have been excited if she thought she was in danger. Which meant the killer hadn't tormented her. Odd. Why would he torment Lynne with that picture, but not try to terrorize Randi?

And why was she excited?

"Did she answer you?"

"Some nonsense about her teenage daughter returning to school. At the time I didn't think anything about it. Now . . ." He deliberately paused. Was it for dramatic effect? "Now I think she was excited because she'd started a relationship with someone else."

"At least you hope she had," Kir said in dry tones.

Bradshaw's expression hardened to stone. He looked like a man who was done with the conversation. "I don't know who killed Randi or the other woman," he told Kir in harsh tones. "It had nothing to do with me. I just don't want any trouble."

Intending to press until he'd determined whether the man was guilty or innocent, Kir was interrupted by the vibration of his phone. Pulling it out he read the text that flashed across the screen.

Can you come to the clinic?

His heart missed a beat. It was from Lynne. He'd put

his number in her phone last night, insisting she promise to call if she needed anything.

Any interest in continuing the confrontation with Bradshaw was forgotten. He did, however, point a finger in the man's pale face and deliver a warning.

"I wouldn't leave town if I was you."

Chapter 16

Nash was enjoying a deep, alcohol-induced sleep when the pounding on his door shattered his dreams. He groaned, pulling the covers over his head. What sort of monster disturbed a man before noon on a Monday? There was a law against that, wasn't there? If there wasn't, there should be.

He tried to recapture the darkness that had offered him a temporary peace, but the pounding continued with a ruthless determination. Whoever was outside wasn't going to leave.

"Christ." Climbing out of bed, Nash pulled on a pair of jeans he'd tossed on the floor and headed through the cramped front room. He was currently stuck in the renovated garage behind his mother's house. If she heard the commotion, she'd scurry across the backyard to poke her nose into his business. "Keep your pants on. I'm coming," he yelled, his head pounding.

How much had he drunk last night? A full bottle of vodka? Pulling open the door, he winced. The morning was gloomy with fat gray clouds hanging low, but it was still bright enough to make him narrow his eyes.

"Morning, Nash," a short woman with a bright red coat wrapped around her full figure said as she brushed past him.

"Shit, Chelsea." He slammed shut the door and whirled to face his unwelcome visitor. "Do you know what time it is?"

She shrugged. "It's almost nine o'clock."

"On a Monday."

"I came by after lunch yesterday. You said you'd be here."

Nash had a vague memory of Chelsea cornering him at church. As if he was going to discuss their sex antics in front of his mother. *Stupid bitch.*

"I was at the Bait and Tackle fixing the toilets." He shoved his fingers through his tangled hair. It wasn't a lie. He'd spent hours choking on sewer gas before he'd managed to unplug the clogged lines. "That damned place is sucking the life from me."

She unzipped her coat and shrugged out of it. No doubt to show off the cashmere sweater that hugged the luscious swell of her breasts. With a casual motion she threw it on the threadbare chair that was piled with empty pizza boxes. The entire place was a pigsty, but he didn't have the energy to clean it, or the interest. Maybe it was time to invite his mom in for dinner. She'd take one look around and start scrubbing.

Chelsea studied him in confusion. "I thought you loved the bar?"

"I love being a bar owner." His lips twisted. "I hate owning a bar."

"That doesn't make any sense."

He snorted. His fleeting attraction to this woman had

nothing to do with her brains. A good thing, since she didn't have any. "Not many things make sense to you."

She stuck out her bottom lip in a childish pout. "There's no need to be mean."

"This is how I am at nine o'clock on a Monday morning."

She wrapped her arms around her waist. As if protecting herself from a coming blow. "We need to talk."

Nash groaned. The only thing worse than being hauled out of his bed when he was nursing a hangover was being harassed by a jilted lover. "Why?"

"Because I have a right to know if you seduced me just to get your hand on those drugs."

"Seduced you?" He laughed. "You've been trying to get into my pants since I started dating Lynne. If anyone was seduced, it was me."

An ugly flush stained her cheeks. There was no way she could deny the accusation. She might be younger than Nash, but she'd been aggressive in her attempts to capture his attention.

"That didn't answer the question," she instead accused.

"You don't want me to answer it."

Her flush darkened. "You used me."

"Bull. It was a mutual exchange."

Her eyes widened in disbelief. "Are you kidding?"

Nash's head throbbed and his gut was queasy. He'd gone past the age when he could drink all he wanted without repercussions. The knowledge only intensified his anger at having to deal with the ridiculous woman. "You were panting to get a good, hard banging and I needed some extra cash," he told her in harsh tones. "Win-win."

He heard the breath hissing between her lips. As if

she'd taken a physical blow. "Everyone said you were a pig. I heard them warning Dr. Gale that you weren't good enough for her, but I didn't believe them. I thought . . ."

"What?" he demanded as her words trailed away. "That I was a bad boy with a heart of gold?"

"Yeah, something like that." She sniffed, jerkily wiping the tears from her cheeks. "I'm an idiot."

Against his will, Nash's heart twisted with regret. What was happening to him? He'd always been arrogant. And selfish. But he'd also been fun-loving, charming, and the life of the party. Now he felt old and bitter. As if he'd squandered his life despite the fact he was still in his early thirties. "Crap. I'm sorry, Chelsea. I didn't intend to be a jerk," he muttered. Then he sighed. "I didn't intend a lot of things."

"What things?"

He waved an impatient hand to indicate the shadowed room. "I'm not one of those freaks who worries about being 'in touch' with my feelings, but it doesn't take a genius to know my life didn't turn out like I expected," he said in sour tones.

"What did you expect?"

"I was going to play Division One football. Maybe even go pro."

She furrowed her brow. "You went to college, didn't you?"

Nash shoved his hands in the front pockets of his jeans. It was hard to remember the eager young man who'd packed his bags and headed off to become rich and famous. "For a semester. Then I got caught cheating on a test and they cut me from the team." He'd been shocked when the coach had called him in to clean out his locker.

No one had cared in high school when he cheated. It'd been bogus to be cut because of one stupid test. Still, he'd known his college days were over. If he wasn't playing football, there was no point in staying. "About the same time my dad died so I came home to help my mom. Worst mistake of my life."

"Pike isn't that bad."

"It's a shithole, but I didn't have the money or the skills to land a decent job, so I was stuck." He shook his head in self-disgust. "I'm still stuck."

She pursed her lips in disdain. As if she was judging him. "I don't know why you think you're stuck. You're still young, single, and free to do whatever you want," she said in peevish tones. "It's not like you have a kid depending on you. Why not sell the bar and move away?"

It was a question he asked himself a dozen times a day. Chelsea was right. He could sell the bar, pack a bag, and walk away. But he didn't. He stayed. Day after day after day.

"And go where?" His voice was equally peevish. "A different shithole in a different state? Besides . . ."

"What?"

He hunched his shoulders. "Nothing."

"What's really keeping you here, Nash?" Chelsea asked, stepping toward him as she searched his face for some hint to his inner motives. "Oh my God," she finally muttered. "It's the vet, isn't it?"

Nash jerked, his face heating with embarrassment. "What the hell are you babbling about?"

"Dr. Gale. Do you love her?"

Nash started to deny any feelings for Lynne, but the words stuck in his throat. "I don't know," he grudgingly conceded. "When I first hooked up with her, I was hoping she had some extra cash to invest in the bar. She seemed like an easy touch." He shook his head at his stupidity. He'd been stressed from having to replace the roof, and looking for an easy way out of his troubles. But it hadn't taken long to realize Lynne didn't have the funds to pay his bills. Still, he'd continued to date her. Why? It was a question he'd refused to consider. He shrugged. "I suppose I got used to us being together. She wasn't like anyone else I ever dated. She cares about everything and everyone." Regret twisted his heart. "Even me."

Chelsea took a step back, as if his words had hurt her more than his betrayal. "So why sleep with me? Or steal the drugs from her clinic?"

"Just a few weeks after we started dating, I could sense her pulling away," he admitted with a rare burst of honesty. It'd been a subtle shift in their relationship. She'd always been busy with her stupid animals, but she started making more and more excuses why they couldn't get together. And her habit of texting him funny pictures or stories during the day had slowed to a trickle. "I knew she was going to dump me."

Chelsea sent him a jaundiced glare. "You wanted to punish her?"

Nash sucked in a sharp breath as she hit the nail on the head. "I didn't really think about it, but yeah, I wanted to punish her."

That was why he hadn't felt guilty when he'd been screwing Chelsea in the storage room or stealing the drugs to sell. He'd been . . . vindicated. He'd gotten Lynne before she could get him.

"And now?"

"I'm realizing I only punished myself." He narrowed his eyes as Chelsea suddenly released a shrill laugh. "What's so funny?"

"I came here because I was pissed you used me. Now I pity you."

Nash stiffened his spine. How dare she laugh at him? He was Nash Cordon, high school football star and the town's favorite son. "Aren't you supposed to be at work?" he snapped. "Or did you get fired?"

Her amusement faded, at his harsh words. "I called in." She looked faintly sick. "I'm not sure I can stay there now that Dr. Gale knows what we did."

Nash knew he'd acted badly, but he didn't have much sympathy for Chelsea. She'd not only been Lynne's employee, but she'd claimed to be her friend. Yet the younger woman hadn't hesitated to betray her.

"Looks like we're both screwed," he drawled.

Chelsea brushed her fingers down his bare chest. "It could be a sign we belong together."

He slapped her hand away. "It's never gonna happen, Chelsea. You need to move on."

She blushed a bright red, whirling to snatch her coat off the chair. "Maybe you should take your own advice," she growled, pulling on the heavy garment and heading for the door.

"Maybe I should," he agreed, watching her leave with a flare of relief.

Hopefully, the woman had gotten the message. He was done with her. End of story.

Pressing a hand to his aching temple, Nash headed toward the bathroom. He was going to piss and go back to bed.

He was standing in front of the toilet with his pants around his ankles when a cold chill prickled through the air. *Dammit*. Had Chelsea returned to try and convince him to give her another chance? About to turn, Nash grunted as a sharp pain hit him in the middle of the back.

"Now what?"

Trying to reach over his shoulder, Nash's lips went numb. Then his knees went weak. He placed his hand flat against the wall. What was wrong with him? This wasn't just his usual hangover. Could it be a heart attack? His father had been in his early forties when he'd had his first one.

Leaning against the wall, Nash tried to bend over. If he was going to die, it wasn't going to be with his pants down. But even as the horrifying thought flared through his mind, a dizziness made it impossible to focus. He wildly made a grab for the jeans, but even as his fingers wrapped around the waistband, he swayed to the side and hit his head on the corner of the vanity.

Pain exploded through his brain. Then nothing but a vast darkness.

Lynne sat at her desk as she watched Kir walk from one end of her office to the other. He looked like the feral dogs she had at the kennel, pacing round and round to release their pent-up anxiety.

She hadn't intended to call him. Even though he'd insisted on programming his number into her phone, she'd reminded herself that she was a big girl who'd been taking care of herself for a long time. And even after discovering there had been another murder and the video that Parker had shared with her, she'd been determined to carry on with her day as if it was any other.

It wasn't like she could be certain that it was the killer who'd stolen and then returned her truck. And even if it was, what could Kir do about it?

Determined to be brave, or at least pretend that she was brave, she'd called the sheriff's office to warn them the killer might have been caught on camera in her truck, then concentrated on her waiting patients. She'd vaccinated dogs, dewormed cats, and lanced an abscess on a horse's hoof.

That's when Sheriff Hancock had appeared.

The woman had stomped up to Lynne as she'd finished loading the horse into his trailer, barely waiting for the farmer to drive away before she launched into a furious inquisition.

It had quickly become obvious that Kathy was convinced Lynne was somehow connected to the murder spree. Maybe not the actual killer—although she clearly hadn't ruled out Lynne as the crazed monster—but certainly involved in the hideous deaths.

She'd refused to believe Lynne hadn't been driving the truck, and it wasn't until Lynne had admitted that Kir had spent the night and he could testify she hadn't left the house that the sheriff had demanded the keys to the vehicle so she could take it back to the station to be searched for evidence.

Lynne watched the deputy drive away in her truck and returned to her office. It was only in that moment she'd been struck by a horrifying realization. Pulling out her phone she'd texted Kir. She had to talk to someone. Someone who could understand her distress.

She'd known she made the right decision as soon as Kir arrived. He'd swept into the office and firmly closed the door on the curious faces of her interns, his large presence settling the panic that had thundered through her.

With remarkable patience he'd listened as she'd detailed the eventful morning in a flurry of words, many of which made zero sense. Thankfully, he seemed to at least follow the main points. Which was the reason he was currently pacing in circles.

Without warning, he spun toward her, his expression impossible to read. "You're sure it was your truck? I've seen a dozen just like it in town."

"Positive."

He nodded, accepting her assurance without question. "Do you keep it locked?"

She shook her head, feeling the color leak from her face. "No."

"Where were the keys?"

"In the house."

He frowned in confusion. "Then how . . ." He at last noticed her pallor. "What about a spare key?"

She reached to pull open the bottom drawer of her desk. "I kept it in here."

"Is it still there?"

She slowly shook her head. "That's why I texted you. After the sheriff took off with the truck, I remembered the spare set. When I came in here . . ." The rest of the words stuck in her throat.

"When was the last time you saw it?"

"I don't remember. I haven't needed it for months, so I never checked." She shuddered. It made her sick to think the killer must have been creeping around her clinic.

Maybe even more than once. After all, someone had taken that picture of her sleeping in this office. And now her key was missing. "God." The word burst out of her, coming from the stewing frustration in the pit of her stomach. "It was so stupid to leave it here, but there have been times when another vet had to borrow my truck. It made sense to make a copy and leave it in a place someone could grab it and go."

Kir moved to crouch next to her chair, grasping her chilled hands in the warmth of his fingers. "It's okay, Lynne. None of this is your fault."

His touch allowed her to suck in the first deep breath since she'd seen the flashing lights next to the park. Not that she accepted his assurance that she wasn't at fault. Not when her truck had likely been used during the murder.

"The killer must have gotten into the office and grabbed the key."

"Did you call the sheriff and tell her it's missing?"

She nodded. She hadn't wanted to call. In fact, she'd been close to keeping the theft of the key a secret. Why would she give the sheriff more ammunition to use against her? Then the realization that the information might be the difference between catching the killer or having him continue to hunt the women of Pike had her reaching for her phone.

"Yeah, I left a message," she muttered. "I doubt they were back to the station yet."

"Did they say how long they were going to keep your truck?"

She snorted, recalling Kathy's hard expression as she'd ordered Anthony to confiscate the truck.

"I'm guessing as long as possible. The sheriff is convinced I'm involved. And honestly, I think she just doesn't like me, for whatever reason."

He squeezed her fingers. "You can use my dad's truck. It's old but it runs fine."

She studied his fierce male features, which had somehow become wondrously familiar. She couldn't imagine going through the past few days without him at her side. Actually, it was becoming increasingly difficult to imagine her life without him. . . .

"Thank you," she breathed.

He held her gaze, his expression grim. "The killer's playing with you."

Lynne shivered at his blunt words. "Maybe."

"There's no maybe about it."

The thought made her stomach clench with terror. "People wander in and out of this clinic every day. I could have been a convenient target."

"You don't believe that."

"No, but I want to believe that," she whispered.

He didn't chide her for her childish desire to stick her head in the sand. Instead he glanced toward the drawer she'd left open. "How did the killer know the key was there?" he asked, speaking more to himself than her. "And if the killer was able to walk in and out of your office, why didn't he take the drugs at the same time?" He glanced back at Lynne. "It's more and more likely the killer was Nash. I'm assuming he was in your office often enough to have seen the spare key, plus he could have taken the picture of you sleeping. And he's already admitted he stole the drugs. It would be easy enough for him to lie and claim he sold them to some mystery man in Grange."

She shook her head. It just didn't make any sense. "Why would Nash kill those other women and not me?"

Frustration tightened his jaw. "I can't find the pattern, and it's driving me nuts." He slowly straightened, lifting his hand to tick off the names of the women on his fingers. "First, Sherry Higgins, the owner of a trailer park on the edge of town who was single, but had occasional lovers live with her. Second, Randi Decker, a married woman with a child who ran a flower shop and lived in a fancy house far away from the trailer park. And now a retired third-grade teacher. Did she have any children?"

"Not that I know of. She never married. I don't think I ever heard of her dating anyone. She was the typical spinster."

He grunted in aggravation. "They were all different ages, different levels of income, and different careers. What do they have in common?"

"Could it be your father?" The question was out of her mouth before she could halt the words.

Kir predictably stiffened. He was still raw from Rudolf's sudden death. "My father? What about him?"

"Could he be the link between all the women?"

His lips flattened, but with a visible effort, he appeared to consider her question. "We know he was very fond of you, but I don't remember him mentioning the other women." He spoke slowly, as if searching through his memories. "Of course, it's a small town. I'm sure he knew all of them."

Lynne suddenly felt foolish. She was grasping at straws. "It was just a thought."

"A good one," he insisted. "How do you feel about having a drink at the Bait and Tackle?"

Her heart fell to her toes. The Bait and Tackle was on her list of places never to visit again. "Is that a trick question?"

He sent her a sympathetic smile. "I know it's probably not your favorite place, but Rita King should be there tonight."

The name meant nothing to Lynne. "I don't think I know her."

"She's my dad's old drinking buddy. She's the only one I can think of who would know if he had a connection to the women."

Lynne pressed her hand to her stomach. It was twisted into a tangle of tight knots. "Can't we just invite her to the house?"

He considered her request before shaking his head in regret. "I'd rather keep our meeting casual. She might refuse to answer if she's afraid of getting involved in police business."

"We're not the police."

"If she gives us information that will help solve the case, we'll certainly turn it over to the sheriff."

"True." Lynne blew out a sigh of resignation. "Okay."

"I'll pick you up here at six. We'll have dinner and then go to the bar," he told her. "We want to talk to Rita before she has more than a couple of beers."

She held up a warning hand. "As long as I don't have an emergency. I'm on call tonight."

His brows drew together. "You can't stay here alone."

Lynne didn't take commands, not from anyone. But right now she understood Kir's worry. She would be an idiot to be alone in the clinic when it was obvious the killer seemingly felt free to wander in and out. "If I have to go out on a call, I'll take one of my interns with me. If someone comes to the clinic, then I'll ask Bernadine to stay a few extra hours."

He looked confused. "Bernadine?

"She worked for Dad as his receptionist until he retired and moved to Florida," Lynne explained. "I asked her to stay on, but she claimed she was overwhelmed by the new computer system." She glanced toward the closed door. "Today I intend to get down on my knees and beg her to return. She's amazing with the patients, and always willing to stay late when she's needed. I can teach her to use a computer, but I can't teach someone loyalty." She shook her head in sad regret. "Either you have it or you don't."

"What about Chelsea?"

Lynne shrugged. She hadn't been surprised when she'd arrived at work to discover Chelsea had already called in sick. It would obviously be best for everyone involved if she decided to find a new job. "I'll talk to Chelsea later," she murmured, eagerly turning the conversation away from the painful subject. "What are you going to do this afternoon?"

"Since I'm spending a few extra days in town, I decided to paint the living room at Dad's place," he told her. "And I'll bring his truck to your house."

She managed a weak smile. "Thanks."

"You're actually doing me a favor. I need to clean out the garage but there's barely room to squeeze in there right now." He grabbed her fingers and gently tugged her to her feet. Then, framing her face in his hands, he brushed his lips over her mouth. "I'll see you at six. If you need anything, just call. I'll come running."

A tingling excitement chased away the dark dread that

had been plaguing her all morning. She'd never been so relieved in her life. Eagerly she arched against his hard body, absorbing his warmth.

"Running?" she teased.

He brushed another kiss over her mouth. And then another, and another.

"Running," he murmured against her lips.

She grasped the lapels of his leather jacket, her knees going weak in the best way. "I'll keep that in mind."

"Don't worry," he whispered. "If you forget, I'll remind you."

Chapter 17

It was nearing eight o'clock when Kir led Lynne into the bar. They'd lingered over their dinner, sipping wine and enjoying the homemade pasta that Bella Russo had been serving in her restaurant for the past thirty years. Kir had savored the sight of the tension draining out of Lynne as they'd chatted about her years in vet school and his early attempts to build his business. They even shared a few laughs as they recalled their childhood years.

They might not have been best friends in school, but they could both recall the day that Kenny Atkins released a flock of ducks in the girls' bathroom. And sledding down the big hill that spilled onto a narrow creek. More than one kid had ended up in the hospital after falling through the ice, including Kir.

At last he'd reluctantly urged her to cross the street to the bar. Not only did he want to talk to Rita before she was too drunk to be coherent, but Lynne had to get up at an ungodly hour in the morning. He wanted her home and in bed as soon as possible.

Stepping into the taproom, they were instantly shrouded in the strange illumination that came from a combination of thick shadows and blinking neon lights. Like being sucked into another world. They stopped to allow their eyes to adjust, and Kir instinctively glanced toward the bar at the back of the room. He saw the woman bartender from the last time he'd been there, and an unfamiliar man who was filling a glass cooler with bottles of beer.

"Nash isn't here," he muttered, turning his attention toward Lynne. "Is that unusual?"

She made a sound of disgust. "He always complained that he worked every night. Now I know he was probably in some other woman's bed." She rolled her eyes. "Jerk."

Kir wrapped an arm around her shoulders and tugged her close. This couldn't be easy for her. Especially not after the day she'd already endured. "We won't stay long," he promised.

"I'm fine."

Keeping her tight against his side, Kir turned. It was no surprise to find Rita sitting at the same table she'd been at before. Alcoholics liked routines. The same bar, the same seat, the same drink of choice . . . Kir didn't know if it helped keep them grounded when their world turned to a drunken mist, or if it was a need to have some sort of control in their chaotic life.

Rita was wearing a different jogging suit. This one was a painfully bright purple, and her hair had been pulled into a messy knot on top of her head. He urged Lynne forward and they took a seat across the table.

"Kir." Rita easily recognized him, her gaze still clear. "I didn't expect you to become a regular."

"We just ate dinner at Bella's and decided on a nightcap before heading home."

"Nothing wrong with a nightcap." Rita grabbed her bottle and shook it to reveal it was empty. "Or six."

Kir obediently lifted his hand toward the bartender and indicated three beers.

Rita smiled and glanced toward Lynne. "Who's your friend?"

Lynne held out her hand, a genuine smile on her face. "Lynne Gale."

"Rita King." Rita shook her hand, then settled back against the leather seat with a faint frown. "Hey, was your dad the vet?"

"Yep."

"I liked him. I heard he moved to Florida."

"He did."

"Smart man." Rita glanced toward the window where they could see the snow falling in lazy, swirling patterns.

"He seems happy," Lynne assured the older woman.

"Hey, Lynne." A new female voice broke into the conversation. "Good to see you again. It's been a while."

It was the bartender. Kir struggled to recall her name. Cherry? Yeah, that was it.

Lynne stiffened, her face pale. "Thanks."

Detecting Lynne's unease, Cherry unloaded the bottles from the tray and hurriedly returned to the bar.

Rita grabbed one of the beers, studying Lynne with a frown. "I remember now. I've seen you with Nash. Are the two of you having a thing?"

"Ancient history," Lynne muttered.

Kir cleared his throat. He'd known this was going to be awkward for Lynne, but it was even worse than he expected. Time for a distraction. "I suppose you know there's been another murder?" he asked.

Both women sucked in a startled breath. Maybe he'd been a little abrupt. Still, it worked to distract attention from Lynne.

"Yeah." Rita took a chug of her beer. "Madeline Randall."

Kir folded his arms on the wooden table. "Did you know her?"

Another chug. "Unfortunately."

"You didn't like her?"

Rita's face hardened, emphasizing the deep wrinkles that made her look closer to sixty than forty-four.

"She was my daughter's teacher in elementary school." Rita's words were slurred. Not from the beer, but from a smoldering, toxic anger. "Nicole went from being a little girl who loved school to one who pretended to be sick every morning. I wanted to choke the dried-up old hag." Rita sent Kir a defiant glare. "I don't care if she is dead. She tormented the kids in her classroom."

Kir didn't look at Lynne but he felt her shudder. "I've heard that a lot."

Rita polished off her beer. "Course, it's terrible there's some maniac out there killing women. It makes you want to lock your door and never come out again."

Kir pushed a full bottle in Rita's direction. "My father tried to warn us."

"He did." Rita grabbed the beer and lifted it in a toast. "To Rudolf."

Kir raised the last beer. "Rudolf." He touched his bottle to Rita's then set it back on the table. He'd already had a glass of wine with dinner. Considering the condition of the road, that was enough. "I've been trying to imagine how the deaths could be connected."

Rita shrugged. "They were all women who lived in Pike."

"But why *those* women?"

Using the tip of her finger, Rita scooped the condensation from the side of the bottle. "Who knows? Convenience? They wore the same shoes. Could be anything."

Kir settled back in his seat, covertly studying Rita's expression. "I wish I'd read my father's mystery letters. There has to be a reason he was the only one to get them."

"You sound like a cop," Rita muttered.

"It's in my blood."

Her lips twisted, a hint of grief in her eyes. "That's true."

Kir pretended to consider his words. "You know, you spent as much time with Dad as anyone."

"True again." Rita took a drink. It was a sip this time instead of a gulp. Maybe she'd decided to pace herself. Or maybe she sensed this was more than a casual conversation.

"Did he know the women who were murdered?"

"I'm sure he did. He knew everyone in town."

"Is there a reason someone might think he was friends with the women? Or even enemies?"

She started to shake her head, then hesitated. "Oh, I guess Sherry Higgins did hire him a couple times when she was serving an eviction notice. I remember him telling me last summer that there was a renter who chained themselves to the fridge. He had to get bolt cutters to get them out. Can you imagine that?" Rita snorted. "People are strange."

Kir frowned. "Isn't it the sheriff's job to help with evictions?"

Rita made a face. "Most people in Pike always thought

of your dad as the sheriff, no matter how many years passed. Besides, I don't think Sherry and Kathy got along that well. Something happened between them when they were younger."

Kir couldn't imagine Sheriff Hancock was very happy with Rudolf performing her tasks, no matter how much she might dislike Sherry Higgins.

"Did he do any work for the others?"

Rita stared blankly out the window as she tried to shuffle through her fuzzy memories. Kir didn't hold out much hope. She'd probably been intoxicated for ninety percent of her conversations with Rudolf Jansen.

"Not that he told me," she at last conceded. "I can't remember him mentioning Randi Brooks or—"

"Brooks?" Kir interrupted with a lift of his brows.

"Oh, I mean Decker." Rita wrinkled her nose. "Brooks was her maiden name. I don't know why I keep forgetting that."

"Wait." Kir leaned forward. The name stirred a distant memory in the back of his mind. "Was her father Charlie Brooks?"

"Yeah, he died around five years ago. Heart attack, I think."

Kir had a vivid image of his father returning home late one night with a bloody lip and a grim expression. He preferred to arrest his fellow citizens of Pike without using his weapon, which meant that more than once he was injured during the takedown.

"I remember Dad arresting him after he tried to burn down the gas station," he revealed. "They'd fired him for stealing or something and he decided to torch the place."

"Yeah." Rita released a sharp crack of laughter. "He

was friends with my husband. Both losers who used their fists instead of their brains."

Kir tapped the end of his finger on the table. "That leaves Ms. Randall."

"No one had anything to do with her," Rita muttered, then her eyes widened as if she had a sudden inspiration. "Well, except the night Rudolf got confused walking home and tried to get into her house. Most people in town just took him to his house, but not that old bat." She hissed in disgust. "She called the sheriff and told them there was a crazed rapist trying to break in. Can you imagine?"

Unfortunately, Kir could imagine it all too easily. There'd been more occasions than he wanted to remember when he'd been awakened in the middle of the night by the sound of knocking. By the time he climbed out of his bed and headed downstairs he would find his father propped against the front door, too drunk to know where he was.

"Was he arrested?" Kir demanded.

Belatedly realizing that Kir didn't find Rudolf's antics as funny as she did, Rita glanced away. "I don't think so." She lifted her hand. "Cherry. Another round."

"None for us," Kir said, turning toward Lynne, who instantly slid out of her seat. He was swiftly standing beside her.

"You're not leaving?" Rita protested.

Kir forced a smile to his lips. He'd had enough of the dark, choking atmosphere of the bar. It held too many old memories that had driven him from Pike. This wasn't how he wanted to think of his father. Not anymore. "It's getting late," he said. "Maybe you should let us take you home."

Rita grabbed the still full bottle, shaking her head. "I can walk. It's not that far."

"There've already been three people dead, Rita," Kir reminded her in firm tones that should penetrate her thickening haze. "I don't want you putting yourself in danger."

Rita took a defiant drink. "Four people."

Kir blinked. Did this woman know something he didn't? "Four?"

"The three murdered women and your poor father."

Her words sent a weird chill through Kir. He'd come here hoping for a connection between the women and his father and Rita had just given it to him.

They were all dead.

With a grimace he shoved away the bleak thought. He needed to get out of there. "If you won't go with us, then have Cherry take you home, okay?"

"You got it." Rita offered a mock salute.

Lynne flipped on the living room light before she closed and locked the front door. With a loud bark King came galloping out of the kitchen to circle her in wild abandon. He grabbed the tip of her glove, careful not to catch her finger before he tugged it off and gave it a good shake. Next he did more enthusiastic circles around Kir, groaning in bliss when he reached to rub a tender spot behind his ear. At last satisfied he'd offered them a proper greeting, the huge dog flopped on the floor and closed his eyes.

A wry smile curved Lynne's mouth. She felt fairly confident that no intruder had dared to enter the house while

King was there. He might be friendly enough with her and Kir, but he would intimidate anyone trying to break in.

Next to her, Kir absently pulled off his coat and boots before he moved to stand in the middle of the room. He'd barely spoken during the short drive to her house, and now he appeared lost in thought.

"Are you okay?" she asked, slipping off her jacket and hanging it on the hook next to the door.

Kir's jaw clenched. "I hate those places."

"The Bait and Tackle?"

"Cheap bars filled with broken people."

"Oh." Lynne silently chastised her insensitivity. How could she have been so blind? She'd been so wrapped up in her own toxic relationship with Nash and the bar that she'd overlooked how difficult it had to be for Kir to re-visit a place where his father had no doubt spent endless hours drinking. "I'm sorry. I know it's hard for you to be back in Pike."

He paused, his hand lifting to press against the center of his chest. As if his heart hurt. "Yes, but I'm beginning to realize that I put off my return way too long."

Lynne frowned. She was accustomed to being with Nash. A man who readily blamed everyone and everything for his failures. Kir was just the opposite. He was too hard on himself.

"You couldn't suspect that your father was going to have such a tragic accident," she reminded him.

Kir shook his head. "It's more than that. I assumed that running from my father's self-destruction would keep me from being sucked into his spiraling darkness."

"It was the only thing you could do."

He nodded. "I needed distance, but I regret allowing

the bad memories to overshadow the good ones. When I was little my dad was a superhero to me. He was strong, loyal, loving. Everything a boy could want in his father." He continued to rub the center of his chest, his voice raw with the wounds that had never healed. "Then he revealed that he had feet of clay and I couldn't forgive him. No matter how much I loved him, there was a part of me that always resented what he stole from me." He clicked his tongue. "Selfish."

"No, just human." Not giving herself time to consider her impulsive need to comfort Kir, she crossed the floor to wrap her arms around his waist. Then, laying her head against his chest, she sucked in the warm, citrusy scent of his soap. "Do you want to know what I think?"

He stiffened, as if she'd managed to shock him with her impulsive hug. Honestly, she'd shocked herself. Then, slowly he relaxed.

"Tell me."

"I don't think you're beating yourself up because your father wasn't perfect, but because you weren't," she murmured. "You're afraid you failed as a son."

She heard his heart miss a beat, as if her words had touched a nerve. Had she gone too far? He was, after all, grieving Rudolf's death.

Then she felt his arms wrap around her and his lips brush the top of her head. "How did you get to be so smart?"

She nestled closer. It felt good to be cocooned against him. Safe. "I spent my childhood convinced that my mom left because she didn't want a child. I knew that if I hadn't been born, she'd still be here. And my father wouldn't have been so sad."

His arms tightened around her. "And now?"

"Now I try to accept that I'm responsible for my own decisions and actions," she told him, her sense of comfort being slowly replaced by a potent awareness. His muscles were deliciously hard as she pressed against them and his citrusy scent was causing her blood to tingle in all the right places. "I can't control other people," she forced herself to continue. "They have to do what they have to do."

His hand lightly skimmed up her side. Lynne trembled as his fingers tunneled beneath her hair that tumbled over her shoulders. She'd taken it out of her usual ponytail before Kir had arrived at the clinic to pick her up for dinner. She'd also dug through her purse to find the old tube of lipstick she hadn't used in months.

She hadn't asked herself why she was going to such trouble. It wasn't like Bella's restaurant was fancy. Just the opposite. Now she knew why. His fingers cupped her nape. Another shiver raced through her body.

"Does that work?"

She licked her suddenly dry lips. "Sometimes."

His mouth brushed the top of her head. "Sometimes is a start."

Lynne tilted back her head to meet his smoldering gaze. She'd heard about a passionate haze, although she'd never actually experienced it. This, however, was just the opposite.

Oh, there was passion. It churned through her as if it was about to explode. But there was no haze. Instead she was acutely aware of the world around her. As if her senses had all been dialed to hyperdrive.

She was vibrantly conscious of the heat of his fingertips as they pressed against the bare skin of her throat.

The accelerating beat of her heart that made her breath quicken. The rush of blood that seared away the lingering chill.

It all combined to offer a sense of magical anticipation.

Even the warm, familiar scent of her home and the faint snoring of King added to the sensation that this was a rare and precious moment.

"It is," she managed to croak.

She reached up, pulling down his head to claim his lips in a kiss that scorched her to the tips of her toes. They curled in her boots.

There were kisses, and then there were soul-destroying kisses. This was one of those soul-destroying ones.

Lynne leaned heavily against his body, her hands burrowing beneath his sweater to skim up his back. He was so warm. Fascinated by the contrast of his hot, silken skin stretched over rock-hard muscles, she inched her hands up to his broad shoulders.

Kir moaned, using the tip of his tongue to widen her lips so he could deepen the kiss. He tasted of the wine they'd shared at the restaurant, and something else. Need.

Pure male need.

The taste sent her stomach somersaulting, like when she was twelve and she finally worked up the nerve to ride her first roller coaster. It'd been terrifying and exhilarating at the same time.

Just like this.

Wanting more, she grabbed the hem of his sweater and with an eager lack of skill wiggled it over his head. She tossed it aside, studying the expanse of his chest lightly dusted with golden hair. It was just as perfect as she'd expected. As if it'd been chiseled by an artist.

Not even trying to resist temptation, she reached to trace the angles and planes of his torso. He sucked in a sharp breath, gazing down at her with raw eyes.

"This is just a start."

Lynne's mouth went dry. "A start to what?"

A wickedly charming smile curved his lips. "If I say 'heaven' would that be too corny?"

It *was* corny. Just like the butterflies in the pit of her stomach were corny. And the way her heart pounded so hard it was hard to breathe. And the sensation her bones were melting as a delicious heat poured through her.

"I'm beginning to think I like corny."

His smile widened as he bent down to hook his arm behind the back of her knees. His other arm braced her shoulders as he swept her off her feet and headed across the living room.

King lifted his head to watch them leave with a sleepy contentment.

Chapter 18

Kir carried Lynne to her room with a sense of . . . He wasn't sure exactly what he was feeling. Hunger. Anticipation. And absolute amazement at just how right it was to hold this woman in his arms.

After lowering her to the bed with the same care he would give to his most prized possession, Kir perched on the edge of the mattress. It was dark in the room and he reached to flip on the lamp on the nightstand. A soft pool of light spread over her face, revealing the vulnerable need in the depths of her eyes.

His heart skipped with a fierce determination.

This woman was so strong on the outside, but she'd been hurt and betrayed by Nash. He wanted her to be one hundred percent certain she could trust him.

"This was the last thing I expected when I returned to Pike," he told her, slipping off her boots.

A shaky smile curved her lips. "Yeah, it wasn't what I was expecting either."

Still holding her gaze, he reached for the waistband of her pants. With a practiced ease he had them unzipped and gently tugged down her legs. "When I saw you at the funeral, I felt relieved," he said, allowing his fingers to stroke over the bare skin of her thighs. Not surprisingly, they were tight with muscles. Her work as a vet meant she was in peak physical condition. It was sexy as hell. His cock reacted with immediate appreciation.

She shivered, her lips parting with an unconscious invitation. "Why relieved?"

His fingers skimmed over her hips, tracing the low line of her satin panties. "You reminded me that even though my dad was gone I wasn't alone." He hooked his thumbs under the elastic and slid the underwear down so he could toss them aside. A growl of appreciation rumbled in his chest as he absorbed the sight of her ivory body contrasted against the dark cover beneath her. He liked the sensation of unveiling her beauty, piece by piece. Or rather, garment by garment. Like constructing a sensual puzzle. "That's why I was so anxious to see you again."

Her breath hissed between her teeth. "So you wouldn't be alone?"

Nodding, he lowered his head to press a soft kiss to her lips. At the same time, he grabbed the bottom of her sweater. "And to discover if the spark that ignited inside me was real or a figment of my grief."

"What did you decide?"

He peeled the sweater over her head, his body clenching with a fierce hunger as he caught sight of the frilly bra. She was so sensible, so ruthlessly down-to-earth. The sight of that naughty bit of lace was a thrilling surprise. As if she'd revealed a hidden part of her . . . a part she never shared with anyone.

One he desperately hoped she would never again share with anyone but him.

The dangerous thought floated through the back of his mind as he unhooked the bra and allowed it to float away. Then, with oddly shaky hands, he yanked off the remainder of his clothes. He was trying to take this slow. He wanted to savor every second of his time with this woman. But his body was hard and aching with a pounding need to possess her.

"You tell me if the spark is real or not," he rasped, pulling a condom out of his wallet and setting it on the nightstand.

Catching him off guard, Lynne reached to wrap her fingers around his straining erection. Kir bit back a curse as pleasure blasted through him. Her touch was hesitant and slow. Painfully, gloriously slow as she pulled her fingers back to the tip of his cock.

"It looks real," she teased.

Kir arched his back, relishing the stroke of her fingers until a familiar pressure built at the base of his arousal. He was about to embarrass himself. Gently pulling her hand away, Kir lowered himself to the mattress, stretching out beside her.

"I'm hoping you have a few sparks of your own happening," he murmured, pressing their naked bodies together. The friction created a velvet heat that vibrated between them as Kir tangled his fingers in her hair and kissed her with a blatant hunger. He moaned as the taste of her hit his tongue. Sweet, feminine temptation. Intoxicating.

Time drifted past, as slow and lazy as the snow falling outside as Kir explored Lynne's slender body. First with his fingers and then with his lips. He discovered that kissing the arch of her foot made her giggle, and that there was a tender spot on her inner thigh that made her sigh in pleasure. He absorbed the scent of her soap that clung to her skin and the plush softness of her breasts.

At last raising his head, he gazed down at her face, which was flushed with passion, her lips swollen from his kisses. His heart contracted, squeezed by an emotion that felt too big to fit inside him. "Are you sparking yet?"

She wrapped her arms around his neck, lifting her head off the pillow to nibble a path of kisses down his jaw. "Do I really have to say it?"

"Yes, please," he rasped.

She framed his face in her hands, her eyes dark and mysterious in the soft light. "I didn't think I could be on fire when the temperature is below zero outside."

Smug pleasure blasted through him. "I want you drowning in flames before the night is over."

Her lips twitched. "Has anyone told you that you're overly ambitious?"

Rolling on top of her, he pressed her into the mattress as he threaded their fingers together. Then, he stretched her hands above her head as he reached for the condom. Quickly slipping it on his aching erection, he settled between her parted legs.

"Isn't there a saying about the pot calling the kettle black?"

She released a low groan as the head of his cock slid an inch inside her body. "I'm not ambitious, I'm passionate," she told him.

He slid in another inch. The wet heat of her wrapped around his tender tip, the sensation unbearably exquisite.

"Ambition and passion," he hissed between clenched teeth. It was increasingly difficult to carry on a coherent conversation. "A match made in heaven."

She squeezed his fingers, her head tilted back as he pulled out and pressed back in another inch. "Heaven, again."

"It seems to be the word I associate with you," he confessed. And it was the truth. Lying on the bed in the shadowed room with Lynne soft and welcoming beneath him was as close to paradise as he'd ever been. "Especially when you're in my arms."

She arched her back in a silent plea for more. "Funny. The word that comes to my mind is dangerous."

"Opening yourself to another person is risky," he readily agreed. "Are you willing to take a chance on me?"

In answer she wrapped her legs around his waist, her expression one of anticipation.

It was the only encouragement he needed. Holding her gaze, he pressed deep into her body. Her slick flesh pressed against his cock, squeezing him in bliss. They groaned in unison.

Rocking his hips, Kir lowered his head to kiss Lynne with a sizzling desire. Could anything be better? This was the sheer perfection of opposites. Cool sheets against hot skin. Hard muscles cradled against soft curves. Low moans and the thunder of hearts.

Moving together they reached for the heavens.

Nash woke with a splitting headache and no idea where he was. Christ. It'd been years since he'd blacked out. Not since his college days.

Lying on the hard floor he had a wistful urge to return to those simpler days. He'd do things differently this time. There wouldn't be any endless parties and sleeping through class. Nope. He'd concentrate on his football, and even if he didn't make it to the pros, he could find a place to coach, or even become an announcer at the games. Anything but returning to Pike as a washed-up has-been.

Nash groaned, wrenching open his heavy lids.

Dark. That was it. Just complete, utter darkness. What was going on? The garage didn't have many windows, so it was always gloomy inside, but it usually wasn't this thick, choking obscurity.

Wondering if he was in that weird place between waking and sleep, he blinked. Still dark. Had he gone blind? No. That was stupid. People didn't go blind from drinking too much. Did they?

Unless he'd slept through the day and it was night.

With an effort, Nash cleared his mind of the lingering cobwebs and battled to recall where he'd been before blacking out.

He had a vague memory of spending the day at the bar fixing toilets. Hard to forget that disgusting task. And then he'd gone home to drown his sorrows in a bottle of vodka. And then . . . Oh yeah, Chelsea had barged in to yell at him. Stupid woman. Was it his fault he wasn't some fairy-tale Prince Charming? It wasn't like she was perfect. Besides, he could barely take care of himself, let alone anyone else.

Dismissing the memory of Chelsea, he tried to concentrate on what had happened after she'd left. He remembered going into the bathroom and then nothing.

No, wait. He'd been standing in front of the toilet when he'd felt a pain in the middle of his back. There'd been a blast of panic as he'd bent over to try and pull up his pants.

That was when he'd hit his head on the corner of the vanity and knocked himself out.

Was he still in the bathroom? No. That room was too cramped for him to stretch out. And it felt like cement, not linoleum beneath him. Icy cold cement he could feel from head to toe because he was completely naked.

His heart thumped against his ribs. *Shit.*

Could he be in the morgue? He'd heard horror stories about people who died and then came back to life in the ambulance or even the emergency room. Maybe whoever found him assumed he was a goner and sent him straight to the death house. God knew the local authorities were a bunch of bumbling amateurs.

Then he gave a small shake of his pounding head. There was a sense of space around him. As if he was lying in the middle of a vast area, not in a cramped cubicle.

Nash was suddenly furious despite the shocking cold. Had someone snuck into his house while he was passed out and hauled him here as some sort of joke?

He was Nash Cordon. Star football player. Business owner. The man who could have any woman in town. The man everyone envied. Muttering a curse, Nash forced himself to a sitting position. He glanced around, unable to penetrate the shroud of darkness.

It was cold. Bone-deep cold, and the faintest hint of a breeze, but he didn't think he was outside. There was the heavy sensation of a roof over his head. Besides, if he was in the open, he should be able to see the sky. Beneath his bare ass he could feel broken cement and a layer of grime. As if no one had been there for years.

Where was he?

Hell. The word whispered through the back of his mind. *I'm in hell.*

Shivering as much from the fear as from the cold, Nash shoved himself to his feet and started walking. If the devil wanted him, then he was going to have to catch him.

His bravado lasted for five minutes. The precise time it took for the brutal cold to sink through his bare skin to cramp his muscles. He stumbled, nearly falling. Crap, his feet were already numb, and he had a terrible fear that he was walking in a big circle.

Tilting back his head, he released a furious howl. The sound echoed eerily through the frigid darkness, masking the approaching footsteps. He had no clue that he wasn't alone. Not until something smashed against the side of his head.

With a grunt he fell to his knees, the sensation of something warm trickling down the side of his neck. Blood? The thought was preferable to his brains leaking out.

"Who are you?" he screeched.

Was there a laugh? Nash panicked. He didn't know what was happening, but he was absolutely certain that he was going to die if he didn't get out of there.

Trying to rise to his feet, he felt something slide over his head.

"Where are you going, Nash?" a voice whispered as a thin wire sliced into his throat. "The fun is just about to start."

Lynne pressed tightly against Kir as they snuggled in the middle of her bed. It was deliciously unfamiliar. Usually she encouraged her partner to leave as soon as sex was over. Most mornings she had to get up ridiculously early. And of course, there was the very real possibility she would get an emergency call in the middle of the night. It only made sense for her date to go home so she could sleep uninterrupted.

At least that was what she told herself, and her partner.

Now she realized she asked them to leave because she didn't want them to stay. She loved her privacy. Especially after a hectic day jam-packed with animals and their owners. Peace and quiet were treasures she guarded with jealous zeal.

Kir was different. She had her arms wrapped tightly around his waist as if she was ready to physically prevent him from moving away.

The thought should have horrified her. She never, ever wanted to be one of those clingy women who were willing to sacrifice their intelligence and pride when it came to men. But holding on to Kir didn't feel like a sacrifice. It felt . . . right. Wondrously, gloriously right.

Tilting back her head, Lynne glanced at the man who was turning her world upside down. She'd expected to find him smiling with a smug satisfaction. After all, he'd made her scream in pleasure. More than once. In fact, they'd made love three times. Each one better than the last.

Instead she found him staring at the ceiling, his brows pulled together in a frown.

She propped herself on her elbow, a portion of her pleasure fading. Was he regretting what had just happened between them? Maybe wondering how to get out of there without hurting her feelings?

The thought made her mouth dry and her heart thud with a slow, aching unease. "What are you thinking about?"

He turned his head, a wicked smile curving his lips. "I have you naked in my arms. What do you think I'm thinking about?"

There was a heat smoldering in his eyes that assured her that whatever was on his mind, it wasn't regret. Relief raced through her and she returned her smile. Later she would chastise herself for reacting like a skittish teenager, not a grown, supremely confident woman.

"Even you have limits," she teased.

His eyes darkened with ready passion. "Is that a challenge?"

"One for later," she murmured, rubbing her hand over his chest. She loved the feel of his silken skin roughed by golden hair. "Now tell me why you're frowning."

"I just realized I didn't call the office today."

Oh. It took Lynne a second to process his words. She wasn't sure what she'd been expecting, but it wasn't that. "Is that bad?"

He arched his brows. "Would you forget to check on your clinic?"

"No, but I imagine you have a well-trained staff who are paid a fortune to make things run smoothly," she said. "I have interns who spend a few months training with me before moving on, and a receptionist who slept with my ex-boyfriend."

"That's true." He rolled on his side so they were face-to-face. "It still doesn't excuse me."

She pressed her palm against the center of his chest, feeling the steady beat of his heart. She hated that Kir was so hard on himself. "Why does it bother you so much?"

"My forgetfulness is either the result of my advanced

age, or I've made my decision to sell the business and I'm already pulling away."

Her hand slid up his chest to cup his face in a silent gesture of comfort. "Or it could be that you're stressed because your dad just died and there's a serial killer stalking the women in this town," she suggested in dry tones. "Maybe it just slipped your mind."

"It's more than that. I've barely thought of Boston since I came back to Pike. It's like . . ."

"Like what?"

He held her gaze. "Like I'm home."

A fragile joy swirled through Lynne at his soft words. Was he saying he might return to Pike? Forever?

Careful not to get her expectations too high, Lynne leaned up to press a kiss to the hard line of his jaw. "You *are* home," she whispered.

Chapter 19

Dear Rudolf,

*Do you know what I hate about kids today?
The incessant whining: Oh, I'm misunderstood.
Oh, I'm being bullied. Oh, I'm harassed. And all
the while they're pasting their pimpled faces all
over the Internet. Look at me, look at me, look at
me. Stupid brats.*

*Every kid thinks they're misunderstood or
bullied or harassed.*

*Except for me. Don't get me wrong, I was
brutalized, but that was a gift from my drunken
loser of a father, not my peers.*

*No, to the other kids I was invisible. I could
walk by and not one person would notice I was
there. Like I was so worthless they couldn't be
bothered to acknowledge my existence.*

*Can you imagine what that does to a person?
Being ignored is the worst. Who cares if you're
mocked for wearing the wrong clothes or pushed in
a locker? You can heal hurt feelings or a few bruises.
No, being ignored erases you as a human being.*

You're nothing.

You don't heal from that.

And then there are the lucky few.

The ones that shimmer and glitter and steal all the attention. They suck it away like a black hole. But do they appreciate what they have? Of course not. Arrogant asses.

They moan and groan and pretend life has been so difficult. And worse than that, they demand constant pampering. As if we were all put here to tend to their needs. Petulant children tossing tantrums.

Ah, but sometimes it's dangerous to get what you want.

Just ask Nash Cordon.

No, wait. You can't. He's dead.

And you know what? It turns out he wasn't nearly so eager to be the center of attention as he pretended to be. Not when it included my personal touch.

Plus, I've discovered something interesting. Death is even sweeter in the dark. You can't see, which is a pity, but there are other senses. You can hear the crunch of bones breaking. And feel the soft flesh yielding beneath a sharp razor. And smell the copper tang of blood as it pools on the dusty cement floor.

And the screams.

Nothing is more sexually fulfilling. I touch myself in private places as those screams echo in the depths of my soul.

Nash Cordon will have one more moment in the limelight and then he'll fade into obscurity.

Crimson blood stains the pure white snow. Life spills from warm to frozen. Don't look. The pain is gone.

It was still pitch-black outside as Lynne finished dressing. Pulling her hair into a high ponytail, she left her bedroom and headed into the kitchen. It was no surprise to discover that Kir was already there along with a drooling King, who was watching him butter a stack of English muffins. She'd smelled the coffee while she was still in the shower.

Her heart did a funny flop as Kir turned and smiled. He was fully dressed in a flannel shirt and jeans, but his jaw was shadowed with a morning stubble and his hair was mussed. She'd never seen anyone look more gorgeous.

"You don't have to get up at this ungodly hour, you know," she said, her voice breathless.

He shrugged, handing her a mug. "I always wake up early. Besides, I'm discovering an addiction to sharing coffee with a beautiful vet before sunrise."

She blushed. Compliments always made her feel awkward. "I'm not beautiful."

He placed a muffin on a plate and set it on the counter next to her. "That's a decision I get to make, not you."

"Oh really?" She nibbled the muffin and sipped the hot coffee. She'd never taken time for breakfast. She showered, pulled on her clothes, and headed for the clinic. Now she realized there was something special about this time of day. A promise of a new beginning with a man who filled her kitchen and heart with a warmth she'd never expected.

"Yes, really."

She held his gaze as she polished off the muffin. Then she set aside the plate. "You might be the boss in Boston, but this is Pike."

He arched a brow. "So who is the boss in Pike?"

"Maybe we can be partners."

"Partners." His eyes darkened with an emotion that made her heart do another flop. "I like the sound of that."

"Me too," she whispered.

Kir turned to place his mug on the counter, a hint of purpose to his quick movements. Was he intending to pull her into his arms? Maybe kiss her until she forgot she had a full schedule waiting for her?

She shivered with anticipation, but even as he started to turn, Kir came to a sharp halt.

"What's that?" he demanded, glancing out the window over the sink.

Lynne pressed against his side, her mouth dry with fear. "What? Where?"

"That light."

Lynne frowned in confusion. "The streetlights?"

He pointed upward. "No, in the sky."

Lynne leaned forward, studying the glow that was reflected against the lingering darkness. It wasn't the hovering dawn. It was something from the ground. "Could it be a fire?"

"It looks too steady for a fire."

"True. Oh, wait." Lynne abruptly recalled where she'd seen that glow before. "It looks like the lights from the football field."

"Do they always leave them on?"

"No. Only when they have a game."

He was silent for a minute, then he squared his shoulders. "I'm going to check it out."

She reached out to grab his arm. Not because she thought he was overreacting to lights. Right now, anything out of the ordinary was setting off alarm bells. No, she simply wasn't going to let him go alone.

"*We're* going to check it out." She squeezed his arm. "Partner."

He shook his head. "Lynne—"

"Have you considered the possibility this is a trick to lure you away so I'm left here on my own?" she interrupted.

He released an aggravated sigh. "You're too smart for your own good," he muttered. "Or my good."

She pulled on her coat, letting King out to do his business before filling his bowls with food and water. They could take him along, but she was still reluctant to leave the house without him there to provide protection. It was going to be a while before she was over the horror that the killer had been sneaking around her property.

Leaving the house, Lynne made sure the doors were locked as Kir started the SUV and scraped the ice from the windows. At last they were driving down the empty street, a tension silencing any urge to chatter. It was probably nothing, she tried to tell herself. Some kids might have turned on the lights last night and no one noticed. Or there was some weird power surge. No doubt there were any number of explanations.

She was still clinging to the hope that it was nothing more than a fluke when they turned onto the road that led past the three-story brick school that had been built a hundred years ago, with a new addition that was awkwardly attached at the back. On one side was a graveled parking lot, and on the other side was a long field framed by a chain-link fence.

They drove past the bleachers that were nearly hidden beneath the snowdrifts, and the scoreboard, until they had a clear view of the field.

Her breath tangled in her throat. Right in the middle of the snow-covered field was a shiny black truck.

"That's Nash's truck," she said in a harsh voice. There was no mistaking the oversized custom wheels and floodlights on top of the cab. "Why would he leave it in the middle of the football field?"

Kir slowed to a mere crawl as they continued down the street. "He seems the type to enjoy reliving his glory days. And you said yourself he's always parking wherever he wants."

Lynne frowned as she studied the truck. It didn't look like it was running. The headlights weren't on and there was no smoke coming from the tailpipe. In fact, it looked frozen in place.

"At this hour, in subzero weather? No." She shook her head. "Nash prefers to relive his glory days in the comfort of the bar with a bunch of his drunk buddies who still think he's a local hero."

Kir pointed toward the gate at the far end of the fence that had been smashed open. That was obviously where the truck entered the field. "Maybe he got plastered and ran off the road."

She slowly nodded, trying to imagine what Nash had

been doing that would lead him to this part of town. It was possible he'd been out selling beer to the local students, but this seemed too visible a location. He preferred the dark alley behind his bar. Not to mention the fact, he would never have turned on the lights. That would only have attracted more unwanted attention.

Lynne stiffened, struck by a sudden thought. "What if the killer stole it to use in another murder?"

Kir cursed and slammed on the brakes. The SUV fishtailed and slid to a halt less than an inch from the fence.

"That murder," he breathed.

It took a second for Lynne to figure out what he was talking about, then her breath was squeezed from her lungs as if a vise were crushing her chest.

"Oh my God." She shoved open the door of the SUV and slid out, wading through the snow to press against the fence. "Nash."

Kir appeared next to her, holding his phone to his ear.

Vaguely Lynne heard him telling someone that there was an emergency at the football field, but her attention was locked on the macabre sight of the stiff body lying directly beneath the back bumper of Nash's truck. It looked like there was a red rope wrapped around his neck that was tied to something in the bed of the truck. He was completely naked with splotches of frozen blood coating his skin and a dusting of snow that almost obscured his face.

She swayed, her stomach threatening to revolt. "No. I don't believe it."

"Get back in the SUV and wait for the sheriff," Kir commanded in sharp tones.

She grimly battled back the nausea. She could be sick

later. Right now she had to focus on Nash. "We have to see if he's still alive. I can do CPR."

She'd started to move toward the demolished gate when Kir grabbed her arm. "Lynne, he's dead."

"But—"

"He's been dead awhile. There's nothing you can do to help." He firmly turned her away from the field. "Go back to the SUV."

She dug in her heels, wanting to cling to the hope she could rush to Nash's side and somehow urge him back to life. It didn't matter that he'd been a selfish jerk who'd humiliated her. Or that she'd dreaded the thought of accidentally running into him. He'd been a part of her life since she was in preschool. How could she imagine Pike without him?

But she'd seen exactly what Kir had seen. If Nash had still been alive when he was brought to the field, he was now frozen to death. A naked, wounded body couldn't survive in this temperature.

She swallowed the lump in her throat. "What are you going to do?"

"I'll be right behind you," he promised.

"Kir—"

"I promise."

A sharp breeze sliced through air, sending a spray of snow into Lynne's face. She shuddered, her stomach clenching at the thought the snow might have been touching Nash's dead body. Bile rose in her throat and she scurried toward the SUV. She could calmly stitch together a gushing wound or dig through cow dung in order to diagnose a particular bacterium.

But this . . .

She reached the vehicle before she threw up.

Chapter 20

Kir held up his phone to take a video of the crime scene. He began at the broken gate and followed the tracks across the field to where the pickup was parked. Next he took several pictures of Nash's body.

He wasn't one of those ghoulish people who were fascinated by train wrecks or dead people. But he wanted clear images he could study later. The local law enforcement would never share information they discovered, and he fully intended to continue his amateur investigation.

There was a vicious monster out there. Kir wasn't going to sit around twiddling his thumbs while the killer came closer and closer to Lynne.

He was trying to zoom in on the footprints leading away from the truck when the sound of an approaching siren had him shoving the phone into the pocket of his coat. A couple minutes later the heavy truck rounded the corner and skidded to a halt just inches from the fence.

The sheriff climbed out along with her deputy, Anthony, both of them looking as if they'd been dragged out of bed.

Stomping toward the mangled gate, the sheriff silently

took in the sight of Nash lying naked in the snow. Then, placing her hand on the weapon holstered on her hip, she turned to glare at Kir.

"Why am I not surprised that you and Dr. Gale are in the middle of yet another murder?" she growled.

Kir arched a brow, refusing to be goaded by the woman. "Hardly in the middle. We happened to be driving down the street and noticed the lights on."

Kathy snorted in disbelief. "Happened to be driving down the street at this hour?"

"Lynne's a vet. She has a crazy schedule."

"And you?"

He shrugged. "I don't think it's safe for her to be out here alone. Do you?"

An ugly smile twisted the woman's lips. "I'm more worried about the safety of other people around the good doctor."

"You can't honestly believe she has anything to with this?"

The sheriff hunched her shoulders. "She just discovered that her boyfriend was cheating on her. Now he's dead and she found the body. If that isn't suspicious, I don't know what is."

Kir ground his teeth. This woman used her badge to bully respect rather than trying to earn it as a good, decent sheriff who cared about those she served. He didn't know if it was a character flaw or just years of being worn down by those who refused to believe she was capable of doing her job. And right now, he didn't care.

"So exactly how did she manage to overpower a man who is a foot taller and twice her weight?" he mocked.

"Not to mention the fact that she had to somehow haul him to this field."

Kathy's jaw tightened, her hand reaching up to grab the bill of her cap as the wind sent shards of ice pelting through the air. "All the victims were drugged with sedatives from her clinic."

"And most vehicles have a winch," the deputy added, pointing toward the bed of the truck. "Easy enough to move a body for anyone."

His words distracted Kir. Glancing toward the pickup he realized the red rope around Kir's neck must be attached to a winch. The deputy was right. It would be easy enough for anyone to wrap the rope around Nash's neck and drag him through town.

"Secure the scene, you idiot," Kathy snarled toward Anthony. "And keep your mouth shut."

The man hunched his shoulders, as if accustomed to being berated by the older woman, and trudged through the snow toward the truck. Kir hid his disgust. He had dozens of employees and not one of them would have tolerated being talked to in that manner.

He shook his head. Not his problem.

"You think the bodies were moved using a winch?" he asked, unable to recall if Lynne's truck had one installed.

Kathy pinched her lips. "I think I've seen Lynne wrestle calves to the ground with no problem. She's stronger than she looks."

He made a sound of impatience. "I was with her the entire night."

"An accomplice would make it even easier to move a body," she countered without hesitation.

Kir narrowed his eyes even as he reached into his

pocket to wrap his hands around his phone. Thank God he had an accurate record of the crime scene. He didn't want to believe Kathy Hancock would alter evidence to implicate Lynne or him in the murder, but he sensed her growing desperation.

He was going to make a backup of the pictures and put them in a secure file. "Do we need to get a lawyer?"

Kathy glanced over her shoulder, glaring toward Lynne. "If she's guilty, she's going to need more than a lawyer. She's going to need a miracle." With her cheesy warning still lingering in the frozen air, Kathy squared her shoulders and followed in her deputy's footsteps.

Kir rolled his eyes and moved to join Lynne in the SUV. Climbing into the driver's seat, he released a low groan as the warmth wrapped around him. He hadn't realized how cold he was.

"I suppose the sheriff is convinced I'm involved?" Lynne muttered, her gaze locked on the law officials who were kneeling next to Nash's frozen body.

"Right now she's ready to blame both of us."

Lynne clicked her tongue. "I'm not sure why she hates me so much."

"I don't think she hates you," Kir assured her, sensing her bewildered hurt. All of this was bad enough without suspecting that the person in charge of the investigation held some sort of grudge against you. "I think she's afraid."

Lynne sent him a startled glance. "Afraid of what?"

"I've realized since coming home that Kathy has never been able to fill my father's shoes," he told her. "At least not in the minds of the citizens of Pike. It must be gnawing at her confidence despite her aggressive attitude. Deep inside she fears she's not up to the job."

Lynne pressed her lips into a tight line. "That's what we all fear."

"Yeah."

The sound of approaching sirens reminded Kir that this area was about to be overrun with official vehicles. He didn't want to be in their way. And just as importantly, he didn't want to get blocked in.

He had things to do.

Reversing his way down the street, he pulled through the parking lot of the school and drove several blocks west before heading back to Lynne's house. It ensured he avoided the approaching ambulance and fire truck, as well as the early morning gawkers who were hurrying to get dressed so they could discover what had happened.

He pulled to a halt in her driveway, swiveling in his seat to study her stern profile. She was silent, lost in thought. Then, abruptly she turned to meet his worried gaze.

"Why Nash?" she demanded. "How does he fit in with the others?"

Kir slowly shook his head, frustration bubbling through him. "I wish I knew. I feel like we're grasping for answers that turn to mist as soon as we touch them."

"Blind leading the blind," she muttered.

"True."

They shared a worried glance, both knowing they were in over their heads. Whoever was out there stalking the citizens of Pike was spiraling out of control. Not only because the kills were happening so quickly, but the method by which the bodies were being disposed had become an even more blatant challenge to the sheriff.

After unhooking her seat belt, Lynne clenched her

hands in her lap. She looked as if she was trying to gather her composure. Or maybe her courage. "Did you notice anything when you were taking pictures?"

Kir hesitated. He sensed that Lynne was still in shock. Who wouldn't be? It was bad enough to stumble across such a gruesome sight. He knew he'd be having nightmares for weeks. It would be much worse for Lynne, who'd had an intimate connection with the victim. Then again, they didn't have the luxury of waiting until her raw feelings had healed. Not when the killer could strike again at any moment.

"He was like the women. Posed naked, although he had a red rope around his neck instead of a ribbon. I don't know if that has meaning or not." His mouth felt oddly dry, as if the horror was sucking away the moisture. "From a distance it was impossible to see specific injuries, but he looked . . ."

"Tell me."

He shuddered. From where they'd first been standing, Nash had looked as if he'd been left to freeze in the snow. Once he'd gotten closer, it'd been obvious that he was bloody and broken in ways that made his gut clench.

"Bad. Really bad. I don't know if he was beaten or hauled behind the truck while he was still alive."

She released a shaky breath. "It doesn't seem real."

He reached to cover her hands with his own. "I'm sorry."

She glanced out the front windshield, her eyes unfocused as if she was lost in her inner thoughts. "I know I should cry, but I'm numb." She shook her head. "I can't feel anything."

"It's the shock."

A minute, then another passed before she finally glanced back at him. "Was there anything else?"

Kir shuffled through the limited information he'd gathered. He was a businessman, not a cop. He'd never learned how to spot clues. "The tracks had started to fill in, so I'm guessing the truck had to have been there for at least an hour or so," he said.

She absorbed his words. "That would mean it was driven there around four a.m. The same time Ms. Randall's body was dumped yesterday."

He nodded in agreement. "There were footprints, but I doubt they'll be much help with the blowing snow." He tried to imagine the killer calmly arranging the body before strolling away from his grisly creation. "Do you know if there are any cameras at the school?"

She wrinkled her nose. "I doubt they would have them at the football field. We barely keep the school open, let alone invest in technology that isn't absolutely necessary."

He wasn't surprised. Pike had never been a wealthy town, and recently it'd been devastated by the collapse of the dairy industry. But surely there were a few cameras around town that had captured the image of the truck being driven through the empty streets? He wouldn't have access to them, but the sheriff would check. At least he hoped she would.

Something the killer would have to realize.

"It's still risky." He tapped his fingers on the steering wheel. "Just like dumping Ms. Randall in the park downtown was risky. Either the killer is taunting the sheriff, or the danger of getting caught must add to his sick pleasure."

"Or the places have a meaning," she suggested in soft tones.

Kir studied her in surprise. He'd never considered the possibility. "Yes. Maybe it's about where the bodies are placed and not who the body belongs to." He considered the implications and then made a sound of frustration. "It still has no rhyme or reason. An empty pasture. A frozen lake. The park. The football field."

"Nash did play football," she reminded him. "Besides, it doesn't have to have a meaning for us. Just to the killer."

He continued to tap his fingers on the steering wheel. "If that's true, then maybe the list my father gave to Pastor Bradshaw is the initials of potential dumping grounds, not people."

He didn't have to say that he desperately hoped she was right. If they were looking for places, not names, it might mean she wasn't a target.

She smiled wanly. Neither of them were reassured by his words.

"I'll let you figure that out," she said, pushing open her door. "I need to get to work."

"Lynne."

"I know." She slid out of the SUV. "I'll be careful."

"Don't go on any emergency calls alone."

"I won't." She rolled her eyes. "Besides, I'm fairly sure the sheriff is going to be spending at least part of the day at my office."

"I'll swing by with some lunch."

He waited until she had his father's old truck running and was driving down the street before he pulled out of the driveway and headed in the opposite direction. He wanted to have a look at Nash's place before the sheriff had a chance to run him off, and then do a quick check on Pastor Bradshaw. If he'd been out and about at such an early hour there might be evidence around his house. Then he wanted to check out the dump sites. It was possible there might be a connection that would finally click in his mind.

Stranger things had happened.

The truck's old heater was still blasting out frigid air when Lynne reached the clinic. Hurrying inside she nearly cried when she saw Bernadine calmly seated behind the front desk. Whatever new craziness the day might have in store, at least she knew her patients would be in good hands.

"Thanks for coming in," she said, her voice thick with sincerity.

The woman waved away her words of gratitude. "I'm here as long as you need me, Lynne."

"How about forever?"

Bernadine clicked her tongue, but Lynne could see the pleasure in her eyes. She was the sort of person who liked to be needed.

"We'll see," she murmured. "I left your messages on your desk and that blond intern is setting up the exam rooms."

Lynne's lips twitched as she headed for her office. Bernadine never bothered to learn the names of the various interns. She said that they came and left too quickly to earn a place in her crowded brain. They still loved her. She made everyone's life easier when she was there.

Lynne pulled off her parka and replaced it with a lab coat. She had a full morning of surgeries scheduled. She needed to get started if she hoped to take a break for lunch. And, it was the perfect way to keep her mind fully occupied. The last thing she wanted was to sit around brooding on the horrifying memory of Nash.

The morning passed in a blessed blur, and she'd just finished placing a sleeping boxer who'd tangled with a porcupine in a heated cubicle to start the healing process when she was distracted by the sound of raised voices coming from the outer lobby.

Her heart sank. *What now?*

She was halfway down the hallway when she finally recognized the shrill voice that was echoing through the clinic.

"Get out of my way, you old bat," Chelsea yelled.

"You use that tone of voice with me and I'll put you over my knee, Chelsea Gallen," Bernadine warned. "It wouldn't be the first time."

Picking up her pace, Lynne entered the lobby to see Bernadine and Chelsea standing in the center of the room. They each had their hands on their hips, glaring at each other. Both were too stubborn to give in and Lynne had a momentary panic that Chelsea might actually attack the older woman. "What's going on?" she demanded in loud tones, drawing the attention to herself.

Chelsea narrowed her eyes. "You bitch—"

"Go to my office or leave," Lynne interrupted, pointing toward Chelsea. "Pick one."

Chelsea tossed her hair, heading toward the hallway. "Whatever."

"You mind your manners," Bernadine called out.

Lynne rolled her eyes, joining Chelsea in the office and closing the door. She wasn't in the mood to deal with the petulant girl who'd betrayed her, but it was the perfect opportunity to sever their relationship. Even if Bernadine decided she wanted to go back to her retirement, Lynne couldn't have Chelsea in the clinic. She would never trust her again.

Lynne took a seat behind her desk, but Chelsea paced from side to side. "Is it true?" she at last burst out. "Is Nash dead?"

Lynne flinched, her stomach clenching. That wasn't what she'd been expecting. In fact, it hadn't occurred to her that word of Nash's murder would already have spread through town. Stupid, of course. There were no secrets in Pike.

Except for the killer who was hunting them.

A shiver raced down her spine. "Yes."

Chelsea blinked back tears, her face pale beneath the layers of makeup. "God. On the news they said . . ." She was forced to stop and clear her throat. "They said it was the same killer who murdered the others."

The girl looked pitiful, but Lynne couldn't manage much sympathy. Did that make her a bad person?

Lynne shrugged. "I doubt anything is official."

Chelsea stopped her pacing to send Lynne a poisonous glare. "They also said you found the body."

Lynne swallowed a curse. How had that particular rumor gotten around? The sheriff? "Kir and I were driving by the school and noticed Nash's truck," she grudgingly admitted.

"Did you see his body? You're sure it was him?"

"I'm sure."

There was a long, painful silence before Chelsea reached up to wipe away her tears with an angry motion. "This is all your fault."

Lynne widened her eyes at the accusation. "Don't be ridiculous. I didn't kill Nash."

"It's your fault," the younger woman insisted, a fevered glint in her eyes. "If he hadn't been obsessed with you—"

"What are you talking about?" Lynne interrupted Chelsea's whining. "Nash and I ended things weeks ago."

"You ended things. He never moved on," she stubbornly insisted.

Lynne snorted. "I would say he moved on before we officially broke up. Or have you forgotten that I know about the two of you in the storage room?"

Chelsea managed to look even more belligerent. "That was your fault too."

"Mine?" The sheer audacity of her claim stole Lynne's breath. Chelsea couldn't be serious?

No one was that self-centered.

"He was trying to hurt you," the younger woman insisted. "That's why he had sex with me and stole the drugs."

Lynne frowned. The babbling made no sense. "If he wanted to hurt me, he would have arranged for me to catch the two of you together. Instead he made sure it stayed a secret."

Chelsea refused to listen to reason. "There was a part of him that still hoped you would get back together."

Lynne shook her head in resignation. "Even if that's true, I don't see how I'm to blame for his death."

"If he hadn't been trying to punish you, he would never have agreed to steal the drugs and sell them."

Lynne's mouth parted to argue, only to snap shut as she studied the woman in confusion. "Wait. Do you think that Nash was murdered because the killer knew he was the one who stole the sedatives from the clinic?"

Chelsea hunched her shoulders. "Why else? The other victims were all middle-aged women. Why would a serial killer be interested in Nash unless he was worried he might be exposed?"

Why, indeed. Lynne tried to wrap her mind around the possibility, but it was impossible to concentrate while Chelsea was glaring down at her. She would have to wait until she was alone to reconsider Nash's murder. "Who knows why a madman kills?" she instead muttered.

Chelsea made a raw sound of fury. "You can try to pretend you're innocent all you want, Dr. Lynne Gale, but I know you're guilty."

Lynne leaned back in her seat, as if she could avoid the toxic hatred that pulsed around the younger woman.

What the hell was going on? She'd always assumed people liked her. Okay, she wasn't Miss Socialite. She didn't spend every night at the bar or her weekends at the golf course. But she was a respected vet who cared about her neighbors. It was unnerving to think there were people in town who carried such hatred in their hearts toward her.

Chelsea. The sheriff. Who knew who else . . .

"Why are you so eager to blame me?"

Chelsea's jaw tightened. "You don't even know what you have, do you?"

"What I have?"

Chelsea waved a hand toward the framed diploma on the wall. "Your fancy education, and a career handed to you on a silver platter." The younger woman made a sound of disgust. "It's no wonder you think you can toss men away like garbage."

Lynne surged to her feet as anger pounded through her. She'd spent eight years in grueling college classes. She hadn't partied, hadn't dated, hadn't gone on spring breaks. She'd either been studying or returning to Pike to help her father. And the demands on her had only increased when she'd graduated. She'd come home expecting to spend years working with her dad before deciding if she wanted to take over the demands of the clinic. Instead her father had taken a nasty fall and the doctor had warned that he needed to retire and take care of himself if he didn't want to end up in a wheelchair. Suddenly, Lynne found herself shouldering the burden of the clinic, whether it was what she wanted or not.

And this petulant girl, who never took responsibility for anything, was daring to imply that it had all just been handed to her like a gift-wrapped present.

"I worked my ass off to become a qualified vet and then worked even harder to keep this clinic running. As for throwing away men—" Lynne shook her head in disgust. "We both know that Nash was a selfish jerk who was incapable of loving anyone but himself."

Chelsea sniffed the tears once again running down her cheeks. "He should have been mine."

Lynne sucked in a slow, deep breath. It was a waste of energy to be mad at this woman. They were complete opposites who would never truly understand each other. "I think it would be best if you cleaned out your desk, Chelsea."

"Fine." With a flounce, Chelsea turned to pull open the door. "I didn't want to work here anyway. It stinks."

"Wait." Lynne rounded the desk, struck by a sudden thought.

Chelsea glanced over her shoulder. "What now?"

Lynne held out her hand. "I need your keys to the clinic."

"I don't have them with me."

"I'll need them by the end of the day."

There was an awkward pause, then Chelsea cleared her throat. "I can't."

"Why not?"

"I lost them."

Lynne's hand dropped, her eyes narrowing. Was the girl lying? She wouldn't put it past her to be that spiteful. Then again, there was a hint of fear in her expression. Was she scared Lynne might call the sheriff?

"When did you lose them?"

"I'm not sure." Chelsea lowered her lashes, hiding her eyes. "I thought they were in my purse, but when I looked for them this morning to bring them back, I couldn't find them."

Lynne's mouth was suddenly dry. She had a bad feeling about this. "When was the last time you used them?"

The girl shrugged. "Maybe last week."

"It's important, Chelsea," she snapped.

"I don't remember." With a muttered curse, the younger

woman headed out of the office and down the hallway. "Just leave me alone."

Lynne followed behind, watching in silence as Chelsea yanked open the drawers of the desk, indifferent to Bernadine sitting just inches away.

She wanted to demand that the girl answer her question. It was imperative to discover exactly when the keys went missing. It might explain how someone had managed to get the spare truck key from her office. And maybe even take a picture of her sleeping. But Chelsea's mutinous expression warned she wasn't about to answer any questions.

It would be easier to turn over the information about the lost keys to the sheriff's office. They had the means to force Chelsea to talk.

Lynne was already dreading the thought of making the call.

"That girl is just like her mother," Bernadine groused as Chelsea slammed out of the office. "Wanting something without having to work for it."

Lynne was instantly distracted. "Why do you say that?"

"Marie Gallen refused to work, even after her husband walked out on them. And she was always asking people for money or a place to stay." Bernadine lowered her voice, although they were the only two people in the clinic. "Not many people know it, but years ago, Chelsea's mother was arrested for stealing money from the booster club. It was almost five hundred dollars. A lot of money back then."

Lynne arched her brows. She'd never met Marie Gallen, and she wasn't really interested in her past criminal habits. But the woman's brush with the law made her consider a new possibility. "Did Sheriff Jansen arrest her?" she asked.

Bernadine nodded. "He did. I overheard him discussing what'd happened with your father." The older woman smiled at Lynne's obvious surprise. "He was on the school board at that time."

Ah. That made sense. Her father was a big believer in community service. She really didn't know how he'd had the time. She could barely remember to breathe. Of course, she did have the sanctuary to deal with on top of the clinic.

"What did they do to her?"

"Your father wanted her to be released with a warning as long as she returned the money."

"I assume she did?"

"As far as I know." Bernadine lifted her hands. "It was all swept under the carpet."

Lynne nodded. Bernadine's words had reminded her that many of the good citizens of Pike had some dealings with the law. Sherry had assistance with her evictions. Randi's father had been arrested. Nash had been in trouble for selling booze to underage kids. Even she had to use the hotline for animal abuse cases.

Her theory abruptly fell apart as she got to Ms. Randall. It seemed unlikely she would do anything illegal.

Lost in her thoughts, she didn't hear the door open. It wasn't until Kir appeared next to her that she realized he'd arrived.

"Ready for lunch?" he asked, holding a picnic basket in his hand.

"Perfect timing," Bernadine said in firm tones. "She needs a break."

Chapter 21

Rita squinted as the sunlight drilled into her eyes. She groaned and slapped on a pair of dark glasses. It'd been so long since she'd left her house during daylight hours that she'd forgotten the sheer brightness.

Most people assumed Wisconsin was a cold, gray place. And they were right about the cold. But when the sun made an appearance it reflected off everything. The snow, the slick roads, the frosted windows of the nearby buildings. Even the trees had a layer of ice that shimmered like diamonds.

It might have been beautiful if the brilliance wasn't like steel daggers being shoved into her eyes.

Wincing in pain, Rita hunched her shoulders and trudged down the street. She desperately wanted to return to her house and climb back into bed. Her stomach was icky from too many beers last night and too little food. But that wasn't why she wanted to scurry back to the safety of her home.

She felt exposed out here with the wind tugging at her shabby coat and the fear that unseen eyes were watching her. It was a stark reminder of who she'd become over the past years.

Poor Rita. The timid mouse of a woman who let her husband beat out his frustration on her face. The woman who finally broke but couldn't even manage to run over her husband without screwing it up. The woman who lost her daughter and any reason to care if she was alive or dead.

Rita King. The spectacular failure.

She shivered, then fiercely battled back her blast of panic.

She'd allowed her anxiety to keep her away from Rudolf's funeral. A weakness that shamed her to her very soul. She wasn't going to let it get the best of her this time.

For the past three nights her old friend had haunted her dreams. As if he was trying to reach out from the grave to warn her. She didn't know why he couldn't rest in peace, but she was going to ask him.

It was the only way to get any sleep.

Reaching the cemetery, Rita was forced to wade through the drifted snowbanks to at last reach Rudolf's grave. The disturbed earth created a mound higher than the other graves, but there was a layer of snow over the top that thankfully softened the sight of raw dirt. It was unnerving enough to be there without the bleak reminder that Rudolf was probably still a frozen corpse in his coffin. It would be months before he would thaw out and start to rot.

Rita nearly gagged at the awful thought.

"Stop it," she muttered. "You're here to talk to Rudolf's spirit, not worry about his dead body."

Stopping next to the recently installed headstone, Rita

concentrated on her friend's name carved into the marble and the heavy urn that was filled with brittle flowers that rustled in the stiff breeze. Slowly the instinctive unease at being in a cemetery was replaced with memories of Rudolf when he was still alive. A sharp pain sliced through her. She desperately missed him. No one else understood her driving need to dull the pain night after night. Or her self-loathing when she woke the next morning with a dull, pounding headache.

Beyond that, he was a good companion. He told stories that made her laugh or gasp at his brave escapades. A few might even have been true.

Rita reached out to touch the headstone.

"Talk to me, Rudolf. Tell me what's bothering you," she whispered.

There was nothing but the whistle of the wind as it pierced the thick line of cedar trees that framed the cemetery.

She frowned. Was she an idiot to think Rudolf was trying to talk to her? Probably. Of course, it wouldn't be the first time she'd allowed her wild imagination to over-take her common sense. But it'd felt so real.

"Come on, Rudolf," she muttered. "I'm freezing."

While stomping her feet, which were going numb from the cold, she accidentally kicked the base of the head-stone, causing a layer of snow to fall off the cement urn.

Rita flinched. The last thing she needed was to desecrate a grave. Wasn't it bad luck or something? Crossing herself despite the fact she wasn't Catholic, she was distracted by the sight of something white poking out of the dead flowers in the urn. It looked like a stray piece of trash.

With a disapproving click of her tongue, Rita reached down to remove it. Who would do such a thing?

It wasn't until she pulled it out that she realized it wasn't a scrap of paper. Instead it was an envelope with Rudolf's name scrawled on the front.

She hesitated. It was probably a personal note from someone Rudolf had helped. There were a lot of people in Pike who owed him their gratitude. So should she leave it there or take it to Kir?

Unsure what to do, Rita at last decided to open the envelope. If it was something that would remind Kir of his father's many fine qualities, she'd take it to him. Otherwise she'd stick it back in the urn.

After reluctantly removing one glove, Rita ripped open the envelope and pulled out the folded paper. It was a handwritten note and it took a couple minutes before she managed to decipher the words.

Then her heart stopped.

That wasn't a metaphor.

Her heart actually forgot to beat as she shoved the letter into the pocket of her jacket.

Then, leaning forward, she glanced into the urn. There were more envelopes. Bile rose in her throat, but biting her tongue she forced herself to reach in and grab them. Tucking them in the same pocket as the first one, she turned to hurry out of the cemetery.

She'd been right, a triumphant voice whispered in the back of her mind. Rudolf had been trying to reach out and warn her. Now it was her duty to make sure the letters were given to . . .

Who?

The sheriff? No, she was worthless. Maybe she should

contact the FBI. On television they were always the one who solved the big cases, right? But how did a person get ahold of them?

Kir would know, she decided. He was one of those people who was a natural leader. She wasn't at all surprised when Rudolf had told her he'd started his own business in Boston.

She reached into the pocket of her coat. She never carried a purse. There wasn't any point. All she ever needed was her phone, her cigarettes, her house key, and a couple bucks. Pulling out the phone, she hesitated before dialing Rudolf's number. She assumed he'd still have his landline. She heard the sound of ringing, then Rudolf's gruff voice echoed in her ear, telling her to leave a message.

Her heart did a crazy dance. The voice was so familiar. As if Rudolf was standing next to her. Sucking in a deep breath, Rita quickly told Kir she'd found something he needed to see. Hopefully, the younger man would think to check the answering machine. If not, she would try to find him later tonight.

Stepping through the trees that marked the edge of the cemetery, she heard the sound of an approaching vehicle. She paused, careful to replace the phone in her pocket. She'd destroyed or lost more phones than she cared to recall. She couldn't afford to buy another one.

Ironically, it was her rare display of caution that was her downfall.

If she'd been looking up, she would have seen the vehicle that was aimed in her direction. She might even have managed to jump out of the way.

So many "if onlys" in her life.

The death she'd been seeking for years claimed her in an explosion of shattering pain.

Kir forced himself to wait before he demanded to know why he'd seen Chelsea Gallen storming from the clinic when he'd pulled up. Lynne was already as thin as a whippet. He didn't want her losing any more weight. Squashing his curiosity, he'd led her into her office and insisted she eat a large helping of the chicken pot pie he'd made along with a salad.

He was ridiculously pleased when she polished her plate. As if he'd managed to achieve some wondrous achievement.

Man, he had it bad.

It wasn't until he'd packed away the dishes that he finally coaxed her to reveal the details of her confrontation with her former receptionist. Within a few minutes his temper was rising. By the time she was done, he was standing in the center of the office with his hands clenched and his blood boiling.

"So anyone could have the keys to the clinic?" he growled.

Lynne sat on the sofa, her face pale. "If Chelsea wasn't lying."

He sent her a confused glance. "Why would she lie?"

"I warned her when I gave her the keys that if she lost them, I'd have to have all the locks changed and that she would have to pay for the expenses. It's not only going to be costly, but it's a hassle I don't need right now."

"It could be revenge," Kir agreed. Chelsea had struck him as the sort of vindictive person who'd take pleasure in causing Lynne problems. But her relationship with Nash had also proved she was willing to sacrifice her pride and morals to please a man. Maybe even to please a friend. "It could be she gave them to someone and didn't want to admit who had them."

Lynne twisted her hands together. "The killer?"

"It's possible."

There was a long silence as they considered the dangers of having the keys in the hands of a murderous monster. Then Lynne heaved a frustrated sigh. "Or maybe she just lost them."

"Yep."

"Going around in circles. Again," Lynne muttered. Then she frowned. "I almost forgot. Chelsea did have an interesting theory."

"What's that?"

"She thinks Nash was killed because of his connection to the drugs that were stolen, not because he was a chosen victim."

"Not bad," Kir said. It was true that Nash didn't really fit the profile of the other victims. "If the killer feared Nash might have information that could expose him, it would make sense to get him out of the way."

Lynne narrowed her eyes. "You don't believe it."

"No." He reached into his front pocket to remove the list that had supposedly come from his father. Then he moved to sit next to her on the sofa. "I went back over this," he said.

"And?"

"And I don't think it's listing locations." He pointed to the first initials. "There's an S. H."

"Sherry Higgins."

His finger moved down. "R. D."

"Randi Decker."

He moved to the next line. "M. R."

She nodded. "Madeline Randall."

"N. C."

"Nash Cordon." Lynne shuddered, her face going from pale to a sickly gray as she reached to touch the next initials on the list. "D. R. L. G. I'm next."

Kir stuffed the paper back in his pocket, swiveling on the sofa to grab Lynne's hands. "You need to get out of town. At least until the killer is found."

She was shaking her head before he ever finished speaking. "You know I can't do that. I have a business. The sanctuary. My house."

He'd already anticipated her arguments. "Your father could return to Pike to take care of things."

"And where would I go?"

He cupped her cheek in his hand. "We could stay at my condo in Boston."

He heard her breath catch, as if she'd been caught off guard by his offer. Why? Surely she understood he intended for them to be together? Whether it was here or somewhere else.

Before he could assure her that she was stuck with him, she was pulling away from his lingering touch.

"We can't hide there forever."

He stared down at her. Hiding away with this woman forever sounded like a perfectly reasonable life choice to him. "Why not?"

"Kir . . ." Her words trailed away as the sharp sound of sirens blasted through the air. Lynne jumped to her feet and raced to the window. "Now what?"

"Let's find out." Grimly Kir straightened and pulled on his leather coat. It was obvious he wasn't going to convince her to leave Pike this minute. They might as well discover what had happened. Perhaps the sheriff had actually done her job and was on the way to arrest the killer.

His lips twisted into a humorless smile. It seemed unlikely.

Lynne bundled herself in her coat and boots, and they headed out of the clinic. He was relieved to notice that Bernadine was at her desk in the outer lobby and he could hear one of the interns in an exam room. He didn't like the thought of anyone in the clinic being on their own. Not when there was a crazed killer stalking Lynne.

Together they climbed into his SUV and Kir followed the fading sound of sirens. Ten minutes later they pulled to a halt in front of a line of low, brick buildings. Most were empty, but it looked like one was used as a café and another had the name of the local real estate company painted on the window.

In the parking lot was not only the sheriff's vehicle, but an ambulance and the news van.

Kir climbed out of the SUV with a frown. Surely the killer hadn't struck again already? He stepped toward the official vehicles only to be distracted as Lynne headed directly toward Parker Bowen, who was opening the back door of the van.

"Has there been another murder?" Lynne bluntly demanded.

Parker shook his head, looking almost disappointed. "Not this time."

"What do you mean?"

Parker shrugged, removing his expensive trench coat

and replacing it with a heavy parka. "Looks like a hit-and-run." He headed toward the driver's door and pulled it open.

"Are you leaving?"

"This is second-team stuff," Parker told her, pointing toward the aged sedan that had just pulled into the parking lot.

A young woman with long blond hair and an eager expression jumped out and headed toward the deputy, who was draping crime-scene tape across the alley between the café and an empty building. Parker got in the van and drove away.

Kir shook his head in disgust. "He's a real winner."

Lynne turned her attention toward the EMTs who were leaving the alley and heading toward the waiting ambulance. She sucked in a shocked breath as they got near enough to see the patient strapped to the gurney they were pushing.

"Oh my God, is that Rita?"

Kir's breath hissed between his teeth as he caught sight of the woman's ashen face heavily flecked with blood. He felt as if he'd just been punched in the gut. "I'll be back," he muttered, shoving his way through the gathering crowd.

By the time he reached the ambulance they had loaded Rita inside and closed the doors. *Damn*. He had to discover which hospital they were taking her to. Jogging toward the front of the vehicle, he was abruptly halted as the sheriff stepped directly in his path.

"Get out of my crime scene," Kathy snapped.

Kir cursed as the ambulance drove away. "Is Rita going to the hospital in Grange?"

"I'm not telling you anything."

Kir whirled back to face her, deliberately towering over her. He was done pandering to this woman's petty need to push people around. If she didn't feel competent to do her job, she should quit. She was putting the entire town in danger.

"Dammit, she was a friend of my father," he snarled. "Maybe his only friend at the end. If she's been hurt, I'm going to make sure she gets the medical care she needs."

Kathy flushed at his fierce tone. "She doesn't need a doctor, she needs an undertaker," she snapped. Kir jerked in shock and the woman released a harsh sigh. "I'm sorry," she forced herself to mutter before turning and walking toward the alley.

Kir stood still, trying to absorb the unexpected pain. Poor, sad Rita. She'd spent years being punished for marrying the wrong man. She should have had a chance to redeem her future. To find peace.

Instead she'd been run down in an alley. Where was the justice in that?

Justice. The word echoed through the back of his mind. Yes. That's what she deserved.

Turning on his heel, Kir scanned the group standing next to the crime-scene tape. He focused in on the clutch of elderly men who were watching the scurry of officials with obvious impatience. He was betting they were waiting to return to the café and finish their lunch. Or maybe they'd been in the middle of a card game.

They seemed the most likely to know something.

He strolled to stand next to the group, trying to look casual. "Did anyone witness the accident?"

A man who Kir was guessing to be in his sixties with a ruddy face and watery blue eyes shook his head.

"Nope. Chester was taking out the trash from the lunch crowd when he saw Rita lying behind the dumpster."

Kir was about to ask where he could find Chester when he was struck by something the man had said. "*Behind* the dumpster? You're sure?"

The man frowned, as if he assumed Kir was one of those morbid people who took joy in tragedy. "Yeah," he reluctantly answered. "Chester said she was jammed against the wall. He nearly didn't see her. He just caught a peek of her boots sticking out. Terrible tragedy." With a shake of his head the man turned away, closing ranks with his friends, who eyed Kir with suspicion.

Kir sighed before making his way back to Lynne, who reached out to grab his hand.

"Are you okay?"

"Rita's dead."

"I'm sorry." She squeezed his fingers. "A hit-and-run?"

Kir glanced toward the alley where the sheriff and her deputy were already clearing away the crime-scene tape.

"That seems to be the general assumption," he muttered.

Lynne stared at him in confusion. "Is there a reason you don't believe it?"

His jaw tightened as the crowd hurried back into the café and the officials crawled into their vehicles to drive away. It was as if nothing had happened.

Was it because Rita King had been the town drunk, without money or friends? Or just because there was nothing left to do but plan the funeral?

And why couldn't he accept that it'd been nothing more than a tragic accident? Did it have something to do with his unresolved grief for his father?

He sighed. So many questions without answers. It made his brain hurt.

"Rita was found behind the dumpster," he told Lynne. "How did she get there?"

She blinked, puzzled by his refusal to accept the obvious. "The impact of the car . . ." Her words trailed away. "Well, she could have been thrown there."

"I suppose."

He was trying to imagine the force it would take to shove a woman behind a dumpster when Lynne reached out to give his arm a gentle squeeze.

"What now?"

He shook away his morbid thoughts, telling himself that it was sheer paranoia to assume this was more than some tragic accident. "I'll take you back to work, then I'm going to make sure someone contacts Rita's daughter," he told Lynne with a shudder. "I don't want the poor woman left in the morgue."

She regarded him with concern. "Are you sure you should be driving? You're pretty shaken up."

"I'm fine." He turned to lead Lynne back to the SUV. "You can call me when you're done, and I'll pick you up."

They crawled into the vehicle and Kir switched on the engine.

Lynne heaved a small sigh as she watched the last of the gawkers drift away. "I'm sorry, Kir," she murmured softly. "Rita deserved better."

Kir gripped the steering wheel, a sick regret in the pit of his stomach. "She did."

Chapter 22

Lynne finished the last appointment and was waiting for Kir to pick her up by five thirty that evening—nothing less than a miracle. She waited in the lobby until she saw his SUV pull into the parking lot, not about to take any chances. Then, after locking the doors and switching on the alarm, she hurried to join him in the thankfully warm vehicle.

"Did you locate Rita's daughter?" she asked as she closed the door and buckled her seat belt.

Kir pulled out of the lot, his face lined with weariness. "I didn't talk to her, but the deputy at the sheriff's office said they'd contacted her, and she was on her way back to arrange the funeral." He sent her a quick glance. "The deputy also told me your truck has been released. You can pick it up tonight."

Lynne swallowed a rude word. "About time."

"We'll take my dad's truck to get it and then run it back to his house. I need to grab some clothes anyway."

"Okay."

They drove to her home and after taking King out for a quick walk, they exchanged the SUV for the old pickup and headed to the impound lot behind the sheriff's office. Twenty minutes later they both pulled to a halt in front of Rudolf's old house and were entering through the front door.

Lynne arched her brows as she pulled off her boots and slipped out of her heavy coat. The shabby furniture and old carpet were the same, but there was a new layer of white paint on the walls and the yellowed blinds had been replaced with new curtains. It was amazing how the simple touches had refreshed the room.

"It looks good in here," she told Kir, turning in a slow circle. "Is there anything you can't do?"

His lips twisted as he took off his coat and tossed it on a chair. "Solve crimes."

She studied him with a flare of sympathy. He looked . . . subdued. As if the pressure he'd placed on himself to expose the killer was taking a heavy toll. Without considering what she was doing, Lynne walked forward to wrap her arms around his waist. "I'm pretty sure that's like brain surgery," she assured him. "A talent that takes both training and experience."

"Unfortunately."

Lynne rested her head against his chest, feeling the soft brush of his lips over her hair. Instantly the lingering chill was chased away. It wasn't just the warmth of his body seeping through her sweater. Or the strength of his arms as they wrapped around her. It was the familiar scent of his skin and the steady beat of his heart beneath her ear.

He wasn't one of those guys she usually dated. He'd put his unpredictable, reckless childhood behind him. Now he was solid and loyal and utterly dependable.

A man who a woman chose for the long haul.

Her heart missed a beat, but before she could panic at the direction of her thoughts, Lynne was distracted by a red flash across the room. "What's that blinking light?"

Kir glanced around. "Where?"

"Next to the television."

Kir dropped his arms and turned to discover what she was talking about. "Oh." He shrugged. "It's my dad's answering machine. I thought I deleted all the messages."

"Maybe someone was trying to get ahold of you."

"Why not call my cell?"

"They might not have your number."

"True." With obvious reluctance he crossed the carpet and bent over the stand that held the old-fashioned phone and machine along with the usual pad and pencil to jot down notes. Her own father had kept a phone just like it until he moved to Florida. Some things you just couldn't change. Kir pushed a button, then another one when nothing happened. "I always forget how to operate this thing. I'm pretty sure it was invented in the Stone Age."

Lynne was about to move and help him when the sound of Rudolf's voice stopped her in her tracks. He sounded as if he was standing in the room with them as the older man told the caller to leave a message after the beep. She closed her eyes, but even as she struggled against the wave of pain, a breathless female voice echoed through the room.

"Hi . . . um . . . Kir . . . this is Rita. Rita King," the woman said. "I just found something at your father's grave you should see. I think they're from the killer." There was the sound of rough breathing, as if Rita was walking as she was talking. "Okay. I'm going home, so when you get this come by. Or we can meet at the bar tonight." There was an awkward pause, as if the woman wasn't used to talking on the phone. "Yeah, so talk to you later."

There was a long beep as the message came to an end and Lynne released a shaky breath. "Rita."

Kir glanced down at the machine. "The message was recorded at eleven thirty. She must have called right before she died."

Lynne pressed a hand against her stomach, trying to imagine what had happened.

Obviously, Rita had her old friend on her mind. Whether it was because of Kir or some other reason, they would never know, but she'd decided to visit his grave. Once she was there, she'd found something—or rather some things—that had alarmed her. She'd called Kir and . . .

What?

Gone to the café and randomly been run over?

No. Lynne didn't believe it. Granted, Rita had probably been distracted by what she'd found. But the chances that she'd wandered in front of a moving car were astronomical. Not when she'd just discovered evidence that might unmask the serial killer.

"You were right," she told Kir. "Rita's death wasn't an accident."

Kir frowned, pacing the small living room with short, jerky steps. "What the hell did she find?"

"She said 'they're' from the killer," Lynne reminded him. "Which means more than one thing."

He came to an abrupt halt. "Letters."

Lynne nodded. It was the first thing that came to her mind. "It's possible."

"Why would they be at the grave?"

"Because the killer is still writing them, and in his mind, that's where your father is."

Kir paled, his hands clenching into tight fists. "So he writes them and leaves them in the cemetery? The sick bastard." There was fury in his voice. "Why can't he let my dad rest in peace?"

Lynne considered the question. She tried to imagine why any killer would write letters to an ex-sheriff. Was it to taunt him? To prove he was superior to the local authorities? But why choose Rudolf? Why not send them to the new sheriff? Maybe he had a grudge against the older man? That didn't seem right either.

Actually, the only thing that made sense was that the killer felt some need to reach out to Rudolf.

"It must have stolen his pleasure to have your father so unexpectedly die," she said. "He obviously considered Rudolf his confidant in a sad, twisted way."

Kir nodded. "Yes."

A silence filled the room as they both considered the possibility that letters had been left at Rudolf's grave and what could have been in them. A couple minutes later Kir was crossing the room to stand at the base of the staircase.

"What's wrong?" Lynne moved to stand at his side.

Kir was pale, his gaze locked on the wooden steps. "I was thinking about something Rita said."

Lynne was confused. "On the message?

"No. When we were at the bar."

"What did she say?"

"That there were four deaths."

"Oh, I remember." Lynne was still confused. "She was talking about the three women who'd been murdered and your father. We didn't know about Nash yet."

"Yes, but she connected them."

"What do you mean she connected them?"

He turned to meet her searching gaze. "She put my father's death with the murdered women."

Lynne wasn't sure if Kir had a point or if he was just remembering his father's untimely accident. Whatever he was talking about, it didn't seem to have any relevance to what happened to Rita. "She was drunk and babbling," she said.

"*Vino veritas.*"

"'In wine lies the truth'?" Lynne translated.

"Too often we make certain assumptions and accept them as truth. Drunks can occasionally see things more clearly."

Her confusion transformed into disbelief. "Are you suggesting that your father was murdered?"

Kir pointed toward the staircase. "I was told he fell down the steps and I didn't ask any questions of the coroner. Why would I? Even before I moved to Boston my father often slept on the sofa because he was too inebriated to make it up to his bedroom. If he had tried, it seemed plausible he could fall down and crack his skull."

Lynne reached out to touch his arm. She could feel the tension that hummed around him like an electric force field. "Kir, the killer was reaching out to your father with those letters. Why would he kill him?"

His jaw tightened. "Maybe he gave away too much. My father might have been a drunk, but at one time he was a damned good lawman. Eventually he would be able to put tiny clues together to come up with a theory."

"If that's true, why didn't he tell you?"

"Maybe he didn't have the chance." He deliberately glanced toward the answering machine. "Like Rita."

Lynne scowled, an unexpected anger jolting through her. Nash's death had been horrifying. His broken body would haunt her nightmares for years to come. And she felt awful for the poor women who'd been murdered. No one deserved to die like that.

But the thought that someone had deliberately attacked Rudolf and shoved him down the stairs made her strangely furious.

"That bastard," she hissed.

Kir had started to nod in fierce agreement when his eyes widened and he was rushing across the floor. "Shit. The list," he rasped. "That's it."

Lynne watched as he grabbed his coat and dug into the pocket. "That's what?"

He pulled out the folded piece of paper and tossed his coat back on the chair. Then he walked back to stand next to her. "I thought at first that my dad had made it." He unfolded the note, holding it so they could both see the printed letters. "But then Rita pointed out that it wasn't my father's handwriting."

Lynne didn't remind him that Rita wasn't the best source of information. She doubted the older woman could recognize her own handwriting let alone anyone else's.

"Do you think the killer sent it to him?"

He rubbed his fingers over the tattered paper. "I think he somehow got his hands on it and made sure it got to me."

"Why not mail it to you in Boston? Or take it to the sheriff?"

"Good questions that need answers."

She recognized the expression on his face. He was plotting something he hoped would lead to the killer. "We need to call the authorities," she urged in an attempt to keep him out of danger.

He pulled on his coat and moved toward the television stand. "Let's drop off the answering machine at the sheriff's office. They can listen to the message for themselves."

Lynne narrowed her eyes. That was way too easy. "Then what are we going to do?"

"First we're going to visit my father's grave." He headed toward the door. "There might be more letters or an indication of who left them."

"And then?"

"Then we're going to find what Rita wanted me to see."

Dear Rudolf,

What's wrong with people? I spent years being savagely abused and not one person noticed. Or even if they did, they turned a blind eye. But when I want to be invisible it feels as if everyone is butting their noses into my business.

First you.

And then your beer buddy, Rita King.

Why would she poke around your grave? It wasn't like she even bothered to attend your funeral. Stupid bitch.

I was going to take her to my special place.

*Why not enjoy her screams? But then I realized it
would be a sacrilege.*

*My special place is for exorcising my demons,
not for getting rid of the trash. I've chosen my
victims with exquisite care. I've spent years
anticipating their punishment. I couldn't defile
what has become my temple, could I?*

No.

*Rita King wasn't my enemy. She was a problem
that needed to be solved. And that's what I did.*

*I stomped my foot on the gas and rammed
directly into her. It was shocking how high she
flew before she landed on the icy street. She
looked dead, but I had to make sure, so I ran over
her like she was roadkill.*

*It seemed appropriate since she tried to do the
same thing to her husband.*

*Then I scooped up her broken body and left her
in a spot you know all too well, my friend.*

*I'm safe again and my attention has returned to
my next quarry.*

*Crimson blood stains the pure white snow. Life
spills from warm to frozen. Don't look. The pain
is gone.*

Chapter 23

Kir struggled to contain the impatience that sizzled through him as Lynne drove at a snail's pace to the cemetery. It wasn't her fault. The street was not only layered with ice, but the turnoff wasn't marked. It was dark enough that it would be easy to drive past the gate. Besides, his impatience had nothing to do with their careful pace.

He was still fuming from their recent trip to the sheriff's office.

It wasn't like he expected Kathy Hancock to be on duty 24/7. Even with a serial killer on the loose, she deserved a few hours to sleep. But when he'd handed over the answering machine, he'd hoped for more than a bored deputy telling him they'd eventually get around to listening to it.

It wasn't like they were overrun with clues on who was killing the good citizens of Pike. And even if they didn't believe Rita's death was more than an accident, they would surely want to discover what she'd found when she'd been at Rudolf's grave.

At last Lynne pulled through the open gate and weaved

through the graveyard. After parking in the middle of the narrow path, she left the truck running with the headlights directed toward Rudolf's headstone as they climbed out and walked the short distance.

Kir's lungs burned as he breathed in the frigid night air. People who lived in warm places had no idea that cold had a smell. It was sharp and steely, like a blade. And just as deadly.

Approaching his father's grave from the side, Kir pointed toward the footprints that were visible in the snow. "Someone was here."

"Yes." Lynne halted next to the marble headstone. Bending down she touched the dead flowers that had spilled out of the heavy stone urn. "It looks like they took whatever was here."

Kir studied the grave. The mound of loose dirt was covered by layers of undisturbed snow. In fact, the only sign of anyone having been nearby was the one set of footprints that he was assuming belonged to Rita. So how had the killer known she had found the letters?

Lifting his head, he glanced around. Although it was dark, it was easy to make out the nearby road. "It would be easy to see the grave from the street," he murmured his thoughts out loud.

Lynne pointed behind him. "Both streets."

Kir glanced over his shoulder. She was right. The graveyard seemed isolated because there were no nearby buildings and the front was blocked by a thick line of cedar trees. But if it was daylight, he would be easily visible to anyone passing the cemetery from the south or east.

"The killer must have been driving by and happened

to see Rita here," he said. "He might even have seen her pulling the letters from this urn."

She frowned at him. "Kir."

"I know." He held up his hands. "I'm just speculating."

She offered a grudging nod. "Okay. Let's say the killer did see her. Rita left you a message after she'd found something at the grave. So he didn't try to stop her from taking them."

Kir gave a slow nod. "It's possible he parked down the street to wait for her to leave the cemetery."

"Then he followed her to the café?"

Kir hesitated, trying to recall the exact layout of Pike. It wasn't a big town, but it'd been a long time since he'd lived there. "Rita said in the message she was going home," he muttered. "She lives in the opposite direction."

Lynne shrugged. "She could have decided she was hungry."

"I suppose." Kir wasn't satisfied. He didn't know much about Rita King, but if she was anything like his father, she would have saved every penny to buy booze. Eating out at a restaurant would have been a rare indulgence. "It was cold to be out walking."

Lynne shivered. "It's still cold."

It was their cue to leave, Kir decided. "I think we've seen all there is to see here."

She didn't hesitate, hurrying toward the truck and taking her place behind the wheel. Kir climbed in beside her.

"Now where?"

"The café," Kir said without hesitation.

"I'm pretty sure it's closed," Lynne warned, putting the truck in drive and easing her way over the snowdrift blocking the path. "They only serve breakfast and lunch there."

"I don't want to eat. I want to search the alley next to the building."

"Search it for what?"

"The letters." He held his hands toward the heater that was blasting hot air. "Or whatever Rita might have found at my father's grave."

They pulled out of the cemetery. "Wouldn't it be easier to search during the day?"

"I don't want anyone asking questions," he told her. "Not to mention the fact that there's a good chance the sheriff is going to block the alley off as a crime scene once they get around to listening to the tape."

Lynne snorted. "*If* they get around to it."

"True." Kir shrugged. "But I don't want to take a chance."

Lynne was silent as she concentrated on the slick streets. The wind had picked up, blowing the snow to create a fresh layer of ice. At last she pulled into the lot in front of the café and parked.

"You can stay in the truck. There's no point in both of us freezing."

She slowly turned her head, studying him with a narrowed gaze. "Do you know how many nights I've spent in the middle of a pasture pulling a calf? If anyone should stay in the truck, it's you. After all, you're the soft city boy."

"Soft?" He leaned across the console, pressing a lingering kiss against her lips. "I'm going to prove just how wrong you are." Another kiss. "Later."

"You promise?"

He nipped her lower lip, savoring her sweet taste. "You have my word. And my heart."

Swiftly she pulled back, her eyes wide. "Kir."

Kir swallowed a sigh. "Yeah, I know. My timing sucks," he admitted, cupping her cheek in his hand. They were parked beneath a streetlight that bathed her face in a silvery light, adding a hint of mystery to her beauty. His heart swelled, filling with an emotion that felt too big to be contained. As if it was going to burst out of him if he didn't share it. Unfortunately, this wasn't the time, and most certainly wasn't the place. "Put a pin in it and we'll revisit this conversation when we're back home."

She hastily scurried out of the truck, reaching behind the seat to pull out a heavy flashlight. Kir followed behind her, using the flashlight on his phone to penetrate the thick shadows of the alley. He pushed away the fear he'd just made an idiot of himself. Men in love were supposed to make idiots of themselves, weren't they? He'd worry later about finding a more graceful way to convince her they belonged together.

For now, he had enough to deal with searching from one end of the short alley to the other.

It didn't take long. Besides the dumpster there wasn't anything to see. The trash had either been collected by the sheriff's department to be searched through later, or no one ever bothered to enter the alley besides the owner of the café. He was betting on the latter.

"Nothing. Not even a stray piece of paper," he muttered in disgust, glancing along the foundations of the brick buildings. "I suppose it was a long shot." He glanced to the side, surprised to discover Lynne standing at the entrance to the alley with her hands on her hips. "Is something wrong?"

"It's too narrow."

With a frown he walked to stand next to her. "What's too narrow?"

"The alley." She spread her arms, indicating the width. "Only a compact car could fit between the buildings. And even then, it couldn't get past the dumpster."

"You're right." Kir cursed. How had he missed something so obvious?

Lynne shook her head in confusion. "So was the car chasing her and she ran down the alley?"

Kir tried to picture it. Had Rita been heading to the café? If so, why wouldn't she have run inside instead of entering the alley? Or had her destination been the alley? Maybe she'd been meeting someone there?

He shook his head. Even if Rita had been in the alley, it would have been awkward to try and kill her there. Why not wait for a more convenient location? "He would have had to back out and pull away after he hit her. It's hard to believe no one noticed anything."

"Especially if it happened around lunchtime," Lynne agreed.

Kir considered the various possibilities. At last he pointed straight ahead. "What's on the other side?"

Lynne took a step back, glancing around as if trying to orient herself. "Empty buildings, I think," she finally said. "It's been a while since I've been around here."

"Let's check it out."

Without waiting for her to agree, Kir was striding down the alley. There didn't appear to be anyone around, but it was possible someone might notice their flashlights and decide to call the sheriff. It would be his luck to have the sheriff show up and toss them in jail for trespassing, even if she couldn't be bothered to listen to the message Rita left.

Their footsteps crunched loudly as they exited the alley to halt on the frozen sidewalk. It was even darker on this side of the block than the other, and he realized the streetlights had burned out. Either no one had bothered to complain to the city, or Pike was too financially strapped to deal with the outage.

He glanced from side to side. Nothing but empty buildings. "Not much to see."

"No." She shook her head. "Pike seems to die a little more each year."

Kir started to sympathize only to stiffen as he caught sight of the store across the street. It was a low building that had cheap siding to make it look like a log cabin and a tin roof. Plastered on the large front window were several faded posters that advertised the various beers and spirits available inside. The door, however, was hidden by a heavy slab of plywood.

"Shit." He pointed across the street. "That used to be a liquor store."

"Yes. It closed down years ago."

"Eighteen years ago."

She glanced at him in surprise. "Did you know the owners?"

"No, but they shut down the store and moved away from Pike a few months after my dad was shot in the middle of this street."

"Oh." She glanced toward the street, her hand lifting to press against the center of her chest. "That was here?"

Kir nodded. "The owner . . ." His words trailed away as he forced himself to recall the night that had destroyed his father's life. It wasn't easy. Not after eighteen years of trying to block it from his mind. "I think his first name was Gordon. Anyway, he called the office to say he'd seen a man loitering in his parking lot. He suspected the guy was selling drugs."

"Your dad came to check it out?"

"Yep." Kir's mouth felt oddly dry. "He'd gone into the store to talk to Gordon, and when he came out he saw the suspect in this alley. He was crossing the street when the dealer pulled out a gun. A few seconds later the dealer was dead, and my father was lying in the street with a bullet in his head."

He said the words in clipped tones, battling back the image of his father lying in the dark street with blood pouring from his shattered skull.

"Did the liquor store owner blame himself?"

"I think so." Kir had a vague memory of a silver-haired man stopping by the hospital, tears in his eyes as he stood next to Rudolf's bed. "He packed up and moved away a few months later."

Lynne wrapped her arms around her waist. "I remember when it happened, but I didn't realize it was here. I'm sorry."

For a pained moment Kir was unable to look away from the spot in the street where his father had nearly died. Then, with a shake of his head, he turned back toward the alley. "It can't be a coincidence."

"What can't?"

He pointed toward the dumpster. "Rita's body being left here."

"Do you mean she decided to come to this location because she knew this was where your father was shot?"

"No." It had never felt right to assume Rita had left the cemetery and headed to the café instead of returning to her home as she'd said she was going to do. Still, there hadn't been any other explanation. Until now. "I don't think Rita came here at all. Not until she was already dead."

Lynne arched her brows. "The killer brought her here?"

"He could have run her down as she was leaving the graveyard, then loaded her into his vehicle." He shrugged. "Rita barely weighed a hundred pounds. It would have been easy to stuff her behind the dumpster."

"That makes sense." Lynne looked sick even as she made a visible effort to remain in control of her emotions. "Why would he follow her into town and run her down in front of a crowd of people when he could kill her in a more isolated area?"

"Exactly. Then he brought her here to dump the body." He swept his hand around the empty street. "If he parked on the street, I doubt anyone would have noticed his car. More importantly, I can't imagine there are any working cameras. Why have security for an empty building?"

"God." Lynne shuddered. "It's so horrible."

Kir moved to wrap an arm around Lynne's shoulders. "Let's go back to my dad's house."

She readily followed him back to the truck. He suspected she was eager to get away from the spot where Rita's broken body had so recently been found. He didn't blame her. It was a gruesome end for the poor woman.

"Do you have a specific reason you want to go to your dad's place?" she asked as she crawled behind the steering wheel.

He joined her in the truck. "There are some old papers I want to look through."

"Okay." She pulled out of the parking lot. "Let's swing by and pick up King. He's going to be ready for his dinner."

Dear Rudolf,

Our time together is nearing its end, old friend.

For so long I have depended on you to be my rock. You rescued me from the depths of hell. And while I was dragged back to the fiery pits, I never blamed you. You even helped me battle my bloodlust after I ended the screams.

I suppose it was too much to hope that the hunger would stay buried. It's too ferocious. Too consuming. And I wearied of the fight.

Why shouldn't I release my demons to feast on my enemies?

And still you were there.

I had to share my dark secrets with someone. Who else would I choose but you? The man who taught me the meaning of courage.

But every good thing comes to an end. Not only did you force me to stop you from interfering in my vengeance, but I am at the end of my list. I saved your precious vet for the last. Not because her death was bound to wound you, but because she has proven to be such a disappointment.

The others were selfishly cruel by nature. Like snakes slithering through the darkness, infecting the world with their poison.

Lynne . . . She is a sweet caring woman. Someone who offers nothing but kindness in a world where no one else gives a damn. Then she

*proved she is as damaged as the others. She
proved unworthy of my admiration.*

*And that was more painful than all the others
combined.*

*She has to be punished. And, if I am honest,
there has been an unexpected pleasure in watching
her squirm. She senses me. She knows I'm near,
but she can't see me.*

*I've savored her fear, and I regret that I don't
have the patience to continue the game.*

I'm once again invisible. Until I strike.

*Crimson blood stains the pure white snow. Life
spills from warm to frozen. Don't look. The pain
is gone.*

Chapter 24

Half an hour later, Lynne was entering Rudolf's old house with a frisky King in tow. She'd fed and walked him around the block despite the frigid air. And while the dog was ready for a longer jog, she wasn't prepared to risk his paws on the ice. Tomorrow she would take him to the office so she could spend her time between her appointments giving him the attention he needed.

Lynne pulled off her coat and boots in the kitchen, then poured out a large bowl of dog food before going in search of Kir.

She found him in a back bedroom that had been a study when Rudolf was alive. There was an old desk and a couple easy chairs, along with a dog bed the old man had never gotten around to throwing away. And in the far corner there was a glass case that held his prized fishing poles. At the moment it was stuffed with cardboard boxes Kir was shifting from one stack to another.

"The box is here somewhere," he muttered as she entered the room. "I should have marked what I put inside, but I . . ."

"Kir," she interrupted, moving to grab his arm.

He sent her a startled glance. "What?"

She firmly tugged on his arm, leading him out of the study and into the small living room. Then, halting next to the leather sofa, she pressed on his shoulders. "Sit down."

"But—"

She pressed harder. "Now."

He sank onto the worn cushions, his expression impatient. "What's wrong?"

She stood over him, her hands on her hips. "You need to take a break."

"I can't. Not while the killer is out there."

"And we're here together, with the doors locked and King on guard duty." On cue, the large dog galloped into the room, his tongue hanging out to drip slobber on the carpet.

Kir arched a brow. "What are you suggesting?"

"Dinner first."

"Okay." He started to lift himself off the sofa. "I can—"

She once again pushed on his shoulders. "Sit down and let me take care of it."

He sank back. "I didn't get to the grocery store. There's not a lot to choose from."

"I can manage." She pointed a finger in his face. "You stay here."

His lips twitched. "Yes, ma'am."

She turned toward the dog. "Keep an eye on him," she commanded. King barked, then with an easy leap he was on the sofa next to Kir.

Kir laughed. "Bossy," he chided, rubbing an affectionate hand on King's massive head.

"Partners," she corrected.

His expression softened and a dangerous emotion smoldered in his impossibly blue eyes.

"Partners," he whispered.

Sensations tingled through her body as she turned and scurried into the kitchen. She didn't mind the desire that heated her blood. Making love with Kir was an uncomplicated indulgence that brought her nothing but joy. In fact, if all she had to think about was cold nights spent in the heat of Kir's arms, everything would be perfect.

But Kir presented all sorts of complications. Not only because he'd started making himself at home. He'd also wiggled his way into a part of her heart that was too vulnerable to deal with betrayal. He could very easily shatter her.

After forcing herself to concentrate on warming the tomato soup and grilling two cheese sandwiches, Lynne carried the simple dinner into the living room. She smiled at the sight of Kir sprawled back in the cushions with King leaning heavily against him. His face was still tense, and there was a paleness to his skin that revealed the strain of the past few days, but at least he wasn't pacing around with that frenetic impatience.

She joined him on the sofa, and they ate the food in silence. It wasn't fancy, but it was warm, and Lynne sighed as she swallowed the last spoonful of soup.

Kir sat back to send her a lazy smile. "Not bad. Did you cook for your father?"

"When he was home." She thought back, surprised by the realization she'd rarely shared a meal with the older man. In fact, her most vivid memory was sitting in front of the television nibbling on a slice of frozen pizza. "I usually ate dinners by myself."

"Yeah, me too." He reached to grab her hand, threading their fingers together. "Were you lonely?"

"I didn't think about it at the time. I understood his job was demanding, and I wanted him to take care of the animals. But I always wished I had brothers and sisters so the house wasn't so empty." She leaned toward him, breathing deeply of his male scent. "What about you? Did you wish you weren't an only child?"

He lifted her hand to press her fingers to his lips. "Until my mother remarried, and I had a brood of step- and half-siblings."

She didn't miss the edge in his voice. "You're not close to them?"

"No. By the time my mom met her current husband and they started having kids I was in Boston concentrating on my career." He shrugged. "And to be honest, none of us tried very hard."

It was sad, but Lynne knew it was probably inevitable after Kir had decided to stay with his father. The sheer distance meant he would never be close with his mother and her new family.

"Once I asked Dad if he'd take my mom back if she returned to Pike," she murmured. "He told me that you can fix broken things, but they're never the same."

He held her gaze, brushing his lips over the back of her hand. "But you can learn from others' mistakes and do better."

"Do you think it's possible?"

"With the right person."

A flutter of excitement clenched her stomach. It felt like she was standing on the edge of a cliff, about to tumble into a bottomless valley.

Did she step back or take the plunge?

She leaned close enough to rest her head on his shoulder. "How can you be certain it's the right person?"

"There's nothing guaranteed in this life, but I know what my heart is telling me."

"What's that?"

He pressed his lips to the top of her head. "To grab on tight and refuse to let go."

The flutters became a flurry of exhilaration. She could barely breathe. "It's . . ."

"What?"

"A little scary," she admitted.

His lips skimmed to nuzzle her temple, his arm wrapping around her. Then, without warning, he was scooping her off the cushion to settle her in his lap. "Of all the things that are scary right now, this is the only thing that feels right," he told her.

She snuggled against his chest, refusing to allow the thought of the killer to shadow this moment. Tomorrow they would once again be on the hunt. Tonight was for them.

"I suppose that's true, although I should warn you that my life is crazy even without a serial killer on the loose," she warned. "I think one of the reasons my father never remarried was because he knew he made a terrible husband, and I'm just as bad. I miss dinners, sleep through movies, and show up to birthday parties covered in mud and smelling like cow dung."

His fingers trailed up and down her spine, igniting sparks of passion that made her quiver with longing. "I've eaten a lot of dinners alone, you can snore on my shoulder during any movie you want, and we'll make a joint agreement to avoid birthday parties if you happen to be smelling dung-like," he told her.

"I'm serious, Kir."

He cupped her chin in his hand, tilting back her head to meet his teasing gaze. "Me too. I love you, but I draw the line at cow dung and birthday cake."

She jerked. There it was. The "L" word.

"Kir," she breathed.

He smiled down at her. "I'm not taking it back. You're just going to have to get used to having me around."

She licked her lips. "And if you decide you want to leave Pike again?"

He lowered his head, capturing her lips in a slow, searching kiss. "You've taught me an important lesson, Dr. Lynne Gale," he said against her mouth.

Barely aware she was moving, Lynne lifted her arms to wrap them around his neck. "What lesson?"

"Home isn't a place," he told her. "It's a feeling."

She didn't know what to say to that. And in the end, it didn't matter. Not when he gently laid her on the cushions of the sofa and stretched out beside her. King grumbled at being dislodged and padded into the kitchen. Lynne and Kir barely noticed his departure as their lips locked and their bodies pressed together in a fierce, overwhelming need.

Lynne woke to discover herself alone on the sofa with a heavy cover tucked around her naked body. She yawned, reaching for her phone, which she'd left on the coffee table. Almost six o'clock. How had she slept so late?

A blush stained her cheeks as she recalled how she'd

spent the previous evening. It'd been past midnight when she'd finally fallen into a deep, dreamless sleep. It was no wonder she'd overslept this morning.

Tossing aside the blanket, Lynne pulled on her clothes and headed into the kitchen. She discovered a hot pot of coffee waiting for her and a recently fed King sleeping near the floor vent. But no Kir.

Usually at this point, Lynne would be sending up a silent prayer of thanks that her lover had the good sense to slip away. She preferred to wake alone. It allowed her to avoid the awkward morning after.

This morning, however, she knew beyond a doubt that Kir would never have left her without waking her to tell her where he was going. So where was he?

Moving through the house, she tracked him down in the back study.

Her breath lodged in her throat as she stood in the open door and studied the man who'd burrowed his way into her heart. He was dressed in jeans and a flannel shirt, but his hair hadn't been combed and there was a shadow of whiskers on his jaw. His dishevelment did nothing to dim his potent masculinity. In fact, it only made him more attractive. At the moment, however, she refused to acknowledge the tempting tingles of awareness that spread through her.

Instead she watched as he crouched next to a box, pulling out old photo albums and stacks of folders. "How long have you been up?" she asked.

He jerked his head around, clearly caught off guard. Then a slow, inviting smile curved his lips and he motioned her to join him. "Not more than half an hour."

Moving forward, she knelt next to him. "What are you looking for?"

He waved a hand toward the boxes that he'd lined up on the hardwood floor. "These came from my father's office after he was forced to retire."

Lynne glanced in the closest box. It was stuffed with trophies and medals that were mounted in velvet cases. "He had a lot of awards."

Kir reached to touch one of the trophies. "He was a hell of a sheriff. I wish . . ."

"I know." She covered his hand and gave his fingers a small squeeze. "What can I do to help?"

"Keep me company."

"I can do that."

Lynne watched in silence as Kir sifted through the various photo albums before turning his attention to the files. She understood how hard this was for him. He wasn't just dealing with the sudden loss of his father. He also had to deal with the possibility that a lunatic had snuck into this house and struck the killing blow.

It made it all so much worse.

"This is it," he at last said, flipping open the file to reveal a collection of newspaper clippings as well as sheets of typed paper.

"What are they?"

"The various reports from my father's shooting."

Lynne made a sound of surprise. "He kept them?"

"I tried to throw them away, but he insisted he needed to be reminded that he'd been injured performing his duty," Kir said, a hint of sadness in his voice. "He told me it didn't seem such a waste when he could cling to the belief that he'd been protecting the citizens of Pike from a dangerous criminal."

"I suppose that makes sense."

Kir sighed. "It would have been better if he could have looked to the future instead of dwelling on the past."

Lynne nodded, thinking of her own father. After he'd broken his hip and realized that his days of being a vet were over, he'd made the sudden decision to leave the area. He'd told her it was because the warmer weather eased the pain in his joints, but she suspected he'd known it would drive him crazy to see her headed out to work every day while he was forced to sit in the office. Or worse, stay home and watch television.

It was a shame Rudolf hadn't chosen to find a way to keep himself occupied. As Kir had said, dwelling on the past had only intensified his need to drown his sorrows.

"Easier said than done, I'm sure," she murmured.

"Yeah, and it didn't help that he was in constant pain."

Lynne touched his arm in sympathy. "You were looking for the file because you think it has something to do with Rita being left in that specific alley?"

"It's a possibility." He shrugged. "And right now I don't have any other clues to follow."

"Okay." Lynne couldn't imagine what they would find, but Kir needed her support. That was exactly what she was going to give him. "We know your dad was called by the local liquor store to investigate a suspicious person."

He nodded, holding up a sheet of paper. "This is my father's copy of his statement." He read directly from the report. "At ten fifty-five p.m. a call came into the station from Gordon Gallen at the Hometown Liquor Store."

"Gallen?" Lynne questioned in surprise. She'd been too

young when the liquor store had closed to pay attention to the place. Now she instantly recognized the name. It seemed an odd coincidence. "I wonder if he was any relation to Chelsea?"

"Possibly her grandfather."

"I'll ask Bernadine. She knows everyone in town."

Kir continued to read from the report. "My father arrived at the store at eleven fifteen and assisted Gordon to file a complaint, then he went to talk to the suspect." He halted, forced to clear his throat. "That's when the shooting took place."

Lynne hurriedly distracted him from the memory of his father's injuries. "What do you know about the suspect?"

"Delbert Frey," Kir told her. "A local drug dealer who my father had arrested a dozen times before."

"Why did he shoot your father?" she asked. "Loitering doesn't seem like it was that big of a deal."

"He was carrying enough crack on him to get him charged with trafficking." Kir's jaw tightened with frustrated anger. "That would have meant several years in the penitentiary, not the usual slap on the wrist."

"Did he have a partner?"

"None listed."

"What about a family?"

Kir shuffled through the papers in the file. "There's nothing in his rap sheet." He paused, glancing at one of the clippings. "Ah. This is the obituary section of the newspaper." He tilted it so she could see the faded newsprint as he read out loud. "Delbert Frey, thirty-seven years old, was cremated and laid to rest in a private ceremony. He was preceded in death by his parents. Surviving are his wife, one child, and a sister. Flowers and memorials can be sent to the Grange Funeral Home."

It was brief and to the point. As if the reporter had dashed it off at the last second. She shook her head in confusion. "Why didn't they give any names?"

Kir dropped the clipping back into the file. "They were probably trying to protect the family," he said. "I doubt they were very popular in town."

She nodded. He was probably right. She could remember the public outrage when it was discovered that Rudolf was in the hospital, fighting for his life after a lowlife criminal had put a bullet in his head. If the drug dealer hadn't died in the shoot-out, there was a chance he might have been hauled to the town square and beaten to death.

"Frey." She tested the name, feeling a vague sense that she should recognize it. "Does it mean anything to you?"

Kir shrugged. "My father probably mentioned him, but I don't remember anything in particular."

"What about witnesses?"

He sent her a startled glance. "I'm not sure, but that's an excellent thought. It's possible the person sending the letters to my father wasn't involved in the shooting, but simply witnessed it." He placed the file back in the box and surged to his feet. "I need to go to the sheriff's office to read through the official report. It should reveal any witnesses. It might also have more information on Delbert Frey."

Lynne rose to stand beside him. "Do you think they'll let you see it?"

A hard smile curved his lips. "One way or another."

She believed him. Kir could be charming, funny, and a delightful companion. But he'd survived an alcoholic father and built a million-dollar business with his bare hands. There was nothing he couldn't achieve once he set his mind on a goal.

Relieved he was going to be spending the morning at the sheriff's office and not out searching for the killer, Lynne turned her thoughts to her own plans for the day. "I need to get home to change for work."

He nodded. "I'll ride along and pick up my SUV at your house."

A half hour later they were pulling to a halt in front of her house and Kir was climbing out of her truck.

She reached across to grab his arm. "Kir."

He glanced at her in surprise. "What?"

She wrinkled her nose, not sure why she felt a sudden chill of premonition. Almost as if something was whispering in her ear that danger was near.

"Be careful."

Chapter 25

Kir glared down at the deputy. Anthony was a heavyset man with an unfortunate squint who was guarding the entrance to the sheriff's office. The deputy had started the encounter with a hint of smug superiority. He'd informed Kir that there was no way in hell a civilian was pawing through official sheriff reports. And even hinted that he might write Kir a ticket for wasting his time.

That was when Kir had taken command of the situation.

He might not have his father's macho bluster, but he could be as intimidating and ruthless as any CEO. Now the younger man had lost the color from his face and he looked like he was wondering if he would fit beneath the desk. Kir could tell him the answer was no. Not unless the deputy was a contortionist, which seemed unlikely.

"I'm not leaving until I see my father's file," he told the man.

"I—"

His protest was interrupted as the door behind him was jerked open to reveal Kathy Hancock.

"I'll deal with this," the sheriff said, pointing toward Kir. "Come into my office."

Kir circled the deputy's desk and headed through the open door. Kathy stepped aside, closing the door behind him.

"Has anyone told you that you're a pain in the ass?" she asked.

Kir shrugged. "Not today."

"Well now someone has." Kathy settled behind her desk, nodding toward a chair in the center of the floor. "Sit down."

For a stark minute, Kir was frozen in place. It'd been eighteen years since he'd stepped foot in this office. Now the sight of it hit him with a physical force.

He could remember peering out the long, narrow windows that overlooked the town square. Or zooming his toy cars over the wood-planked floor while he and his mother waited for Rudolf to finish up his paperwork and take them to dinner. Or the memorable weekend his father had made him stand in the corner for endless hours after he'd been caught smoking in the garage.

Glancing around he realized he could barely recognize the place. The wooden floor had been covered by a thick carpet and the windows were hidden behind heavy drapes. The leather furniture had been replaced with IKEA close-out specials, with lots of shelves and filing cabinets on rollers. Even the chairs had wheels. And the walls had been stripped bare of the framed pictures of the town that his father had collected over the years, to be replaced with bulletin boards covered with MOST WANTED posters.

It looked sterile, and bland, and the sight of it caused a visceral pain inside Kir that nearly sent him to his knees.

Clenching his hands, he sucked in a slow, deep breath.

And then another one. At last he managed to make his way to the chair and sit down, although his emotions remained raw.

Kathy watched him with a frown, easily sensing his distress. "Why are you terrifying my deputy?"

Kir glanced toward her desk, which appeared remarkably tidy. His father usually had stacks of files and notebooks filled with his scribbled reminders or details of his ongoing cases.

"Did you listen to the tape?" he abruptly demanded. He hadn't expected to see the sheriff. He wasn't going to waste the opportunity to discover if she had any new information.

There was a short silence before she gave a shake of her head. "No."

"Christ." He shoved himself upright, the chair wheeling away. "Are you deliberately trying to let the serial killer run loose?"

She sent him a fierce scowl. "Sit down and shut up."

"I—"

"Do you want me to explain or not?"

Kir ground his teeth, grabbing the chair to steady it before sitting down. "This had better be good."

Kathy pressed her hands flat against the empty desk, her expression sour. "I haven't listened to the tape because I've turned the case over to the task force that's arriving today."

Kir blinked. He hadn't been expecting that. "What task force?"

"When I was in Madison to deliver the evidence from the crime scenes, I asked to meet with the Feds. It's obvious we don't have the staff or the resources necessary to track down the killer."

That was astonishingly reasonable, Kir silently conceded. And completely out of character for the sheriff who'd been aggressively possessive about the investigation. He studied her in confusion. "Why didn't you say so?"

"Because I don't answer to you," she snapped.

Her harsh response rasped against his exposed nerves. He leaned forward, his eyes narrowed with annoyance. "All I want is for the killer to be stopped," he said between clenched teeth. "Why are you trying to make Lynne and me the enemy?"

"You're interfering in official law enforcement business. I have enough on my hands without amateur sleuths bumbling around creating chaos."

"It's more than that. From the beginning you've had a chip on your shoulder."

Kathy flushed. "Bullshit."

Kir refused to back down. "Are you trying to claim you weren't determined to pin the murders on Lynne?"

"I was following the evidence," the sheriff stubbornly insisted. "Not only were the victims knocked out by dart guns that are regularly used by vets, but the sedatives could be directly traced to her clinic. Or have you forgotten that fact?"

"That was easily explained by Chelsea."

"Too easily."

Kir stiffened. There was an edge in her voice that made the hairs on his nape stand on end. "What are you talking about?"

A humorless smile curved the woman's lips. "Did you

ever consider the possibility that your girlfriend convinced her lover to seduce Chelsea?"

"Why would she do that?"

"To have a fall guy in case things went south." Kathy said the words with a coup de grâce flourish. As if she'd made some point that should have stunned Kir with its brilliance. Instead he was baffled by her logic.

"So who's the fall guy? Chelsea or Nash?"

"Either one. Maybe both." She made a sound of annoyance. "Neither one had the brains to realize they were pawns."

Kir remained confused. "Why would Lynne go to the trouble of stealing her own drugs? Wouldn't it be easier to convince one of them to steal from another vet? Or even to buy the drugs in Madison or Green Bay?"

Kathy's jaw tightened. Obviously, she didn't have an answer. Instead she sat back in her chair with a huff. "As I said, I was just following the evidence."

Kir shook his head. He accepted that the sheriff had to interview Lynne when the dart gun and sedatives were discovered. But the fact that the older woman had continued to place Lynne at the top of her suspect list, even after it was obvious the items had been stolen, went beyond normal caution.

"You wanted it to be her why?"

Kathy glanced toward the bulletin board, as if seeking inspiration. "I wanted the case solved," she finally muttered. "She looked guilty."

"To use your own charming phrase . . . bullshit."

"You're blinded by your feelings for the vet."

"I'm not the only one blinded," he shot back. "I'm at least honest enough to admit my feelings."

"You want me to admit my feelings?" There was a brittle pause before Kathy released a sharp bark of laughter. "Fine. I quit."

Once again Kir was caught off guard. "Quit?"

The color drained from Kathy's face, leaving her looking pale and oddly vulnerable. "When my term as sheriff is over, I'm leaving Pike."

"You're leaving?" Kir struggled to wrap his mind around what she was saying. "Why?"

She shrugged. "Because I've discovered what I've always feared."

"And what's that?"

"I shouldn't be a sheriff." Her gaze moved to the windows that were covered by the thick drapes. It seemed like a metaphor. While his father had cherished the view of the town, Kathy had done everything in her power to block it out. "At least not in Pike."

"Is this because of the serial killer?"

"No, this has been coming for a long time. Probably from the day I took the job."

Kir was genuinely dumbfounded. For as long as he could remember, this woman had been working to take his father's position. She'd started as a part-time juvenile officer before being promoted to a deputy sheriff. Now she was just going to walk away?

"I don't understand. It's what you wanted, isn't it?"

"I thought so." She ran her hands over the desk, as if trying to find comfort in the faux wood. "But let's say that it didn't happen as I expected."

"Because of my father's shooting?"

"Yes. He was a fixture in this town. They couldn't imagine anyone else as sheriff. It didn't help that he was removed from office as a hero." Her hand moved to touch the star sewn onto the front of her uniform. Her fingers lingered, clearly reluctant to let go of the badge. "I was never given the chance to prove I was up for the job."

Kir frowned. She couldn't be insinuating that his father's tragic misfortune was the reason she'd failed? "That wasn't his fault."

"Maybe not." She hunched a shoulder. "But it was easier to blame him than to blame myself."

"Why would you blame yourself?"

Kathy studied his face, as if searching for some hidden emotion. "Your father never told you, did he?"

"Told me what?"

She rose to her feet, pacing toward a shelf that held several potted plants. Kir wondered how they survived without sunlight.

"He wasn't supposed to be on duty that night," Kathy blurted out, her back to him.

Kir gripped the arms of his chair. "The night he was shot?"

She nodded. "It was my shift."

The floor seemed to buckle beneath Kir. As if his entire world had just been turned upside down.

For eighteen years he'd lived with the repercussions of that night. The months of painful physical therapy after his father had left the hospital. The deep depression after Rudolf learned he couldn't return to his job. The drinking. The fights with his mother until she'd packed her bags to leave forever.

"Why did my dad take the call?" he finally demanded.

She kept her back turned. "I was home with . . . with the flu."

There was something dodgy in her answer. Why? It had been a Friday night. Had she been out with a boyfriend? Maybe a girlfriend? Had there been a party she couldn't bear to miss?

"So . . ." His mouth felt so dry he could barely speak.

"I should have been the one shot." She turned to face him, her expression defensive.

Kir wanted to agree. How different would his life have been if Rudolf hadn't been injured? Certainly the older man would have stayed as the sheriff, and it was doubtful he would ever have become an alcoholic, which meant his mother might very well have stayed.

Then again, would he have developed the grim drive needed to start his own business? Or have learned to search for loyalty and kindness and independence in the woman he hoped to make his wife?

Who could say?

He released a slow, shaky breath. "No one should have been shot," he forced himself to say.

"If I hadn't called in sick—"

"The only one who is guilty is Delbert Frey," he interrupted. He didn't feel sympathy for Kathy Hancock. She wasn't a victim of circumstances. She'd made choices that had consequences. But she hadn't been the one to pull the trigger. There was only one person who had destroyed Rudolf Jansen's life. "And he's dead."

Her mouth twisted into a humorless smile. "I might have accepted that if the entire town didn't whisper behind my back, blaming me."

Kir snorted. "That's your imagination."

"And I suppose your father's resentment was my imagination as well?"

"Yes," he said without hesitation. For all of Rudolf Jansen's many faults, he was never one to cower and point fingers at others. He took his hits on the chin and kept his mouth shut. It didn't make him right or wrong, that was just how he was. "My father never held you responsible."

"He did. It was in his eyes." Her voice rose an octave, her face darkening to a weird shade of magenta. "Just as it was in your eyes."

Kir shoved himself out of the chair, surprised to discover that his legs threatened to buckle. Long ago he'd been stupid enough to get into a boxing ring with a friend who'd challenged him to a bout. The friend had promised he wouldn't hit him in the face, and Kir had ridiculously assumed that gave him the upper hand. It'd taken three body blows to send him to his knees.

He felt exactly like he did then.

"My eyes?" He met her accusing gaze with a frown. "I didn't even know you were supposed to be on duty."

She licked her lips. "No, but you thought I was responsible for ignoring your father's warnings that there was a serial killer in town."

"You did."

"No one believed him." She clenched her hands, glaring at him in frustration. "He told a thousand crazy stories. But then the women started dying and you returned with your judgmental attitude. That's why . . ." Her words trailed away.

"Why what?"

Something raw and painful darkened the woman's eyes. "I suppose that's why I wanted to believe Lynne was responsible for the killings."

Kir tried to follow her convoluted logic. An impossible task. "That doesn't make any sense."

"It was obvious from the moment you returned to Pike that you had a thing for Dr. Lynne Gale. It would have served you right if she was the killer."

Kir flinched. It was one thing for Kathy to behave like a petulant child because she didn't feel like she was getting the respect she deserved. Or to bluff her way through a job she was obviously incompetent to hold. It was another to try and land an innocent woman in jail. Or worse, to allow the people she was supposed to protect to be hunted like animals. "You know, your petty insecurities might very well be the reason Rita and all the others are dead."

The color once again receded from her face, leaving her a shocking shade of ash. "I realize that now. Too late."

Kir swallowed his words of fury. There was no way to change the past. The woman's selfish decisions had created havoc in Pike, but right now it was more important to concentrate on the future.

"Maybe not too late. What do you know about the night my dad was shot?"

She jerked, as if he'd punched her. "I told you, I had the flu—"

"I'm not interested in why Dad was on duty," he sharply interrupted. "I'm asking about the details of what happened when he got to the liquor store."

"Oh." She looked impatient. "I don't know what sort of details you want. Rudolf got a call from the local liquor store that someone was hanging around the parking lot peddling drugs. When he got there he took a statement and then went in search of the perp. He was crossing the street when the dealer pulled a weapon and they exchanged gunfire."

He ignored her offhand tone. He needed information, not another bout of self-pity. "Were there any witnesses?"

Kathy frowned, as if trying to recall the events of the night. "Just the store owner."

"And the shooter was alone?"

"Yep."

"Were there any cameras in the area?"

Her impatience became more pronounced as she planted her fists on her hips. "Not that I know of. Your father gave his statement and all the evidence corroborated what he said. It was an open-and-shut case so there was no need for an investigation."

That was no big surprise. Pike was a small town with limited resources. If Rudolf's explanation was backed up by the store owner, everyone would have been happy to close the file and move on.

"What do you know about Delbert Frey?"

Kathy glanced away. Was she trying to remember the man? Or was she hiding her expression? Impossible to know for sure.

"He was a regular guest in lockup. Petty theft. Drunk and disorderly. Drugs. A real creep."

"Where did he get his weapon?"

"I think it was stolen."

"From someone local?"

"I don't remember."

Kir swallowed a curse. It felt as if the woman was deliberately keeping her answers vague. As if she didn't want to give away more information than absolutely necessary. "Did Delbert come from Pike?"

"No. I think he grew up in Grange and his wife came from Madison," she said. "I remember her sister came to pick her up the day after the shooting. She didn't even bother to arrange a funeral for her husband."

Kir considered his limited options. He wasn't ready to give up on his suspicion that the killer had some connection to that night. Unfortunately, he was running out of means to get more information.

"I want to see the files from my father's shooting," he abruptly demanded. If nothing else there might be a way to contact the liquor store owner listed in the report. Or maybe Delbert Frey's wife.

"Come back this afternoon and ask the task force."

Kir scowled. "Why can't you get them for me?"

She folded her arms over her chest, the very image of implacable resistance. "I'm no longer on the case."

"But—"

"I won't tell you again," Kathy interrupted. "Come back this afternoon."

"Shit." Kir whirled on his heel and headed for the door. There was no point in trying to argue with the woman. He'd do as she said and return that afternoon. Maybe someone on the task force would be willing to listen to him.

Until then, he intended to search Rita's house. There was a very small possibility she might have returned home before she was murdered. If the letters were still there, he intended to find them before the killer did.

Chapter 26

It was midmorning when Lynne returned to the office. She'd spent the past few hours with her intern driving from one end of the county to the other. Farm calls were always a draining, physical ordeal, but the brutal weather made them even more difficult. She was frozen to the bone by the time she'd peeled off her outer clothing and entered her office.

Like an angel from heaven, Bernadine followed behind her, placing a steaming mug of coffee on the desk.

"You sit down and warm up," the woman commanded.

"Thanks." Still shivering, Lynne slid into her seat and cupped the mug in her hands. "I'm becoming more convinced with every passing day that my dad made the right choice to flee to sandy beaches and sunny skies."

Bernadine heaved a small sigh. "I miss him."

Lynne sipped her coffee. She'd always wondered if Bernadine had harbored a secret love for her employer, but she'd never tried to probe. She adored the older woman and would never do anything to hurt or embarrass her.

"Me too." Lynne wrinkled her nose. "Especially now."

"There's evil in this town." Bernadine pursed her lips. "You should go spend some time with your dad. Get away from this place for a while."

Lynne smiled wryly. "You sound like Kir."

"That's not a bad thing, is it?" Bernadine's expression softened. Clearly she'd fallen victim to Kir's potent charm. "He strikes me as a smart, highly competent young man."

"Yes." Lynne smiled. "He is."

"And he's not hard on the eyes."

"Not hard at all," Lynne readily agreed.

Bernadine cleared her throat, as if considering whether to speak the words hovering on her lips. "Perhaps I shouldn't say anything," the older woman said in an apologetic tone, "but you've done worse."

Lynne felt a stab of regret. It didn't feel fair to compare the men she'd dated over the years to Kir. They hadn't been bad men. Not even Nash, despite his weaknesses. But they'd never been right for her, and in her mind they would never rival Kir. Not on any level.

"Yeah," she breathed.

Bernadine studied her with a searching gaze. Lynne struggled to keep her expression from revealing all the emotions she wasn't prepared to share.

"Is he returning to Boston?"

"We haven't really discussed the future." Lynne took another sip of her coffee, her stomach clenching as she allowed herself to recall how Kir was spending his morning. "Right now it's enough to stay alive."

"God, yes." Bernadine clicked her tongue. "We are all praying the monster is caught and put behind bars. Better yet, put in his grave. The sooner the better."

Lynne set aside her coffee. They were going to need more than prayers. "That reminds me."

"Yes?"

"Do you know anything about Delbert Frey?"

Bernadine stared at her with a blank expression. "Who?"

"He was the drug dealer who shot Rudolf Jansen."

"Oh, I remember that." Bernadine shuddered. "Just awful."

"Did you know the shooter?"

"Not really." Bernadine shook her head. "I'd heard his name around town. He was always causing trouble."

"What sort of trouble?"

Bernadine glanced away, as if trying to capture some elusive memory. "It seems like I remember something." She snapped her fingers. "Oh, yes. There was some sort of fight at the trailer park. They had to call in the state police and everything."

"The trailer park that Sherry owned?"

"It must have been. I'm not sure there's ever been any other trailer park in town."

"What happened?"

Bernadine leaned toward her. Like all people did when they were about to share some juicy gossip. "I wasn't there, of course, but I heard some people talking, and they claimed Delbert Frey was beating his wife and one of the neighbors tried to stop him. The neighbor ended up in the hospital, barely clinging to life, and Delbert ended up on the street after he was evicted from his home. They also said he threatened to burn the entire town to the ground."

A sharp stab of distaste sliced through Lynne. She

didn't remember the man, but she'd met others like him. They were so angry with the world that they tried to destroy everything and everyone around them.

"Do you know his wife's name?"

Bernadine considered the question. "It was something odd. Marrow?" She shook her head. "No, that's not right. Merrill? Yes, that was it. Merrill."

"What do you know about her?"

"Nothing." Bernadine lifted her hands in a gesture of apology. "They never came to this clinic. To be honest, I don't think they mixed with the rest of town. At least not the decent folk."

Lynne leaned forward, opening her laptop. Then she typed a name in the search engine.

"Merrill Frey," she said out loud. "It isn't a common name. I wonder if I can find some information on her."

Bernadine moved around the desk, allowing her to see the computer screen. "Why are you so interested?"

"Kir suspects the killer's obsession with his father might have started the night Rudolf was shot," Lynne said, distracted as she scanned through the links popping up.

"That was twenty years ago."

Lynne's lips parted, only to snap shut. She didn't want to reveal that Rita had left a message for Kir. Not only because she didn't want people gossiping about the woman and the way she might have died, but it was possible the sheriff would want to keep the information secret. Her personal opinion of Kathy Hancock and her staff didn't mean she wasn't anxious for the killer to be caught and convicted.

"It's just a theory."

"I suppose it's as good as any other."

"Exactly." Lynne concentrated on the computer screen.

There were plenty of hits on businesses and a few people with the last name Merrill. Even a Facebook page with a cat called Merrill.

"There's no Merrill Frey," she muttered in frustration. Then a link to a newspaper announcement caught her eye. "Wait. Merrill Bowen-Frey weds Ernie Rucker from Warsaw."

"What's the date?"

She clicked the link. "2005. A couple years after Delbert was killed."

"That could be her."

Lynne read through the short announcement. There wasn't anything beyond the bare facts that they'd been wed at the courthouse in Warsaw and planned a short honeymoon in Green Bay.

"Merrill Rucker." Lynne typed the name in the search window. "Maybe I can get an address or where she works. . . ." Lynne's words trailed away as the obituary popped onto the computer screen. She leaned forward, her heart lurching at the sight. "No."

With a shaky hand, she clicked on the link. It had to be another Merrill Rucker, right? What were the odds that the woman had died just a few years after her first husband?

But it wasn't another Merrill Rucker. And worse, she hadn't just died. She'd been brutally murdered.

"What is it?"

"She's dead," Lynne rasped, sitting back in her seat as she tried to regain command of her shaken composure.

Bernadine made a sound of surprise. "She must have been young. Was it a car wreck?"

Lynne shook her head. "She was found murdered in her backyard New Year's Day 2007."

"Murdered?" she demanded in disbelief. "Are you serious?"

"Her throat was slit."

Bernadine swayed, grasping the back of Lynne's chair. Obviously, the older woman had the same stunned reaction as Lynne. "My God. Just like here," the older woman muttered. "How did it happen?"

With an effort, Lynne forced herself to lean forward and reread the article. It was high on drama and sketchy on details. "There isn't much information," she said. "Just that the body of Merrill Rucker was found naked in her backyard with her throat slit."

"Did they find the killer?"

Lynne skimmed to the end of the article. "They arrested her husband, but they eventually released him due to a lack of evidence."

"Where is he now?"

There was no further information in the article. Lynne clicked back to the search engine and typed in the name Ernie Rucker. She found a dozen links to the trial, and one that connected to his high school graduation. But there was nothing after 2007.

At least no public information.

"There's no record of him. As if he disappeared." A chill spread through her, an icy dread that was intense enough to make her teeth chatter. "I need to tell Kir."

She was reaching for her phone when the sharp ring

of a bell echoed down the hallway. The front door had just opened.

"Sounds like your next appointment is here," Bernadine said, hustling out of the office to greet the client.

Lynne glanced at her watch. She had two more appointments and then she was free for lunch. She'd wait until then to call.

Kir drove toward Rita's house with a prickling sense of foreboding.

He tried to tell himself he should be relieved. The task force that Kathy Hancock promised was going to arrive in a few hours and they would surely be capable of tracking down the murderer. Pike was too small to hide a serial killer.

But he couldn't shake the sensation that the clock was ticking. And that they couldn't wait for anyone to ride to the rescue.

It didn't matter if his sense of impending doom came from his frustration with the sheriff and his certainty that her incompetence had put Lynne in danger. He had to keep moving, keep trying to track down the killer before he could strike again.

Circling the town square, he was headed toward Rita's house when he glimpsed the steeple in the distance. The sight abruptly reminded him that he wanted to speak to Pastor Ron Bradshaw.

He angled toward the church, his mind still sorting through his encounter with the sheriff. Someday he was going to have to deal with her confession that she should have been on duty the night his dad was shot, and the fact that her wounded pride had allowed her to ignore Rudolf's belief a monster was writing him letters.

Not that he was going to place all the blame on the woman's shoulders. She couldn't have known what would happen when she called in sick. And she'd been right when she claimed no one had believed Rudolf's drunk ramblings, including Kir himself.

Still, he needed to find some sort of peace with the past.

A worry for another day, he acknowledged as he parked in the graveled lot next to the church. He was just switching off the engine when he caught sight of a figure darting out of the front door and scurrying down the street.

Was that Chelsea Gallen? It was hard to tell since she'd been bundled in a heavy parka with a stocking cap pulled over her hair. But he could have sworn it was Lynne's ex-receptionist.

After climbing out of his SUV, he moved up the steps and entered the church. Instantly he was surrounded by the humid warmth that only came from an old-fashioned boiler. It drove away the chill in his bones but left behind a moist layer of heat on his skin. Not the most pleasant sensation.

Glancing around the shadowed pews, he noticed the altar that had once been decorated with Randi's flower arrangements. Now it looked . . . barren. As if it were mourning the passing of the woman.

Kir frowned at his odd musing, wondering if stress was affecting his brain. He was a tediously logical person. Not someone who believed in omens or spirits or premonitions.

Thankfully, his thoughts were interrupted by Bradshaw. The pastor stepped into the nave, a smile pasted on his face.

"Welcome to . . ." His words stumbled to a halt, his expression becoming hostile as he eyed Kir. "Not again."

"The proverbial bad penny," Kir quipped. "Was that Chelsea Gallen I just saw leaving?"

The pastor clenched his teeth. He clearly wanted to tell Kir to go to hell, but he bit back his words. Was he afraid Kir might reveal his secret connection to Randi Decker? Probably.

"She stopped by to ask if she could speak at Nash's funeral." Something that might have been genuine sympathy darkened his eyes. "Unfortunately, I had to tell her that it would be up to his mother to decide who would be allowed to have a part in the service."

Kir arched a brow. "You're officiating Nash's funeral?"

Bradshaw looked at Kir in surprise. "He was a member of my flock, even if he didn't attend as regularly as his mother might have wanted." He smoothed his hands down his chunky sweater. "In fact, I'm preparing my sermon now. So, if you don't mind . . ."

Kir folded his arms over his chest. He wasn't going anywhere until he had the answers he wanted. "I have a few questions."

The pastor rolled his eyes. "Of course you do."

"These questions aren't personal. These are about my father."

"What about him?"

"I want to know what happened the day the two of you met."

"I already told you. And as I said, I have work to do."

"This is important, Bradshaw," Kir snapped as the man waved a dismissive hand.

Bradshaw stiffened with a defensive anger. "So is my sermon."

Kir ground his teeth. He didn't want to bully the man into answering. Not this time. What he needed wasn't a confession, but a detailed account of exactly what Rudolf Jansen had told him on that fateful day. He was only going to get that if he could convince the man that he wasn't his enemy.

"I'm sorry," he forced himself to apologize, his tone strained. "I need your help." He held Bradshaw's gaze. "Please."

A portion of the man's stiffness eased. "Why?"

Kir considered how much he wanted to reveal. Right now, the only person in Pike he trusted was Lynne. Everyone else remained suspects. "I think the day my dad came to this church he'd discovered something about the killer," he told the pastor.

Bradshaw looked confused. "That was before any of those poor souls were murdered."

"I know, but I think the killer was already in Pike."

The man arched his brows, as if considering the possibility. "You know, I recently heard rumors that your father claimed to be getting letters from a crazed lunatic before his death."

"Yes, he was," Kir said in firm tones. "I'm assuming they must have given him some clue to the identity of the person sending him the letters."

There was a short pause before the pastor asked the obvious question. "Did he tell you who it was?"

"Not in so many words." Kir reached into the pocket of his leather coat to remove the list, holding it in front of Bradshaw's face. "He left the answer with you."

Chapter 27

Bradshaw glanced toward the paper with a confused expression. Kir had no way to know if it was genuine or not.

"What is that?" the pastor asked.

"The note my father left with you," Kir said.

"Oh, I remember." Bradshaw glanced back at Kir. "What does it have to do with the killer?"

"I'm not sure, beyond the fact that it's a list of initials that correspond to the victims."

"You . . ." The pastor's mouth hung open, as if he couldn't form the words. "Is that a joke?" he eventually demanded.

"See for yourself." Kir unfolded the paper and turned it so Bradshaw could see the column of initials. "Sherry Higgins. Randi Decker. Madeline Decker. Nash Cordon." He pointed toward the bottom line. "I'm worried that the last initials refer to Dr. Lynne Gale."

The color leached from Bradshaw's face. "Did your father write this?"

"No."

"Then where did he get it?"

Kir's lips twisted. If he had that answer, he wouldn't

be standing in this church digging for information. "I'm assuming he got it from the killer."

"He sent it to him?"

Kir heaved a harsh sigh. "Perhaps. After my father's death I discovered someone had broken into his house to steal the letters." He waved the paper. "It's possible the killer was trying to get this back."

Bradshaw frowned. It didn't take a genius to realize that Kir had more questions than answers. "Why send it if he didn't want your father to have it?"

"Cold feet, maybe? Perhaps my father started to put clues together and it spooked the killer." Kir shrugged. The explanation didn't feel right. His father had told him the letters he was receiving were filled with gruesome desires. As if the person writing them was wallowing in his self-indulgent fantasies. Why suddenly send a boring list of initials? Kir made a sound of impatience. "Or maybe he found the list," he continued. "Whatever happened, I think my father was desperate to keep it out of the hands of the killer. That's why he gave it to you for safekeeping."

"Why me? Why not the sheriff?"

That one was easy to answer. "Because the sheriff didn't believe him."

Bradshaw didn't look convinced of Kir's logic. "Surely he had friends he could trust?"

Kir considered the people who'd been a part of his father's life toward the end. Rita. Perhaps a couple other drinking buddies. Certainly no one who could be depended on to keep their lips shut. Plus, Rudolf was still a sheriff at heart. He would never put one of his buddies in danger.

"I'm still trying to work it out in my mind," he vaguely told the pastor. "Which is why I need your help."

"Okay." Bradshaw nodded, although there was no missing his hesitation. The pastor didn't really want to get involved, and Kir couldn't blame him. There was a killer on the loose. And if Kir was right, then both his father and Rita had been murdered when they'd gotten too close. "I'll do what I can," the pastor offered.

"Tell me what happened the day my father gave you the note."

Bradshaw furrowed his brow. "It's hard to remember exactly."

"You told me after the funeral that you were arriving at the church when my dad stopped by."

"Yes." The pastor slowly nodded. "I was unlocking the front door when he pulled into the parking lot and waved his arm to catch my attention."

"Then what?"

"He climbed the steps and introduced himself. We chatted for a few minutes and then I asked him to come inside. He refused."

"That's when he asked you to speak at his funeral?"

Bradshaw nodded. "I was surprised since he didn't attend my church, but he insisted."

"Did he act like he'd been drinking?"

Bradshaw looked shocked by the question. "No. I would never have let him get back in his truck if I thought he was drunk."

Kir nodded. His father had many faults, but as far as Kir knew he'd never gotten behind the wheel when he was inebriated.

So what had been in the older man's head that caused him to worry about his funeral? Did he have a premonition? No. Kir shook his head. His father didn't believe in anything remotely mystical. He was a lawman who dealt in hard facts. Which meant he must have realized he'd done something to alarm the killer.

"Was he nervous?" Kir asked the pastor. "Afraid?"

"He said he was tired."

"Tired?" Kir frowned. Did Rudolf mean he hadn't slept well? Or that something was weighing on him?

"I thought perhaps he was sick, but he denied it," Bradshaw retorted. "I think he even said he was as healthy as a horse. That's why I was afraid he might have deliberately fallen down the stairs when I heard about his death."

It took Kir a second to realize what the man was implying. "Suicide?"

"I don't judge."

Kir snorted. "Rudolf might have been willing to drink himself into an early grave, but he would never have deliberately broken his own neck," he said in firm tones. Even when Rudolf was at his lowest point, he'd never been suicidal. He would have considered it the easy way out. "Someone else ensured that he fell down those stairs."

"Someone else?" Bradshaw repeated. "Are you saying he was murdered?"

"I think it's possible." Kir paused, allowing the pastor to consider the possibility. Then he turned the attention back to the past. "What else did my father say to you?"

Bradshaw's fingers nervously tugged on the sleeves of his sweater, his face pale. "I really don't remember."

Kir narrowed his eyes. Was the man being honest? Or was he being deliberately evasive? Hell, it was possible his father had never come to the church at all. Kir only had Bradshaw's word, which he'd already proven was less than dependable.

Kir grimaced. What choice did he have but to accept the man was telling the truth? At least until he could prove he was lying. "He gave you the note, right?"

"Yes." Bradshaw continued to fidget with his sweater. A fine layer of sweat covered his face. "He'd asked me to arrange his funeral and I told him he needed to make an appointment so we could discuss the details. He promised he would call." He glanced away, seemingly shaken by the thought that Rudolf had been killed. "I remember that he stepped closer to me to hand me the note and he lowered his voice as if he was afraid someone might overhear him when he asked me to keep it until after the funeral. In fact, he made me swear I wouldn't let anyone see it except his son."

"You didn't think that was odd?"

"I've had a lot of odd requests over the years. One elderly lady insisted that I be in the room when the undertaker prepared her body, and another asked me to speak at her cat's funeral. Last year a man insisted his funeral service be nothing but Beatles lyrics," the pastor nervously babbled. "As I said, I don't judge."

Kir bit back a curse of impatience. "So what did you do with the note?"

"I placed it in a folder and locked it in my filing cabinet."

"You didn't look at it?"

"Certainly not."

"And you didn't tell anyone that my father gave it to you?"

Bradshaw stiffened, his face hard with unmistakable indignation. "My meetings with my parishioners, regardless if they attend my church or not, are sacred," he rasped. "I would never compromise their privacy."

Kir nodded, ignoring the man's outrage. He was forming a theory of why Rudolf had chosen to leave the note with Pastor Ron Bradshaw. "My father would probably have known that," he spoke his thoughts out loud.

"What?"

"If my father was trying to find a place to hide the list, it would make sense to choose a person who had no connection to him, and someone who could also keep it secret until they could give it to me," he explained. "Who better than a man of the cloth?"

Bradshaw looked skeptical. "Why not send it to you directly?"

Kir's lips parted to say he didn't know why, but then he snapped them shut with a grimace. He did know why his father hadn't sent the letters to him. He just didn't want to admit the truth.

With an effort, he swallowed the lump that was forming in his throat. "Because he didn't trust me."

"I'm sure that's not true."

Kir smiled wryly at the pastor's shocked expression. "It is, unfortunately. I was just as bad as the sheriff. For years I ignored his claims that he was receiving letters from a killer. If he'd sent me the list, I probably would have thrown it in the trash. But after he died . . ." He shook his head, familiar regret weighing heavy on his heart. "Everything that belonged to him was suddenly important."

Bradshaw seemed to consider Kir's words before giving a shake of his head. "That doesn't explain why he would have chosen me. There are six other churches in this town. Most of them much larger than mine."

Kir didn't have a ready answer. There were certainly churches closer to his dad's house. And there wasn't a bar within blocks, so it seemed unlikely he would have spent a lot of time in the area. Of course, the road that ran past the church was the access road heading to the nearby highway.

"Maybe he was driving by and happened to see you," he absently suggested.

Bradshaw made an odd sound. As if he was choking. "Yes, that's right!"

Kir sent the younger man a startled glance. "What is right?"

"You just reminded me that when your father first walked up to me, he looked uncomfortable, as if he didn't know how to start the conversation," the pastor said. "It's something I'm accustomed to, so I happened to notice his boots were covered in snow and I asked if he needed any help shoveling his driveway. There are several young men in my congregation who are always looking to make some extra money." He paused, as if waiting for Kir to commend his consideration toward his flock. When Kir sent him an impatient glare, he flushed and continued. "Your father said he hadn't been shoveling snow, he'd been out fishing that morning. I happen to be an avid angler myself, so we spent several minutes chatting about a new pole he'd gotten from his son for Christmas."

Kir hissed as the words hit him like a physical blow. When he'd bought the pole for his dad, he'd intended to fly home for Christmas and give it to the older man in person. Instead he'd gotten caught up in being wined and dined by the corporation that was hoping to buy his business, and he'd wrapped up the gift and sent it through the mail.

When had he become such a selfish prick?

"Yeah. He'd been talking about it for years, but he refused to spend the money to get it," Kir said, his voice thick with regret.

Bradshaw glanced away, as if giving Kir a sense of privacy. "Anyway, I asked if he'd been to the lake and he said no, that he had his own slice of heaven where he liked to fish."

Kir grimly forced himself to focus on what the man was telling him. The only way he could make amends to his father now was by catching his killer. And keeping Lynne alive. "The road in front of the church would lead to my grandparents' old farm," he conceded.

Bradshaw shrugged. "I don't know if that helps or not."

"Me either." Impatience crawled through Kir like a living force. He needed answers, but he didn't know where to look. Hell, he didn't even know what questions he needed to ask. "Is there anything else you can remember?"

Bradshaw shook his head. "No."

"Thanks for your time." Retracing his steps, Kir was pulling open the door when Bradshaw spoke.

"You should let the authorities deal with this."

"Not as long as Lynne is in danger."

"Have you heard the proverb that 'a prudent man fore-seeth the evil, and hideth himself: but the simple pass on, and are punished'?"

Kir glanced over his shoulder. "I'll face down the devil himself if I have to."

Chapter 28

Lynne shoved aside her half-eaten sandwich and reached for her phone. Nothing. She tossed it back on her desk with a grimace.

She'd texted Kir twenty minutes ago but he hadn't responded. It shouldn't be a big deal. He could be busy with the official files. Or eating lunch. Or driving. Or . . . Or a hundred other things. It wasn't like she instantly responded to texts. Not unless it was an emergency.

Still, his silence was starting to wear on her nerves.

She was impatiently drumming her fingers on her desk when Bernadine stuck her head through the open doorway with a questioning expression.

"Well?"

"I haven't heard back yet."

Easily sensing Lynne's seething concern, Bernadine stepped into the office and pasted on a reassuring smile. "If he discovers anything, I'm sure he'll call," she assured Lynne.

"Maybe."

"If you're worried, we can go find him," Bernadine suggested. "You don't have any appointments this afternoon."

Lynne shook her head. It'd only been a few hours. It was likely he was still at the sheriff's office. She had enough worries without fretting every time Kir was out of sight. "No. I have to go to the sanctuary to film the 'Pets' Corner.'"

Bernadine looked confused. "I thought that was on Friday nights."

"That's when it airs, but we always film on Wednesday afternoon."

Reluctantly Lynne rose to her feet. She wasn't in the mood to parade around dogs and cats and even goats for the camera, but the weekly segment had allowed her to rehome over a dozen animals. She wasn't going to miss an opportunity to have a new episode of "Pets' Corner" for the Friday night news.

"How long does it take?"

Lynne pulled her purse out of her desk drawer and grabbed her phone. "No more than an hour."

"If you haven't heard from Kir by the time you're finished, we'll go and find him," Bernadine said in decisive tones.

"There's no *we*."

"You're not leaving this clinic without me."

Lynne frowned, confused by the older woman's tenacious insistence. "But I need you here."

"You have interns who can handle things for a couple hours."

"Bernadine—"

"I promised Kir I wouldn't let you run around without someone with you," Bernadine interrupted.

Lynne was caught off guard. She had no idea Kir and

her receptionist had been scheming behind her back. "When?"

"It doesn't matter." Bernadine's expression had never been more stubborn. "I intend to keep my promise."

Lynne sighed. "You're going to insist on this, aren't you?"

"You betcha."

"Fine. Get your coat."

It took a few minutes to get bundled up and to discuss the schedule for the afternoon with her interns. Then, helping Bernadine climb into her truck, Lynne drove to the sanctuary, parking between the old farmhouse and the large barn that had been converted into kennels.

"Oh my. I haven't been here since you had your open house." Bernadine took a slow survey of the long, L-shaped stables and huge paddock that held a dozen horses and several mules, along with a couple llamas. In the attics of the stables Lynne had created a heated aviary. "I had no idea it'd gotten so big."

Lynne sighed. "I'm afraid it's getting out of hand. When I opened the sanctuary I was thinking about a few stray dogs and cats, but so many people in the area are struggling." She shook her head in resignation. It was hard enough for families to care for their children during these hard times, let alone feed their pets or livestock. Still, she couldn't keep accepting more animals if she couldn't keep them properly sheltered. "I'm going to have to start thinking about cutting back or find the funding to hire more employees." Switching off the engine, Lynne glanced around. "Parker must be running late."

It wasn't unusual. The ambitious reporter worked even more hours than Lynne.

Bernadine's gaze moved toward the old, weathered house. "Do Grady and Monica still live here?"

"Yep. They've been great, but once they're done with their degrees I can't imagine they'll want to stay." Lynne reached over the back of the bucket seat to grab her medical bag. "Yet another problem to be solved."

"I'm sure you'll figure it out."

Lynne smiled wryly at the woman's confident tone. "I'm glad one of us thinks so."

Bernadine turned back to face Lynne. "Your father was a beloved part of this community."

Lynne blinked, not sure where the older woman was going with the conversation. "Yes, I know."

"He was everyone's friend and he volunteered for every community event," Bernadine continued.

A wistful sadness settled in Lynne's heart. Although she was happy to know that her father was happily retired in Florida, she missed him every single day. "I'm still amazed by his energy," she murmured. "I'll never be able to live up to his reputation."

Bernadine clicked her tongue. "You've already surpassed him, my dear."

"That's kind, but not true."

"It is true," the receptionist insisted. "There were many folk worried when your father retired. They thought it would be too much for such a young woman to handle, but you've proven you're just as good a vet as your father. Maybe better."

Lynne felt her cheeks warm with pleasure. She'd been equally worried. It was one thing to dream of being a vet and another to take on a clinic that had hundreds of clients.

"That's the nicest thing anyone has ever said to me," Lynne told her companion.

"Your phone wouldn't be ringing off the hook if the citizens of Pike didn't think you were the best vet around," Bernadine told her. "They have too much invested in their livestock to take any risks."

Lynne didn't try to argue. It would be false modesty to claim the clinic wasn't flourishing under her care. But she was honest enough to admit that she would never be capable of replacing her father. "I still don't have Dad's ability to mix with the community," she reminded Bernadine.

"There are more ways of helping people than just sitting on school boards or library committees or shooting the breeze with the guys at the VFW." Bernadine pointed toward the outbuildings. "Just look at what you've done here. So many animals saved. It's exactly what we needed."

Lynne impulsively reached to grasp Bernadine's hand, giving it a tight squeeze. "Have I mentioned how much I've missed having you around?" Bernadine blushed, but before she could speak, Lynne nodded toward the house. "If you want to go inside and say hi to Monica, I want to run and check on a couple of puppies that were dropped off this morning."

"I'll go with you," Bernadine swiftly offered.

"It's only going to take a minute, I swear." Lynne pointed toward the side of the barn. "I'll leave the door open so you can see me the entire time."

There was a pause before the older woman grudgingly nodded in agreement. "Very well."

Lynne rolled her eyes. "I now understand the term 'mother hen.'"

"You've always needed one."

Not giving herself the opportunity to imagine her life with a mother who fussed over her, Lynne jumped out of the truck. "Save me a hot cup of coffee."

After scurrying over the hard-packed snow, Lynne entered the barn, leaving the door open. There was an explosion of excited barks as she passed by the kennels, pausing at each one to greet the eager dog inside. Eventually she located the two recent additions to the sanctuary in the quarantined section at the end of the barn. She would come back later to do a full checkup and start the two puppies on their vaccinations. For now she just wanted to make sure they didn't need any immediate medical care.

Less than half an hour later she was stepping into the kitchen of the farmhouse. It was like the rest of the property—old and a little shabby, but built with a solid durability that promised it would be standing long after many newer homes had tumbled into piles of cheap plywood.

She glanced around, surprised to find the room empty.

"Hello? Monica? Bernadine?" she called out.

No one answered, but she could hear the sound of the television coming from the living room at the back of the house.

She pulled off her heavy coat and draped it over a ladder-back chair. Ignoring the alluring scent of coffee that wafted from the pot on the stove she stepped into the hallway. She would say hi to Monica before she poured herself a mug and settled in to wait for Parker.

The area was shadowed, but Lynne easily caught sight of the large woman sprawled on the wooden floor.

Bernadine. She came to an abrupt halt, terrified the older woman had a heart attack.

Dropping to her knees, she reached out her hand. She intended to check for a pulse. It wasn't until she felt the sharp pain in the middle of her chest that she realized her mistake.

Bernadine hadn't suffered a heart attack. She'd been tranqued.

Grabbing the silver dart that was stuck just above her heart, Lynne yanked it free and dropped it to the ground. But the damage had already been done. Even as she struggled to her feet the world was starting to fuzz as the drug spread through her body. She swayed heavily to the side, smacking her shoulder into the wall. Someone was approaching. She could make out a dark form at the end of the hallway, but her double vision was making it impossible to focus enough to make out the features.

"Crimson blood stains the pure white snow. Life spills from warm to frozen. Don't look. The pain is gone," a voice whispered.

Kir drove from the church to Rita King's house. He still wanted to look for any clues that the woman might have found at his father's grave. Especially now that the task force would be swooping in and keeping any evidence tightly locked away.

After parking down the street, he circled the small, cottage-style home and tried the back door. Locked. He muttered a curse. When he was a boy, no one locked their doors. These days, however, he didn't blame people for doing whatever necessary to stay safe.

Tromping through the heavy snow, he made his way to the front porch and climbed the steps. It seemed unlikely that the front door would be unlocked if she'd bothered to secure the back one, but stranger things had happened.

And continued to happen.

He was just reaching for the knob when a voice brought him to a startled halt.

"Are you a friend of Rita's?"

Kir turned his head, searching for the source of the voice. At first, he couldn't see anyone. Just the small, tidy houses that lined the snow-packed street. In this residential section of town most of the people were at work at this hour. So where had the voice come from?

It was the sound of a television that drew his attention to the next-door neighbor. A closer look revealed an open side window where the face of an elderly woman was peering through the screen.

He stepped off the porch and crossed the short distance toward the house, which was even smaller than Rita's, with faded aluminum siding and a weathered roof. He stood directly in front of the window, catching the scent of stale cigarettes and day-old cabbage.

He squashed the urge to grimace and pasted a smile on his face. "I'm Kir Jansen," he said. "And you are?"

"Leah Meadows." The woman tilted her head to the side, like a bird eyeing him with open curiosity. "You're Rudolf's boy, aren't you?"

"Yep."

The hard suspicion eased from Leah's narrow, heavily wrinkled face. "I thought you might be one of those horrid reporters that have started to descend on the town. Like ghouls, taking our tragedy and trying to make a buck off it."

Kir bit back a curse. He hadn't realized the media had taken an interest in the murders. The last thing any of them needed was a horde of invaders spooking the killer into the shadows. What if he decided to lie low until the task force and reporters grew tired and moved on?

He clenched his teeth. The sheriff had called in the task force, but the reporters were there because of Parker Bowen and his ambitious desire to attract the attention of a national network. "I agree," he muttered. "Our local ghoul is bad enough."

"Local? Oh, you mean Parker Bowen?" The woman sucked in a loud breath, her hand patting the silvery curls that appeared to be shellacked by layers of spray. "I wasn't talking about him. He's such a lovely man."

Kir resisted the urge to roll his eyes. Instead he concentrated on the reason he was there. "I don't suppose you have a key to Rita's house, do you?"

She narrowed her eyes. "Why?"

"Rita called me just before she was killed and said that she had something to give me," Kir admitted with blunt honesty. He had no idea how well the two women had been acquainted. The last thing he wanted was to get caught in a lie. Not when Leah might have some information that might help him.

"What could she have for you?"

Kir shrugged. "I assume it belonged to my father."

"Ah." Leah nodded her head. "That makes sense. The two of them were thick as thieves over the past few years."

"Do you have a key?"

"No." Leah pursed her lips. "But I believe her daughter

is coming back later today to plan the funeral. I'm sure she'll be happy to help you."

Kir squashed his flare of frustration. It was a long shot to think the woman had a key. Or, even if she did, that she would let him go in and search through Rita's belongings.

About to return to his vehicle, Kir halted as he was struck by a sudden inspiration. "Did you happen to see Rita leave the house yesterday?"

"I did." Leah jerked her thumb over her shoulder, indicating the room behind her. "I was sitting in my easy chair watching my favorite game show when I caught sight of her stepping off the porch. It was quite a surprise."

"Why a surprise?"

"Rita never left her house during the day," Leah said. "In fact, she used to joke she could be a vampire since she never saw the sun."

Kir glanced toward the fading, empty house. It was sad to think of Rita in there alone, refusing to leave until the darkness could hide her from the world.

He shook his head, returning his attention to Leah. "Did you see what time she came back?"

"She didn't, poor soul," Leah said without hesitation. "She walked down the street and never came home. As if the daylight just swallowed her whole." Leah turned and Kir heard the scratch of a lighter before a cloud of smoke drifted through the screen. "Maybe Rita was a prophet. Maybe she knew she was destined to die beneath the sun."

He wrinkled his nose at the nasty smell of tobacco, but he remained standing next to the window. "You're sure she didn't come back?"

Leah nodded her head in an emphatic motion. "Yes. I was worried about her."

"Did she appear afraid? Concerned?"

"Not really. But like I said, she never left the house that early, so I kept watch for her. I wanted to ask if she'd been sick and went to visit the doctor."

Kir accepted the woman's explanation. The citizens of Pike were nosy, but they possessed a genuine concern for each other. Anyone in trouble could count on their neighbors to step in and lend a hand.

"I was hoping . . ." He shook his head in defeat.

If Rita hadn't returned to the house, that meant whatever she'd found at the grave was on her when she'd been run down. Which meant it was now in the hands of the killer.

Leah pressed her nose against the screen. "Hoping for what?"

"Never mind." He forced a smile. "Thanks for chatting with me."

"Do you want me to tell Rita's daughter to give you a call when she gets here?"

"No. I'm afraid I'm too late. Again," he said, turning away.

Once in his vehicle, Kir pulled out his phone to discover he'd missed a text from Lynne. Quickly replying that he was fine, he drummed his fingers on the steering wheel.

His instinct was to head to the clinic and discuss his morning with Lynne, but what did he really have to tell her? That a task force had been formed? That Pastor Bradshaw hadn't been able to reveal anything about his father that they didn't already know?

Kir frowned. That wasn't quite true. He'd discovered

where his father had been the morning he'd taken the list to the pastor.

He absently glanced at his phone. Lynne hadn't answered. Which probably meant she was busy with a patient. Tucking the phone back in his pocket he started the engine and headed out of town. He would retrace his father's journey that morning. Maybe there was something along the way that would give him a clue to where Rudolf had gotten the list. Or what had spooked him into seeking out the pastor to arrange his funeral.

It was probably a wild-goose chase, but anything was better than sitting around twiddling his thumbs.

Chapter 29

Lynne woke with a throbbing headache and her body stiff with cold. Even worse, she was shrouded in an impenetrable darkness.

Where was she? What'd happened?

Time ticked past as she struggled to clear the cobwebs from her mind. Something that would have been easier if her heart hadn't been hammering and her breath coming in short, painful pants.

At last she managed to conjure up the fuzzy memory of driving to the sanctuary. Yes. Bernadine had been with her, and she'd gone to check on the puppies. Once she was done, she'd gone into her grandparents' house and found the older woman lying in the hallway.

Then someone had shot a dart into her.

Forcing herself to a sitting position, Lynne pressed a hand to her aching head and tried to peer through the gloomy shadows. She couldn't see anything, but she had a sense of a vast space around her. As if she was in a cavern. That would also explain the sharp chill in the air.

But where was there a cavern near Pike?

Unless they'd traveled away from the town. After all,

she had no idea how much time had passed. She assumed she'd been hit with the tranquilizer that had been stolen from her clinic, but without knowing how much had been in the dart, she couldn't begin to calculate whether she'd been out a couple minutes or half an hour.

Panic burst in the center of her being. Somehow the thought that she'd been driven far from her home was even more terrifying than the darkness.

"Hello," she called out, wincing as her voice echoed through the shadows. She could sense someone was out there . . . watching. "Who's there?"

"Did you know that fear has a smell?" a low, male voice whispered through the air. "It's thick and rich, like an expensive spice."

Lynne stiffened. She was too frightened to try to identify the speaker.

"Who are you?"

There was the sound of approaching footsteps. "The invisible man."

She placed her hands on the cold floor. She knew she was too weak to try and stand, but she covertly felt around her, inanely hoping for something she could use as a weapon. There was nothing, but she did determine that there was cement beneath her.

Which meant she wasn't in a cavern. So where?

"I don't know what that means," she managed to mutter.

"Invisible. Unseen." A soft, rasping laugh. "A ghost from your memories."

Memories? She was forced to clear a sudden lump from her throat. "We know each other?"

"Not as well as I'd once hoped."

She shuddered at the mocking words. "Show yourself."

"If you insist."

There was a crunch of boots against the crumbling cement, then a loud click. Far overhead a single fluorescent bulb flickered to life and Lynne could see her surroundings.

She frowned, confused by the huge square of a room with a high ceiling lined with heavy steel beams. There were stacks of old steel desks and chairs shoved in a corner and the walls looked as if they'd been built out of concrete blocks. It wasn't until she caught sight of the window that revealed a cramped inner room with dozens of old-fashioned computers and radar screens that she realized where she was.

This was the abandoned air base.

The knowledge hit her at the precise moment that someone stepped into the pool of light. A gasp of shock was wrenched from her throat as she allowed her gaze to take in the familiar man with dark hair and gray eyes.

"Parker?" she rasped. "Parker Bowen?"

He was wearing an expensive trench coat with a cashmere scarf and leather gloves. The elegant attire made him look like he was about to report the news, not create it.

He offered a mocking bow. "Surprised?"

Lynne blinked. She wasn't just surprised. She was stunned. She'd made the stupid mistake of assuming the killer would be a ruthless lunatic, not an intelligent, successful man. A man who had shared countless hours with her at the animal sanctuary.

How was it possible?

"Why?" she eventually managed to choke out.

He flashed his white-toothed smile, pacing from one

edge of the pool of light to the other. Like an actor on a stage. "Let me tell you a story."

Lynne shuddered. Like she had a choice? There was no way anyone was going to find her. Not in this remote, abandoned building. And certainly no one suspected Parker was the killer, so even if someone noticed he was absent from the station, they would never connect him to her disappearance.

Her only hope was to pacify the man and wait for an opportunity to escape.

"Okay." She forced an expression of interest on her face. "Tell me."

Another charming smile. "There was once a little boy." He paused, pretending to consider his words. "Let's call him Carl. He was very shy. Very quiet. Like a mouse. Do you know why?"

Lynne swallowed. She'd always thought those mystery shows where the detective spent the last half hour of the movie revealing his brilliance were goofy. Now she understood. Parker didn't care about sharing the details of his psychopathic mind. He wanted to be the center of attention.

Even if she was his only audience.

Play along, Lynne. Just play along.

"Because he was scared?" she forced herself to question.

He clicked his tongue with disappointment. "Ah, you know the story."

"Not really, but a puppy makes himself small when he's scared."

"Yes." He nodded. "Invisible. Meaningless."

"What happened to—" She bit off her words, well aware that her life depended on keeping Parker from snapping. "Carl?"

"He tried to make himself small. He even pretended he was a shadow, not a real person. That way nothing could touch him. That was a fantasy, of course. Nothing could help him avoid the blows."

"Carl was abused?"

"Abused." Parker spat out the word. Like it was a curse. "Such a pointless word. These days everyone is abused." He waved his arm in a dramatic gesture. "You sneeze in a room and someone cries they've been abused."

Lynne slid back an inch. The feeling was returning to her legs. It was a tingly, painful sensation that intensified the cold chills shivering through her body, but it meant she could stand. And eventually walk. Then run.

At some point, she was going to try. If she had to die, it wasn't going to be sitting on her ass.

"Then what happened to Carl?"

Parker returned to his pacing. "He was tortured."

Lynne dared another inch. "I'm sorry."

He snorted. "Are you?"

"Yes."

"You don't even know what I mean by torture." He sent her an accusing glance, thankfully unaware she'd moved. "Shall I describe the sound a forearm makes when it's being snapped in two? Or the smell of burning flesh when you press a hot iron to the skin? Or the exact shades of color that surround a black eye?"

In spite of herself, Lynne made a sound of distress. Was he describing his childhood? Yes. She could see it in the empty gray of his eyes. The deadness that came with the inability to connect to the world after years of abuse. She'd seen it in animals. Why hadn't she seen it in Parker?

Because he'd created a façade to fool the world, she silently realized.

A cruel smile curved his lips. "Does that trouble you?"

"Yes."

His mocking expression faltered, as if he was caught off guard by her genuine sympathy.

"I haven't gotten to the true torture," he told her. "It's the waiting. The cowering in the dark as you listen to the screams from the next room. The suffocating fear as you hear the footsteps coming closer and closer to the bed. The pleading for mercy that falls on deaf ears."

There was a chilling intensity in his voice. "Did you—"

"Shh." He snapped his fingers, his jaw tightening. "We're talking about Carl."

She forced herself to take a deep, calming breath. It didn't ease her panic, but it helped her to focus. Obviously, it was important she separate Carl from Parker. Deadly important.

"Did Carl escape his torture?" she asked.

His smooth composure returned as he resumed his pacing. "One night a brave lawman put a bullet through the heart of the monster."

Her breath was slowly squeezed from her lungs. "Rudolf?"

"Yes. He was Carl's hero."

Lynne struggled to work through exactly what Parker was telling her. As far as she knew, Rudolf had only shot one man during his years as sheriff.

Delbert Frey.

So that meant Parker Bowen must be his son, Carl Frey. And he obviously grew up in Pike. Had they gone to school together? The name didn't ring any bells, but then the combination of the lingering sedative and sheer terror wasn't helping conjure up her childhood memories.

It also meant Kir had been right. His father was at the center of the killer's obsession.

"What did Carl do after . . ." She hesitated, unsure if his father's name might trigger Parker into violence. "The monster was dead?"

"He foolishly thought life would be better." He reached the edge of the pool of light and smoothly turned to retrace his steps. "And it was. For a couple years."

Lynne scooted another inch. Didn't dare look over her shoulder, but she could feel a breeze on her nape. There had to be an opening somewhere back there. "Then what happened?"

"A new monster appeared. Along with the screams." Parker's expression remained coolly composed, but his hands clenched into tight fists. "Those endless screams. That's when Carl realized the truth."

"What truth?"

"There was only way to get rid of the monsters."

"How?"

He sent her a startled glance, as if he couldn't believe she was so stupid. "Stop the screams, obviously."

"Carl's mother?" Lynne croaked.

"Exactly." He drew his thumb across the front of his throat. "A quick slice across the carotid arteries and there was nothing but blissful silence."

Lynne's blood ran cold. Merrill Frey hadn't been

murdered by her new husband, but by her own son. The betrayal must have been staggering for the poor woman.

"You . . ." Lynne forced back the words at the dangerous glimmer in the gray eyes. "I mean, Carl murdered his mother?"

"No, he put her out of her misery." He pointed a finger at her. "Like you do when you have a sick dog. It's called mercy."

Lynne winced. It was the toughest part of her job, and a decision she never made without regret. To be compared to a ruthless killer was enough to make her stomach twist in horror.

"Carl's mother was a victim," she insisted.

"By choice," Parker spat out. "It could have been her and her son. Together. No pain. No fear. No screams." He made a sound of disgust. "But she was too stupid. She had to be silenced."

Lynne's mouth was dry, her mind stuck on the image of Merrill Frey lying in the snow with her throat slit open. No one deserved such a fate. No one.

She resisted the urge to ask what happened to Ernie Rucker. Right now Parker was enjoying the limelight. If he thought she was distracted by other actors in his melodrama, he might decide to end the performance. "Where did Carl go?"

"To his aunt in Madison," Parker answered.

"Was he happy?"

He mulled over the question, as if he'd never considered whether he'd been happy. "She was a decent woman who tried to help," he at last conceded. "But Carl was damaged. Like Humpty-Dumpty who couldn't be put back together again." He came to a sudden halt, studying her with a curious gaze. "Have you been to therapy?"

Lynne paused. Was this a trick question? "No."

"Carl went to a place for troubled teens," he told her, his gaze lifting to study the light overhead. "It's odd. Kids who've been brutalized can be sorted into three categories."

"Categories?" Lynne said, using his distraction to scoot farther away.

"Yes. There were the angry kids. The ones who used their pain as an excuse to spew hate and violence toward everyone around them. They thought they were so tough, but actually they were just boring. Like an endless cliché." He curled his lips in disgust before continuing. "The second category were the suck-ups. The ones who thought that if they were good enough, they would eventually be loved. They were even more boring." He made smooching noises. "Always looking for an ass to kiss."

"And Carl?"

"He was the third category." He smoothed a hand down his expensive coat, an odd, wistful expression softening his features. "On the outside he seemed fine. He was no longer the timid mouse. Now he was charming, good-looking, even popular. Other kids wanted to be like him. But inside . . ."

"He was broken," she finished for him.

"Yes."

She licked her dry lips. "It wasn't his fault."

The hardness returned to his face. "You're damned right it wasn't his fault. Which was why those responsible had to be punished."

* * *

Kir shivered as he stood in his father's favorite fishing spot next to the lake. He didn't know why he was there. He'd driven the route that Rudolf always took to the farm, hoping to see something that would spark his imagination. So far he'd accomplished nothing more than wasting his time. If his father had seen something that had given him a clue to the killer, or had made him fear for his life, Kir wasn't seeing it.

Just the same stretch of empty highway followed by remote roads and snowy fields he'd seen hundreds of times before.

"Talk to me, Dad," he muttered in a harsh voice. "Tell me what you would have said if I hadn't been too stupid to listen."

The whistle of the wind and the cry of a nearby crow were his only answer.

Glancing toward the ridge where the house had once stood, he allowed his gaze to trace the hillside down to the frozen lake. Then he studied the line of pine trees in the distance. He was just turning away when he noticed the radar towers of the air base etched against the blue sky. And something else. The outline of a truck parked in the vast, empty lot. Why would someone be there? The place had been shut down for years. Plus the government had big signs posted that it was off-limits. Not that the warnings had stopped him when he was a teenager.

Kir narrowed his eyes, trying to make out the details of the vehicle. It was definitely a pickup. And even at a distance he was guessing it was a dark color. Black or navy or . . . red.

Just like Lynne's.

Muttering a string of curses, Kir whirled around and battled his way through the snow to where he'd left his SUV.

He'd had the answer the minute the pastor had told him his father had been fishing at his little slice of heaven. What else was out here to see except the old air base?

Now he could only hope his inability to recognize a clue beneath his very nose hadn't made him too late. If something happened to Lynne, he would never forgive himself.

Chapter 30

Lynne pressed her hands flat against the cement, preparing to shove herself upright as fury darkened Parker's eyes. Obviously, she'd made a mistake to remind him of how helpless he'd been as a child. But then again, he was crazy. She was fairly certain that every subject had the potential to set him off.

Besides, her attempts to pacify him weren't offering her an opportunity to escape. Maybe if she rattled him, it would . . .

Well, she didn't know what. But the longer she sat on the frozen floor, the more likely her legs were going to go back to sleep.

"When did Carl become Parker Bowen?"

He stiffened, and for a heart-thumping second she was terrified she'd pushed too hard. Parker had clearly managed to separate the child he'd been from the man he'd become. Not a split personality. But an indestructible barrier that kept him from drowning in the pain of his past.

She wanted him rattled, not ballistic.

His nose flared, as if he was sucking in a deep breath, then he surprisingly forced himself to answer her question.

"When I went to college. My middle name was Parker, and Mother's maiden name was Bowen, so it was easy enough to get it legally changed."

"You started a new life?"

"That was the plan."

She studied his finely chiseled features and glossy dark hair. On the surface he looked so normal. Not that she expected the killer to creep around in a black cloak and hockey mask. But surely such evil should have left some mark on the surface?

"Something went wrong?"

He slowly nodded, his eyes distant as if he was recalling the moment he'd decided to become a serial killer. "It started with the dreams."

"About the monster?"

He sliced his hand through the air in a gesture of denial. "No. He's dead and gone. He never enters my thoughts."

"What were your dreams?"

"The blood in the snow."

A sharp shiver raced through Lynne. Not just from his whispered words, but the image that formed in her mind.

A terrified woman whose life had been shaped and ended by violence.

She struggled to speak. "Your mother?"

"Yes."

"Did you regret what you did to her?"

He jerked his head toward her, seemingly astonished by her question. "Regret? No. I . . ."

"You what?"

A strange, taunting smile curved his lips. "I fantasized about doing it again."

Revulsion rolled through her with a physical force. "Oh."

He turned to fully reveal the sick pleasure that made his face glow beneath the fluorescent light. Suddenly the evil was all too easy to see.

"It was so beautiful. Her naked body lying beneath the moonlight, the dark pool of blood staining the snow."

"Beautiful?" she choked out.

"I wanted to see it again, but at that point in my life I still hoped I could be normal." The glow dimmed, his lips pursing. "So I had to purge my dark desires."

Lynne scooted back another inch. She was almost at the edge of the pool of light. "What does purge mean?"

He waved his hand in a broad gesture, returning to his flourishing gestures of a man onstage. "Rather than performing the deliciously evil deeds that filled my dreams, I wrote them down in letters."

Lynne didn't have to guess where he'd sent those letters. "Rudolf."

"Yes."

Pity for Kir's father tugged at Lynne's heart. The older man had not only been forced to leave the job he loved after putting his life on the line to protect the citizens of Pike, but he'd gone into a deep depression that had only been aggravated by the taunting letters from a madman. It was a blunt reminder that life was rarely fair. "Why him?"

He arched a brow at the edge of anger in her voice. "He was my savior. The only person who'd battled my demons."

"And you rewarded him with evil letters?"

Parker snapped his brows together, predictably offended by her barely hidden scorn. "He was the sort of man who took pride in helping those in need, wasn't he?"

Lynne clenched her teeth. She had to be careful. After

all, the letters Parker had sent to Rudolf had been the least of his crimes. "I suppose," she murmured.

"Besides, he had his own demons." Parker shrugged with blatant indifference. "Who better to understand mine?"

Accepting that the man had no ability to feel remorse for the pain he caused, Lynne asked the question that had been niggling since he'd told her he'd gone to live with his aunt in Madison. "Why did you come back to Pike?"

"This is my home."

She didn't remind him that this was where his father had been shot and killed. Not exactly the childhood trauma most people would want to relive. "That's the only reason?"

He sent her a sly glance, wagging his finger in her direction. "It's what I told myself. Although deep in my heart I already knew what was going to happen."

"You came back for revenge."

The white teeth flashed in response to her accusation. "Sweet, sweet revenge."

Lynne stopped trying to inch away. Instead she clenched her muscles, preparing to shove herself to her feet. There was a strange tingling in the air that warned her Parker was spiraling toward a meltdown.

"You killed Sherry because she evicted your family out of your trailer?" she asked, desperately trying to keep him focused on anything but her.

"How did . . ." He bit off his startled words, his eyes boring into her with dangerous intensity. "Have you been snooping on me, darling Lynne?"

Feeling like a deer in the headlights, Lynne tried to remain perfectly still. "A lucky guess," she lied.

"Doubtful. You're such a clever girl." He shoved his

hand in the deep pockets of his coat, continuing to watch her with that unwavering gaze. "But, however you discovered we'd been kicked out of our home, that's not the reason I killed Sherry."

"It wasn't?" The words came out in a hoarse rasp.

His sharp crack of laughter echoed through the empty space. "No, we'd been kicked out of a dozen places. Either because we couldn't pay the rent, or more often because my father was fighting with the neighbors."

Lynne frowned in genuine confusion. "Then why?"

"Because she laughed," Parker said, his expression flinty. "As if it was some great joke that a child was being tossed out like trash." His jaw tightened. "She wasn't laughing when I stood over her and sliced her throat open."

Nausea rolled through Lynne's stomach, but she grimly hid her reaction. She wouldn't give the man the pleasure of seeing her revulsion.

"And Randi?"

Parker shrugged. "She used to babysit me. Or actually, she pretended to babysit. As soon as my mom walked out of the house, she would lock me in my bedroom so she could have sex with her boyfriend." Parker visibly shuddered in disgust at the memory. "I'd hear them in the living room, grunting and groaning while I was caged like an animal. I spent my time fantasizing about picking the lock of my bedroom door so I could get out and use my baseball bat to bash their heads in. That would have stopped the grunting."

"And Ms. Randall?"

"She knew."

"Knew what?"

He took a step toward her and Lynne swallowed her

scream of frustration. He'd just erased the small amount of space she'd managed to put between them.

"The dried-up bitch knew I was being abused and she did everything in her power to make it worse," he hissed. "At least once a week she would send home bad reports or keep me after school for some minor mistake to make sure I would be beaten."

Lynne parted her lips in disbelief. "Surely she didn't realize—"

"She saw the bruises, but she just kept doing it." He cut through her protest with an icy fury. "As if she took pleasure in knowing she was causing me pain."

Lynne quickly nodded. Not just to pacify Parker. The truth was that she couldn't be sure the older woman hadn't taken some perverse pleasure in knowing she was condemning a little boy to violent beatings. Ms. Randall had a mean streak that had made her classroom a misery for all the kids unfortunate enough to have her as a teacher.

"What about Nash?" She asked the question that had been nagging at her since she'd realized the killer was Parker Bowen.

"Ah, Nash." There was an ugly edge in his voice. "The great Nash Cordon. Star football player. Local golden boy. I hated him."

"Why?"

"Do you remember me?"

"What?"

"It's a simple question." The words were snapped out, hitting Lynne like the crack of a whip. "Do you remember me?"

Her mouth went dry. Did she lie? It obviously was

important to Parker. But then again, he might be laying a trap. What if she said yes and he started quizzing her on the past?

At last she went with the easiest answer. "No, I'm sorry, but I don't remember you."

"Of course not." A darkness flared in the depths of the gray eyes. "I was the mouse. The shadow in the corner."

"It wasn't you," she hurriedly protested. "I didn't pay attention to anyone. I had a few friends who I would hang out with, but my mother wasn't around so I never had birthday parties or sleepovers. I didn't really fit in."

He slowly nodded. "Yes, you were different from the others."

"Were you in my class?" she demanded, scrambling through her memories for any hint of a Carl Frey.

There was nothing. He truly had been a shadow.

"Two years back." He shrugged. "At least when I was allowed to go to school. My mom would yank me out and pretend I was being homeschooled whenever my father was at his most violent. I think she was afraid someone might call the authorities and have me taken away. She didn't have to worry. No one made the call." A flush was crawling beneath his skin, as if he was beginning to lose control of his emotions. "And after we were kicked out of the trailer park, we moved to a cabin outside town. It made it even easier for my mom to find excuses not to take me to school."

Lynne didn't allow herself to think of the horrors he must have endured as a child. He'd grown up to become a monster. Once she assumed had brought her to this remote location to slit her throat and dump her body in the snow. Her only emotion should be determination to escape.

"I still don't understand why you killed Nash."

"He was everything I wanted to be, but did he appreciate what he had?" The flush on Parker's face darkened at the mention of the older man. "No. He pissed it away on a cheap bar filled with regrets."

Lynne blinked. He killed Nash because he didn't think he appreciated his life. "That's . . ."

"Insane?" His flashed a too-white smile, his eyes glittering with a hunger that he'd managed to hide until this moment. "I told you I'm broken."

Lynne dug her heels into the cement. She was going to have to try to make her move. But first she had one question that had to be answered. Otherwise it would haunt her for the rest of her life. Well, what remained of her life, anyway.

"Why me?" she demanded. "I've never done anything to hurt you."

He lifted his brows. "Just the opposite. You showed me a kindness I never forgot."

Okay. That wasn't what she'd been expecting. "I did?"

"Yes." His smile softened until it appeared almost genuine. "I was seven, maybe eight years old and I found a stray puppy. I knew my dad would never let me keep it, so I hid it in an empty shed near the school. Every morning I would visit and bring him food." His smile faded. "One morning my dad caught me stealing bacon and forced me to take him to where I'd hidden the puppy. He was going to kill him when you passed by."

Lynne stiffened in surprise as the memory of that morning rose from the recesses of her mind. She'd been walking to school when she'd seen the man holding the squirming puppy by the scruff of the neck. He'd been shaking the poor thing so hard it was obvious he was going to end up breaking the tiny dog's neck. Instant fury had overcome her as she'd charged toward the stranger, indifferent to the fact he was an adult with what was obviously a violent temper.

"I remember."

"You started throwing rocks and screamed so loud that a dozen people came running." His nose flared with pleasure as he recalled what she'd done to his father. "My dad slunk away like a scared rat and I took the puppy to the woods where no one could find him. It didn't matter that I was punished when I got home. I had my dog. It was the only thing in the world that ever loved me."

She shook her head in confusion. "Why are you angry with me?"

"I'm not angry," he protested. "I'm disappointed."

"Disappointed?"

"In my mind you were nothing less than an angel come to earth," he told her, that hunger still smoldering in the depths of his eyes. "I held on to that image of you, and when I returned to Pike I discovered that nothing had changed. You were still the fierce protector of the vulnerable. Such a beautiful warrior. I decided I was going to make you mine."

She shuddered at the mere thought. Even when she'd assumed he was a handsome, fairly successful journalist there had been something about him that had squashed any attraction toward him. Almost as if her inner alarm had been warning her there was something sketchy.

A damned shame she hadn't paid more attention to her instincts.

"I . . ." She had to stop and clear the lump of horror from her throat. "I had no idea."

"Because of Nash," he snapped in a harsh voice. "I couldn't believe when I first heard the two of you were dating. How could my angel be with that . . . Neanderthal?"

"It was a mistake," she assured him.

He wasn't satisfied. In fact, his face darkened to a strange shade of puce. As if he was having trouble breathing. "Not just a mistake. It was a betrayal," he insisted. "I expected others to disappoint me. It was as inevitable as the sun rising. But not you." He paused, visibly regaining control of his temper. "That's when I realized I had to do something very special to punish you."

"Special?" That didn't sound good.

He smiled, pulling one hand out of his coat pocket to reveal the switchblade clutched in his fingers. With a smooth flick of his wrist the long blade was revealed, the razor-sharp steel shining with lethal promise.

Chapter 31

Kir halted at the edge of the opening that led to the massive octagon-shaped room in the very center of the air base.

After a frantic call to 911 he'd driven straight across the snow-packed fields and jumped out of his SUV to scale the chain-link fence with more haste than grace. Then, dropping to the other side, he'd jogged across the frozen runways. He didn't try to hide his approach. If someone was watching, there was no way to get across the wide, empty space without being seen. Besides, he was in too much of a hurry.

Passing by Lynne's truck, he came to a sharp halt. He was going to need a quick getaway once he managed to rescue Lynne. Pulling open the driver's door he was relieved to discover the keys still in the ignition. Obviously the killer hadn't expected anyone to enter the abandoned parking lot. Kir switched on the engine. Then, remembering Lynne's heavy flashlight, he reached behind the seat to grab it before slamming the door and continuing forward.

Once at the main terminal, he shoved open a loose door and slipped into the darkness. A heavy cold shrouded around him, the shadows so thick he was virtually blind. He paused, tapping into the knowledge he'd gained as a boy sneaking around this building. Moving forward, he made a hard right and entered the narrow space between the outside wall and the inner wall. The construction of the terminal followed ancient castle designs with layer after layer of cinderblock to offer protection against explosions. The result was a spiderweb of tunnels that led to dead ends and occasionally into the various rooms. It'd made an awesome place to play hide-and-seek when he was young, or to keep away from prying eyes when he got older and wanted someplace to party in privacy.

Traveling through the tunnel, Kir passed by the hallway that opened to the inner rooms and instead searched the wall until he found the small, rusty latch near the low ceiling. There was a sharp squeak and Kir winced. He'd forgotten how noises echoed through the tunnels. Then, after pushing on the wall that now swung free, he entered a hidden escape passage that led down to the bunker room.

If he were a serial killer, that's where he'd take his victims.

Ignoring the terror that pulsed through his body at the thought of Lynne in the hands of a maniac, Kir slowed his pace to a mere crawl as he caught sight of the faint light just ahead of him. He'd been right. There was someone down here. Which meant he had to be careful not to kick a stray pebble, or worse, trip over something he couldn't see in the darkness. He couldn't alert the killer that his evil lair had been discovered.

As he reached the opening, Kir came to a halt. The sound of voices drifted through the air and a vast, overwhelming emotion swept through him, nearly sending him to his knees. Until that precise second he didn't realize there'd been a deep, terrifying fear that he was too late.

Pressing his hand against the wall, he struggled to regain his balance even as he recognized the voice of the man speaking. *Parker Bowen.* He nodded, feeling an odd lack of surprise. It wasn't that he'd suspected the man. Parker Bowen seemed like a typical blowhard who was all wind and little substance. But now that his identity was revealed, Kir allowed the puzzle pieces to fit together.

Parker could travel around town in full view, and yet not be truly noticed. He was expected to be everywhere, even at the crime scenes with his toothy grin and obnoxious questions. And Kir had sensed the man's interest in Lynne, although he'd dismissed it as predictable male lust.

He cautiously inched forward, absently listening to Parker blather about his reasons for killing Nash and his perverted need to make Lynne suffer. He refused to allow the words to sink into his brain. Not now. Later he would brood and stew over the man's twisted logic.

In the center of the space there was an oblong glow spilling from the ancient fluorescent light overhead. It allowed him to see Lynne seated on the hard cement floor with a man standing over her.

His jaws locked as fury pounded through him, but once again he battled back his emotions. Later he'd have an epic meltdown. For now he had to remain laser focused on getting to Lynne. Especially since he didn't dare wait for backup. It would take time for them to drive out to the air base. Assuming they bothered to come at all. And once they were there, it would be a miracle if they could find their way through the maze of hallways and tunnels.

Taking a second to confirm that Lynne was unharmed,

Kir shifted his attention to the man standing a few feet from her.

Parker Bowen was wearing his expensive coat and cashmere scarf, and leather boots more suited for the television station than an abandoned air base in the middle of nowhere. But while he appeared harmless, Kir could see the lethal blade he held in his fingers with practiced ease.

That blade had already sliced at least four throats, maybe more. Kir had no intention of underestimating the level of danger this man posed to Lynne.

"Very special," Parker was assuring Lynne, a smug pleasure in his voice. Obviously, the bastard was taking pleasure in having her at his mercy. "My mother was a stupid woman. It didn't matter how many times she was beaten or raped or humiliated, she would always go back for more. And she'd take me with her. Then I allowed myself to be attracted to you, only to discover that you were just as stupid. Throwing yourself away on that piece of shit." His fingers tightened around the knife. "It wasn't enough to see you bleed. I wanted more."

"More what?" Lynne's voice was amazingly steady as she defiantly stared up at her captor.

Kir felt a strange glow of pride at her unshakable courage.

"I didn't know," Parker admitted. "I just wanted to see you suffer. I first tried to set your sanctuary on fire. But when I managed to break into the kennels the dogs made such a racket it woke the people in the house."

That explained the break-in at the sanctuary, Kir acknowledged, bending nearly double as he entered the control room. There was no easy way to get across the massive, empty space, which meant he had to hope he was close enough to make his move before Parker realized they weren't alone.

Across the room he heard Lynne's gasp of sheer horror. "You would have burned those helpless animals?"

Parker shrugged, clearly indifferent to Lynne's outrage. Of course, he was a stone-cold killer. It was doubtful he even understood things like love, empathy, or regret.

"I had second thoughts after I returned to town. I decided instead to destroy your clinic," the idiot blathered on. "I was certain that would hurt deep in your soul. The trouble was that I didn't know how to do it. Not until I caught sight of Nash and your slut of a receptionist doing the nasty in your storage room." His laughter echoed through the emptiness. "I realized I could kill two birds with one stone. Or rather kill two birdies and torment a bitch."

Kir's gaze darted toward Lynne. Predictably, her face was flushed with a seething fury. Lynne was the most even-tempered person he'd ever known, until it came to her beloved animals. But threaten one of them and she was like a crazy woman.

Terrified she was going to do something stupid, he straightened and waved his arms to attract her attention. If she said or did anything to alert Parker that he was approaching from behind, they were both dead. But that was a risk he had to take.

For a second she was too focused on her captor to notice his movements, then he watched the shock that spread over her face as she caught sight of him. Her lips parted, but

Kir sharply shook his head, fiercely hoping she would understand he wasn't ready to give away his presence.

Almost on cue, her lips snapped back together, and she returned her gaze to Parker. "You were the one who bought the drugs from Nash," she said, obviously realizing she needed to keep the man distracted.

Kir released a shaky breath. Once again Lynne's courage was on full display. *Amazing.*

Parker tilted back his head to laugh in twisted pleasure at her accusation. "He was so easy to manipulate. He had the brains of a slug."

"What about the dart guns?" she asked as Kir took a silent step forward, and then another.

Parker shrugged. "I'd seen the kind you used in the clinic and ordered them online."

Kir took two more steps, wincing as the cement crumbled beneath his feet. It wasn't loud but the silence that filled the room was absolute. Not to mention the fact that the space was built like an echo chamber. Even the smallest noise reverberated.

Almost as if sensing his burst of fear, Lynne loudly cleared her throat. "And deliberately left them behind?"

"Of course." Parker waved his hand, the light glinting off his knife. "I had to be tediously obvious to lead the dumbass sheriff in your direction."

"And you left the photo on the shed?" she continued, her voice overly loud, as if she was deliberately trying to conceal his approach.

Kir didn't let her efforts go to waste. Bypassing one of the metal columns that held up the high ceiling, he edged closer and closer to Parker.

"Yes, I couldn't resist letting you know I'd seen the

real you." Parker sliced the knife through the air. Kir's heart missed a beat. He couldn't see the man's face, but he sensed his increasing agitation. It was in the edge in his voice and the stiff angle of his shoulders. "The woman beneath the mask. Just like I revealed my mother for the weak coward she was."

Lynne licked her lips. Did she feel the tension in the atmosphere? Probably.

"When did you take the photo of me?"

"Months ago. I'd gone into the clinic to see you and of course your receptionist was nowhere to be found. She was probably in the room with Nash. When I got to your office, I could see you sound asleep on your couch. I considered joining you to teach you how it would feel to have a real man holding you in his arms. But in the end, I decided not to soil myself."

He paused, as if thinking back to that moment he'd seen her alone and vulnerable. The thought made Kir's stomach cramp with what might have been.

Parker stepped toward Lynne. "Instead I took a picture to savor later."

Lynne scooted backward, nearly out of the pool of light. "How did—"

"No more," Parker abruptly interrupted.

Kir tensed as Lynne studied Parker with a wary gaze. "What?"

"No. More. Talking." Parker lifted his arm, the knife reflecting the overhead light. "It's time for screaming."

There was an odd sense of unreality to the moment. As if Kir had somehow strayed into a cheesy horror flick. The gloomy, abandoned air base. The damsel in distress.

The ruthless villain with a knife clutched in his hand. The bumbling hero attempting a rescue mission . . .

Swallowing a curse, he cleared his head. Parker had plunged into the dark side. The time to move was now.

Coiling his muscles, Kir leaped toward the man's back, yelling at the top of his lungs. "Run, Lynne."

He slammed into the man, taking them both to the ground. Luckily, Kir landed on top. Parker released a growl that sounded like a rabid animal as he struggled to turn over. Behind him, Kir heard footsteps as Lynne rushed to stand next to them.

"No, I'm not leaving you," she panted.

"Go." Kir switched on the flashlight in his hand, then with an awkward twist of his body, he tossed it toward the opening he'd come through. He didn't want Lynne going out the main exit. Not when Parker might have laid booby traps to keep her from escaping. "Follow the tunnel," he told her. "It leads out of the building."

"No."

Kir used his weight advantage to keep the man pinned to the ground. He didn't miss the glint of the knife that was still clutched in Parker's hand. If he didn't keep him contained, all sorts of bad things were going to happen.

"We need help," Kir gritted, his muscles strained to the max. Who the hell would have suspected the smoothly sophisticated Parker Bowen would be as strong as an ox? Maybe it was a serial killer thing. You'd have to be buff to haul around the bodies. He shook away the inane thoughts, sending Lynne a pleading glance. "Your truck is running in the parking lot. Take it to town and find someone—"

"My truck?" she interrupted, her eyes widening. "It's here?"

"Yes, it's in the parking lot." Kir grunted as Parker managed to elbow him in the ribs. "Now go."

Astonishingly, Lynne turned to run across the wide space with adrenaline-fueled speed. In less than a minute she'd disappeared from view, swallowed by the darkness. Kir breathed a sigh of relief. He'd assumed he'd have to plead for her to go, but now he could concentrate fully on the man squirming beneath him.

"You idiot," Parker rasped, managing to get enough space to swing his arm backward.

Kir jerked back his head as the knife threatened to plunge into his eye. The tip of the blade sliced through the flesh of his cheek. Instantly he felt the ooze of blood flowing down his face. It was intensely hot against his chilled skin.

Distracted by the pain, Kir was shoved aside as Parker scrambled to his feet. The man glanced toward the tunnel where Lynne had disappeared, clearly debating whether to try and stop her.

With a surge of desperation, Kir jumped to his feet and stepped directly in front of the man. Parker was going to have to go through him first.

As if accepting that he would have to deal with Kir before he could track down Lynne, Parker sent him a vicious glare. "Just like your dad," he ground out. "Poking your nose in where it doesn't belong."

"Is that why you killed him?" Kir demanded, glancing around the cement floor. The place had once been an active air base. There should be something lying around to use as a weapon.

He shuddered as he caught sight of the dark stains on the broken cement. Was that blood? With an effort he forced himself to ignore the gruesome splotches and continued his search for something that could help him fight off the lunatic.

Nothing.

Parker waved his arm from side to side, circling Kir as if looking for the perfect place to strike. "Very good. I wondered if anyone would ever figure out what happened to Rudolf," he drawled, flashing a smile that was all white teeth and aggression. Like a wolf. "There's a beauty in working in the shadows and I have perfected the art of invisibility. But every artist desires his creations to be properly admired."

Kir's gut clenched with fury. It'd been difficult when he thought his father had died in an accident. It was brutally hard to accept that he'd been murdered by this worthless piece of scum. "You think you're an artist?"

"Of course, it might not be everyone's taste, but you have to admit there's a drama in the bodies I displayed for your pleasure." Parker leaped forward, stabbing the knife toward the center of Kir's chest.

Kir jumped to the side, longing to smash his fist into the center of Parker's face. It was only the knowledge that the man was deliberately taunting him that allowed Kir to ruthlessly crush his blast of anger. Emotions were the enemy right now. He had to think with crystal clarity if he was going to survive until help arrived.

"No one took pleasure in your sick displays." Kir curled his lips into a sneer, edging back toward the tunnel.

"And it doesn't take any skill to drug vulnerable women, or to throw a helpless old man down the stairs."

"You would know Rudolf wasn't harmless if you ever bothered to visit him," Parker countered, twirling the knife with the ease of a man who'd practiced that particular skill. Then, with the speed of a striking snake, he slashed toward Kir's face. "What kind of son abandons his father when he needs him the most?"

Kir dropped to his hands and knees, hearing the whistle of the knife just above his head. *Shit.* He was going to have to get out of there before he was turned into a shish kebab.

But how?

He might be able to overpower Parker and wrench the knife from his fingers, but the man was stronger than Kir had expected. He wasn't sure he could get the upper hand before the blade was sticking out of his heart.

What he needed was a distraction so he could make a run for it.

It wasn't until a sharp shard of cement cut into his palm that he was hit with inspiration. Clenching his teeth, Kir tightened his fingers around the broken piece of cement, then twisting his torso, he threw it directly at the overhead light.

The fluorescent bulbs burst in a shower of glass, plunging the room into a deep, impenetrable darkness. Exactly what Kir needed.

Remaining on his hands and knees, he crawled away from Parker. Immediately he heard the scrape of the man's boots as he moved to block his escape to the tunnel. He'd already expected that. He intended to lead Parker toward the main entrance before circling back. It was his only hope of escape.

"You can't hide forever," Parker called out, frustration in his voice.

"And you didn't answer my question," Kir answered in a loud voice. He needed the man to follow him.

Parker paused, as if considering whether he was being led into a trap. Then at last he stepped toward Kir.

"Because he broke the rules of the game," the man said.

Kir shuffled backward, the rough cement bruising his knees. "The game?"

"Yes, the one we'd been playing since he shot my father."

"How did he break the rules?"

"This is my personal lair." Without warning, Parker kicked out, managing to connect with Kir's ribs. "This is my Fortress of Solitude. Just like Superman had. This is the place I come to be alone with my dark fantasies and plan my revenge."

Kir grunted, rolling to the side a mere second before the knife scraped against the cement just inches from his hand. Refusing to consider how close he'd come to having the blade in his back, Kir instead concentrated on Parker's words. He could easily see the man down here, hiding like a spider as he brooded on the past and scratched down his list of . . .

"The list," Kir muttered, surging to his feet and scurrying backward. His cheek was on fire and he suspected at least one rib was cracked, but he needed to be ready to run toward the tunnel.

"Do you have it? I was afraid . . ." Parker made an impatient sound. "Where is it?"

"My father sent it to me," Kir smoothly lied. The last

thing he wanted was for anyone else to die because of the stupid thing.

Parker's footsteps crunched toward Kir, the blade whistling through the air. "Liar."

"Did my father know you were the killer?" Kir demanded, leaping to the side to avoid the man's determined slashing.

"I assumed he did. One day I noticed that my list was missing. I checked the video from my cameras, and I discovered your father had intruded into my lair days before and pawed through my papers."

Kir silently reconstructed what had happened. His father must have been fishing and noticed something at the air base that stirred his curiosity enough to enter and find the list. No doubt he'd gone to the sheriff, who ignored his warnings, and then decided to investigate on his own. He couldn't have known Parker had caught him on a security camera.

That explained why it'd taken a few days between Rudolf handing the list to Pastor Bradshaw and falling down the stairs. Kir wiped the blood from his cheek as he battled his urge to howl in frustration. If only . . .

The thick darkness only emphasized Kir's wave of bleak despair. As if it were a living force that was sucking away his will to continue his futile fight. Then, with an effort, Kir forced himself to concentrate on the sound of Parker's movements. Dammit, he was going to end up dead if he didn't keep himself focused.

"You killed my father because he trespassed?" he demanded in sharp tones.

There was a pause, as if Parker was surprised Kir hadn't curled in a ball of fear. Did the lunatic sense the evil that pulsed through the frigid air? Or was he the cause of the evil?

"I went to his house to confront him. It wasn't until I demanded the list that I realized he hadn't known it belonged to me," Parker at last revealed. "Then it was too late. I had to silence him."

Parker was still speaking when he struck out, but this time he didn't slash with the knife. He instead kicked out. Kir managed to dodge a direct blow, and even got in a kick of his own. Parker grunted as Kir's foot slammed into his knee.

"Silence him by breaking his skull?" Kir demanded, feeling something icy on his nape. A breeze. He was close to the entrance.

"You have no idea how painful his death has been to me," Parker protested, managing to sound genuinely aggrieved. As if he wasn't the one who'd thrown Rudolf down the stairs. "Unlike you, I truly cared about your father."

Kir ignored the man's false pity as he came to a halt. The sound of Parker's footsteps had moved to the side. Was he trying to cut him off? Or was he hoping to flee through the exit and go in search of Lynne?

Either way, Kir sensed things were about to happen. He needed to be ready.

"And Rita?" he asked, determined to keep the conversation going so he could pinpoint Parker's exact location.

It felt as if they were in a standoff, neither willing to make the first move. Eventually something, or someone, was going to break.

"That bitch," Parker spat out. "She should never have stolen those letters from the grave. They were private."

"You ran her over?"

Parker chuckled. "Like a dog."

Kir hissed at the mocking words. The pig. The cruel, evil-hearted pig.

"You can't silence everyone," he rasped.

"There's just you. And Lynne," Parker assured him. "Then I'll disappear and become someone new. It was my plan all along."

Kir clenched his muscles, prepared to make his dash toward the tunnel across the room. "Have you heard the saying about the best-laid plans?"

"Yes."

Without warning a brilliant flare of light flooded the room. As if the sun had suddenly crashed into the air base. Kir blinked, momentarily blinded by the high bay lights that flared to garish life.

"Which is why I always have a backup," Parker drawled.

Narrowing his eyes, which felt as if they were being stabbed by the harsh glow, Kir belatedly realized Parker had dropped his knife and was holding a handgun.

"Shit." He lunged to the side as the deafening explosion reverberated through the vast space.

Kir hit the ground, the breath knocked from his lungs. His rib ached and his face still burned, but he didn't have a bullet in his head. He was going to take that as a win.

Unfortunately, he doubted he would be so lucky the next time. Already his vision was starting to clear. Which meant Parker's vision would be clearing as well.

Rolling to the side, he planted his hands flat on the cement and then shoved himself upward. He glanced back even as he bent low and prepared to race toward the tunnel.

What he saw halted him in his tracks.

Parker was standing near the main entrance to the control room, his arm still lifted with the gun clutched in his hand. But he wasn't looking at Kir. Instead he was reaching up with his free hand to grab the long silver tube sticking out of his neck just above his scarf. Kir frowned. What was that thing? It wasn't until it dropped to the ground with a clatter that he remembered where he'd seen it before.

A dart. Only this one was twice the size of the ones he'd seen in Lynne's clinic.

Swiveling his head, he caught sight of Lynne standing at the edge of the tunnel with what looked like a rifle in her hand. That's why she'd been so eager to get to her truck, he acknowledged with a flare of pride. She'd known she had the tranquilizer gun in there.

Shaking off his strange sense of unreality, Kir turned back toward Parker. The man was grimly moving his arm to point his gun in Lynne's direction, his actions sluggish but still deadly. Without hesitation Kir leaped forward, planting his shoulder in the middle of the bastard's chest as he drove him to the ground.

Parker collapsed like a limp doll, the drugs Lynne had shot into him taking full effect. But just to be sure—okay, it was just because he couldn't resist temptation—Kir untangled himself from Parker's limp arms and sat up. Then, not bothering to check if he was awake or unconscious, he slammed his fist directly into the middle of Parker's face.

Bones crunched as the man's nose was broken and blood spurted from a split lip. Feeling amazingly better, Kir turned his head to send Lynne a wide smile.

"Good shot."

to disappear after the sheriff had finally arrived at the air base and Parker had been hauled away. Now that the killer was locked up and the mystery of the list left to Kir by his father was solved, there was no reason for him to remain in Pike.

But he had.

Each morning Lynne woke to find herself wrapped tightly in his arms. And each night she came home to discover a warm meal waiting for her.

It was . . . paradise.

Slowly, cautiously, she began to trust in his promise that he was there to stay. Just as she began to depend on his companionship to fill the emptiness that had been a part of her life as long as she could remember.

The only disruption in the smooth, welcome peace of Lynne's life was Kir's secret project.

She knew he was working on something he promised would help raise funds for her shelter, but he refused to explain what he was doing or allow her to help. It tested her control-freak personality to the very limit of her endurance. At last he'd told her to buy a new evening gown and get ready for her surprise.

Not sure what to expect, she allowed Kir to lead her up the stairs of the local VFW hall. The three-story brick building was the only spot in town that had a large enough space for a decent-size crowd to gather. Unless you counted the community center at the lake, a place that could only be used a couple months out of the year.

They entered through the double oak doors and climbed the stairs to the top floor. Stepping into the long, narrow room, Lynne came to a startled halt.

"Oh my God," she breathed. The room had been transformed from a plain space with wood paneling and a low

Epilogue

Although it was mid-April, spring was more a promise than a reality as Lynne slipped out of Kir's SUV. At least the snow had melted. A good thing, since she had on heels for the first time in years. And she'd replaced her heavy parka with a light shawl that matched her beaded black gown.

Waiting for Kir to join her, she took a moment to appreciate the sight of him attired in an exquisite tailored suit that had arrived with the rest of his belongings from his condo in Boston. Right now the majority of his stuff was piled in his father's house, but Lynne knew it was a temporary arrangement. Already Kir was sketching out blueprints for a new home to be built on his grandfather's land. It was a huge, sprawling farmhouse that included five bedrooms, an enclosed conservatory, and a fenced meadow that would be perfect for kids and pets, including King, who'd become a permanent fixture in her home. He warned her that he hoped to have several of each.

Warmth spread through her as she allowed her gaze to sweep over his starkly male features and hard body shown to perfection in the dark suit. She'd expected him ceiling to a spring fairyland with twinkling lights draped from the ceiling and trellises decorated with her favorite pale pink roses lining the walls. At the very back a long table had been arranged with uniformed servers offering plates of hors d'oeuvres and fluted glasses of champagne.

It wasn't the decorations, however, that made her breath catch in her throat. "Kir." She sent him a startled glance. "This is your definition of a little fundraiser?"

He sent her a wicked smile. "What did you expect?"

"Bake sales. Car washes." She turned back to study the mingling crowd stuffed into the room. There had to be at least two hundred people who were all dressed in their finest clothes. And while she'd never rubbed elbows with the most powerful citizens of Wisconsin, she recognized faces that she'd seen on television. "Not senators and corporate CEOs."

Kir shrugged. "Bake sales aren't really my style."

"I don't know." She sent him a small smile. "You make a mean cheesecake."

"True," he readily agreed. "But senators and CEOs bring in more money than cheesecake."

She returned her attention to the crowd. Was that woman in the corner an anchor for a major network? Lynne was certain she'd seen her on the late-night news. More importantly, Monica and Grady were there, all healed up from being knocked unconscious by Parker, along with a beaming Bernadine, who was now a full-time receptionist at the clinic.

"How did you convince so many people to come?" she asked.

"You are a very popular person in Pike."

She snorted. "Not this popular."

"Don't underestimate yourself, my dear."

"I'm a realist. I doubt the senator who is currently eating a shrimp cocktail has ever heard my name."

"I have a wide web of connections from my business," Kir said in a casual tone. As if everyone could pick up the phone and gather prominent citizens from the upper Midwest. "And the fact that we recently survived the local serial killer didn't hurt. Everyone wants to meet us." He paused, touching the scar that was starting to fade from his cheek. A visible reminder of his encounter with Parker Bowen. "And of course, to catch sight of this beauty."

Lynne instinctively pressed against Kir's side. He was the rock she had grown accustomed to leaning on. It was a wondrous feeling.

"So they're here because we're notorious?"

"A few of them."

Lynne shuddered. "I'd be offended if this wasn't for the sanctuary."

Since Parker's arrest she'd done her best to throw herself into work. She didn't want to think about how many hours she'd spent with the smooth, charming journalist when he'd been plotting her death. Or the pain and terror he'd caused to the people of Pike. She didn't even want to consider Rudolf Jansen's brutal end.

It would take time to process the destruction that had started with Delbert Frey and the torture of his son. The evil man had created a monster who had nearly destroyed them all. For now it was enough that they were alive.

Kir wrapped a protective arm around her shoulders. "We can leave if you want. I'm sure we'll make enough from the door tickets alone to be able to hire extra help and expand the kennels."

Lynne wondered how much Kir was charging for the

tickets even as she tilted her chin to a defiant angle. "No, I need to face this."

Kir frowned down at her. "If you're trying to prove your courage to me, let me assure you it's not necessary," he told her. "Not only did you face down a serial killer, but when you could have fled to safety, you instead returned to shoot the bastard."

Lynne blushed at the warm pride in his voice. It was ridiculous. She hadn't done anything special. When Kir had yelled out that her truck was in the lot, she'd known exactly what she had to do. In fact, she couldn't believe how stupid Parker had been to drive her truck instead of his van, although she supposed he was worried someone might catch sight of the vehicle and realize he was at the air base.

Still, it'd taken less than five minutes to run up to the parking lot and grab her long-range gun. She used it on cattle or horses that were in the pasture and too skittish to get close to. Or occasionally deer that the local conservation department wanted to test for disease. After grabbing her rifle, she'd syringed enough sedatives into the dart to put down an elephant and headed back down to the bunker. The dosage was potentially lethal to humans, but Lynne didn't care. She wanted Parker knocked out as quickly as possible.

"It isn't about courage," she insisted. "It's about accepting the past so we can move on to the future."

"I'm good with that." He lowered his head to brush his lips across her forehead. Then straightening, he swept a searching gaze over her upturned face. "Are you sure you're okay?"

She started to nod, then sent him a rueful smile. Kir

had a sixth sense. He always knew when she was lying, which wasn't the most comfortable talent to have in a partner.

"I'll be better when Parker, or rather Carl Frey, is locked in the penitentiary and the key thrown away," she admitted. The nightmares had started to fade, but the knowledge that she was going to have to endure the trial kept her up at night.

"Yeah." Kir shrugged. "I called the prosecutor again today, but she said they're still investigating. It's going to be months or even years before he goes to trial."

"Did they ever discover Ernie?" she asked, referring to Merrill Frey's second husband.

"No. Either he realized his stepson was a psychotic killer who murdered his own mother and decided to disappear before he could become the next victim, or Carl decided to get rid of him." Kir heaved a resigned sigh. "That's part of the ongoing investigation."

Lynne leaned her head against Kir's shoulder. "So much death."

"Yes." He dropped a kiss on top of her head. "But not tonight."

He was right. Lynne straightened, pulling away from Kir to allow the happy chatter of the guests to wash over her. It felt good to be surrounded by her friends and even those people she'd never met. It reminded her that there were still good things in the world worth celebrating.

"No, not tonight," she agreed with a smile.

Kir's eyes darkened as he studied the curve of her lips before allowing his gaze to drift down to the plunging neckline of her gown. "First we're going to convince these very fine guests to hand over obscene amounts of money," he said, his voice roughened with desire. "And then we'll return to your house and I'll continue my efforts to convince you to marry me."

An answering desire swirled through Lynne, warming her in delicious places.

She sent him a teasing glance. "You do know that I might have already agreed to the proposal if you weren't so good at trying to convince me."

A low growl rumbled in his throat. "I sense we're going to have a very long, very interesting future together, Dr. Gale."

"Would you have it any other way, Mr. Jansen?"

Sliding his hand down the curve of her spine, he led her into the crowd. "Not in a million years," he whispered in her ear.